Books by Barbara Probst Solomon

THE BEAT OF LIFE
ARRIVING WHERE WE STARTED
SHORT FLIGHTS

Horse-Trading and Ecstasy

ESSAYS BY

Barbara Probst Solomon

1989
NORTH POINT PRESS
San Francisco

I would like to thank the Centre de Documentation Juive Contemporaine and its archivist, Vidar Jacobsen, for making its archives on Otto Abetz available to me and for its excellent guidance and assistance in my research. I am particularly appreciative of the encouragement of Eugene Winick, Eva Pryor, my editor, Ross Feld, and of the unquestioned backing of my decision to cover the Barbie trial by Juan Tomás de Salas, the publisher of *Cambio 16*. I also want to thank Joan O'Connor, curator at the Kennedy Library, for her help with its Hemingway Archives. I feel enormously lucky to have the abiding support of my family, my daughters, Carla and Maria, and my mother, Frances Probst.

The following essays have appeared in these publications in a slightly different form: "The Politics of Passion: Marguerite Duras" and "Ernest Hemingway's Real *Garden of Eden*" in the *New Republic*; "Diego's Diego" and "1948: The Resistance Goes Modern" in *Culturas/Diario 16* (Madrid); "For James Baldwin," "The University: Everyone's Gold Mine," "The Person Alone," and "The Ordeal of Jean Harris: Adrift in Westchester" in *Dissent*; "Notes from New York" in *Views* (London); "The American Mood: Kerouac and Mailer" in *Socialist Commentary* (London); "Günter Grass: There Are No Fascists in Greenwich Village," "In Texas Spanish Is Fashionable Now," "Jacques Vergès," and "Otto Abetz: King of Hitler's Paris" in *Cambio 16* (Madrid); "Dwight Macdonald's *Against the American Grain*" and "Spain: Who Really Won?" in the *New York Review of Books*; "Days and Nights in Texas" and "Life in the Yellow Submarine: Buffalo's SUNY" in *Harper's*; "Conversation with Lewis Mumford" in *Sites*; "Horse-Trading in Female Ecstasy" in the *Nation*; "Pierre Jean Jouve's *Paulina 1880*" in the *Washington Post Sunday Book Review*; "Ellen Hawkes's *Feminism on Trial*" in the *Partisan Review*; "Conversation with Norman Mailer" in *El País* (Madrid); "Spain After That War" in the *Village Voice*; "The Lively Literary Revival," "Paul Nizan," and "Klaus Barbie and the Conscience of the Literati" in the *New York Times Book Review*; and "A Diary of the New Spain: The Spanish Elections" in the *New York Times Magazine*.

Remembering Paco Benet, Pepe Martínez, and Josep Pallach,
who made Peninsula,
and for Miriam Rugel and Augusta Wallace Lyons

Contents

IV. FALLEN ANGELS

V. SPAIN LOST, SPAIN FOUND

VI. FRANCE, ITS OCCUPATION, AND THE BARBIE TRIAL

"You must not think you are saved because you are happy at the sight of green wheat."
Paul Nizan,   *Aden, Arabie*

I.

Writers, Artists, and Exile

The Politics of Passion

Marguerite Duras

1987

The grand *monstres* of French literary culture—Jean-Paul Sartre, Roland Barthes, Michel Foucault, Jacques Lacan—are all dead. Marxism and the *nouveau roman* have, almost inevitably, lost their former luster. French literary vedettes like Philippe Sollers and Nathalie Sarraute have jumped ship and are writing highly accessible autobiographical novels. And the absolute reigning queen of the new Parisian literary life, in which readable novels have become suddenly acceptable, is Marguerite Duras.

Her autobiographical novel *L'Amant* [*The Lover*] won last year's *Prix Goncourt*, France's most prestigious literary prize, and has sold over 700,000 copies; it is now a best-seller in the United States, too. Duras also has been in the spotlight this season because of the publication of *La Douleur* [*The Sorrow*], a more straightforward account of her experiences in the French Resistance in Paris at the end of World War II. (She says she found the four brief fragments contained in the book in a cupboard in her country house.) The book's subject is heroism, but it also sheds considerable light on the obsessions that Duras has dealt with much more obscurely in her other work. For years one had heard in French literary circles about the "Duras problem"—that one of her assignments in the Resistance had been to become more or less the girlfriend of a French collaborator, whom she then turned in, and who was subsequently executed. In *La Douleur* she explicitly discusses the "Rabier incident"; she also reveals that she ordered another collaborator to be tortured and had sexual longings for a third collaborator on the eve of his execution.

Horse-Trading and Ecstasy

In the case of Duras, born Marguerite Donnadieu in 1914 in Saigon, there are many different pieces of the puzzle to be sorted out. She is an odd hybrid of poetry and skewed politics. Most of her 15 novels—*The Ravishing of Lol V. Stein, Moderato Cantabile*, and her own favorite (she considers it a great twentieth-century classic), *The Vice-Consul*—have been highly stylized, moody *nouveaux romans*. Yet there is another side to her, an intensely political side, that may be found, for example, in her script for Alain Resnais's film *Hiroshima mon amour* and in *La Douleur*.

From the outside, Duras has always very much seemed a literary star, but it appears that during the last decade she felt her work neglected. In the early 1980s both she and her current companion, Yann Andréa, a writer in his thirties, became reclusive, depressive alcoholics. Eventually she signed into the American hospital in Neuilly-sur-Seine for a detoxification program. Andréa also took the cure; *M.D.*, his demonic account of their joint descent into an alcoholic hell, was published in 1983. During her shaky recuperative period, Duras started *The Lover*. It was conceived as a text to accompany a book of photographs she wished to publish of her early life in Indochina, and written in a speedy three months. In the novel a Chinese man and an adolescent French girl conduct a torrid liaison for a year and a half, to the shock of local French colonials. The man picks her up in his limousine every afternoon after school, and she sports a bunch of expensive new clothes. The affair ends because the man's father insists that his son marry a Chinese girl. The narrator leaves for Paris, for the Sorbonne.

Though *The Lover* has the familiar elements of Duras's style—displaced, disjointed eroticism; hypnotically repeated incantations about death and eternity; and the skilled use of a classically French intense confessional style, all done in short takes in a nonchronological sequence—it is unusually accessible. Duras has reworked the same material about her family and her adolescence that she used in one of her earliest novels, *The Sea Wall*, published in 1950. The family is ramshackle French colonial. The widowed mother is a schoolteacher in a half-caste school. She instills in her daughter and two sons a sense of grandeur about their genteel poverty: a houseboy serves them skimpy dinners, a loyal French maid sews for the adolescent daughter badly cut dresses with smocking in the wrong places. The mother's enterprises invariably fail; her schemes to develop rice paddies in the south are wrecked because the locals have given her the wrong information. Still, there is enough money for the family restlessly to go back and forth to France.

The book is presented as a piece of autobiography, but Duras has always liked manipulating myths. Her portrait of the ravaged little woman—of the frail-shouldered, sexually perverse, tiny white girl in the thin silk dress, the man's fedora, the glittering paste high heels, forced in effect to whore for her

4

beloved and despised family—is very reminiscent of that other teenage *maudite* Edith Piaf. Here is *la petite môme en Indochine*. Indeed, the way Duras at 71 seems suddenly to have seduced all of France—the public accounts of the gamine and her sexually abused childhood, of her near-death from alcohol, the almost national celebration of the doomed amours of her past and of her new life-saving young lover—all evoke the way it was with Piaf. "The little sparrow," however, really did have a beat-up childhood. In the case of Duras, who went on to study law at the Sorbonne, reality seems to have been more complicated.

A tiny white girl is despoiled in the heart of Saigon. The Chinese man "does it" to her again and again, only a thin window blind separating them from the teeming Chinese masses just outside. Meanwhile, the Chinese's father is lying on an iron cot in a room in another town, counting his millions and smoking opium: this corrupt and evil old man, who steals from the poor, has the nerve to prevent his son from marrying the poor little French girl, who needs money to help her widowed mother and two brothers, thus condemning her to permanent ruin. She becomes known as the "little white whore from Sadec." The novel's *sotto voce* message, in short, is pure French colonial: rather oddly xenophobic, almost as though the author were sitting in a Loire kitchen, telling the local concierge the lurid details of what it was like to have been the orphaned *môme* of France *outre-mer* in those days and nights when France still possessed its empire in Indochina.

Duras wants to have it both ways. As a former mainstay of the French left she would be the first to call the next fellow *raciste*, but she adroitly knows just how most of her French readers will respond to her cautionary tale of sex in the Orient. The narrator's mother is quite symbolic of how the average Frenchman perceived his role in Indochina. The widowed schoolteacher tries to bring French culture to unappreciative half-castes, but later she is exploited by unscrupulous locals who sell her bad land in the south for her rice paddies, while Indian moneylenders harass her. Now, Duras can be an exceedingly politically precise writer. Why, then, are the Chinese, the locals, the Indians always perceived as the bad guys with the money? Were the French really the exploited in Indochina? What of the hunger riots of 1930, for example, which were savagely punished by the French? What of the almost slave labor recruited by the French for the rubber plantations in Cochin China? Just *who* was meant to work mother's rice paddies? Anyway, in 1930 the antiwhites were Ho Chi Minh's young revolutionaries, not Chinese millionaires.

One wonders how France's imperial colonialism organized itself inside the head of the young Marguerite Duras, of the singularly intelligent young woman firmly preparing herself for her departure for the Sorbonne and her true future in France. I imagine her as a lonely young girl in Saigon, conjuring up images of France through her one real link to the mother country—the marvelous libraries the French installed as a monument to French culture in every outpost of their colonial empire. I see this troubled, imaginative Creole girl (Duras's own label for herself) rummaging through French literature, rolling off the tip of her tongue, in her best invented Paris accent, grand incantatory phrases—perhaps a touch of Corneille: *Rome qui t'a vu naître, et que ton coeur adore!*—mixing centuries, lofty ideals, and notions of place and country with her own desire. Once in France, she was to Frenchify herself in the handy manner used by those who needed to gain a quick sense of belonging there—through the French Communist Party. (She was expelled from it in 1950.) The trouble with the French is that so few of them feel that they really *are* French.

In *The Lover* the sexual exotic, really, is the French girl, not the man. In the important first seduction scene she is in control. (She also lusts for her classmate Hélène, whom she likes to imagine in a *ménage à trois*.) The 15-year-old narrator commands the horrified man to seduce her: "Treat me like you treat other women." But would a Chinese millionaire's son, who had lived in Paris and known many French women, be weeping and mewling like a stuck pig at the thought of making love to a sexy French girl he had picked up? Who exactly is this lover? Duras's talent for myth may be as active in her account of her sexual history as in her account of France's colonial history. Speculating on the subject, Michel Tournier observed in a review of *The Lover* that Duras has the half-caste features found in Chengdu and concluded that it was her mother who had the affair with the Chinese man. "And so this short, harrowing novel should have been entitled not *The Lover* but *The Father*. A father who is hated because he is yellow, because he is compromising to the mother, who has 'fallen,' and compromising to the daughter, who carries on her Eurasian face the shame of her origin." My own hunch is that the mysterious Chinese lover stands for Duras's brother, that this is a tale of incest disguised as a tale of miscegenation. Many passages in the novel suddenly make emotional sense. ("I asked him to do it again and again. And he did it in the unctuousness of blood. And it really was unto death. . . . ") And this would explain why, after the narrator leaves for Paris, she receives only one short letter in ten years from her younger, much-adored brother: an oblique message that he is all right. And, why, in the family scenes, when the Chinese takes the narrator and both her brothers out dancing, he seems to her, suddenly, so powerless and nonexistent. During the Japanese occupation of Indochina, in 1942, the brother dies of pneumonia.

Whether Tournier is right and the lover is the father, or my hunch is more on the mark and he is the brother, or whether he is some combination of all these figures, clearly this may not be the straightforward piece of erotic autobiography that Duras would have us believe. Indeed, Tournier's explanation could help to account for the strange mixture of erotic attraction and xenophobic repulsion toward "others" in all of Duras's work. According to Tournier, Duras has said in an interview that in the detoxification clinic she hallucinated that a Chinese man was persecuting her. There is a truly mad scene in the novel about purification, in which the mother suspects the daughter's affair, strips and locks her in her room, and while the older brother is outside, egging her on, she beats the girl: "[she] . . . comes to me and smells my body, my underwear, says she can smell the Chinese scent, goes even further, looks for the suspect stains on my underwear, and shouts, for the whole town to hear, that her daughter's a prostitute. . . ."

At the end of the book Duras describes the Chinese man—or whomever he might symbolize—visiting the narrator many years later in Paris. It is a common wish, that one's first love will return, pledging undying *amour*. More subliminally perhaps, Duras may be mixing a private fantasy with a public fantasy. The return of the lover to Duras may stand for France's dream that its lost Indochina will be restored, and will eschew its marriage to "the other Chinese woman."

> *It must have been a long time before [the Chinese man] was able . . . to give [his Chinese wife] the heir to their fortunes. The memory of the little white girl must have been there. . . . For a long time she must have remained the queen of his desire, his personal link with . . . the immensity of tenderness. . . .*

Here, with her skilled use of incantation, Duras magnificently fuses the Chinese man, her son (the child is born shortly before the novel ends), her adored dead brother, France, and its lost colonial empire:

> *And with the trembling, suddenly, she heard again the voice of China. He knew she'd begun writing books, he'd heard about it through her mother whom he'd met again in Saigon. And about her younger brother, and he'd been grieved for her. Then he didn't know what to say. And then he told her. Told her that it was as before, that he still loved her, he could never stop loving her, that he'd love her until death.*

Unfortunately, the political echoes of *The Lover*, its shrewd mingling of erotic experience and racist nostalgia, do not end there. Duras has saddled the novel with a highly inflammatory subplot that can't quite be ignored, and which sheds light upon both *La Douleur* and *Hiroshima*. At one point in the narrative Duras abruptly turns to mattters in France during the German occupation. The narrator's hated older brother has become a small-potatoes collaborator. The two siblings are quarrelling over their mother's money. The narrator's husband has been deported. And she has become a fond friend of Betty Fernandez, the wife of Ramon Fernandez, a French writer and collaborator who had literary "at homes" during the German occupation. Suddenly—as in *Hi-*

roshima—Duras mixes real history into the poetic haze: "Once Drieu la Rochelle was there. . . . Maybe Brasillach. . . . Sartre never came." And, in almost a throwaway sentence, Duras casually says:

> . . . *collaborators, the Fernandezes were. And I, two years after the war, I was a member of the Communist Party. . . . The two things are the same, the same lack of judgment, the same superstition if you like, that consists in believing in a political solution to the personal problem.*

The Fernandezes are described as rather charming, cultivated sophisticates, and as loyal friends.

> *Ramon Fernandez used to talk about Balzac. He spoke with a knowledge that's almost completely forgotten . . . as if he himself had once tried to be Balzac. He had a sublime courtesy. . . . He was sincere. It was always a joy to meet him in the street. . . .*

The collaborator is portrayed as the sincere, courtly preserver of French tradition, as the guardian of Balzac. Amazing, the way Duras suddenly becomes a party to the worst clichés of *la vieille France*.

The fact of the matter is that Drieu la Rochelle and Brasillach were France's two most famous literary fascists. They actively worked with the Gestapo. At the end of the war Drieu la Rochelle killed himself; Brasillach was executed in France's most important trial of collaborationist intellectuals. Along with him were executed Georges Suarez and Maurice Bunau-Varilla, the owner of *Matin*, a newspaper publisher who was known for his fancy parties for the Gestapo. (He liked flowers molded in the shape of a swastika as a table centerpiece.)

Despite the blurred pale violet photograph of the young author on the cover of *The Lover*, presumably the publisher's indication that this is a misty erotic tale, there is nothing misty about Duras's explicit references to men like Brasillach and Drieu la Rochelle. Was being a collaborator really the same as being in the Resistance? Duras may be abusing the privilege of the writer; of course she may juxtapose and rearrange the bits and pieces of her erotic life as she pleases, but perhaps not to the extent of distorting and displacing moral meanings and historical facts. To be sure, one might argue that the execution of Brasillach was too vengeful, that too many abuses were committed in France at the war's end. But that is not Duras's point. She is espousing, rather, a notion that enjoyed a certain amount of literary popularity in Europe in the 1960s—that everything is relative, that there are legitimate standpoints from which victims and aggressors may be viewed as equals.

Duras recently vented her spleen against Sartre on French television. She said that he was not a writer. Well, perhaps he won't be best remembered for his novels, if that was her implication. Still, tipping the balance against Sartre and his world in favor of Brasillach, Drieu la Rochelle, and their world is outrageous. The real question for France, which lost nearly two million people in World War II, remains not who resisted—it is not human to demand that others risk their lives, and anyway there were many forms of resisting—but who collaborated. And the problem for French literary culture is that so many of its fine stylists were active French fascists. What Sartre, Camus, and the others of their circle provided for France in the immediate postwar period—despite their many quarrels, despite their misjudgments about Marxism—was a defense against a beautifully styled French prose that had been used in the service of atrocity. Thus Sartre's emphasis on plain prose was deliberate. So, too, was his philosophy; existentialism's controlling idea—that one is the sum of one's acts, that words only have power when attached to an act—was an essential moral medicine for France. As the only major power to have been occupied by the Germans, with its culture in shreds, France badly needed a vision by which to recoup its lost moral and literary self-esteem.

But now Duras offers to a new generation a view of writers like Brasillach and Drieu la Rochelle as elegant, thoughtful romantics. Her subtle comparison of occupied France to the body of an innocent raped child is another twisted rewriting of history. (To be sure, these matters are in vogue now, part of the French appetite for *retro*; the biggest best-seller in France is Régine Deforges's *Gone With the Wind* of the Resistance: *La Bicyclette Bleue*, a two-volume saga with a Joan-of-Arc heroine, semi-hard-core pornographic sex, scenes of extraordinary sadism, and figures of every political hue.) Appearing at a time in its country's history when explosive trials concerning the collaboration of French officials with the Gestapo are about to begin, and when the country is witnessing a new upsurge of racism, the subtle subplots of *The Lover*—the poor French girl defiled by rich Orientals, the sincere collaborators who are the true defenders of Balzac—are more than a little troubling. And in *La Douleur* Duras also describes the collaborator she betrays as a man whose true desire was to own a bookstore of rare books. (She seems fond of this link between collaboration and the love of fine literature.) In June the Paris weekly *L'Evénement du jeudi* published a series of letters, released from government archives, written by Frenchmen to Pétain to save Jewish lives. It was striking how many spoke to Pétain in his own language: they stressed that Jews weren't to be considered enemies of France because they did not defile the purity of French culture, despite their accident of birth. Unlike the Germans, the French were not concerned with purity of blood, but with purity of culture. That is how their fascist intellectuals rationalized themselves as the true saviors of France.

Duras, of course, was in the Resistance. Indeed, she saved Mitterrand's life—he is "Morland" in *La Douleur*. He was a close friend of Duras's husband, "Robert L." This book is her expiation not for crimes committed, but for her

9

own sadomasochistic impulses and obsessive feelings of guilt for having participated in the punishment of collaborators. In a note at the beginning of one of the sections of *La Douleur*, she calls these extraordinary pages her *textes sacrés*; they are about the things closest to her, the hidden recesses of her homely, less grandiose, everyday heart. We don't need Duras's declaiming on television about her eternal love (for her Chinese lover) to understand that her deported husband mattered to her: her description of rushing through Paris to grill his friends who had returned from the same camp to find out whether he and his sister might still be alive is devastating. Robert finally was located by fellow members of the French Resistance, dying and delirious in Dachau; the sister was found in Ravensbrück. She dies on the way home; he is saved, but is returned to Duras almost a living cadaver. Her description of not being allowed to feed him the *clafoutis* she had baked for him because his stomach had so shrunk—survivors were dying from being fed too quickly—is shattering. The husband looks at the food being withheld from him; sometimes he steals scraps. The denial is a repetition of what he suffered in the concentration camp, but it is the only way his life can be saved.

Duras may perceive herself as a rebel, an outsider, a Creole, but her work is really rather exemplary. It is a reflection of the contradictions of French consciousness, of its noble and its ignoble reality. This is one of the reasons she remains an interesting and important writer. But again, by way of being such a representative writer, Duras can have it both ways. Consider *Hiroshima mon amour*, made in 1960. It was unusual because it was the first French film, with one minor exception, to mention World War II. (*The Sorrow and the Pity* wasn't made until 1970.) Touted as being a universalist antiwar film, which it was not, the film deals with French feelings of guilt. But there comes a twist. There are no French males, no soldiers, in *Hiroshima*. The French understandably didn't wish to recall World War II, or Algeria, or Indochina, and so Duras created a film about the war with a heroine.

And then there came still a further twist. Duras managed to equate the suffering of the Japanese after the bomb with the suffering of the French during the occupation. In this upside-down thinking, France becomes an imaginary wasteland, filled with carnage. By expropriating Hiroshima's tragedy, Duras released her country from the unpleasant memory of having submitted to the Germans. Moreover, by a further involution, since the United States was guilty of the senseless destruction of Hiroshima and yet helped to liberate France, Duras gave the French a chance to direct their anger outward; antiAmericanism in de Gaulle's France was at a peak. The only foreigners to escape blame, in fact, are the Germans. All this was in 1960. Ten years later *The Sorrow and the Pity* gave evidence of the country's growing ability to examine its past; Claude Lanzmann's *Shoah* is even grander and more somber evidence. *La Douleur* continues to make the subject of the German occupation more explicit, which is badly needed by the French.

Duras's writing has real power. Her strength is in her images, in the music of her prose. Though she probably wouldn't see herself this way, this daughter of *outre-mer* is, for better and for worse, her country's most successful nationalist writer. And somewhat like Céline, though not nearly of his genius, Duras seems to have absorbed into her consciousness her country's profound xeno-phobia, which in her love-hate relation to France she speaks for even as she ceaselessly attempts to overcome it, as she gets beneath the French skin with her imperfect, luminous art.

Diego's Diego

1986

I had forgotten the existence of my movie footage of Diego Rivera until the recent Philadelphia Museum retrospective of his work. I knew one of the people involved in the show and remarked, one day this past summer, quite casually, that somewhere in my closet I had films of Diego Rivera working on his unfinished mural at the University City in Mexico. I had shot this brief footage while a student at Columbia, during a summer vacation in Mexico. My friends were amazed. Who had introduced me to Rivera? Several of the nosier ones were even more blunt: In my youth had I had an affair with Diego Rivera?

I really never knew him, nor he me. Writers love to embellish, so it crossed my mind that it would make a great story to *hint* perhaps that a love affair had taken place—but as Diego Rivera and I never even shook hands, or exchanged addresses, it struck me as too nervy even to hint at such a whopper. Anxiously I began to wonder if the footage still existed.

I took a ladder and searched in the upper shelves of my closet. Finally I found steel boxes of sixteen-millimeter reels. I decided to transfer the films to video. When this was accomplished, I took the videocassettes home from the processing lab and that evening—suddenly, magically—on my television VHS there appeared my youth—Spain, France, Mexico—and finally Diego. I watched the movement of his hands, the close-up of him instructing his workers what to do next, and I saw myself, brown hair parted in the middle, somber

This was published in the Sunday literary review of *Diario 16*, in Madrid, in a group of one hundred international writers celebrating its one-hundredth number. We were asked to write a short piece involving memory. The American writers included John Irving, Allen Ginsberg, John Updike, Diana Trilling, Mary McCarthy, Clancy Sigal, Lionel Abel, Daphne Merkin; the foreign writers included Edna O'Brien, Marguerite Duras, Octavio Paz.

green eyes, intense, unsmiling, and aloof. Who took the pictures of me? I do not remember.

So there Diego has been, all those years, on the top shelf of my closet. Although I didn't know him in 1952 when I shot the films, with the passage of so much time his permanent place in my home movies, which I had meant to be a cinematic autobiography of my youth, now brings us together. Once a meeting between two people has been recorded, preserved and remembered, it ceases to have been an accidental, random encounter: Diego Rivera now has become part of my remembering.

That the films were so well preserved was an accident of *forgetting*. As was the fact that they exist at all. Before I went to Europe in 1948, though I was still in my teens, it had crossed my mind that it would be handy, for the postwar, to have a movie camera. I bargained with my parents. I pointed out that, as I had refused to go to school, I was saving them tuition money. I also promised not to buy clothes for a year. Finally I convinced them to let me have a 16-millimeter movie camera and lots of color film. I wandered through Normandy, went to the Omaha beachhead and photographed considerable footage of the American ships, rusted and dank with seaweed, sinking into the sea. In another set of reels taken in France, Paco (my Spanish friend who was studying anthropology at the Sorbonne), his brother, (the future novelist) Juan Benet, and I, play-acting, were pretending to shoot a surrealist "thriller" in the forest in Rambouillet. Though I was fairly adept at splicing in titles for the different sections, I was always a lousy speller—the Café Gijón in Madrid, I spelled "Hijon."

It was during the summer of '52, at the end of my five-year postadolescent journey through the world, that I spent an August in Mexico. I felt I had come home from Europe for good—I had made a crucial decision—my future was going to be emphatically in America. Most of my Spanish Paris friends had been scattered; France didn't have enough postwar jobs for the French—the country obviously couldn't accommodate the children of Spanish exiles. So my friends had left France for Latin America, Mexico, and the United States. Pepe Martínez, one of the few of our group who stayed behind in France and who in the early 1960s in Paris founded the famous Spanish exile press, Ruedo Ibérico, at that time was an anonymous out-of-work young Spaniard in Paris. He'd been thrown for a time into a French civil prison for not having had the right papers; he had already served some years in a Spanish prison for being part of the libertarian youth movement. It was a depressing time. I was weary of saying goodbye forever to my closest friends at the Gare Saint Lazare. I knew we, as a group, would never be united again. Before going to Mexico I had sold my last vestige of happy days in France, my Dyna-Panhard Levassor, which was as small a blue car as its name was long. I had gone through France with it. General Motors wanted my car because they wanted to tinker with its water-cooled motor—they had tracked me down through customs; apparently I was the only American crazy enough to have brought the tiny Dyna back from France. I handled my sadness and my homesickness for Europe by telling myself I loved New York. Discovering Mexico City was part of the internal sales-pitch I was giving myself about how wonderful it was going to be to live in America.

With one of the few friends I had in Mexico City I visited the University City. Diego Rivera, in crumpled blue denim, was standing on a scaffold directing his crew who were hammering at his great mosaic on a wall by the stadium. He looked down, saw me, saw that I had a movie camera, called to me, came down from the scaffold, and we talked in Spanish for a few minutes. He asked my name. I said Barbara. I didn't ask his—he was Diego Rivera. He said to leave it all to him; he would climb up the scaffold again and direct what should be filmed. I should just point my camera upward at the right moment. It would be, he said, his gift for my future. Then he climbed back up the scaffold. I waited, and when he smiled, waved, and moved, I clicked the camera. I waved him thanks in return, then walked on and rejoined my friend.

Why didn't I cajole him into making more of the moment? An interview, a visit to his studio, a longer film? I was shy; also, I was nothing. I would have had no place to publish an interview; I didn't become a "young published writer" until '59. There are always good pieces of a dying generation, of older talent, lying around for the taking when one is young; I didn't grab because my compulsions were anti-archivist. I was more intent on creating myself. I wanted to be of "my time, my generation," which I was convinced had nothing to do with anything that had gone on before "my time." I was scared that if I looked back and stared too long at the already famous, like Lot's wife, I would lose something of unnameable value and turn into a pillar of salt.

No, there was more to it than that. When I met Diego he was a big floppy aged old man, and I was still a sleepwalking girl encased in a dream of finding a perfect unblemished odorless future love that would last unto eternity: I needed to divorce all possible parental figures from any suggestion of their sexuality. I preferred men near my own age. Now, so many years later, I watch my Diego footage, and I am disappointed. It is so short. It tells me nothing.

But the next time I look at the film I realize Diego's hand is pointing to plumed serpents embedded in the mural. Rivera's first wife, Angelina Beloff, adored his tales of serpents. Is he saying that, by putting his Russian-souled Angelina's adored "plumed serpents flying through the skies" in his last mural, he had not totally forgotten her? Frida Kahlo, his third wife, already was gravely ill that August 1952 afternoon I walked by the University City. According to her biography, Rivera's happiest memory was of their first meeting: he was working on a mural in Mexico City and on top of a scaffold, she called up to him, a young dark-haired girl; he called down to her, Frida and Diego started to flirt, they fell in love. *When I walked beneath Diego's scaffold, he called to me, but I did not call back. I was in my private trance.*

Again and again, I play the footage of Diego on my video, until I fathom, thirty-four years later, what he gave me. "My gift for your future," he had called out to me, hurling into my unknown destiny, with all his artist's power, the condensed anguish of his multiple lives lived. *He, Diego, existed, Angelina existed, Frida existed*, his erotic past recorded and held, to become part of my future, waiting for some quiet time when I could look back unblinded and take an old man's story, without fear of turning like the wife of Lot into only salt. What I will never know is what *he* saw. The stubborn timeless child within me plaintively wonders if he guessed I would become me.

For James Baldwin

"I am on my way—I'm coming through."
JAMES BALDWIN

1988

The air snapped and crackled. December weather. The white Christmas mini-lights were already lit in New York. It was a funny day, this eighth of December. Overnight one had got accustomed to the American flag and the hammer and sickle intertwined on television. It reminded me of my childhood in this city, the World's Fair and World War II. In the media, again, Russia and America were positioned as allies; it was as if nothing had happened in between—to me or the world. Maybe we were living through historic times. This afternoon Reagan and Gorbachev were signing their nuclear arms agreement; we were into a new era.

In New York, far from the parties in Washington, there was a sense of things ending. At noon in the Cathedral of Saint John the Divine, on Amsterdam Avenue up near Columbia University and the border between white New York and Harlem, near the streets García Lorca wrote about in his time in New York, James Baldwin was being buried. He was sixty-three years old. He had had a heart attack a few years ago; after an awful year of stomach cancer he died in Saint-Paul-de-Vence.

I took a taxi across Central Park. A crowd was gathering in the Strawberry Fields opposite the Dakota to sing Beatle music—it was also the seventh anniversary of John Lennon's death. Lennon was an international symbol of the sixties. James Baldwin became a symbol to the black civil rights movement. But before that—and I think ultimately—he was a true New York writer, particularly of the fifties and early sixties, that literary moment when conversations were quick with ideas, when essays dazzled and everyone listened, everyone fought, when words were so important. Jimmy was a novelist at that precise crossroads when the *idea* of a novel was beginning to falter, and he taught all of us the rhythms of the essay. In *Notes of a Native Son* (1955) and *Nobody Knows My Name* (1961) he combined a high-style Parisian classy urgency he had picked up in France—he first went there in '47—and a special American intimacy born of the tempo of all the American writers that had gone before him—his hero was Henry James, also a self-exiled novelist, a great essayist. Biblical cadences too, moral messages that were the birthright of a Harlem storefront preacher's stepson, mixed with the beat of jazz, and the anger of having been born black. Baldwin was my youth. He would be the only writer of my time to have earned such a funeral.

Though some American novelists have made lots of money, writers have no official place in our society—we have no tradition of the grand funeral for *hommes des lettres* that has been so integral a part of French history. Jimmy's funeral, then, was extraordinary. There probably were about five thousand people at the cathedral. Students, blacks, Columbia University professors, writers, people from publishing, people from Harlem—all sorts and all ages came.

Understandably the speakers stressed Baldwin's role in creating a written moral language for the civil rights movement. But as I sat in that vast solemn space, I thought, finally, how *American*, and full of dreams invented and acted upon, Jimmy's life had been; even his years in France had been shaped by the books our generation had devoured about Hemingway and Fitzgerald in places like Cap d'Antibes. In the late forties, when Jimmy went there, France still had literary resonance for Americans. Jimmy yearned for quality—in writing, in ideas, in the look of things, the style of life. He was the first person I knew to own a sheepskin coat, to sport a fur hat, and wear an oversize muffler. I see him before me in that wonderful outfit; he had the special delight in magical luxury of a kind who grew up bone poor in Harlem and who washed dishes in Greenwich Village night spots before bolting to Europe. His stepfather had been a Harlem storefront preacher—he had no real church, just an odd occasional room somewhere. And here was Jimmy's funeral. Finally he was being buried in the biggest cathedral in the world, in one of the grandest writers' funerals in New York ever. The services were High Church Episcopalian, which is the fanciest and most snobbish American religion can get, but it was the rhythms of black jazz that soared through the vaulted cathedral. First came the Processional—the Babatunde Olatunji African Drum Salute reverberating through that great gray stone space like a wailing for dead African kings. The High Church Episcopal ministers in their long white lace robes carried their tall gold crosses, followed by the mourners—a sad family, an aged mother, conservatively dressed members of the black bourgeoisie, Columbia professors in beige Burberry coats, occasionally glorious women dressed in the phantas-magorical lush stuff of a Josephine Baker. There were 1960s hippies, and small children, and Ossie Davis and Ruby Dee and Max Roach. Odetta sang "The Battle Hymn of the Republic." There was jazz. Jimmy Owens played the trumpet and horn and Danny Mix was on the piano. They played "When the Saints Go Marching In" with almost unbearably pure pitch. The horn just floated at us. Then the speeches and the music were over. The mourners carried Jimmy's coffin down the cathedral steps to the waiting black limousine parked on Amsterdam Avenue, and the funeral cortege drove slowly back up through Harlem, on the way out to the cemetery.

But was Baldwin's ambition, really, to have been known as a "black writer"? Despite his anger at the deprivations whites have inflicted on those born black, I don't think so. The eulogies about him by Maya Angelou and Toni Morrison—both of the women were his close friends—indicated his lit-erary complexity. As Toni Morrison said, there were many Jimmy Baldwins, and many different things will be written about him. Jimmy had so much to combat. In his own eyes he was born short, puny, ugly—and homosexual. And poor. And black. In a period when even Tennessee Williams didn't quite dare to write overtly about homosexual love and desire and despair, Jimmy took the plunge: he wrote *Giovanni's Room*. I suspect he learned a lot from Henry James, some of it about style—some of it about how to convey a certain special sort of male anguish. But I felt a chill inside me during the services when Amiri Baraka delivered his revolutionary Marxist-Leninist tract in Baldwin's name. What flashed through my mind was that angry period in the 1960s when what had seemed to start out wonderfully fell apart, and disintegrated into slo-gans and violent polemics—Baraka, then known as LeRoi Jones, lashing out in hatred of the white audience who came to see his play, *Dutchman*. Andrew Goodman had just been killed in Mississippi, his parents were in the theater; it was an awful night.

Emmanuel de Margerie, the French ambassador, spoke, but no white American writer; I felt this shortchanged and distorted Baldwin's real literary place. He was proud of having been given the *Légion d'honneur*, but his pride was at having merited it as a writer. He didn't leave America just to get away from the unbearable conditions of black life here—after all, he didn't go to Af-rica but to Paris, because he had that very American idea, specifically of his generation, that it was the civilized place where writers went. His rage at the bitterness of being black in America formed him, but his writing transcended color—his style and way of writing has had an enormous impact on a whole generation, black and white.

Jimmy's relation to the civil rights movement was more ambivalent than the eulogies indicated—indeed certain segments of the movement attacked him for escaping the battle and living in France, and even for his writing so much about being homosexual. But some of his best essays were about his discovery in France of his abiding "American-ness." Neither Hemingway nor Fitzgerald ever wrote so concretely about being aliens in Europe. What Baldwin did was new—he "liberated" our generation from the lost-generation idiom—he leapt back over those twenties writers, fished up Henry James, held on to him for dear life, modernized him: after he wrote about Europe in his special way, we all picked up from him a permission to write about our encounters with Europe minus awe for Europeans. Jimmy's greatest anguish as a writer probably was that despite the emotional power of his early novels *Go Tell It on the Mountain* and *Giovanni's Room*, he didn't write a single book as great as Ellison's *Invisible Man*, undoubtedly one of the three or four great American novels of the second half of the twentieth century. But in his combination of novels and essays, Baldwin developed a special literary voice, moral and angry, that shaped American writing far more than has been acknowledged.

Though the emphasis in the funeral was on Jimmy's blackness, in many ways he was a product of the primarily white New York post–World War II literary scene. His first essay, on Harlem, was published in 1948 in *Commentary* magazine. The lead article in the first issue of *The New York Review of Books*, in December 1963, was a review by F. W. Dupee of *The Fire Next Time*. Baldwin had a tremendous influence on Styron and Mailer. In Styron's case he led him to *The Confessions of Nat Turner*. But with Mailer it was different. Real love-hate. (Peter Manso's book on Mailer records some of it.) They were always taking each other's measure. Baldwin had a devilish side, he accused Mailer of not daring to be homosexual, of being a Harvard boy, a bourgeois—"my mother took in your mother's washing." But together they also impishly gave a party in New York in the late fifties celebrating the end of the Beat Generation—neither one defined himself as Beat. (Baldwin would sharply criticize the Beats in the foreword he wrote for my novel *The Beat of Life*: ". . . the dubious protection of the uniform, the pose, the shrillness, the fake poetry and the fake jazz . . .") Unlike the Beats, both Jimmy and Norman were moralists. Baldwin's taunts about Norman's Harvardness resulted in lifting Mailer out of his lumbering Dreiserian-moralist-mode into something swifter, more modern: he helped create Mailer's sixties vocabulary: "The White Negro" was Mailer's retort to Baldwin. It was like a good tennis match. They volleyed with each other to win, and each improved the other's style. That volley deeply changed American writing. Literary anger—black and white—wasn't a result of the civil rights movement, but preceded it.

I wasn't a close friend of Baldwin's, but I felt a piece of my youth die and go with him in that sealed coffin carried down the steps of Amsterdam Avenue. He gave me my start as a writer—he "named" me. When I was still at Columbia in 1960, I wrote *The Beat of Life* which, ironically, was about Columbia students who lived near Saint John the Divine in the then Puerto Rican Upper West Side. Cork Smith, my editor, sent galleys of the novel around. To his and my astonishment, James Baldwin, whom I had never met, replied with an amazing foreword, and thus changed my life forever. It was hard in 1960 to emerge as a female writer and be taken seriously. Even harder if you were "bourgeois" and had never in obvious ways suffered or could be thought to be the voice of ill luck, the mute, and the marginal. How to describe those times? I remember that after my book came out I met John Updike at a Cambridge dinner party. He said to me: So, publishers put a picture of a female author on the back of a book—and in come the reviews . . . Undoubtedly Updike thought he was being gallant in even recognizing that I had written a book; and in those times, and in those Harvard circles, his remark came out sounding vaguely like a compliment. What would never have been questioned then was his subtle distortion of reality—his suggestion that female writers because of their gender were getting more than they were entitled to and had an unfair advantage, something totally askew with the actual situation for women writers in 1960. It was no accident that two of the writers who eulogized James Baldwin were women—early on he accepted women as writers, as beings capable of thinking. Maya Angelou's remark, that he knew that black women need brothers, wasn't merely a warm eulogy but a rarely commented-upon truth about Baldwin. A decade before the feminist movement he expressed those thoughts in what he wrote about my book: " . . . it is about the death of love, the hideously whistling space where all our values used to be. . . . There has probably never been a generation so ill equipped to deal with reality on any terms whatever. The sons never had any fathers to kill and so never became men, which failure is having a disastrous effect on everybody's daughter."

Jimmy's true obsessions had to do with human emotion and its arrests, the claustrophobic anguish of one generation beating incommunicably against another—he reminded me of Chekhov's fragile brittle hero in *The Seagull*. It is always risky when committees, even good committees, try to mobilize the kind of urgent autobiographical anger born out of something deeply private within a writer into something useful and usable. Baldwin desperately wanted the civil rights movement to succeed, but their special need of him placed strains on him in ways beyond their imagining. People in charge of Causes never understand that a writer's voice can't be *owned*. Because Jimmy wanted to be loved, to please, he sometimes was too vulnerable to the demands of the outside world.

During the funeral I thought of that day in the early sixties that I bumped into him during a Chicago winter snowstorm. "Come hear me speak," he insisted. It meant driving that night to Northwestern, up to Evanston. But I did, because Jimmy had a certain lonely urgency to him, a charisma—a way of making you do what he wanted. I drove in the middle of a blizzard, and then stayed on and talked with him and his friends until three in the morning. I went home driving inch by inch through snowdrifts.

After the funeral I went across the street to the Green Tree. Elegantly dressed blacks who had come to Saint John's for Jimmy were gathered at the next table. Then a white man walked in, and we ended up seated together. He said he was Arthur Geller, an old friend of Jimmy's, but that in the sixties they had had some falling out. We had something to eat and coffee, and he talked about knowing Jimmy in New York in the 1940s. I wasn't sure how it ended up that we were so separated from the blacks in the restaurant. Why didn't we talk to them about Jimmy, or they us?

Later I walked the few short blocks between the cathedral and Columbia. I thought of my time in the fifties as a student there. Fred Dupee had been my professor. Images of different deaths, different funerals connected to the place came to mind. Galindez, the Spanish professor kidnapped by Trujillo's agents and dumped out of a plane to crocodiles, never was given anything official at Columbia. Trilling had had a discreet on-campus Columbia Chapel memorial, which had suited him. And Jimmy had the biggest, grandest cathedral funeral as befitted his life—he had started out as an ordained preacher in Harlem. While I was standing on the street looking for a taxi, two young black women came up to me. I assumed they had been at the funeral—why stop me on the street? No, that wasn't it. One of them was a designer. "Your coat is such a different way of working fur—where did you get it?"

"I brought it home from Paris—I got it the summer the dollar was high."

"That was smart of you—it really is beautiful."

I blinked. Why were we having this conversation on the corner of Amsterdam Avenue about fur coats right after Jimmy's funeral? I was glad they had stopped me, it took away from the bad feeling I got in the restaurant at the color-separateness of the tables. I kept talking so much to them, they must have thought me garrulous. I nearly hadn't worn it, but then I had thought of Jimmy and the flashy stylish way he dressed and thought what the hell and why not. In the taxi on the way home, I thought about those days, and those unexpressed covert landmarks, even angers, that connect people in a generation to each other. Maybe other books could have been written, or people should have said different things, or fought some battles harder and left others unfought. But that's like saying nobody should have died. On the way back I simply wanted to remember the way it had happened.

Ernest Hemingway's Real
Garden of Eden

1987

Last spring Scribner's published Ernest Hemingway's posthumous novel *The Garden of Eden*. It was, inevitably, a great event; Hemingway's modernist experiments shaped the twentieth-century American novel and gave us our literary language. *The Garden of Eden* stayed on the best-seller list for 13 weeks. It was stylishly published, too; the jacket reproduces Juan Gris's *Woman with a Basket*, which evokes the spare modernist style of the early Hemingway. The image has a Mediterranean flavor, very apt for a novel of the 1920s described by its publisher as "a story of love and obsession . . . about a young American writer and his wife on an extended honeymoon in Mediterranean France and Spain, and about the woman to whom they are both attracted."

The book's critical reception was mixed, in part because the reputed length of Hemingway's manuscript caused many reviewers to raise questions about the liberties that had been taken with it. Some scholars immediately expressed skepticism about editorial propriety, despite the publisher's disclosure in the preface to the book that in

> preparing the book for publication we have made some cuts in the manuscript and some routine copy-editing corrections. Beyond a very small number of minor interpolations for clarity and consistency, nothing has been added. In every significant respect the work is all the author's.

Scribner's indicated in its promotional material that in fact there had been no fewer than three versions of *The Garden of Eden*. There was one draft of 400 pages; another of 1,200 pages, of Hemingway's typescript and holograph; plus 300 pages he added later. According to Edwin McDowell's report in the *New York Times*, Tom Jenks, Scribner's editor, worked from the longest version.

The published book starts out well enough. David Bourne, a writer, and Catherine Bourne are a couple in their early twenties honeymooning in Le Grau-du-Roi, on the French Mediterranean. Hemingway describes them coming down from Paris to Avignon with their bicycles, a single suitcase, a rucksack, and a musette bag. Only a few pages later, however, there occurs a rather baffling change. David says of Catherine:

> *She had always looked, he thought, exactly her age which was now twenty-one. He had been very proud of her for that. But tonight she did not look it. The lines of her cheekbones showed clear as he had never seen them before and she smiled and her face was heartbreaking.*

The paragraph feels a little senseless—one hardly thinks of a woman of twenty-one as being well preserved. All of a sudden, the cycling innocents are gone. The couple begins to sound older, jaded. It is the first sense we get that something is wrong here, that something is hidden beneath the surface of this novel.

Catherine bobs her hair. She insists that David make love to her as though she were a boy. She takes David away from his novel in progress and to Spain. With the speed of light, David and Catherine move to Biarritz, to Hendaye, to Madrid, then back to the south of France. They settle in La Napoule, near Cannes. By then Catherine has had three short, boyish haircuts, each time bleaching her hair a whiter blond. By my reckoning, she should have been almost bald from all the clipping. And by page 143, Catherine's hair is being referred to as gray, or as toneless silver. Now (according to my mother), the only blond bleach to be had in the twenties was brassy. Again I sensed that somehow in this story Hemingway's later life was being interpolated into his earlier one, and the abruptly lurching narrative made me wonder about Scribner's scissors. Just what had Hemingway's publisher removed from his work?

In La Napoule, a *ménage à trois* develops. Catherine falls in love with Marita, a younger woman. (But at twenty-one, what is younger?) She means to share her with David, but instead David and Marita fall in love. Catherine's mental imbalance becomes apparent; a breakdown begins. In this state she jealously burns David's unfinished manuscript, making it impossible for him to write anymore. Catherine suffers terrible guilt, she relinquishes Marita to David, she departs for Paris. And David finally overcomes his block by finishing a short story about his father's experiences in Africa during the Maji-Maji rebellion in the early 1900s. The novel ends, then, on an upbeat note: David has Marita, and his power as a writer, and peace with his father.

Just before Catherine burns the manuscript, she rather peremptorily informs David and Marita that she is taking David's rough unfinished draft to Derain, to Dufy, to Picasso, to Pascin (Scribner's calls him Pascen), for them to illustrate. What happened to the innocent kid with the bike and the rucksack? Is she merely hallucinating? Probably not; by this time their luggage is pricey Vuitton. Catherine and David seem oddly secure about approaching Picasso and Derain with David's work. Perhaps David is really a somewhat older, somewhat more successful writer.

And there is the strange choice of hotels in the critical Madrid scenes of *The Garden of Eden*. When the Spanish novelist Juan Benet and I were kids in Madrid, in the late 1940s, we stumbled on the modest pension where Hemingway lived during his early days on the Calle San Jerónimo. To this day Juan mourns the fact that we didn't filch the Hemingway novel—I don't remember which one it was—that was dedicated to the owner of the pension and prominently displayed in the heavily shuttered, threadbare, olive-oil-smelling pension parlor. Why would Hemingway, with his great sense of place, his supreme gift for mood, have switched his young, bohemian couple from a pension like that to the Palace? That is rather like describing a great love affair in the Greenwich Village of the twenties and setting it at the Plaza.

The Garden of Eden has always been described as Hemingway's last major effort. He wanted to experiment, to move away from his early style; and he struggled with it from 1946 until his death in 1961. His son Patrick told me that in his post–World War II period, Hemingway was fond of saying to his critics: "Gentlemen, you are criticizing my arithmetic when I am long ago into calculus." Would Hemingway, in the final test of his literary ambition, really have written the thin and disjointed novel that Scribner's published?

After *The Garden of Eden* appeared, the original Hemingway manuscripts at the Kennedy Library in Boston were made available to scholars. I wanted to read them, so I went up to Boston. And now, after studying them, I feel that Hemingway's publisher has committed a literary sacrilege.

There is no way that the manuscript that I read, an extraordinary mass of unfinished work, written in the troubled last years of Hemingway's life, could have been made into a smooth popular novel without the literary equivalent of "colorization." Just as the black-and-white movies of the 1930s have been defaced with rosy colors, robbing American culture of part of its patrimony, so, too, has Scribner's interfered imperiously with what Hemingway left us. It has transformed these unfinished experiments into the stuff of potboilers and pulp. Read *The Garden of Eden* and you will be reading Hemingway through a scrim. The pity is that buried beneath the editorial violations is some very important Hemingway.

Nobody can finish an unfinished novel for a writer, and nobody should presume to try. Would that Hemingway's editors had had the editorial dignity of

Ernest Hemingway's *Real* Garden of Eden

Edmund Wilson, who presided scrupulously over the posthumous publication of Fitzgerald's *The Crack-Up*. A scrupulous edition of this significant manuscript of Hemingway's is crucial for our understanding of his most profound artistic preoccupations. It is important to know, for example, what Hemingway wrote when—for the second part of *The Garden of Eden* seems to be an almost directly autobiographical account of his anguished last years. In the original, the description of Catherine burning the manuscript has a hallucinatory effect, and it appears next to a frightening paragraph about a flier being burned in a plane; these sections were clearly written after Hemingway's two plane crashes in 1953. (In the second accident, he was abandoned in the downed plane because he was too big to get through the door; he had to smash his way out.) It is perfectly obvious from a close reading of the manuscript, and from its correlation with the events of Hemingway's last years, that the difficulties of composition mentioned toward the end of the novel really have to do with Hemingway's anxieties about his deteriorating physical and mental powers. It is disgraceful to confuse these pains, courtesy of a cutting-and-pasting editor, with the banality of a young man's writing block.

What we have in the best parts of the original, in other words, is something far more precious than the novel Scribner's has published. The manuscript reveals a consummate craftsman mixing fictional narrative with the record of his own inner voyage as an artist, with the careful development of his own views on art. More than in any previous work, Hemingway allows the reader to see him overtly engaged in the process of thinking. The real *Garden of Eden* is a sort of *summa* of Hemingway's aesthetics.

Even at the level of plot, the original novel is different. In the manuscript, there are four men, and two of them (David Bourne and his friend Andy) are writers. The other two are artists—the extraordinarily gifted Nick Sheldon, married to Barbara, and Picasso, who comes into the novel toward the middle. The relations between these two couples and other artists are the substance of Hemingway's story. It shows, then, a more various world, not just a single couple. For example: in Hemingway's *Garden of Eden*, it is Barbara, not Catherine, who is the temptress; she sets the infidelities in motion by desiring Catherine. (There are hints of Zelda and Scott in the portrait of the Sheldons.) More important, the folders in the Kennedy Library reveal that Hemingway wrote two endings. (They are the final chapters in the manuscript, though someone has marked them as "stories.") Both are tragic. In the first, Nick is killed in a car crash after Barbara has been unfaithful to him with Andy, and some time after that Barbara commits suicide. In the second, which is perhaps a continuation of the first, Catherine has partially recovered from her mental breakdown in Switzerland; she rejoins David, and the two of them walk along the beach near Le Grau-du-Roi recalling earlier, happier times.

The latter part of the manuscript at the Kennedy Library is a sad text to read.

It documents Hemingway's growing emotional stress toward the end of his life. It is in these passages, which conform to the chronology of his last years established by Mary Hemingway in her autobiography, *How It Was*, that Hemingway's alter ego, David Bourne, becomes most obsessed with the pain of writing. At stake, quite clearly, was Hemingway's attempt to keep himself intact, to recover his strengths after the airplane crashes, after the multiple damages to his body and his mind. At times the manuscript reads almost like a coded record of his inner torment and of his troubles with Mary. He even has one of the characters wonder whether the narrative (which includes the African story David Bourne writes) really is Bourne's secret diary.

Patrick Hemingway confirmed for me that the African story had to be a late addition to *The Garden of Eden*, since it was based on the 1953 safari during which Hemingway was nearly burned to death. There are passages in the manuscript about a pilot burning in his plane—dark, traumatic passages in which Hemingway writes "so lonely, so lonely . . . , " and instructs himself to take hold and not kill his wife. The tortured master writes:

> *He had never in his life as a man been impotent, but in an hour standing at the armoire on top of which he wrote he learned what impotence was. . . . He could not write more than a single sentence. And the sentences themselves were increasingly simple and completely dull.*

How could any of this have led to the happy, beachy ending of the book Scribner's produced?

It is in this later, more troubled section of the manuscript that Marita becomes important, but the relationship described suggests more a young woman helping a suffering, aging writer than it does hedonistic, sun-drenched young love on the Riviera. There are some echoes in Marita of Renata from *Across the River and Into the Trees*, but she most closely resembles Hemingway's real-life last love, Valerie Danby-Smith, who after Hemingway's death married his son Gregory. In the manuscript, for example, Hemingway links the love affair with Marita to a lovely afternoon spent by the banks of the Ignati River. Mary Hemingway, in her book, writes that it was in Madrid, during Hemingway's trip to Spain in 1958, that he befriended the young Irish journalist. They went to the bullfights at Pamplona and picnicked along the banks of the Ignati. (Ironically, it was Valerie Danby-Smith and Mary Hemingway who, according to Mary's book, had the difficult task of sorting out the manuscripts of *The Garden of Eden*. This must have been rather difficult, as they both appear to have been, in part, models for the women in the novel.)

Critics have made heavy weather of Hemingway's dealings with sex change in the novel, of the fact that Catherine and David swap roles in bed. They have also found David Bourne curiously passive, and speculated about the appearance in *The Garden of Eden* of a new kind of male Hemingway hero. David Bourne does indeed come out sounding rather like the weak slave of a blond dominatrice. In truth, however, his passivity is due to the editor rather than the author, to the fact that Scribner's cut out his manner of talking, with other *men*, about art. Also cut is Hemingway's raunchy use of smell in David's sexual appreciation of the women. Scribner's excised all indications that David's age grows to 60. The publisher wanted youth, and produced a wimp.

In the Scribner's version, the heart of the matter has been chopped away, and in its place are peroxide bottles and bobbings. But Hemingway was writing about immortality, not peroxide. In the very first chapter of his *Eden* he makes it clear that his theme is metamorphosis, which includes androgyny. In a crucial love scene, David and Catherine attempt quite explicitly to reproduce with their androgynous sex Rodin's statue based on Ovid's *Metamorphoses*. This statue fascinated Hemingway because of Rodin's success in conceptualizing a *continuous chain of metamorphoses*. Ovid shaped from the erotics of real life his creations: the manual on the varieties of lovemaking and his verse *Metamorphoses*. Centuries later, Rodin, as artist, again repeats the process and takes from real life the models for his re-creation of Ovid the poet. Catherine and David—Bourne-of-Ovid (David and Ovid also sound alike)—in their lovemaking, become part of an endless universal chain of love fused with art, in which men and women fusing and changing sex roles become part of a larger continuum. By totally removing Rodin, the Scribner's version loses all connection to Hemingway's *Eden*. Not only is the Rodin connection germane to the lovemaking scene, it is the foundation for the work.

The men in the original version—David, Nick, Andy, and, further along, Picasso—relate and are fused to one another through their art and literature. Thus, when Nick dies, the narrative switches to Andy, who "absorbs" Nick's story. In a very funny scene Catherine visits Picasso because David wants Picasso and Nick to illustrate and become part of David's narrative; aware of the grandiosity of the enterprise, David now calls his narrative his "production." Catherine relates that Picasso will help David. "He says you're a fine man too, but he kept calling you a savage. He said Nick was the only good American painter." According to Mary Hemingway, Hemingway indeed tried to persuade her to pose seminude for Picasso, which she refused. Did Hemingway secretly wish, like David Bourne, that he could do a sort of Rodin on Ovid by incorporating Picasso's portrait of a Hemingway wife into his own narrative? In the original Hemingway manuscript Hemingway's views on male/female roles remain classic: men sublimate their relation to each other through art—women may be bitchy or supportive, erotic and lesbian, they may play sex games and demand to be called the boy, but they are never in command; they are the models, never the artists. Hemingway meant his readers to keep Rodin in mind.

Recall the words that introduce the love scene in the Scribner's version. David observes:

> *She had always looked, he thought, exactly her age which was now twenty-one. He had been very proud of her for that. But tonight she did not look it. The lines of her cheekbones showed clear as he had never seen them before and she smiled and her face was heartbreaking.*

In Hemingway's version, however, David says that "her face was heartbreaking *in its sculpture*" [my emphasis]. And on the next page David asks Catherine:

> *"Do you remember the sculpture in the Rodin museum?"*
> *"Which one?"*
> *"That one."*
> *"Yes."*
> *. . . He lay back and did not think at all.*
> *"Are you changing like in the sculpture?"*

They keep talking about the Rodin. Then Catherine says:

> *"Will you change and be my girl and let me take you? Will you be like you were in the statue? Will you change?" He knew now and it was like the statue. The one there are no photographs of and of which no reproductions are sold.*
> *"You don't think I'm wicked?" . . .*
> *"Of course not." . . .*
> *"How long have you thought about that?"*
> *"Ever since we were there that day in the Rodin."*

Scribner's has also banished the other key to Hemingway's meaning, Hieronymus Bosch's triptych at the Prado representing "The Garden of Eden," "Earthly Delights," and "Musical Hell." In his novel, Hemingway ceremoniously leads his characters on their march toward a grand fiesta at the Prado; he assembles the whole *Eden* cast—the Bournes (born) and the Sheldons (shell)—in Hendaye, the Basque town next to San Sebastián, with its great shell-like harbor. Hemingway's pause here is significant. His characters are like warriors setting camp before a great battle.

His expatriate Americans talk literature—interestingly, it is Proust who clearly has Hemingway bedazzled. *Eden* is the only place that I know of that Hemingway, who was a Joyce man, seriously considers Proust, who, for the modernists, was a dark horse coming from another mountain; it was not until the end of the 1920s that the modernists caught on to the fact that Proust was a major challenge to their conception of avant-garde. David asks Catherine when she had decided to imitate Proust's style of speech.

> *"When did you start talking like Proust?"*
> *"Reading him, I suppose. Reading is terrible for how you talk."*
> *"How long have you been reading Proust?" Andrew asked.*
> *"Only since Hendaye. . . . I bought them all for me to read when I went up to Biarritz one time. I promised David I wouldn't skip although, of course, naturally I wanted to read Sodom and Gomorrah first, and I did read some—having encountered numerous examples of that sort of person, as you would naturally, having gone to school in Switzerland, as I did."*
> *"Where are you without skipping?" David asked.*
> *"Almost half through the Côté, poor Swann. It's easier to read, and I suppose nicer when you know Paris."*

Later, in the more hallucinatory sections in the manuscript, Proust is mentioned again. His art seems to make Hemingway anxious and angry. One senses Hemingway's anguish at the recognition that it was Proust who had written the sort of inclusive narrative—a novel about the art of writing a novel, about art and literature, about androgyny and homosexuality—that Hemingway was striving after, that he wanted his own late work to be. But what writer could be more unlike Proust than Hemingway?

Obviously in *Eden* Hemingway was after complexity; he makes a point of including in his work digressions in the manner of the Old Testament, legend, myth, narrative, secret diary, novel, Taras Bulba, charades, the tales of Scheherazade, and the Holy Grail. In the pause at the beach in San Sebastián, before the slow literary march on to the Prado, Hemingway also discusses Henry James, a passage Scribner's also removed in editing.

But for his most successful experiments Hemingway always turned to the painters. This time there was inspiration to be found in Bosch—in his whole alchemy of colors (his androgynous, wicked Eve with two apples is black because black, in Bosch's time, symbolized something charred, something changed); in his depiction of universal metamorphosis, with its androgynous couples, zoomorphs, birds, and fish, each contained in individual cracked eggs like little narrative conceits. *The Garden of Eden* has got to be the "eggiest" novel ever written—there is no end to egg references and egg jokes in the longer version—but like the rest of Hemingway's wacky but meaningful humor, most of the eggs have been removed in the published book. Maybe that's just as well: in this distortion of Hemingway's text his jokes might not have been understood.

Hemingway has done many different takes on the journey from France to Spain reflecting *rites de passage* and ceremonies of love and light. In *The Sun Also Rises* the journey involves the lost generation, fishing, impotence, and disillusionment. *Death in the Afternoon* is about the art of bullfighting; it was also Hemingway's attempt to create a new English-born-of-Spanish, and *For*

Whom the Bell Tolls was his second war. According to my reading of the original *Eden* Hemingway conceived of it as his expatriate artist's march to a special fiesta at the Prado. The structure of Hemingway's original novel is very much the structure of Bosch's triptych—the innocent gathering of the protagonists before the journey to Madrid is the Garden of Eden, the great voyage toward the Prado is the beginning of the Garden of Earthly Delights, and, finally, the ending in La Napoule is the Musical Hell. Seen this way, it makes sense, in a way it does not in the Scribner's version, that Hemingway, in the Madrid scenes, places his characters in the Palace Hotel. He paints his magical scene of the outdoor café in front of the trees and the Prado by moving the outdoor gardens of the Ritz, which does have a view of the Prado, to the Palace Hotel, which has never had an outdoor café. In this novel about change, Hemingway makes Madrid eternal by fusing three hotels—the Ritz, the Palace, and the Pension Aguillar of his youth. And Catherine and David's love scene in the Palace occurs after their visits to the Prado: again, metamorphosis.

In the Scribner's edition, the chapter about the Prado ends on this blunt note:

> *"Let's first lie very quiet in the dark," David said and lowered the latticed shade and they lay side by side on the bed in the big room in The Palace in Madrid where Catherine had walked in the Museo del Prado in the light of day as a boy and now she would show the dark things in the light and there would, it seemed to him, be no end to the change.*

But the manuscript, Hemingway's more poetic version, reads, starting with David speaking:

> *"Let's first be very quiet in the dark."*
> *"All right. Only our thighs touching. Can I start first and try too?"*
> *"Can you?"*
> *"Oh, yes. I thought about it while you were asleep. But this is only until I know you'll have to invent too."*
> *"I can try."*
> *"Isn't it fine that neither of us knows?" We'll know he thought.*
> *"Just to kiss is enough now," she said, "please." Then in the dark it was all changed for him as it had been for her since the day before and since she had walked and gone to the Prado.*

Hemingway then added, and later crossed out, "He had never thought that he could do what he did now happily and completely and he did without thinking and with delight what he could never do and would never do." Throughout the manuscript, Hemingway has various turns of mind as to how oblique the lovemaking should be; but his main intent is to show Catherine and David's erotic life deepened, first by the Rodin, then by Bosch.

In the lovely final passage with which Hemingway seems to have wanted to end *Eden* he writes of temporal change, and the nature of life. In a scene almost deliberately evoking *Tender Is the Night*, Catherine and David, reunited, walk along the beach at Le Grau-du-Roi. Catherine says: ". . . I made everything in my image. I could change everything remember. Change me, change you, change us both, change the seasons, change everything from dark to light and then speed it up, speed it up, and then it went away and then I went away."

He meant *Eden* to have been his final summation on art and literature, on the nature of love and the body, on the possibilities of human life. But you won't find any of these strong conceptions in the book that Scribner's has published in his name. To paraphrase the publisher, in almost no significant respect is this book the author's. With all its disfigurements and omissions, its heightening of the trivial and its diminishment of the significant, its vulgarization of Hemingway's struggle to grapple with the great theme in his tragic final years, this volume is a travesty. Literature is art and must be treated that way, as Hemingway knew when in his final novel he kept his gaze on the clear white light of the Prado.

II.

Tableaux Vivants

Life Among
the New York
Intellectuals

Notes from New York

1964

I was born in New York City and grew up in one of those tall midtown apartment buildings in the center of Manhattan near the Central Park Zoo, child of
New Yorkers, grandchild of New Yorkers, all of which geography—emotionally and literally—makes of me, I am told, a *genuine* New Yorker. Having
kept up an easy rhythm of leaving and returning to this city, I had this place
itself on my mind when I received a letter asking me to do a piece on morale
among New York intellectuals. Ideas, problems—political and sexual—
zoom with jet rapidity across all oceans. In Japan they read *The Catcher in the
Rye*; in New York we are up on the meaning of the Mods and Rockers. As for
nothingness, everybody is on to that. It is the quality of life that is different
here—the *way* we live here that makes women, men, intellectuals, homosex-
uals, teenagers, etc., what they are.

I came back here last year after time spent in Texas and Chicago to find that
the city, always frantic and electric, had taken on the frenzied quality of an ab-
stracted fright. Little things. In the lobby of my building I noticed the legs of
the chairs had iron chains securing them to the wall. "Nothing is safe," the elevator man muttered. "*They* even steal the plastic plants." He hands me a special key for the lobby door. "Now we keep it locked at night." Locks. All over
the city the lock business is booming, everyone stocking up (door chains,
peep-holes, inner bolts) on safety the way people rush to buy food when there
is a war scare on.

Everyone has his own "they." The whites are afraid of the blacks, the

Written in response to a request by the British journal *Views* for a piece on New York intellectuals.

blacks of the police, the taxi drivers of the passengers who might hold them up late at night, mothers are afraid to let their children use the parks—dope addicts, lunatics, random murders, and violence: New York has it. The atmosphere exudes an air of mistrustfulness and apathy to a degree of almost mass paranoia.

I walk outside of my building with the chained furniture and overhead an advertising blimp is circling, leaving behind its white cloudy message in the sky. SUPPORT MENTAL HEALTH VACATION IN MIAMI BUY GOODYEAR TIRES. I don't know whether to laugh or cry. Later, in that mixture of discarded old people and transient poor that is Upper Broadway, I stand talking to a friend. A woman passes us by. "Goddamn you," she yells at the peopled street, "Goddamn all of you, go back to Levittown where you came from." Her arms are flailing, nobody looks up, we are used to the senseless, the mad and the lonely.

To use one's eyes in New York is to see ugliness, abnormality, the worst rat-infested slums in the world, and endless blocks filled with people living in utterly impersonal misery. So finally we train ourselves to see and hear nothing. I am in a bus. A boy, maybe ten or eleven, has gotten lost. He starts to cry. The driver tells him to move on, everyone bursts out in sudden, nervous laughter. Feeling slightly unreal, as though perhaps there is something comical in the situation I have failed to grasp, I move, nonetheless, toward the boy and get him on the right bus. Now, this is hardly an act that would strike one as anything but normal behavior in other parts of America, or in London or Rome. Yet—as tourists who came to visit the World's Fair found out—New York, while perhaps A SUMMER FESTIVAL, is not a place for people.

In the melody that language makes, the clue it gives as to whether we are civilized or not, I hear women and men seriously referring to their lovers as this or that "conversation piece" they were with at a party. Or somebody mentions that "distressed" is very expensive. "What is distressed?" I ask. "A certain type of antique furniture." Talk about confusion between sexes—we have leapt way beyond that, into a realm where the furniture is grief stricken and the people are pieces, the coldness of the original confusion helping to breed the unreality of the latter.

Dream-country, dance-country. One day I go through the city with a photographer. We are trying to do a documentary on dance studios. There is the B.D.L. studio—down-to-earth information, no strings attached—the MATA AND HARI, where "ethnic" is being taught. Over on the East Side little girls are dreaming their way upwards into becoming women by flinging leftover Isadora Duncan veils high above their heads. They are expressing themselves. "You are a seed, you are a tree, you are a woman, you are a little girl, breathe in, breathe out." On the Upper West Side, in a basement apartment near Columbia University, a sociology professor's wife is teaching the belly dance. (The sands of a floating future have leapt ahead ten years; the little girls are now twenty-year-olds.) I listen to the hootchy-kootch, note the book collection of Sartre, Malraux, Pearl Buck, etc., and I wonder—who does she want to become? The young women are wriggling their way into being Egyptian princesses for an hour. It is a sexy dance, so the professor's wife's myth is that it is "health giving." One woman is gone, swaying with the music, a fake diamond glittering in her naval; she is enthralled by her own magnificence, her eyes are never off the mirror. Something is wrong. It is a room of fantasy, and a room of no men—and if one dreams of being an Egyptian belly dancer, at least let men be in the fantasy. The women are doing it only for themselves. Ten minutes later the queen of the velvet tassels and diamonds is a young girl wrapped in an old raincoat, slumped and tired, her magic view of herself gone. "Gotta go home and make my husband his tuna fish," she mutters crossly.

"Are you planning on becoming a dancer?"

"Who—me? *Belly* dance?" she seems puzzled and shocked.

I ask her what she does during the day.

"I sew costumes for myself," she points to the elaborately worked velvet skirts. "Then I come here. Then I go home." She is twenty years old. An American dream-girl, an American lonely-girl.

Back across town, safely snuggled in the expensive solid warmth that Fifth Avenue exudes, is the Jewish Museum. Built as a monument to the traditions of the Jewish past, it is now the home of Pop Art. I look at the wild throwaway art on one side of the room and the Torahs on the other, and I laugh. The Pop Artists do not know what they are doing in the Jewish Museum, and the good middle-class Jewish matrons of New York are baffled equally by their guests. Oh, who is in charge? Who is he? Who is me?

Views has asked me some serious questions, such as Who is an American intellectual?—and I have responded by telling of dream people who walk through the streets of the city. Though I have thought about the exacting, precise questions the magazine has asked me, I prefer not to answer in your terms, your framework, which is too British, too Marxist, too logical, and would tell you nothing about America. Oh, one can say that New York is the supposed home of the intellectuals; most intellectuals are Jews; their political orientation came out of the thirties, and the postwar group has no political orientation, but these are superficial facts that are perhaps important to you, but not to us. As politely as I can, I would like to remind *Views* that it is your obligation to enter into our confusion, not ours to enter into your clarity. To feel the rhythm of our political thought, or our lack of it, remember that an intellectual is an American *before* he is an intellectual, a Jew is an American *before* he is a Jew, and a black is an American *before* he is a black. The current style of thought and writing in New York is the rediscovery of intensely Jewish or black childhoods in the most clichéd terms imaginable. Suddenly everyone has had a Jewish or black mama, and everyone has sprung up from nicely defined origins. This myth, at the heart of which exists a terrible lie and a spurious form of literary and intellectual con game, represents more our own inability to stomach the intensity of our present and past chaos, to impose an order, if only an ethnic order, on the unbearable. So it is back to the womb, the Jewish womb, the black womb—but the womb in a safeness, an orderliness and completeness that never was.

An American child learns of his history by being told of the American Revolution, which truly is our great pride, our great achievement. And whether rich or poor, white or black, the majority of children immediately must make a leap of the imagination. Were these our forefathers? Were they *my* forefathers? Half the time he is pretending that his forefathers *were* there, and the other half of the time he is trying to fathom the puzzle of where his ancestors actually were during the time when they were supposedly battling the British. Whichever truth he accepts, half of himself is continuously inventing. This creates a tremendous sense of detachment toward our government, which assumes a sort of phantom-like existence at best—and for our country the sense of nothing, not even place, ever being known or fully possessed.

An American goes through life haunted and driven to find the "givens" that every European child knows by the age of six. When a European is discussing politics, he generally sticks to the political. An American either drifts off abruptly into the personal world of his childhood—a world that remains eternally dark, subterranean, dream-like, and chaotic—or he leaps over that void into a pragmatic discussion of moral behavior, the puritan ethic. In our daily lives, and in our thinking, we now are committed in a most exhausting way toward a mode of life with a wildly lurching rhythm. On Monday . . . "Ah, America is on an upward swing," on Tuesday "Chaos has taken over!" on Wednesday "Well, nothing has *really* happened, just a bad dream, just a momentary nightmare." At the moment most of us are completely split in our own view of ourselves. Are we making daytime history or nightmare history?

Instead of cafés or pubs, the current mode of communication between New York intellectuals is to voice their intimate musings over paid TV or the symposium circuit.

What was striking about the symposium this past year that caused the most furor—the *Dissent* one on the Eichmann controversy—was not so much the controversy (about which much has been written) but the mood of the evening.

I walked into that midtown hotel, into that strange mixture of Jewish intellectuals and Jewish survivors: the survivors knowing nobody, the intellectuals turning heads, aware of who was there and who wasn't; the Jews discussing their past, seen in the light of masochism, while nearby, in another meeting, the black intellectuals were discussing their present, seen in the light of unfair suffering (and never mind theories of "masochism"). A crowded evening for midtown theater-district New York, a place where ordinarily the crowds gather for Richard Burton and Elizabeth Taylor.

The dead were not there that night, though their sins and bones were picked upon and tasted; it was a night when individual personalities, on either side of the debate, were flamboyantly making their presences felt. We are not a country accepting of death, and what was so strikingly different from the way a similar debate might have been carried on in a European country is that, beneath the static of fashionable ideas on masochism, etc., the underlying cry was, Tell me, tell me, people do not die. Tell me, tell me, *we* will not die. Or: What is it *like* to die? How do people act when they are about to be killed?

We do not know what it is like to die, and our intellectuals do not know either. America has never been invaded, never knelt down and never been humiliated, never lost. And so what has been, in one way or another, the major experience for European countries in this century, we see vaguely, through scrim. In the two generations represented there—the two that make up the current intellectual "scene" in New York—many of the older missed direct action in the last war by age and the younger group by youth; they have in common great gaps of experience. Because of this, some fairly elementary and sound ideas, such as it is not in one's own interest to be overly masochistic, take on wildly exaggerated and hysterical forms, owing to the fact that all is being evaluated in the abstract. With our native genius for finding happy, forward, optimistic, and positive solutions, the past became a utilitarian lesson in first aid for the future. "Surely," said one expert, "those who died would not want us to weep for them . . ." (Why not, I wondered.) "They would like us to profit by their deaths, learn for the future . . ." And a woman near me muttering "Oh, God, I hope we don't have too many of those survivors."

Hysterical and confused, the meeting became a shambles of itself, a study in brilliant disorder. Indeed, the Jews became so hysterical over the notion that Eichmann had been judged by Jews, and condemned by Jews (a hysteria that seemed to baffle the few Protestant intellectuals in the audience), that I seriously began to wonder if some uneasy memory of having been called

Christ-killers was bothering them. The notion of Jews publicly judging and executing a man, on their own, was throwing them into an indescribable panic.

And people who are afraid cannot be compassionate. I felt a sense of shock when I suddenly realized that something had happened in that meeting. Here were all of us, calmly listening and judging, while a timid soft-voiced woman, one of the heroines of the Warsaw ghetto uprising, was trying to explain, to justify herself—and I felt a terrible sense of shame, that whatever the intellectual ramifications and pickings, it had ended in this woman almost saying "please" to us who had not been there. True, she was applauded—but true also, she had to justify. A visiting Frenchman turned to a friend as the meeting disintegrated. "Les Américains," he said, "Vous êtes fous? Et pour Varsovie? Rien?"

I think he was thrown by the strange lack of somberness in the midst of ideas and statistics batted back and forth, the sophisticated knowingness of New York intellectuals, the utter lack of personal behavior, of knowing when and how, by the personalities interrupting and stamping up to the platform unasked, the lack of ritual, the lack of feeling.

I went home and thought that night of another meeting. I was seventeen—wandering through Europe—and had stopped in the lobby of a hotel in Montreux for a cup of hot chocolate, as I remember. There was a crowd gathering in the lobby; someone told me they were declaring the state of Israel—"You can go in if you like." What I remember of it now is that solemn roll call, those who weren't there made more important than those who were present. The names of small towns in Poland, odd-sounding names, and numbers—five hundred people, twenty people—and men weeping. Maybe I am simpleminded, sentimental, or simply not an intellectual, but that afternoon, I knew who I was, and something stuck, something that I would not forget. And how many years, and centuries, had passed since that hotel in Montreux at the *Dissent* meeting where we Americans had made that woman from Warsaw justify herself, and tell us over and over, like some invisible wall preventing the message from coming through . . . "We were alone, we were dying." And I wondered: If there was anyone seventeen at the *Dissent* meeting in that atmosphere of chaos, ambition, and self-hatred, would he have known who he was?

The New York year was open season on the Jewish debate, everyone getting in the act. Holocausts of the twentieth century degenerated into a private family battle: letters to one another—"Dear John, you and I have always been friends, but on the Eichmann matter. . . ." A private debate of maybe forty people talking to one another—and in it all that is wrong with New York intellectuals, their insularity, their insolence, and finally, what weakens them: their lack of desire to feel that "out there" there is anyone worth writing for.

Last year, as everyone knows, was a bad time for America. It started with the murder of the children in Birmingham, followed by the assassination of the President, murder of Oswald, chaos and death in Mississippi, violence in New York, and it was also the year that newspapers here felt called upon to remind this city of eight million that if thirty-five people see a woman being murdered they should not turn away. In that short space of time between Kennedy's death and now, America has dizzily embraced another ideal of the future, and we are now going to the polls with a choice, as the jokesters put it, between a crook and a madman. One would assume from all of this that the mood of New York intellectuals would be grim. As a matter of fact, their morale has never been better. It has been observed that people whose illness takes the form of withdrawal from their fellow human beings are often prone to suicide at the point when they still are capable of feeling loss—those who reach a state of complete loss of reality are less likely to kill themselves. And the "beyond" is where New York intellectuals are existing right now.

For them the Hudson River is a moat protecting them from the unknown barbarians "out there"—the rest of America—and their fortress is *Partisan Review*, *Commentary*, *The New York Review of Books*, et al. They are social critics who are afraid to know their own country, political experts divorced from politics, and literary critics whose smugness and insularity have created an atmosphere from which most writers have chosen to flee.

True enough, literary cliques have always existed. But this is a group with an especially unsavory history. To understand them, one has to go back to the America of the early fifties, the period when the American intellectual left signed its own moral death warrant by turning its back on the Red-baiting and, in fact, at times even contributing to it. Spiritually floundering, they came to the convenient conclusion that there was to be no more politics, no more literature, and no more ideology. In a sort of curse and death-wish toward the future, they spawned a curious group of heirs for ex-left-wingers.

Usually it is the sons who are rebels and the fathers who are businessmen. Neither writers nor critics themselves, what separated these second-wave heirs from their contemporaries who went the way of advertising agencies and Time, Inc. was merely that their ambitions were more grandiose. They set out to be the grand entrepreneurs of the intellectual; young men of the future, they sensed that the safest way to proceed in those uncertain years was by packaging the past. Cliques form for all sorts of reasons—anything from *épater la bourgeois*, to dada, to socialism, to belief in free love—but rarely do young men in their mid-twenties get together for the express purpose of bringing fame and fortune to a generation already established. At a time when in other countries youth was trying to break away from the Establishment, in New York energy was being directed toward the formation of a closed institution. The atmosphere this bred is also what accounts in part for the violent anti-intellectualism of the Beat Generation, and finally the death of New York—apart from the act of publishing—as the literary center of America. New York "belonged" to the intellectuals and their huckster sons, and neither generation could be respected.

The final achievement of the combined talents of these two groups has been *The New York Review of Books*, the dazzling new successful critical magazine of middle-aged brilliance. There is no doubt that the caliber of the individual articles is excellent. People read it, write for it, and buy it. Yet even those who appear on its pages seem to be somewhat ambivalent about their connection with it. The reason the magazine is disliked is because of the political history behind its birth, and because it is tangible and embarrassing proof of the American intellectual's success at leading the double life.

If Europeans are baffled by the ease with which our intellectuals have adjusted to Kennedy's death, their calmness over Goldwater's nomination—indeed, Americans were touched that Europeans took the President's death so personally (we could not seem to grasp that amount of feeling), and bemused that Europe is so concerned over the American "crisis"—it is because Europeans simply do not realize that, though America may be in trouble, American intellectuals have never had it so good. After all, the same ambitious Mama who produced the tycoon son also produced his brother, the tycoon intellectual. Now both brothers are on equal footing and, essentially, are leading the same lives. This has never before been true here, and our intellectuals are currently acting like the new-rich who don't know what to do with their money; the present mood of assurance that America can never be shaken, that the right-wing radicalism will never have serious consequences and that Mississippi is "somewhere else" reflects less a meshing with any current reality than it does contentment with their own personal status. The new "political realism" isn't *realpolitik*, it is ". . . if I can make it, so can America."

Older critics are fond of giving younger writers advice. And it can be a nice thing. One may go one's own way, but it is also good to have people from a previous generation whom one can admire. When I am in New York and see these critics they say to me what they say to all writers these days. "Stay away from the claque, they are ruthless, destructive, and they hate books." True. And it is also true that one can do one's own work and be published without having any contact with the literary mafia of Morningside Heights.

But what bothers me is that when they talk of the claque, they are talking of their own sons—the young men *they* created. And I think it is fair to judge people not only in terms of their own personal brilliance but also in terms of what they have inspired, what heritage they leave after them. I often ask them, in reply: If younger writers can do without entrepreneurs, why can't you? And if you believed in politics, why did you choose silent heirs? And if you believed in literature, why did you surround yourselves with those whom you say are capable of destroying it? What does what you say have to do with the way you have lived your lives? I have never been given a straight answer.

The American Mood

Kerouac and Mailer

1959

Anyone curious about the undercurrents of feeling during the Eisenhower administration would do well to look at Jack Kerouac's *On the Road*, which, amidst great fanfare, burst forth on the literary scene last year. He would do well, also, to examine its reception by both the public and the critics.

No doubt Kerouac is known abroad as the voice of the "Beat Generation"— a much misused phrase which has come to be a convenient tag for those fond of constantly categorizing the new young. Kerouac is certainly not a rebel, and it is doubtful whether he is a leader of the kind of young the critics have in mind for him. He, himself, is well on in his thirties and a product of an excellent New York private school as well as of Columbia University. What he has expressed, though, are the dreams and the conscience of an adult postwar America—what they might do if they had sufficient daring. His heroes are symbolic of the fantasies of our conventional society in the same way that the wandering protagonists of the Jack London, Horatio Alger, and Hemingway novels were symbolic of the dreams of the stay-at-homes of their time. In the name of God, purity, and sweetness he has provided a fantastic rationale for the insular, nonpolitical, apathetic man. Underneath the careless, boyish smiles there is raging ambitious ugliness, indeed, hatred.

It is no accident that in the society that produced Eisenhower as president, a writer like Kerouac was hailed with acclaim. Eisenhower also likes the good-natured ingenuous approach, and his solution to the problem of the cold war, atom stockpiles, radiation, etc., is innocently to proclaim our God-fearing goodness by broadcasting to the world Merry-Christmas-peace-on-earth mes-sages from our satellites travelling in space. Once the Kerouacian sentimental-ity is scraped away, he resembles something a good deal worse than Eisen-hower; he is more like a stream-of-consciousness blood brother of *Mein Kampf.* Just as officials bemoan juvenile delinquency as an obscure disease of teenagers and refuse to face the cause—a corrupt adult society—so it has been convenient to insist that Kerouac is writing about the prankish young and to ignore that this kind of festering sore afflicts all ages, all classes.

Many writers have shown evil, but Kerouac's special twist is that he must justify it, turn it around, bury it in confusion, chaos, speed, sentimentality, and religion, until ultimate evil becomes ultimate good. Many critics have ob-served that Kerouac might be a good writer if he straightened out his wander-ing style a little. This is impossible. His confusion, lulling rhythm, and lack of clarity is essential—as a cover-up. His world is the world of the "gang." His people travel in packs, but are friendless. A guy must have a "pal," but then he becomes suspicious, turns on him, and rushes off in search of a new friend, preferably someone thousands of miles away. Nothing is felt, but the yawning mouth of sensation must be filled, so newer and different kinds of violence must constantly be discovered.

Kerouac is in love with a world of "leaders" and "supermen." There are or-dinary people whose duty it is to follow (or be killed or robbed—the victims) and the exceptional men whose duty it is to lead us all. Old Bull Lee is a typical leader. He is a "great knower of life," having learned a great deal in Europe dur-ing the thirties. His exclusive concern, apparently, is the international cocaine set—the rumblings of the Second World War are strikingly absent from his European experience. His great literary heroes are Spengler and the Marquis de Sade, and his life's work is the study of the drug habit. He himself is a shining example of its salutary effects. He is keen and powerful, his wife and children are happy creatures of nature who make no demands. Their economic needs are mysteriously provided for by tolerant relatives somewhere in the back-ground. Old Bull Lee wallows in the myth of the America of long ago when men were men, life was free, and there was a rip-roaring lack of law and order. He preaches a violent hatred for his enemies—liberals, intellectuals, unions, and government—while the young gather at his feet and listen in awe.

The book is filled not with anger but with this sullen paranoid hatred. The only thing glorified is power, and the characters yearn for a mighty man who will show them the way.

> . . . *I'm a hotrock capable of everything at the same time and I have unlim-ited energy. . . . All the evil skulls of this world are out for our skin. It is up to us to see that nobody pulls any schemes on us. They've got a lot more up their sleeves besides a dirty arm. . . . I can go anywhere in America and*

45

get what I want because in every corner I know the people, I know what they do. . . . Every one of those things I said was a knife at myself. Everything I had ever secretly held against my brother was coming out: how ugly I was and what filth I was discovering in the depths of my own impure psychologies. . . . "It's not my fault! It's not my fault—" I told him. "Nothing in this lousy world is my fault, don't you see that? I don't want it to be and it can't be and it won't be."

Only conventional society escapes Kerouac's hatred. And why should he hate it? Indeed, why should society hate him? He is the perfect postwar consumer. He and society work hand-in-hand. Among other things, they share the same lack of respect for goods. Today the main thing is to buy and throw away. Kerouac's characters go one step further. They steal and they smash. Money is of no concern. A Cadillac is ruined "just for the hell of it"—but the owner does not object. Why should he? He can always buy a new one. This fantastic waste and destruction, which goes on about us daily, does not stem from a society liberated from money and materialism, but from a society where self-respect has been lost. Though Kerouacian characters live badly, this is out of *choice*—they are always confident that some benevolent relative will stake them, and that when they are ready some sort of job will be available in this past era of the fast and easy buck. A job is only a job. They are not interested in what they are employed in, or in doing a thing well. Though on the surface Kerouac is totally unlike the "responsible" members of the community, underneath, in a subtle way, his writing has touched a responsive chord. He makes people "feel good." He has made a pious cause out of indifference and violence and calls on that age-old God who is merely a servant of man, a whitewasher of guilt.

As an individual Kerouac has provided the public with its own image of what a writer should be—an impish boy-child of thirty-six or -seven who makes no pretense of mixing into the serious business of life, a writer who knows his proper place. His publisher proudly commented, about his TV and radio appearances, that Kerouac approaches all this "with the somewhat diffident air of an innocent bystander who accidentally got into the act."

Kerouac goes along with the tradition that a writer is apart from the community. In recent years our great writers like Hemingway, Faulkner, Tennessee Williams, plus the newer ones like Salinger, have all maintained a gentlemanly distance from the world. The common cliché is that intellectual contact will freeze a "creative writer" and that conversation will "ruin the material." Thought interferes with artistry; as for critical writing, of the sort that James and Proust indulged in, this is the greatest sin of all. The old-fashioned notion of the writer as a complete person—one who talks, writes, and takes an active part in society—is completely gone.

This low view of a writer's place in society has been absorbed by the critics themselves. They seem to have accepted a standard of evaluating writing and thinking (of a nonscientific nature) as varieties of hothouse flowers—ornamental, entertaining, nice to have around, but without effect on "real life," and perhaps this accounts for their lack of shock toward Kerouac's ideas.

Considering the intensity with which we play the literary game of who-is-our-national-spokesman? one would assume that, when a candidate appears, the critics would be interested in what he has to say. Despite the fantastic wordage written about Kerouac, nobody seemed to care what the book is about—with the exception of Norman Podhoretz in the *Partisan Review* and a few others. Some critics immediately treated Kerouac as a big joke—reflecting the intellectual's false pride in assuming that the stupid cannot be important. Others dwelt on his style, either praising his marvelous, peculiarly American sense of rhythm, or else damning the sloppiness of it all.

At a time when the newspapers were filled with articles decrying the growing crime rate, the *New York Times* referred to *On the Road* as:

> . . . *a long affectionate lark.* . . . *Moriarty is a good-natured and slap-happy reform school alumnus, is pathologically given to aimless travel, women, car stealing, reefers, bop, jazz, liquor and pseudo intellectual talk, as though life were just one long joy-ride that can't be stopped.*

Yet:

> *He is Mr. Kerouac's answer to the age of anxiety—and one of the author's real accomplishments is to make him both agreeable and sympathetic.*

An accomplishment indeed! Another *New York Times* review rated it as the major novel of our age and noted that:

> . . . *inwardly these excesses are made to serve a spiritual purpose, the purpose of an affirmation still unfocused, still to be defined, unsystematic.* . . . *It does not know what refuge it is seeking, but it is seeking.* . . . *The absence of personal and social values is* . . . *not a revelation shaking the ground beneath them, but a problem demanding day to day solution. How to live is more important than why.*

Violence in the name of "spiritual purpose" has cropped up over and over in the course of the History of Man—and never yet has produced anything but evil. Another reviewer felt impelled to grant that:

> . . . *what is attractive about it is not its wildness or its desperation but a certain unmistakable simplicity and openness of mind* . . . *when Mr. Kerouac says "whow!" he can convey a certain sense of wonder and innocence that is affecting.* . . .

Today Kerouac is beginning to be *passé*—but that is the wheel of fashion rather than an act of judgment. Actually the one writer, Norman Mailer, who has concerned himself most seriously with what he calls a new personality in America—the hipster who is an emotional outlaw—has met with tremendous public antagonism. The only book of his that has been accepted has been *The Naked and the Dead*, which deals with the more remote subject of war. Without attempting to analyze Mailer as a writer, it is interesting to note that *The Deer Park*, which dealt with hipsters and nonhipsters in postwar America in lucid and nonflattering terms, was considered to be a degenerate novel and met with a wrath never given to Kerouac. Mailer's view of the hipster is far sharper than Kerouac's—he is a moralist and a critic of society, while Keroauc is a *defender* of society, which is not the same thing at all. The public is intuitive about this, they know Mailer is not on "their side" . . . and while many people confusedly lump together Mailer's recognition of the importance of the hipster with Kerouac's glorification of violence, they have the sense to know Mailer is the one to dislike. There is no Mailerian cult—the motorcycle brigade doesn't read him at all. As he so aptly observed in an article called "The White Negro—Superficial Reflections on the Hipster":

> . . . *it is possible, since the hipster lives with his hatred, that many of them are the material for an elite of storm troopers ready to follow the first truly magnetic leader whose view of mass murder is phrased in a language which reaches their emotions.* . . .

The existence of this explosive energy, which has no outlet (unless we go to war again) in people who have become dehumanized, is something to be dealt with. The fact that Kerouac's defense of this violence has been ignored points up a sad heritage of the McCarthy era. Fear is gone, we are free to write what we please—because it doesn't matter any more. Some surprise was expressed abroad that while in England and France a censorship war over *Lolita* was raged no issue was made here. It is not surprising at all—we have better things to fuss about than books. Naturally if critics are eunuch custodians of an impotent literature, moral judgments are beside the point. Which is why they see in Kerouac only a shy little word-clown, and are indifferent to his appealing apologia of fascism new-style—a grinning, friendly, romantic fascism of the spirit.

The University:
Everyone's Gold Mine

(Diana Trilling and
Allen Ginsberg
at Columbia)

1960

In the last decade or so the American university has been put to unprecedented use by industry, the mass media, and research teams, as well as by intellectuals who find it a handy home base. One result has been a failure on the part of the university to maintain itself as a value center for the young. Even worse, the student tends to become a public animal, fair game for all comers.

Today's student is proclaimed a failure before he starts. In the name of necessary research, scores of studies such as *The Unsilent Generation* by Otto Butz have been made. The thoughts, ideals, and private lives of the students have been picked at and probed into by teachers, behavioral scientists, and critics. Now the popular media people have also joined in. Generally, the conclusions of these studies show the young to be a rather dismal, apathetic lot. Obviously the mass magazines and TV have a stake in the student because their business is to explore whatever topics are currently in vogue. But as for the more serious studies, why are they made? What use do they serve? Why all this attention to the adolescent's views on society? Why all the negative conclusions? So far as I can see, it is a case of hoping that the blind will lead the blind. The educators and intellectuals have lost their way; they are no longer sure of their own ethical values. In the Greek sense, they have ceased to be teachers. Instead they have turned on their students.

Turnabout is fair play. The world and the university have examined the student. Now, how does that same world and university size up from the student's point of view? The first thing the student becomes aware of in the new university atmosphere is hurry: hurry and a fantastic respect for success. In an attempt to do away with the ivory-tower approach to education, the universities have endorsed a quick, slick professionalism. Their relation to business is becoming inreasingly intimate. More and more courses which are essentially apprenticeship courses aimed at specific careers are available to the undergraduate student. Indeed, apprenticeship is replacing scholarship.

Years ago, the freshman student in English composition was of interest to no one but himself, his teacher, his friends, and his relatives. His teacher was generally someone who thought of teaching as a full-time profession. Today his young counterpart quickly gets to a "creative writing workshop" and as a "young writer" has a direct marketable value to the publisher always on the lookout for new talent. (I am using writing as an example, but, in different ways, the same essential experience occurs in the language, engineering, science, journalism, drama, and government "fields.")

We've come a long way from the time when the Pepsi-Cola prize was unique. Today, industry besieges the university with student prizes. The student is grateful for the recognition and the financial reward—but he also realizes that industry is conducting a talent hunt on the campus. What possible harm is there, one can ask, in allowing a young writer publication in a respectable, established magazine? On the surface, none. This practice, however, has its repercussions. One, the prestige and importance of the undergraduate magazine has suffered. A student has his eyes on *Mademoiselle* or the *Paris Review*; he no longer devotes his interest or energies to the local publication. Two, subconsciously, at a very young age he molds his talents to what he thinks is wanted of him. The future is so golden and so little is asked of him. He need only not appear an amateur!

The other publication which beckons invitingly to the student comes from within the university. This is the little magazine serving the needs of the intellectual community which has come to rely on the universities to provide a good address. In focusing on these magazines rather than on the genuine undergraduate publication, the student is unaware that he is up against another kind of professionalism—intellectual professionalism—and that the attitudes of this world are just as preconceived and rigid as those of the commercial world.

Unless he is an extraordinary human being, the new part-time teacher, with his commitments to other worlds, both intellectual and industrial, carries into his classroom the sense that what really counts is happening outside. He is under all sorts of pressures. In today's busy world of conferences and meetings, schedules have a way of overlapping. The part-time professor hired by the university to give the students a chance to study with an "expert in the field" is in reality a man harassed by two jobs. Often assistants have to take over the classes and the student quickly learns that he is of only secondary importance to the busy teacher. The relationship between the part-time expert and the university is vague and impersonal. This new, rootless Academia has little awareness of itself and no real notion of its obligations to the university.

The modern teacher-student relationship is more practical than spiritual. Scholarship is no longer an end in itself. It has been replaced by an excessive emphasis on career. Both the professors and the university administration shower the student with opportunities to meet his future employers, and, of course, the new American way of life has become ever onward and upward with fellowships and grants. Some of these gatherings are of more benefit to industry on a talent-hunt than to the students, who are of an age when they should be more concerned with learning and less aware of "jobs." What is the effect of all this on the student? He concludes that the university has tremendous awe and respect for this outside world and wholeheartedly embraces its values. He also gets a premature notion of his own success or failure. The clever ones quickly learn how to navigate. They pick the professors who can "help them along professionally." The atmosphere is filled with tension and artificial stimulation, where the message of "get smart quick" is constantly blared forth.

The university serves industry in more ways than by merely being a free employment agency. Affiliation with the *name* of a good university is an excellent way for business and advertising to buy prestige cheap, and prestige is a very valuable commodity these days. In this era of the "new Nixon," the intellectual and liberal is coming into his own again; he is now blue-chip stock.

A good example of business's misalliance with the university is *Esquire* magazine's "cultural" get-together with Columbia University a year ago last fall. Because of competition from the new pseudo-girlie magazines like *Gent* and *Playboy*, and a decline in its advertising sales, about a year or so ago *Esquire* decided to become more respectable. This metamorphosis finally culminated in a wedding—a literary symposium at Columbia University's McMillan theater with *Esquire* as the aggressive groom, Columbia as the uncertain bride, and the students as the embarrassed bastard children.

Now, I have no quarrel with *Esquire* for trading its half-naked females for the works of established serious writers, peppered with an occasional newcomer, and I realize that this is the way they started out many years ago. (I do fear, however, that it will remain a publishing source of good writers only so long as quality writing has a good trade-in value with the advertiser, and it is not to be counted on when times get rough for the intellectual.) But I am concerned when a mighty university like Columbia, to the disgust of its own students, sells itself short to Madison Avenue.

Students receiving the silver invitations announcing the two-part symposium in honor of *Esquire's* twenty-fifth anniversary co-sponsored by *Esquire* and Columbia's School of General Studies failed to see any connection between the two institutions. Why any magazine? But especially, why *Esquire*? Indeed, what does one of our greatest universities have in common with a magazine that until recently most parents preferred their children not to see? Does the Columbia faculty think that you can buy a good name and honest intellectual conscience overnight? My own guess is that *Esquire* managed to appear very shiny, powerful, and magically impressive to the Columbia faculty. This is the "real" world, and to it one must pay homage. Most teachers tacitly accept the public view of themselves as second-rate citizens and are much more easily intimidated by the business world than people realize.

The theme of this symposium was the writer's place in America. Discussed at some length was the new phenomenon of the writer-teacher. Listening to the speakers argue back and forth about the relative merits of the campus as being a good or bad atmosphere in which the writer could "create," I had the uncomfortable feeling that I was listening to some voyagers remarking on the merits of plane travel over sea travel. But what about the students? Not one of the speakers mentioned his role or obligation as a teacher.

The most shocking feature of the symposium was the way Arnold Gingrich, editor of *Esquire*, treated the students while he was presiding over the second meeting. Apparently he had been angered by the earlier session, which had been conducted by a faculty member in a leisurely university manner. Too slow, and too much student participation. True, he wanted questions from the audience, but they were to be short and snappy. Above all, he warned, no student opinion. He was Gingrich, the editor, trying to organize a "brainstorm." The speakers on the platform looked uncomfortable as they watched him lose his temper. Unable to make his audience respond with the precision of a business conference, Gingrich was reduced to the obscenity of insulting and mocking them, producing only a hostile silence for his troubles.

At the end of the evening the chic and fashionable crowded up front to meet the speakers, and the students went home. Walking along Upper Broadway I heard one student excitedly remark to his friend how much he would have liked to ask a certain question of one of the writers, but he hadn't wanted to make a fool of himself in front of that Gingrich character. His friend shrugged his shoulders. "Oh well," he replied. "Viva *Esquire*."

I was reminded of Gingrich's fiasco at Columbia when I read Diana Trilling's account, "The Other Night at Columbia," in the Spring 1959 *Partisan Review*. On the surface Diana Trilling and Arnold Gingrich are quite different. He represents the commercial world; she the world of the intellect. She, as a critic, writes only for the most rarefied reviews. Her husband, Lionel Trilling, an outstanding critic and writer, is also a professor at Columbia University. Gingrich merely pretended to be interested in the student, as a backdrop for his anniversary celebration. Diana Trilling, in her article, expressed apparent serious concern for the student, and one student in particular. This was Allen Ginsberg, also an ex-student of her husband. Yet she and Gingrich do have something in common, and that is an underlying contempt for the student.

Presumably she wrote the article because she was worried that the intellectual and teacher have failed to lead the student. She examines the case of Ginsberg and implies that if the teachers had not turned their backs when Ginsberg and all the other "lost boys of the forties" had wanted to talk, there might not be a "Beat Generation" today. I have no quarrel with this suggestion—but the tone of her article is incredible. Her concern is mixed with antagonism. The core of her article deals with Ginsberg's triumphant return to Columbia for an evening of poetry reading. She quite casually writes of how she and other faculty wives had scores of back-and-forth telephone calls: should they go and watch the freak show, or should they not? The brave ladies finally decided to attend the poetry reading, prepared to hold their noses against the stench.

Mrs. Trilling saw nothing amiss in stating that she, as a faculty wife, went to a Columbia University function expecting the audience, of whom a large part were obviously Columbia students, to "smell bad" and look seedy. Are these same students, after being called "rabble" and "hordes of barbarians" by Mrs. Trilling, expected to face her husband in the classroom with the respect to which he is entitled? Or should they feel mollified because Mrs. Trilling did not find them as dirty as she had expected?

Mrs. Trilling echoes the concern of university administrators throughout the country over the chaotic, frenetic atmosphere created when writers such as Kerouac are invited to speak. The universities, however, have brought this on themselves by *making* the student body into a public animal. They, not the students, have called the outside world in; they have conducted the studies encouraging the students to reveal their private lives; yet now they are worried about student exhibitionism. Mrs. Trilling deplores the ugliness of the *Life* cameraman with flashbulb poised at Ginsberg's poetry reading. Yet she sees nothing wrong in revealing intimate facts about Ginsberg's life known to her only because her husband was his teacher and confidant.

Who, indeed, has ever thought to teach this generation reticence? The faculty cannot solve this problem, which has gotten out of hand, by storming off the platforms at these gatherings, or by presiding half-heartedly, just to get the whole show over with. They cannot abdicate responsibility and teach responsibility. What they can do is let the students invite their own speakers and close the meetings to the general public and press. Is there a law that says *Life* magazine must attend student functions? I doubt that last year's Hunter meeting, when Kerouac spoke, would have been such a mess if the presence of the cameramen and radiomen had not been a stimulant to the wildness for the purpose of mass audience entertainment.

Unfortunately, this will not occur until the large university rediscovers its own attitude toward its prime function. One reason the individual professor cannot be more forceful in maintaining his position against the onslaught of the outer world is that in today's society it is hard to feel strong and worthwhile when one earns substandard wages. The professor is forced to eke out his income in ways he regards as not being wholly honest—grants, international junkets, excessive publishing, etc. The university's complex alliance with the subsidizing world of big business, mass media, foundation grants, and research projects, plus its role as home base for the footloose intellectual, leads to regarding real education as a minor concern.

The greatest damage done to the student, however, is the *attitude* taken toward him by the generation which should be showing the way. Undoubtedly, the majority of educators, critics, intellectuals, and sociologists of a certain age come from the ranks of pre-Second World War political liberals. Having been obsessed with feelings of confusion, guilt, and bewilderment since the war, they have buried their own self-hatred and frustration by turning on the next generation and damning it in advance. If the ship sinks, let's all go down together.

Critics like Mrs. Trilling (and Leslie Fiedler is another) are more forthright than the sociologists. Angrily she describes the Columbia audience as being *crazily* young . . . so few of the girls are pretty, so few of the boys manly. (The reverse is that the young are too old.) According to her the thirties was a glorious time, and intellectuals never had it better. She feels that those were the days when Jews were real Jews, blacks were real blacks, and Stewart's Cafeteria was a wonderfully gay, witty Village cafeteria, not like the dreary West End Bar today's Columbia students have to put up with. Though she is proud that her youth was a time of passion and feeling, she, like Fiedler, seems a little ashamed of what the feeling was about. For her (and all the others) the great overwhelming and irrevocable tragedy of today's youth is that they were not born in her time.

But one's birth date is never one's "tragedy." We cannot transport ourselves into the glory that was Greece, the brilliance of the Renaissance, or the golden age of Stewart's Cafeteria. Nor should human beings have the egotism to feel that they *should* live in an "ideal" time. But we can absorb the past. And if the thirties was such a valid experience, why are the survivors unable to communicate and make it meaningful today? In all good things there is historical continuity, one generation gives to the next. Why has that generation drawn a curtain of silence? It is they, uncertain and ashamed of their attitudes, who have isolated their life experience rather than let it take root and flower.

No, the loss of today's generation is not in our having to make do with the West End Bar instead of Stewart's Cafeteria in the Village. For if we are to survive anything, we will survive by being of our own time. But our moral destruction may come ever so gently via the Drake Room.*

*A fancy place popular with *Esquire* staff.

Günter Grass

There Are No Fascists
in Greenwich Village

1983

The other day, riding in a taxi up Madison Avenue, I noticed a group of New Yorkers gathered over a felled pedestrian; his body was crumpled flat out in the gutter. When we neared the accident I realized that the body was a robot—and that nobody in that crowd struck me as experienced in handling this sort of situation. Does automobile insurance cover the knocking down of robots? Should an ambulance company be notified? Would the callous escaped motorist be accused of hit-and-run driving? The robot—he, she, or it—had collapsed into such a pathetic fetal position, I yearned to provide some comfort to the poor thing.

Later at home I brooded about the injured robot; this has been the season of the writer and the technological revolution, and machines are on my mind. Obviously none of the folk at Sony or IBM have noticed that the yearly average income of the writer is deep below poverty level. Yet, overnight, despite the cost, every writer in Manhattan has been struck with computer fever. Between Christmas and New Year's day my Smith-Corona old-faithful portable electric had become a piece of prehistory and my snooty choosy thrift shop wouldn't even let me *give* it away. I was one of those caught short: before Christmas I was still proud that my 1968 portable Smith-Corona plugged into the wall, and that I knew how to put a Duracell battery into a cassette machine.

By mid-January, writers' seminars that would turn us into jiffy technological experts had mysteriously proliferated between Tribeca and Morningside Heights. My writer friends instantly had become competitive about their new-found expertise. One bragged that her machine had one thousand pages of memory, and plugged into Japan, the *New York Times*, and spelling programs in fourteen languages. My friends gave their machines names like AU-THORITY, PRETTY BABY, and SMART BOY. I felt too squelched to admit that I never kept "information" (my father once cautioned me: remember your mind is not a garbage pail; a library is for storage, but your mind is for thinking)—and I also scurried out and bought my computer.

But while we New York writers have been busy hoarding the world's information and tinkering with software, the visiting Europeans—not realizing we were involved with our word processors—were flocking to our shores trying to engage us in some other kind of dialogue that, more often than not, has to do with their private and public agendas. Earlier this season Yves Montand had a nice go at it in his New York press interviews, apropos his jam-packed sentimental retrospective concert here of the sorts of French cowboy songs that made him famous. Rather abruptly, I thought, he suddenly accused America of being too soft on Russia; we were, he said, *naïve* about Russia. Since during the previous thirty years he had steadily berated America for being too anti-Russian, this turnabout took real *chutzpah*. Even more nervy was his surprising statement about being pleased with himself that he had made Marilyn Monroe so happy just before she killed herself. Clearly these visiting European luminaries are not in any real dialogue with an American audience; in their blasts to our press they are stage-directing a clever form of transatlantic make-believe. I have learned over the years (and because I read the European press) to decipher some of their more off-the-wall criticisms of us by mentally conjuring up their broadsides as probably headlined (European correspondents always blow up to full scale the American statements made here by their visiting artists) in *Le Monde* the next day. To a Frenchman drinking coffee in a Left Bank café such bravado reads as though, single-handedly, a French Robin Hood has told "Amerika" en masse to shove it. That most of America never got the message, or even cared, never gets reported.

The Germans launched their big transatlantic cultural happening—their first Book Fair in New York—this past March. I went with some of my friends down to The New School for the star event: to hear Günter Grass talk about the responsibility of the writer. I admired *The Tin Drum*; indeed, the novel had a special meaning for me. My grandfather on my mother's side had been born in Grass country, and after reading Grass's novel, I got a better take on the family history. My great-grandmother had smuggled whiskey in a wagon across the Polish–German border near Königsberg; she supported my grandfather with her bootlegging while he piously read books. So I am the American descendent of pious Baltic smugglers. (My father's folk were sporty unpious Viennese.) My family's tales about the Baltic Sea—the good fishing, the border smuggling, the high and low town life, and the urban mixture of Poles, Germans, Jews, and other assortments—are of the world Günter Grass re-created in *The Tin Drum*.

I was chagrined that Günter Grass, as soon as he started to speak in the overflowing New School auditorium, found us Americans so wanting: Why, he complained, weren't we more like Gabriel García Márquez or Carlos Fuentes? What was curious was that it had been Günter Grass who had *insisted* that John Irving should be the American novelist on the platform. Now John Irving has all sorts of talents, but it doesn't take much wit to know he obviously never meant to pattern himself on the European *engagé* mode. I mean, if you want to debate with a Marxist intellectual, why request a flamenco dancer? But our urban intellectuals generally have held little interest for visiting Europeans—they appear to be too mundane, too middle class. What's always been wanted is our exotics. European writers admire our Southern writers, our Gothics, our jazz, whether the ancient jazz beat of Harlem or, now, break-dancing. Our fast junk-food and Clint Eastwood.

While Günter Grass took over and pounded out the ugly historic traumas of the twentieth century, ride-'em-cowboy Irving and the more dream-like Joyce Carol Oates, the other American novelist on the panel, were in orbit on other planets. An eerie evening. It felt rather like watching a Fassbinder movie about America. Nobody was making even enough contact for a real argument. Though Günter Grass obviously had chosen not to be pleasant (and to ignore that he had drawn such huge crowds of admirers that many people had to be turned away at the door), some of his political questions to Irving were deserving of a serious response. Grass's point was that one couldn't see as entirely separate events the occurrences in Argentina—it is estimated that thirty-five thousand people were killed or disappeared during Argentina's military dictatorship—and positions taken by the American government toward that dictatorship. What, he was asking, was the American writer's response to all this?

One could answer Grass in many different ways. I squirmed because John Irving chose to play American *enfant terrible*, acting like a know-nothing, which he is not. So, from the audience, Jacobo Timmerman tried to intervene: he attempted to reach Irving by repeating that what Grass meant was that the existence of those Argentinian torture camps had been partially the result of America's policies in Latin America. Though Grass had been wildly simplistic and propagandistic in his statements, his question still demanded a reflective reply. Irving, from the platform, peered down at Timmerman, who was in one of the front rows, then drawled: "Well, you are a journalist, and I am an imaginative novelist—I have blood in my stories." Irving was equating his ketchup and Grand Guignol effects with Timmerman's personal suffering and the traumatic tragedies of the twentieth century! I sank back in my seat, mortified at having the United States so represented to Europe. The audience was intelligent; there was an embarrassed silence. A man seated in the row ahead of me whispered not so *sotto voce* to a friend: "I think it was H. L. Mencken who said God protects women, children, invalids, and Americans."

The atmosphere in the auditorium became sullenly diffuse. Grass's remarks were increasingly belligerent—we Americans have become the new Nazis, etc.—and he seemed disconcerted that neither those on the panel nor his audience seemed willing to argue with him. A student seated near me wondered aloud: Didn't Grass realize that Americans are more adept at producing anti-American data than the Europeans? "Hey, Grass," the student then called out, "defending American right-wing military policies is not what we do here—there are no fascists in Greenwich Village." Joyce Carol Oates and John Irving behaved as though Grass, with his twentieth-century historical fetish, merely had gone to a university in a town unfamiliar to them and had been taught to play a different game of baseball with different ground rules.

Grass, left to himself, finally began to accuse himself for having been part of the Nazi Youth group. He turned to Joyce Carol Oates and asked her why Americans weren't worried that they might be proliferating Nazis the way Germany did in 1933. She thought, and then, in her small-girl flat upstate-New York cadence, succinctly replied: "Because Americans aren't Germans." Though Grass clearly had been asking for it, the evening regressed into an ethnocentric shambles: your country against mine.

Jakov Lind, the Austrian Jewish novelist who as an adolescent (he was separated from his family) managed to spend the war in Berlin without his identity being discovered by the Germans, finally got up and said, "Enough, Günter. We don't want your guilt—it's *over*."

After the evening ended, and the auditorium emptied, I noticed that Jakov and Grass went off to have a drink together. They shared a mutual history; they came from the same time and place. Several of us walked toward Fifth and Washington Square Park. The weather was an end-of-winter drizzle. Silently I thought about it all. It had been such a bizarre evening. Grass had seemed so unaware of the multitude that had waited in line several hours to hear him and had been turned away for lack of space. He had blind spots, seeing only the enemies he carried around in the pictures inside his own head. His America was a cliché; where, he sighed, was the marvelous America of Dos Passos, the good old days of the 1930s? Though Rooseveltian America did have some wonderful qualities about it, I suspect that the dream America Grass romantically extolled came from the Hollywood films of the thirties and forties. In truth

America then was more bigoted, more narrow-minded, and far more politically slumbering than now. I felt sad. It was a waste of time for good writers to get caught in such provincial cultural politics.

Since everyone is evoking the imaginary snows of yesteryear, I would like to believe that when Gertrude Stein, Picasso, and Matisse broke a croissant together in that Paris of the twenties that exists as a dreamscape in my mind, they didn't come to the café with flags waving.

The Person Alone

In Edward Albee's two-character play, *The Zoo Story*, the publisher asks the young man who accosts him in Central Park if he lives in the Village. The boy, who eventually forces the publisher to kill him in a desperate attempt to experience some human contact, replies that he lives in a rooming house on the Upper West Side. He describes the dreariness of his home and tells how he tried first to make a friend of the janitor's mangy dog, and when that didn't succeed, at least an enemy. Anything, anything, is his mute cry, just to be among the living. For Albee it is a shabby West Side rooming house; for Saul Bellow, in his somber *Seize the Day*, it is a run-down West Side hotel.

The West Side is not only the familiar sandwich with a hard crust on the Park and River sides of semi-fashionable large apartment houses, the homes of the wealthy Jewish middle class of an older generation, and the soft in-between of slum avenues and side streets crowded with Irish and newly arrived Puerto Ricans. It is also a subtle composite including residents of no particular ethnic or economic group. The most notable recent change during the last decade has been the invasion of the neighborhood by actors, TV people, and young couples who can no longer afford the Village (witness the tremendous success of the Reform Democrats here). But what is least apparent is that all along the West Side—from the fifties up to Morningside Heights, which is the home of students and professors, in the endless brownstones, whitestones, small tenements, and once-upon-a-time well-kept hotels of World War I vintage—lives, almost unnoticed, the anonymous wanderer, the single person hopelessly lost in the city.

In canvassing the neighborhood during an election one expects to meet, all in their proper habitat, the Puerto Ricans, the Irish, the Jews, and now, the young marrieds. As you climb up the last flight of stairs of some battered five-story brownstone, you recognize the peculiar stale odor that emanates from the rooms of old people—the underweared, housecoated recluses who have a bit of a job or a tiny pension, some at the bottle, some fussing over eggs at the stove, some reading and rereading yesterday's newspaper. Then there are the countless times you knock at a door—and this comes as a real shock—only to be confronted over and over again by a neatly dressed young man or woman immobilized in a small clean room. The expression on their faces is a strange mixture of expectancy and resignation—almost as though they are waiting for the world to come in and find them. Despite the vast numbers of young people living alone in this broad area there is little in the neighborhood that indicates their silent presence. You don't see many of them on the street; there is maybe one genuine café in a sixty-block radius and hardly any bookstores.

Who are they and why do they come here? Most are from out of town. In the past few years there are more foreigners; students from Europe, Asia, and the Middle East in a turnabout trend are now discovering America. Since the Village is becoming the home of the well-heeled, and has always had more apartments to offer than rooms, it is now uptown for the true transient, who is neither solvent nor shrewd enough to "make it" in midtown or on Bleecker. His (or her) plans are indefinite; with no roommate to split the costs it is useless to lease or sublet a real apartment. In the newspaper ads the rooms on the West Side appear the most inviting. Low rents, good space, and one can pay by the week or month. No furniture is necessary. A few paperbacks, a plant, and some dishes from Woolworth's and you're in. You are convenient to subways, it's nice to be near a river, nice to be near a park—and as for the bleakness, the shabby atmosphere, you assume this is the way of the city, you know no different. What the stranger doesn't realize is that it is fatal to be alone in the city and to have found no "style."

The worst off are the almost-talented. These are the discontented who are not discontented enough; the adventurous who are not adventurous enough; the seekers who are unsure of what they are seeking. As men are more quickly forced to resolve themselves in their work, it is particularly the women who flounder in this nether land. They take mediocre jobs during the day and by night haunt the lectures, the courses. Those who neither leave the city nor "make it," curling inward in a shy defeat, search for a less threatening existence. What they do not find—the women who do not wish to become suburban matrons but who do not possess either the shrewdness to become fashionable careerists or enough sense of self to become true individualists—is the sympathetic way of life they assumed the city could give the "sensitive" person.

As for the genuine bohemians or intellectuals (a group so unsure of its own existence that the American language has never had a fitting noun: student? bohemian? intellectual?), though they are drawn to the city, the city is not always equally drawn to them. In the flat, arid time from which we are just pulling out, life for the intellectual has been particularly hard. The pall McCarthyism cast over the country not only instilled fear but in all sorts of intangible ways robbed the younger generation of communication with those who preceded them. Political lethargy, prosperity, plus the fantastically young marriage, which is directly related to the political and economic framework, have all had a numbing impact on the youth of the city. The person between twenty and thirty who is past college yet not completely adult, who is neither married nor a homosexual, finds he is almost a misfit. Thus the abrasive effect of what should be the true formative years is being experienced only by a tiny "oddball" minority— a minority tragically forced to grow up alone.

Not only is there no moral home for the person who comes to the city but there is also no physical home—no place to go. The West Side, which in recent years has become the habitat of the artist, writer, musician, and intellectual, as well as the footloose floater, barely recognizes the existence of this "subterranean" population. Where does one go to talk? I remember a particularly frustrating afternoon when I wished to discuss a manuscript with a friend—we walked along the Upper West Side finding: 1) cafeterias where you couldn't smoke, 2) bars that were too dark, and anyway we didn't want to drink, 3) restaurants that expected you to order a full meal. We ended, incongruously, chatting in the stilted atmosphere of the lobby of a large once-grand hotel.

In place of the European café, where with a little initiative and the price of a coffee you can meet your own generation, we have instead the specialized school for the nonspecialist. Art and drama schools have become extremely popular in the past ten years partially because they provide a safe haven for the wanderer, a world within a world. The new type of actor is not so much a member of the economically underprivileged seeking a short cut to fame, but the "poet actor," who desires, more than fame and money, to "find himself." One of the great appeals of the Method is that, as a school, it offers tolerance for the unrooted, the person who in different times might never have considered being an actor. One of its great limitations is that its appeal rests on a private emotional situation that has nothing to do with the theater.

Of all the artists, the writer has suffered most during this period. He has no natural place of congregation such as the concert hall, the art gallery, or the theater where he can meet his contemporaries. Traditionally, he learns his craft through his own experience. The writer is the first to feel the pinch of political repression, and he is especially harmed by the rigid separation of the university "academic intellectual" from the "creative personality."

A strong theme this past decade in all the arts—painting, sculpture, writing, the theater—has been the isolation of the individual caught in the prison of an overcrowded but lonely civilization. Why does the person alone, the artist, the intellectual, persist in coming to New York if life here is so hard? Because life in the rest of the United States is even more isolated; and here in the city there is always the magic possibility of sudden change. Why do writers and artists stay less long in Europe than they did in the twenties and thirties? Because, for better or worse, we are a world power. New York may represent the "decline of the Roman Empire," but it is Rome nevertheless. In all its violent electric beauty of buildings, bridges, mechanization, and its infinity of nameless people, with all the virtues and vices of this time, it is the true twentieth-century city.

Experimental theaters, bookstores, and cafés are now springing up where before there was nothing; students are beginning to picket Woolworth's and oppose civil defense programs where before they were silent. I observe this, and I suspect that in the next decade things will be more open. Yet despite some improvements, loneliness in the city is, unfortunately, never a mere question of decades. This is not a "scandal" one can get angry about or protest nor is it a condition that a committee can correct. I remember being eighteen and hearing for the first time in the warmth of a Paris café the word "alienation." Everyone was violently disagreeing with one another about the meaning of the word, but essentially they were all speaking the same language. And I remember coming back to New York with its rooming houses, its poverty and prosperity, its fabulous life and its nothing life, and discovering, emotionally, what the word meant.

Dwight Macdonald's
Against the American Grain

1963

Though the essays in *Against the American Grain* date from the last ten years—a time when Dwight Macdonald substituted literary concerns for political inquiry—his orientation is still basically political. In "Masscult and Midcult" he takes a long look into History, admiring the ordered preindustrial revolutionary world when there was no bad art or fakery purposely produced. What separated good from bad was degree of talent rather than difference of intent. By the end of the nineteenth century there was a solid market for trash, and, at the other extreme, artists and writers who created a private art and who were speaking only to themselves. By the mid-twentieth century the avant-garde, the good, the bad, and the fatal in-between have all become mixed in one indigestible bouillabaisse, and Macdonald has assigned himself the position of pointing out which is which. His concern is "not so much with the dead sea of masscult as with the life of the tide line where the decisive struggles for survival take place between higher and lower organisms."

This is precisely the spot Macdonald attacks over and over again, getting at a political view through literature. Somewhere in "Masscult and Midcult" Macdonald finds it in Ortega y Gasset's bed—the masses are destructive of civilization, the elite, the preservers of tradition. It is a perfectly valid conclusion, and yet once Macdonald arrives at it he shies away from the implications. A world for the elite? It is not easy for a longtime left-winger who is also American to say: "I am Charles de Gaulle." At least the radical philosophies held out the promise of a super-democracy, room for one and all—but there is a very real problem when one's sense of moral values and one's highly developed cultural tastes are in battle with one another. After hastily leaving Ortega y Gasset's elite in mid-air as being too undemocratic, Macdonald pokes around for a bit in some continental philosophy, but the moody dark-night-of-the-soul approach to making theory out of chaos is not really his way either. Again, he goes along with the ideas of Kierkegaard whom he quotes as representing his own outlook; but again, it is not his temperament to sit too long in darkness.

Finally, he comes full circle and triumphantly finds his method of attack—he is, indeed, at home in "The American Grain." His way of thinking is closest to those profoundly pessimistic, skeptical men in eighteenth-century America, who, after taking account of man's ever-continuing potential for evil, busily set about defining, through the "word," a government which would protect man from other men, man from government, and finally, even government from government. Their style was balanced and rational. The word defined the ideal.

For Macdonald, too, "an idea doesn't exist apart from the words that express it. Style is not an envelope enclosing a message: the envelope *is* the message." Curiously, though Macdonald expresses a personal dislike for the legal mode of inquiry with its undue emphasis on "what are the facts?"—his own method *is* very legalistic. He destroys middlebrow values, getting rid of this class, if not in actuality, at least literarily, by a merciless breakdown of style which shows just what "the facts" are in what we consider to be good. Behind the fuzzy sentences that fill our literature is the celebration of even fuzzier values. Fortunately, Macdonald's facts are a lot funnier than most lawyers'. "The disposings of accustomed practice, the preparations of purpose and consent, the familiar mute motions of furtherance" is *not* a legal document but one of those famous Cozzens *echt* sex scenes. He delights in following this with another quote from critic Jessamyn West: ". . . the passages having to do with physical love have a surprising lyric power." Or, as Cozzens himself says of his hero, "The unbending intricacies of thought . . . seem to send his sentences into impossible log jams."

Macdonald does a hatchet job on the updated version of the King James Bible; it commits the double crime of being stylistically inferior to the old version and of obliterating old traditions. The language is dead, Jesus gathering the children unto himself has been replaced by what sounds like a mother calling the kiddies in from a picnic. Things are no better across the Atlantic. Along with rock-and-roll we have exported the American adolescent genius. Macdonald notes, with horror, that the British were as unthinkingly enthusiastic over Colin Wilson's *The Outsider*—a swinging, get-hip-with-pessimism grabbag of literature and philosophy—as Americans were over Cozzens. Macdonald does dispose of the mediocre extremely well. But by focusing so much on what is bad taste he risks reducing everything to matters of style and "good taste."

Macdonald is a great admirer of Norman Mailer—but is it Mailer's clarity of style that gives him his force? Where does Dostoyevsky fit in among the rational thinkers? I prefer Ralph Ellison's work to John Updike's—but Updike writes some very beautiful sentences. One reaction to middlebrow is the romanticism of the Beats—the desire to smash the language entirely—and at the other extreme we have our stylists, as epitomized by the current fiction in *The New Yorker*, who distinguish themselves from middlebrow precisely in the area of "taste." Their literary manners are perfect, but their work is lifeless.

Now, who is the villain really? Just how destructive is this tasteless middlebrow of the genuine artist? Isn't the writer concerned with a deeper loss of values than a failure of judgment on the part of some critic or culture-hopping matron? Shakespeare noticed a long time ago that the majority of people weren't very bright. As for the artist himself, can *Time* magazine culture affect him? Or—why is he reading *Time* magazine?

Macdonald shows his ambivalence toward the real villain in the different standards he applies to Hemingway and Agee. Though he is dismayed by Hemingway's disintegration as a mature man, he pays him a certain compliment in holding Hemingway responsible for Hemingway. In Agee's case he says that the times failed the man. Agee, the man, had all the qualities Macdonald admired. "Agee, I think, had the technical, the intellectual, and the moral equipment to do major writing. By 'moral,' which has a terribly old-fashioned ring, I mean that Agee believed in and—what is rarer—was interested in good and evil."

But did the times destroy Agee? Macdonald gropes for answers. Agee's talents were too diverse, too big, he loved life too much . . . this is an age of specialization. Agee was out of step with the *Zeitgeist* in America in the way that D. H. Lawrence was out of step with the England he was born into. Then Macdonald stops, recognizing that, after all, D. H. Lawrence did become D. H. Lawrence in a way that Agee did not become Agee. Was the waste of his talents a vice of the times or a personal problem of Agee's? Macdonald describes his own experiences as well as Agee's in working for Luce. But Agee was to remain in the Luce organization for years. "What a waste, what pathetic docility, what illusions!" Then Macdonald very honestly takes a second look at his and Agee's relationship to Luce and comes up with a far soberer answer than that the times destroyed the man. He finally asks, who used whom? There is a very sad and moving sentence at the end of the Agee essay—the most personal sentence in the whole book. It comes after the letter in which the young Agee thanks Macdonald for helping him get the job with Luce. Agee writes: "Words fail me re: the job: besides the fairly fundamental fact that I don't want to starve, there are dozens of other reasons why I want *uh* job and many more why I am delighted to get this one." And Macdonald says: "But I didn't do him a favor, really."

Now Macdonald is doing the rest of us the favor he feels he should have done Agee. Once and for all he is disposing of Time, Inc. and the mentality behind it. He has chosen to do this by recognizing and concentrating on his own special gifts—a fine ear for the English language, a talent as a polemicist, and a supreme wit. What is he—and should that really matter? No, he is not a Freudian literary critic, not a sociologist, not an academic, and he has chosen not to be Kierkegaard. Many of his conclusions are debatable—but his essays do not leave the mind like so much mush. And, speaking of good and evil, it would be a very, very great sin to be wasteful of such wit.

III.

A New Yorker
Outward Bound

Days and Nights in Texas

1963

In the way of a native New Yorker I had taken many trips, but always to the other side of the Atlantic—never West. Then, when Hal joined the University of Texas law faculty, we packed up our two daughters, belongings, and pets, and abruptly set out for Austin. The first train took us as far as St. Louis, where the Missouri sluggishly gives up mud-brown water ending in factory-town squalor, the industrial North and the sleepy South joined in mutual decay. Walking through the lackluster streets it occurred to me that T. S. Eliot was an American, not an Englishman, and *The Waste Land* came out of his roots, not his sophistication. Around St. Louis, America seems to slow down and die.

After a night on the Missouri Pacific, the steady rhythm of small Midwestern towns gave way gradually to open land. I kept hoping to see East Texas until it finally came to me that the scrub oaks, a tractor left in a field, a large Victorian Gothic house in the distance, a Falcon near a new split-level, a turkey depot— scattered objects appearing and disappearing in the midst of nothing—*were* Texas. The only break in the stillness was the movement of the train. We walked through empty corridors, past vacant roomettes, and ate dinner in a deserted dining car, choosing from a menu cut to the bone. Well, railroads belonged to another time. I felt a little sad. We were a small family living temporarily in a ghost town on wheels. Later I learned that in Texas you drive a car or go by jet; trains are for cattle. Feeling the lack of people both on the train and in the flat land outside, I asked the conductor what people in this part of the country did in case of some emergency—like a car breaking down.

"They wait," he replied cheerfully.

I looked again out the window, still seeing nothing. My thoughts wandered. Covered wagons, families traveling to places unknown—my God, they really did it. What had previously been a myth—*the* myth—about America slowly penetrated into my reality, commanding its own respect.

About twenty minutes before the train was due in Austin, I started looking for the town's existence. More flat, somnolent countryside. Then, abruptly, without any New England city slum as warning, we were at the station. A friend of Hal's met us. The town seemed a conglomeration of modern insurance buildings, convention hotels, and the usual Woolworth's. The only remnant of the horse and cattle days were the extra-wide streets and high sidewalks. Hal's friend dutifully pointed out the lone star on top of the very grand State Capitol. "Well, you're not very far from things," he remarked. "Austin has a brand-new airport—better than San Antonio. Five hours to New York, three to Mexico City, two to New Orleans." Later, while wiping away three days' worth of soot, and making my acquaintance with the omnipresent Texas sun, it occurred to me that I might be seeing a great deal of that airport in the future. No more train rides through Texas. Or was that slow, silent, uneventful trip the only way you could get from Manhattan to Austin?

The first thing I lost was the English language. Texas vacillated between rambling rhetoric, a linguistic amusement-park maze with all exits sealed off, and clipped abruptness. I shopped at Kash Karry. At school my children studied readin', ritin', 'n 'rithmetic.

We lived near one of a chain of eateries called Pig Stand. This was Pig Stand Number 14. All over town I saw Pig Stands, and when I didn't see Pig Stands, I ran into the Somewhere chain. You could get a Someshake at the Somewhere and a Mooreburger at the Mooreburger. If you want cottage cheese, ask for Less. Turn Less into Les and noncaloric ice cream arrives. At a restaurant you order a dinner of Eight-, Ten-, Twelve-, or Fourteen-Ounce beef. When skillet culture marries supermarket culture with nothing in between to soften the shock, soft spongy "flannel" bread is the offspring; food is named strictly in terms of quantity.

Desperately hungry for something that wasn't Moore, Less, Some, or Eight-Ounce, we tried a local exotic restaurant, the East-West House. The advantage of having a foreign restaurant in Austin is that you can invent your own country. We made our way through the bamboo curtains, gongs were pealing, there was a place to leave your shoes. A Brahms symphony, piped in on a loudspeaker, competed with the gongs. There was a copy of Erich Fromm's *May Man Prevail*, books on Yoga, a huge Buddha, and a large Jesus Christ. Squatting on pillows on the floor, we ate a mixture of cabbage leaves, limp Southern rice with canned tomato sauce, health bread, and for dessert, sponge cake with frozen raspberries and Reddi-Whip. On the spur of the moment Hal decided we should go to Mexico City for the weekend.

In Mexico it was good to see the *New York Times* again, only one day late instead of four. We were news-starved. Texas newspapers not only avoid world events, they bury the real happenings in their own state under a cloud of Who Will Be the Reigning Queen of Pflugerville? Fortunately the university has an independent student newspaper, the *Daily Texan*, and there is also the *Texas Observer*, an intelligent, old-fashioned, in-the-grain political journal run by an intrepid ex-University of Texas student, Ronnie Dugger. Its writers travel continuously throughout the state, committed to reporting the silent tragedies of small Texas towns. For many liberals the *Observer* gave more than news; it was written proof of their very existence, and its office served as their social nucleus.

I went with Willie Morris, then the *Observer* editor, to the state legislature. One of the representatives invited me to sit down, the session was called to order, and somebody played the guitar behind the speaker's rostrum. The representative was afraid I might be bored. I told him no, it wasn't at all like the East. The lobbyists, very much in evidence, were gathered in large groups on the balcony. An old-time Mexican-American politician joined us during the luncheon recess.

The wife of the young legislator from "down in the Valley" was giving a free-floating party. A group of us drifted over to her rented apartment, Japanese-American villa style, and ate *boeuf bourguignon* while lounging on the floor. The hostess, as fashionable as her cuisine, handed me a drink and sort of sighed. A pretty and charming woman in her early twenties, she was Texas-rich. Not comic-rich, but sad-lonely rich. She was committed to spending most of the year in a small border town that her husband's family dominated and where she felt very alien. "You know what I'm going to do?" she said softly. "I'm going to build lots of beautiful houses in my lifetime—houses with real feeling and real beauty—and I'm going to move out of each one of them and hope to God someone nice moves in after me. That's a way of being creative, leaving Texas prettier than it is now—don't you think?" She sighed again. "Austin is an oasis, I hate to leave." Many people during the year were to echo that phrase.

More people drifted in. Paradoxically, being a liberal in Texas, with its mixture of enclave-isolation and easy physical life, at times is like being a colonial in India in the days of the Empire. Everyone knew one another, everyone avoided the natives (the extreme right), and parties had a way of breaking out from one in the afternoon to three in the morning.

An argument stirred up between the Mexican-American politician and one of the young representatives. (I shall call them Fernandez and Richards.) Richards had contempt for the old Mexicans, but was also a little confused by the new ones. Maury Maverick, Jr., a member of a great liberal Texas clan and son of the late New Deal congressman from San Antonio, had been defeated in a recent U.S. senatorial race when Henry Gonzalez, a Texan of Mexican descent then in the state legislature, got into the field, causing a split ticket. "How could a Gonzalez run against a Maverick?" Richards cried in Southern anguish. "Why, Maury's old man sweated blood for the Mexicans. Better that he's gone, it would've broken him."

Fernandez shrugs. "My name is not Gonzalez."

Symbolically, in the way a son displaces the father, the Mexicans in San Antonio had to challenge a Maverick in order to cease being Mexicans. The ultimate demand a majority seems to make of a minority is gratitude, the one thing that a minority improving its position does not grant collectively. Anglos and Latinos . . . I rolled the words on my tongue. Why do so many Texans, when they become emotional, use the foreign word to define themselves? We Anglos, they say. Or is this one of the things they mean by built of the land?

Yet Texas has other qualities. As I adapted to the nonchanging seasons, and as my eye grew accustomed to a subtler, more limited range of color, I began to find a somber beauty in the beige landscape. In the late afternoons I would watch my children riding horseback, and see the color of fire settle over still, empty land. There were days I drove beyond Speedway, beyond the new motels and supermarkets, and went along smaller, older roads . . . Red Bud Trail, Bee Cave Road, Purgatory Road, Bridle Path . . . towns named Marble Falls, Dripping Springs. "The Yellow Rose of Texas" was once meant to be a love song for a mulatto girl. "Originally all those things meant something else."

If the beauty of Texas comes early, so does the hurt. It is a sadness sometimes concealed by statistics—five juvenile parole officers for the entire state, judges without legal training, no state income taxes. From all that richness so little money is poured back. As I walked along one of those streets where the town ends—white dust on the road, a caged parrot in an outdoor junkshop, the muted sound of bastardized Spanish in the air—the distance back into the days of the dustbowl, Depression, and drought didn't seem so very great. "EL PASO 585 miles." The sign points toward an isolated country where human beings grow up hearing few words and no news, toward the silence of distances.

The Texas flag was flying. Politicians, oil millionaires, and cattlemen swooped down on Austin. The band was full of razz, the drum majorettes full of wiggle. The Texas team, the Longhorns, were on the field, clad in majestic orange, their star Jimmy Saxton ("he used to race jackrabbits as a kid") was proudly pointed out to us. The Lord's name boomed across the plains, and there was solemn tribute to Sam Rayburn. Awards were bestowed on past Longhorn heroes. We rose and sang "The Eyes of Texas." The game was like a group bullfight without the mystique. An Ivy League team would have been slaughtered within minutes. Saxton was carried from the field three times; as he wobbled back in, the crowd roared approval. He temporarily misplaced a bit of his memory; the Longhorns had their first defeat of the season and were knocked out of their position as Number One team in the nation. That night Austin was plunged in despair. . .

A legislative meeting was called to examine the question of "slanted" history textbooks. Censors and anti-censors jammed the room. Professors from the university gave their testimony on academic freedom. The first question the legislators asked Roger Shattuck, one of the professors now active in attempts to liberalize Texas, was: Did he go to church on Sunday? A young boy testified that he was given a copy of the Gettysburg Address with God deleted from the text. The lady next to me busily copied down names of those she called the "slanted" professors and writers. One of the professors quoted from *Areopagitica*. "John Milton?" she whispered to a companion, pen poised in midair. "Who's he?"

We ran into a friend at the neighborhood liquor store, where you can also buy shotgun shells. He had talked with someone else who had just visited Lyndon's ranch. When Lyndon, as he is called by every Texan, heard that Walter Lippmann was in town he apparently arranged a small party for him that included some professors, newspapermen, and the governor. Lippmann was whisked off to Johnson City, sixty or so miles west. Lyndon drove several of his guests around the ranch in a white Lincoln convertible. He pressed hard on a horn that sounded off a mating call and all the Johnson cattle thundered faithfully after the car.

The New Forty Acres Club finally opened. Built by a private contractor on a site adjoining the campus (hence avoiding restrictions concerning the sale of liquor on private property), its purpose was to serve faculty, alumni, and friends of the university. The administration sent out letters urging all professors to join. Invited to dinner, we found ourselves walking into a surrealist nightmare of orange, red, and black Shamrock Hotel *moderne*. Upstairs, past the tilted fake palms and tilted gaslights in a mammoth bar, a local combo was drearily singing mildly off-color songs. Some older members of the faculty, nervously nibbling peanuts, seemed uncertain as to whether they were sitting in the dark of a nightclub or the dark of a new-style faculty club. *Viva* the new Academia! We went on a tour of the bedrooms. The chef-d'oeuvre is the Royal Suite, named after the football coach. White and gold furniture was set off in a blaze of red plush. I opened a white closet, and a white TV set peeped out at me. No desks, but there was a satin kidney-shaped sofa.

The new scientist or new poet can then enter the bedroom and lie down on an oversized gilt bed that might have been snatched from a bordello. He can open the other side of the white closet and the white TV will conveniently swivel around to greet him. When he looks at himself in the mirror while shaving, he will find his face framed in a halo of naked cherubs and birds on the wing. He has his choice of two colors of toilet paper. A white telephone is located handily next to the toilet. As it turned out, it was meant for the white professor with instant white thoughts. Shortly after the place opened, a visiting black member of the Peace Corps was refused admittance. Faculty members protest, students picket, and the university loses its chance for a quarter-million-dollar government grant intended for the creation of a Peace Corps training center. The administration tries to disentangle itself from the club. Who was in charge of policy? For whom was it built? Suddenly nobody knows.

Austin's topography is split dramatically, built on a great geological fault—the east is flat and dark, the west is beautiful hilly lake country—and psychologically it also has its extremes. It has its native homegrown liberals, its East Texas bigots, its old-time frontier values, the isolationism of West Texas, and the quality of transiency inherited from a recently floating population. As a result there is no single attitude shown toward the black student. Dormitories and varsity sports remain segregated. During the year the university rolled from crisis to crisis. The students continued their sit-ins, the regents attempted to be punitive and remained at loggerheads with the faculty. In Austin, painted on a huge rock, are the words, "REGENTS IS PIGS," a remnant of older and stormier days. It is also typical of Texas that nobody has ever attempted to remove the sign.

Despite faculty and student support on integration, the black students on campus lead solitary lives. They are divorced from the older black community in the town and socially they remain apart from the white students. Occasionally the black women's cooperative would ask various members of the faculty over for dinner. One night Hal, another professor, and myself were asked. The dingy gray clapboard building was a striking contrast to the modern dormitories on the rest of the campus. The women communicated a mood of uncertainty. Was it all right to ask a professor a question after class? How could you tell how the faculty really felt? How far would they go? What did the students really think? Which students? Which faculty? It can be a very perilous town for a black because one minute it acts like the North, the next like the Deep South.

"You want to know what I really think of Texas?" one of the women said, her voice moving from softness to swift anger. "I hate it. So you get a degree, but just try to get a job worth having. And I'm not"—she smiled—"going to push the ignorance stick."

"What's the matter, baby? You don't like housework?" They all laughed.

I was surprised that by the winter of 1962 most of the women, all actively involved in the integration cause, had heard of neither James Baldwin nor

Ralph Ellison. (They had read Richard Wright.) Up North we tend to see the black students down South as battling for their rights in an atmosphere of cohesive solidarity, as though there is some master plan, and they are all communicating with one another. These women seemed unsure of what to do next, of what their rights were, of whom to ask about these things. Though they could discuss moral issues with the faculty, they realized that a line had to be maintained. They confessed that though they worked with the Students for Direct Action they maintained a guarded distrust. Once a Southerner, always a Southerner? Then I underwent a sort of third degree as a Northerner. I doubted that my answers were very helpful. As a child I had not gone to an integrated school, growing up I had known hardly any blacks, yet Harlem was a ghetto. One of my daughters seemed not to notice color, the other had been puzzled at having a black teacher in nursery school.

We had some black friends, but the proportion was small. Curiously they examined my prejudices; then the conversation drifted into something more female. What were the stores in New York like? Is the beehive hairdo popular? Did I go to the theater? A friend of theirs had seen *A Taste of Honey*. Had I? What books? What music? How much would it cost to study at NYU? To live in New York? Describe other places, other people; what, oh, what does the world look like?

How life looked to me—that part I could answer. What was the shape of experience for a black woman student up North? That, in honesty, I could not. I mentioned Baldwin, Ellison, Paule Marshall. They wrote down the names. "Come back anytime," one of them said, no expectation in her voice that we would or wouldn't. Several women drifted off into a parlor to study. There was an old upright piano against the wall. The woman who mentioned the ignorance stick stood in the doorway and watched us get into the car. Later we went to the movies.

I thought of many of the white students I had met. They also were a combination of tremendous eagerness and complete ignorance as to the shape of life. Why should I have assumed that these students would be familiar with contemporary black writers? I felt a terrible anger at the crime of America that allows vast sections of its population to reach adulthood in such isolation and exposed to so little knowledge that they cannot even find their own world.

There were slow Deep South days and brisk Western frontier days. Hal and I take Carla and Maria to visit a friend's ranch. They run free, naming the different kinds of horses, examining fossils on the bank of a dry creek. Later, in the ranch house, my eldest notices the collection of rifles stacked in a corner. "They're not loaded?" she asks rhetorically. Hal's friend explains that the guns are *always* loaded. He says, "When you see a gun, remember it is a real gun." Then he takes us on a long truck ride. At one point he shoots an armadillo.

"It's dead?" The girls are surprised and unhappy.

"Yes. They eat duck eggs." He explains that sometimes you kill animals and sometimes you don't. Later he gives them some venison to take home. He says it came from a deer he shot and everyone will eat the meat. Then he advised us not to picnic at random.

"Why?" Maria asks.

"When people say no trespassing, they mean no trespassing."

On the way home Carla is lost in thought. At school, she tells us, she has learned how to spot a coral snake and what to do if the snake bites you. Also how to make yourself comfortable in uncomfortable places. In the afternoon I rarely see my children. They take their bikes and disappear with friends. Their world is changing.

I have acquired a new accent, a combination of Texas drawl and staccato Cambridge, England. Texas loves Englishmen, they love Texas. I keep bumping into the British. "I am Cyril Satorsky from London," a man at a party says to me in a voice filled with doubt. "I have been here six weeks. . . . I keep reminding myself, I am Cyril Satorsky from London." Cyril, in pursuit of life, has been wandering through Austin at night in search of a city. Jorge Luis Borges, visiting for the semester, is in search of a sidewalk. A young Southern writer arrives in a hearse he bought in Dallas for practically nothing. A local belle wants everyone to inspect her new paraffin-stuffed breasts. She doesn't like academic types, prefers activists. What's an activist?

"Why, babee, an activist is someone who sits in the suhn, enjoys life, goes swimmin'. . . ."

Hal wants to know about the effect of all that suhn on the paraffin, but the activist actively disappears.

Bill Arrowsmith, of the classics department, who sees the hills of Austin as Tuscany, is busily trying to turn us all into the Greek gods and goddesses of his translations of Aristophanes. Ronnie Dugger sits glumly by himself. He has just come back from a murder trial in Galveston where a man, who has had more stays than Chessman, is going to be quietly electrocuted. No motive for the murder was ever established, the evidence looked inconclusive, and the trial was poor.

We join John Henry Faulk and his wife on their small houseboat on Lake Mansfield. A native of Austin, he had returned home with his family after being libeled and blacklisted several years ago by "Aware." He had lost his job as a radio entertainer. Though his libel suit (Louis Nizer was his lawyer) was now creating a furor up North, that night on the still lake it all seemed to John a remote dream. There are party nights in Austin, and dead, frog-croaking, sonic-boom nights when nothing glows except the ghostlike glimmer from the "moontowers"—mammoth street lamps installed many years ago, though nobody seems to know why. Then there are highway nights when you give up the struggle to walk in a modern American town and you drive fast—ending up in San Antonio, maybe at a Somewhere, maybe nowhere.

Though you can get stuffed paraffin breasts and five-dollar shower caps, it is often hard to do regular shopping. There is no intermediary range between sleazy and Neiman-Marcus. Bloomingdale's, the Southwest awaits you! We give a party; I remember I have a mother, telephone her, and some things arrive twenty-four hours later.

A native Texan listens solemnly while I explain that sometimes New Yorkers find it easier to have food shipped from Manhattan. "Barbara," he says, "you are to Texas born."

Another Texan dives into the *pâté de foie gras* and Brie; appreciatively he pats me on the back: "Say, this Jewish home-style food is great."

Oh, the Texas problem! Oh, the Jewish problem!

While Austin swings precariously from provincial to cosmopolitan, dead to wild, conservative to radical, everyone hurries through. General Walker tries to run for governor, Norman Thomas attends a picnic for pacifists, Norman Mailer comes to give a speech and stays a week talking to students. To do him honor they offer to take him parachute jumping. A young Kennedy man with a briefcase breezes through; he has an hour to talk about the poll tax. We get French intellectuals, Lady James from England, Ladybird from Austin, Welch, the Holy Rollers, and Dwight Macdonald.

Sometimes all that vigor and individualism forced into a lonely intelligence turns in upon itself, spluttering off into mere eccentricity, bright young men hiding behind a cloak of folksiness until the attitude becomes ingrained. Individualism can quickly turn into ugliness. And sometimes—well, sometimes there are very young Texas days. There is the spring evening we spend casually drinking beer under the trees behind Scholz's Beer Garten with a blue-jeaned state senator, still in his twenties, from San Antonio. Many people feel he will someday be governor—or more. Other young politicians lounge in the straw-bottom chairs at other tables, plotting campaigns for Congress or for a tax bill with the *Observer* writers. I think of the students who work their way through law school by getting a seat in the legislature, and suddenly an older, less complicated America glimmers, a place where the youth is still Western-young, not Kennedy-young. Texas loses intellectual freedom because of its bigness, yet, paradoxically, it provides the small freedom of being close to the source. Having grown up in New York, I have never felt the possibility of my ideas physically changing the shape of the place in which I live. But young Texans know they will leave their mark on the state. Young Easterners associate this kind of power with the rat race, with "making it."

In May, homeward-bound, we traded the romanticism of the Southwest, where the future means possibility, with the romanticism of the East, where the future means disaster. Hal wanted to go to New Orleans; we took a jet from Houston. We spent the evening listening to jazz at Preservation Hall, the humidity in the air right for the timbre of Dixieland. We ran into some friends of Ronnie Dugger. "How are things in Austin?" In this part of the country, towns have their own special links and connections. Does America slowly give up and die around St. Louis? Or maybe it just comes and goes.

We took another jet the next day, in two hours we were in New York, Carla and Maria busily talk about Appaloosas, palominos, and Tennessee walking horses; everyone wants to show them the new children's zoo in Central Park. During the summer I am amazed at the number of Texans drifting into New York. But then, it is only five hours away.

Life in the
Yellow Submarine

Buffalo's SUNY

1968

I used to think that Los Angeles—the place where when you are looking to buy a home you are told you are buying "prime dirt" and the houses are called "structures"—I used to think *that* was the American nightmare of the twenty-first century, but things have speeded up, and now New York State is rivaling California. We now have our multi-university system, our State University of New York (SUNY); and in the midst of the dying elms of the dying town of Buffalo we have our own LA gone wild not far from the choked defunct Erie Canal.

I came to Buffalo last fall as a writer-in-residence and spent a few days walking through the city. In certain parts of Buffalo you can still hear the Polish of another century. On the east side of town, along East Ferry, are the scars of the summer riots, open American wounds of summers past and summers to come. Poles, blacks, a thriving Mafia, a Peace Bridge to Canada, the Albright-Knox Art Gallery, four Frank Lloyd Wright houses, sprawling old Victorian homes with the smell of the East and the shape of the Midwest colliding together—this is the landscape of Buffalo. There are, to be sure, new suburbs built in classic American monotonous style, and it has its dying Main Street—with the usual steady stream of garages, Sears Roebuck, and milk-shake stands—and there are, too, the surprising parts of Buffalo, rather beautiful circles, parks, and homes that on a foggy day recall Paris and the Luxembourg Gardens, some of that air of faded comfort that one associates with Proust and the avenue Foch.

Walking through the west side of the old parts of Buffalo I am reminded that at the turn of the century it was a prosperous middle-class town; the ladies of Pittsburgh and Cleveland wrote to Buffalo for their patterns and silks, until, perhaps symbolically, all that seemed to end with a post-Victorian shot in the air. An anarchist rebuffed by Emma Goldman as "unstable" shot McKinley at the Pan-American Exposition. Because of a doctor's reluctance to use a new X-ray machine McKinley died of gangrene. Buffalo, too, slowly died of gangrene. The turn-of-the-century wealthy middle class wished nothing to be changed, and no new industry has come into the town—though in the belt of dying Northeastern towns Buffalo is a little luckier than most in that it is one of the major seats of the Mafia in the U.S. In the summer of 1967 its citizens were surprised that they, like the rest of America, had their riots.

Off Main Street, with its Sears Roebuck, its garages and highway interstices, its delicatessens and malted delights, is the State University of New York at Buffalo, part of the explosion that includes Harpur and Stony Brook, and into which the state is pouring the usual billions of dollars. At present it sits on a postage stamp of a campus of old buildings that was six years ago the private University of Buffalo—a small second-rate university famed primarily for its law school, which, way back in the thirties, was the seedbed for better schools. Louis Howe and David Riesman came out of it.

Old pseudo-Gothic, new slabs of Germanic concrete, and pink and blue Army-type Quonset huts crammed together is what Buffalo looks like now, a crowded mishmash. Everybody's breathlessly waiting for the enormous new building that is to serve as "campus," a presumed architectural glory that will, I gather, cost billions and be the largest single building outside of Brasília. In the meantime, the student population is expanding at a galloping pace: some are locals, left over from the days when this was a trolley-car university; the majority are pouring upstate from greater New York City and environs—they jet into Buffalo and are part of the experiment known as mass education. Martin Meyerson, formerly of Berkeley, presides over the vast complex. What he has to deal with is a microcosm of America *Now*: new young hippie faculty, expensive "star" faculty, deadwood old faculty, eager students, hippie students, sullen students, an alien, generally hostile town, and a bureaucratic mess.

After one week in the Quonset hut known as the English department I felt I was going completely crackers. Like Yossarian in *Catch-22*, I decided there was nothing else to do but go *with* it and hope for survival.

One result of this decision—someone having noticed that at one point in my life I had done some film criticism—was that in a moment of weakness I found myself being prevailed upon to teach a course on film. Within a week my identity went from writer to film critic to *film expert*, and everybody, in breathless enthusiasm, pounced upon me as if I were personally bringing the latest word from Godard, Warhol, etc.

While we are having the usual tensions and storms over Dow Chemical and the CIA, one of the students comes into my office shrieking that he's had it, he wants to blow "it" to smithereens. I assume he means the CIA. "No," he cries, "the milk machine! It's a thief. Eating my dimes, eating my dimes." I sympathize. I feel he has got to the heart of the problem.

Buffalo, a university without a true past, is at present a Blanche du Bois, living off its electronic fantasy future. The basic timidity and uncertainty about its own image make it lack the courage to be at times conventional, so fearfully and provincially it is desperately grasping at the "new." Filthy rich, it is buying up scholars and, along with them, supersalesmen who have no idea what they are selling or who the "customer" is—and, in line with its futurity, it is of course buying equipment like mad. This plethora of money creates total chaos. Events pile upon pseudo-events. More poetry readings are held, more East Europeans invited, more movies shown on any given day than anyone can absorb. Buffalo, like all provincial towns, vacillates between thinking that everything is going on elsewhere and that everything is going on in Buffalo. As a result, in order to make up for lacks and simultaneously prove its lack of lacks, there are the poets, the East Europeans, and the movies—in a greater density per square inch than anything on Morningside Heights. The University suffers constantly from indigestion.

The equipment is bought in bulk. We own a reactor that no one can locate or use. In the basement of the classics department is a printing press grinding out ancient Byzantine. Though library facilities are appalling, we are told not to worry—within a year we will have a new dial-a-matic book system.

Daily there are dreams spun to relieve the dreariness of Main Street, Buffalo, and most of the dreams center around the wonders of the Pentagonesque new campus to come: a movie theater that will show films twenty-four hours a day, a complex of seven theaters for a drama school complete with prosceniums to fit each theatrical era—one administrator groaned to me that the best thing that could possibly happen to Buffalo is to get it to "hold still" for a moment. "Do you realize that when examined closely to scale the theater they have planned is only slightly larger than Lincoln Center?"

At the heart of this is the good old-fashioned American principle that the past does not exist—and a tendency to put all one's chips on ideas about the future and progress which are irrevocably bound to a notion of happiness and goodness that is our natural national birthright, like manifest destiny.

One faculty member breathlessly announced to me that studies have been made about academic children. (Statistics are floating around for just about everything.) "We are producing a race of mental giants." The children are better, the campuses are unique, the future is glorious; meanwhile the fog in Buffalo is awful, and one professor has just bolted. To Haifa!

I quickly realize that one of my main functions is to read the torrent of messages that are ground out daily by the purple mimeographing machine bought by the English department. There are memos for grants, for feelings, sentiments, sporadic student underground pronunciamentos, and lots of memos about MONEY. For people who live in the future, present time has no meaning. One of the first memos that comes my way is an apology to new faculty suggesting that if one has been in the university for less than four weeks it would be better to wait until spring before applying for summer grants. At the end of the day I am exhausted by the financial opportunities offered to me.

Well, I quickly adjust to the rhythm that nobody knows what is going on and if nothing works, it doesn't matter, because Buffalo is a child of the future. My second adjustment is to paranoia. I've always been fond of paranoia as a life style, but paranoia on a grand scale, preferably in some major European capital with good restaurants to plot in. Of course, for paranoia to work, I've always believed you have to have a lot of spare time: with the new small teaching loads (average of two courses a week), the placing of sixty-five assorted geniuses, would-be geniuses, poets, writers (Lionel Abel, Robert Creeley, John Logan, Leslie Fiedler, John Barth among them), the scholars looking nervously at writers, writers feeling sullen among all those Ph.D. types, all crammed together in a cinder-block Stalag 17 office, additionally huddled together because the university has no connection with the town of Buffalo—and even more intensely huddled because the Life of the Mind is being carried on in brutal weather and with an ugliness of surroundings that took imagination to produce—one is often overwhelmed by the sheer weight of the paranoia. I am greeted in the morning by a young assistant professor, Howard Wolf; he looks at the corridors with their attempts at McLuhan, posters frantically placed on every wall to cover the cinder blocks. "*Veh is mir,*" he groans, "the leftist gabardine axis, basement of the mind!" Freud, Jung, Maoism, existentialism, Marcuse, agrarian anarchism, you name it, we have it, Buffalo gray, Bloomingdale's basement of the mind.

Buffalo, like all instant universities, in order to combat a physical environment that is hell, acquires faculty by offering high pay and low teaching loads. While it flounders searching for an image of itself on paper, in practice its own style takes form. Many of its faculty come from California, bringing with them their mode of Western mobility and enthusiasm for new ideas, and a casualness of dress and life-style: cramping Westerners into Dostoyevskian-cum-American physical conditions results in a high degree of nervous tension. There are no crannies here to buffer professors' eccentricities, neither the electric feeling of a large city nor the trees and buildings of a country campus to absorb any cultural or emotional shocks; here among the cinder blocks, every-body's emotional problems assault you.

The placing of a jet strip at the Buffalo airport three years ago has converted Buffalo into a suburb of New York City. More of its students are coming from Queens, Brooklyn, and the Bronx: for them, Buffalo, forty-five minutes' flying time out of La Guardia, is merely an extension of the New York mega-lopolis. Sitting in the English department one day, I looked down the hall and realized that the jet professor is truly here. I live in New York City, my home, my children are there. We got used to traveling when my husband—a peripa-tetic law professor—was alive; now distances truly meant nothing to me and my children.

I often gave my daughters breakfast in New York in the morning, saw them off to school, spent forty-five minutes on a jet to Buffalo, taught a few classes, and then returned home to New York not long after they got home from school. In looking down the hall it came to me (and I'm not talking about the $100,000-per-year elite, but ordinary associate professors) that one man com-mutes between Houston and Buffalo, another is on the New York-London cir-cuit, another is on the Toronto-Buffalo-New York circuit, etc. In actual prac-tice I see as many people from Buffalo in New York, at the end of a week, as I see in Buffalo during the week. Obviously the university is coming more and more to resemble the city, with all the problems of the city: it is inchoate, vast, confused, overly mobile, caught in a series of happenings and pseudo-events and visiting lectures. The students "watch events" with all the anonymousness of the city; one professor was deeply shaken when he questioned a student about the problems of draft exile in Canada and realized that the student simply didn't know what he was referring to by way of place, family, home—the very words had lost their meaning.

The new professors are a cross between credit-card intellectuals, business-men, and performing artists. Within five, ten years, professors will be based wherever they choose to live and will essentially be delivering a series of lec-tures at a series of universities—which is more or less what is being done now. If the university resembles the city, emotionally it also resembles the army. Al-legiance is not to a specific post (a given school)—one is based at some post and transferred around within the total system (the university in America). The student is also on the move. This excess mobility has become a frightening real-ity. The least discernible consideration, behind all the new academic window dressing, is the question of who is being taught what, and when.

Feeling a little discouraged, and often restless, I would have been glad to do more teaching than I was scheduled for—free time in Buffalo is boring—but I quickly understood that to suggest such a thing would brand me a subversive in the system; they have graduate assistants for *that*. I once asked one of the uni-versity's vice presidents if any faculty ever, well, like did they ever discuss actual teaching, and he thought for a minute and said, well no, he couldn't remember any time offhand; occasionally students dropped by, but never faculty. At some point (he was showing me a great many graphs, and like those of every administrator I ever saw on the campus, all his graphs had to do with life ten years hence) I asked him how many students were on the campus.

"Do you mean real bodies or FTEs?"

"I mean *students.*" I shuddered at the "real bodies," and I could not avoid imagining them stretched out, ready for a grave somewhere. "What's an FTE?"

"A full-time equivalent," he rattled off. "You add up a number of credits, which is the equivalent to one real student—"

I shuddered again, told him I had a slow mind.

"We have *two sets of figures,*" he explained, shoving yet another graph in front of my face, "one for real students."

"One for full-time equivalents," I repeated after him, my eyes following the double graphs that look like a series of Mount Everests in combat with one another. I gave up. As I was leaving, the vice president began to question me about, well, what exactly seemed to be going on around the place.

There are all types of paranoia. The form that that of the administrators takes—and the only thing I remember about my conversations with any of them, which I presume weren't very interesting—is the conviction that someone "down there," the reverse of the faculty's "someone up there," actually knows what's going on. That someone probably being a computer.

Administrators, I rapidly found, weren't worth talking to, as they seemed primarily to be armed with statistics pulled together for the purpose of implying that a student had to give some evidence of genius in his high-school average in order to get into Buffalo. But one evening, downstairs in Hays Hall, as I waited for the snow to let up so I could leave, I talked with two students, one of whom said she liked it here but she had worked harder at the University of Miami, it had been a more serious place. So what, I mentally asked of a graph, has intervened since high school?

Later in New York an architect friend of mine explained the whole thing to me. He's out at Stony Brook, our fellow university in the state system in Long Island. He said to me, "I am designing multi-interdisciplinary units for your full-time equivalents. *Capiche?*" Buffalo believes in the rebirth of the humanities.

I walked across campus with Warren Bennis, the provost of social sciences, a rather thoughtful, reflective man, who had recently come from M.I.T. He asked me if I had noticed that people tended to behave *strangely* in Buffalo. "I get the oddest calls," he mused, "people threatening to leave because the heating system breaks down for a few hours . . . you know damned well it's not the heating system. . . ."

I muttered that I had observed a rather, shall we say, high degree of hysteria.

"I think," he said, "it is the business about the future. Buffalo has the lure of promise, of possibility, of change, people come here, they are beguiled (conned?) and all of a sudden they want to act out all their pent-up dreams, all their fantasies, all their ambitions for their own brave new worlds, and, boom, then they are in Buffalo, and unless they are here on a very specific project, boom, the dream explodes, and they find themselves in Buffalo. . . . Some of them will be here for the rest of their lives, trapped by a bit of money, a company town." He sighed. "It is very sad."

I thought of California, where the idea of this sort of dream began. Fifteen years ago, the Eastern professor stood in his Eastern suit gazing out at the Pacific Ocean, walking along Malibu Beach, or later La Jolla, or watching the bay at San Francisco's Golden Gate, and if the dream did not become a reality, the landscape gave him room to sustain the illusion just a while longer, which is after all what life is, the sustaining of things through time. Now, for the young California professor in his California dungarees, to stand on the edge of Main and Bailey and behold the future is closer to Dick Diver come home from the Riviera.

Many afternoons are spent in the Buffalo gray of the English department, with young professors out of Berkeley discussing the look of California, Buffalo *outre-mer*, Buffalo *cafard*.

People *do* behave differently in Buffalo. I sit in my office, wistfully talking to Bruce Jackson about Austin and the pull of the Texas landscape. We have both been there at different times of our lives, and like all children born of the cement and twenty-stories high of New York City, found that that kind of landscape had a pull. He was showing me his photos of small Texas towns, they had a look I recognized and understood, and he was playing Texas prison songs on the stereo in the office, when someone thrust a lost visiting scholar in at us, whispering, entertain him—he's meant to be hired.

A middle-aged graying man, a German university stacks-and-papers type, he looked dazed. "I'm so glad to find you," he kept muttering. (Buffalo has a way of inviting people and often losing track of them, so that would-be chairmen are just sort of left lost in the halls as some other activity claims the host's attention.) We tried to give the man a chair, a cup of coffee, and to reassure him about Buffalo—though, to be sure, it was certainly far from the center of the universe (when strangers hear that, they often get a certain dazed, disoriented, and frightened look on their faces, seeing the parachute they'd been told to leap with suddenly fail to open in mid-air, that look of tumbling to earth). Finally the professor named his price; what he wanted from Buffalo was a mistress.

Horse-Trading and Ecstasy

It was the first time I had seen Bruce Jackson lose his cool. His mouth fell open, and as if he suddenly remembered that professors are perhaps not supposed to sit perched on the tops of desks but on chairs alongside of them, he jumped down, turned off the stereo. I myself stared at the wall on which was affixed a poster of Jean-Paul Belmondo. Definitely this shy Humbert Humbert had been given the word about the "swinging English department at Buffalo" and was manfully trying to live up to what he thought was expected of him. The poor man seemed to be suffering from some sort of temporary cultural shock, and on and on he went, quite seriously explaining his needs (in Buffalo people spend a great deal of time discussing their emotional states of mind). I think what he was describing was actually a housekeeper, but anyway there was no doubt about it, he was standing his ground. Bruce looked at me, I looked at Bruce. Bruce said, "Oh, you can make uh . . . a social life here."

"A mistress. A *permanent* mistress."

"Well, you can't put it in the contract. . . ."

"I think I'd be lonely in Buffalo."

"Graduate students? Female faculty? Townies?" Bruce gave up.

I decide, this one wants a mistress, like hell he wants a mistress. I leaf through my mind, figuring out what is the unmentionable an academic can't bring himself to say.

"Money?" I try.

The man looks relieved, he blushes slightly. "I'm glad to find someone, uh, so realistic. I need . . ." he looks up at me. "How much? That is, I don't mean to sound avaricious, but uh—"

I look at him. "Plenty."

The tone changes, briskly we are talking facts and figures. He names his. Bruce shrugs. "Ask for it," he says. We settle the money question; now down to the nitty-gritty; his favorite library of course is in some other city. "Possible," Bruce grunts. The man looks at us slowly, "Well I think I do have a better idea of where I stand." Abruptly he leaves. I stare out my window, watching the students crossing the campus. Of one thing you can be sure, conversation with academics may start with mistresses, or Bloomingdale's basement of ideas, or academic freedom, but in the end it generally boils down to time and money.

Buffalo's basic problem is that it is a rapidly growing Goliath of an institution dealing with students who, despite the fancy statistics, arrive at the university as mixed-bag products of the bad American secondary schools from which they spring. Rather than concerning itself with this as a genuine educational problem—that is, how to give these students a general corpus of knowledge in which they are sadly lacking—the university has chosen to cover the basic mess with a quick and thick coat of fashionable instant gloss. Most of the professors have too much professional ego at stake to come to terms with the type of students they should be educating; and since the faster route to establishing the prestige of a university is via the graduate school and the Ph.D., the undergraduates, who should be the most important part of the process, get the short end of the stick. They are taught by the graduate assistants. Meanwhile there is no adequate advisory system for the students, and no structured program. The present facilities are intolerable, and the present crop of students, like a generation of guinea pigs, are quite unmistakably being sacrificed to some fantasy of Buffalo's future greatness. One expects a new university to have problems; what is disturbing about Buffalo—and many other state institutions—is the sense one gets of the fraudulent, of the abrogation of faculty responsibility to the student, which the student in turn reflects in a lack of responsibility toward his own work.

Many of the faculty don't seem to be in the least aware that the idea of the "new" is old-fashioned American nativism, or that all their talk about "free expression" is in fact a pretty stale inheritance from the 1930s (progressive education *in extremis*), that it was tired and proved a dismal failure, and that true intellectual freedom is hardly identical with chaos.

I watched the students one day when a visiting European novelist soberly contradicted a faculty member who referred to his work as "experimental." He replied that talk of the experimental is always nonsense, that everything he wrote was real, and came out of his experiences with a nightmare world. He told the students that nothing existed except reality, one had no "choice" in the matter, and proceeded to give them a solemn lecture on twentieth-century history. I felt their response, their eagerness and thirst for some sort of genuine encounter with true knowledge, their own fatigue at the word games that made up most of their instruction. Most of all, I felt their ability to perceive the truth when it is being told them. This is something they rarely get from their own faculty, especially those members of it who appear to have spent their own adult lives on the Ph.D. track.

What then about Martin Meyerson, president of this whole complex? As former acting chancellor of Berkeley he has been burned once. As an urban planner, his dream is for the open campus—the university related to the town—a hard feat to accomplish in a sullen city that intensely dislikes the university and whose newspapers often heckle it for the wrong reasons.

Perhaps the most sophisticated man on the campus and perhaps its most valuable asset—a man who does not come across well in public and is much more at ease in private conversation—Meyerson is faced with almost insurmountable problems. He is quite aware of the problems he has inherited—a new faculty, which veers spastically in a thousand directions at once, too many students, and these added to the worst kind of traditional, hidebound, rigid faculty inherited from the past regime. The combination is explosive. Then, too, there is Albany, one minute handing the university too much money for the wrong reasons, the next minute cutting the budget, also for the wrong reasons, creating more chaos of another kind as programs started cannot be finished; treating the university, in the way of state legislatures, as an angry parent treats a child, now I will be nice to you, now I will punish you.

Toward the end of the second term I begin to get nightmares about the whole thing. In the middle of one of those graying Buffalo nights, I sit up in bed, dreaming of solutions. The only groups I had seen actually make something *work* on the campus were the Maoists—at least there was bright-eyed organizational discipline in their teach-in. Everything went off on schedule. Certainly there was good in Buffalo—the sense at least of life going on in the place, if at times a bit mad, it was better than no life at all. I thought of the children playing with balloons in a psychedelic tent with strobe lights and music, while nearby the old heated Marxist-Leninist rhetoric of the thirties was blanketing the teach-in, and there was something oddly moving and wistful about this American university, this "Buffalo is a Winter Carnival" ambience that one didn't want to see altogether disappear—and something quite moving in Martin Meyerson's dream of a free and open campus. Still, something had to be done to make the whole thing work, so that geniuses, poets, students, and faculty could all go about their business in peace. Now the Maoists, they definitely had discipline—down to the last man, they would make far better administrators than the ones we had now. Meyerson, for a sort of gentle sobriety, a mediator . . . and to give the place a touch of intellectual elegance. But for someone to do a crash job on the chaos . . . McNamara. Two weeks with him clearing up the yellow submarine, Pentagon-style, and everything would be shipshape. He could lead the Maoists, and together they could attack. Mao and Mac, Mac and Mao, I went to sleep happily.

In Texas
Spanish Is
Fashionable Now

1984

Hispanics, now numbering fifteen million, are the fastest growing minority in America. Texas is most changed by this rapid growth. San Antonio, which despite its Spanish traditions had been frosty to its ethnic population, now has Mexican-American Henry Cisneros as mayor. In the old days, the city's ruling oligarchy mumbled about their cultural links to matters Spanish. What they meant was French or Spanish as in Europe, not as in Mexican-American. The amazing, lanky, 36-year-old Henry Cisneros is adept at projecting a Harvard Latino Kennedyesque charm with just-plain-folks Texas style. In San Antonio, he has managed to appeal to the snobs, the dispossessed, and big business—quite a feat.

The McNay Art Museum is one of those small, perfect, jewel-like museums, such as the Frick or the Fundación Miró in Barcelona. A PR person informed me when I went to the party honoring the new Tobin wing that, had I arrived a day earlier, the place would have been wall-to-wall Rockefellers. Well-dressed Texas women and their husbands swiftly moved between the outdoor museum patios and the indoor rooms, where there was a pleasing blend of fresh flowers, German Tex-Mex (the German touch in Texas cooking is the tortes and sausages), good architecture, and paintings. Until recently, at that sort of gathering, there would have been only a few token Mexican-Americans. At this event many Mexican-American couples were present. When an ethnic group in America gets real clout, they begin to resemble the dominant culture; their prior exoticism fades. I leaned back against a door and watched; in that slightly moist southern air, just right for the sound of jazz, the Hispano men moved with grace and know-how, ushering their well-groomed wives, a protective arm for the women offered just in case, while with the other they casually balanced their champagne. The Latin men would put a hand on the shoulder of a society Anglo with ease; they weren't feigning power. They had got "a bunch."

The Tobins have meant money and culture for a long time in Texas, and Robert Tobin has the impish air of a man who isn't going to tell the world how much fun he had the day he played hooky or what was in the picnic basket. Tall, he looks like the beaky, elegant son of a Greek aristocrat crossed with hardedged British money, the sort of man who never placed at Oxford because during final exams he had found something better to do with his time—like chatting with Robert Graves in Deya, Majorca.

"And just what . . . *view* of Texas will you be writing about?" he asked me.

"I've come back to check up on *my* Texas—Scholz's Beer Garten and the *Texas Observer*."

"So—you were at the University of Texas?" San Antonio may be every Texan's hometown, but the U. of Texas in Austin is everyone's youth; Scholz's Beer Garten on San Jacinto was the main university hangout.

I explained that my husband had been brought down to the university in the early sixties, during the civil rights movement, to teach "northern" law at the Law School and to help with the desegregation of the university. Tobin at this became the *Texas* Robert Tobin. "The university was a battleground in the sixties. Those were the days of glory." We talked about those times: Roger Shattuck, William Arrowsmith, Ronnie Dugger, Willie Morris, and a younger, more radical John Silber. Tobin ruminated about his past. "Intellectually, I'm a product of the U. of Texas. Everything I became, I owe to that place. So, you mean to write about *our* kind of Texas. . . ." He paused. "Let me know if you need help."

The weather in San Antonio was balmy. The next morning I splashed in the Four Seasons' heated outdoor pool. Tobin had read me right. What had happened to the liberal Texas I had known? Had it served as midwife to the new, powerful Hispanic community, then died? Or was this odd vote-getting alliance between Hispanics, blacks, women, and gays a new phenomenon independent of old, progressive Texas? Then I went to the Mayor's office.

Mayor Henry Cisneros was sixteen when Kennedy was shot. After Dallas, Kennedy had been intending to go to Austin, just an hour from San Antonio. What were the fantasies of an intelligent, ambitious, dreamy adolescent—an accidental meeting with Kennedy? Or perhaps a firsthand report from a pal in Austin? Whatever child's rendezvous was meant to take place had been shattered in Dallas. Cisneros spent his youth during the angers and furies of the civil rights years—in addition to the Kennedy nightmare assassination there were the fears about what would happen with integration. Cisneros is half Spanish and half Mexican. Like Kennedy, he doesn't come from the class he wishes to represent. His grandfather and father did well; Henry went to private school before attending Texas A&M. Cisneros picked up a mass of impressive degrees in urban studies at the Kennedy School of Government, M.I.T., and George Washington University.

In his city council meetings he switched effortlessly between Spanish and English. He is the most important Mexican-American political candidate in the country, casual enough to please a youthful rebel, with a somber seriousness that would disarm a corporate executive. The next night he had time to see me. He came over to the deserted City Hall after a V.I.P. dinner; it is a quiet building with enough Spanish touches in its design to make one feel at the doorway to Taos. He murmured a few pleasant remarks about a piece I had written. He does his homework.

Pasted in one corner of his mind seemed to be those figures from his youth he appeared bent on pleasing and emulating: he said how attractive John Lindsay, then mayor of New York, had seemed to him when he first went north to college. What a tremendous effect reading Jane Jacob's *The Economy of Cities* had had on him. "I became aware of the urban crisis in Harvard in '68. Before that, I thought public service meant the military."

Like his father before him, Cisneros started out in the military at Texas A&M. San Antonio is an army town. But Harvard in the seventies had gone ethnic. So up north, in Cambridge, Henry Cisneros, the army colonel's son, was reborn as Henry Cisneros, the Chicano leader. He even learned Spanish.

"What was the best thing you took away from Harvard?"

"Confidence that I could engage in intellectual debate and perform competitively with people who seemed beyond my level. When you learn to compete well, few things later in life seem difficult."

Cisneros gazed out at the darkness of San Antonio's inner city. His language, his train of thought, still struck me as army.

Becoming a world leader on Hispanic issues appeals to Cisneros. It would give him continuous national exposure. The army, Kennedy, and John Lindsay all had served as role models. What he now needed was the image of a young, moderate Hispanic. He asked me about Spain's Socialist president, Felipe González.

"González," Cisneros said, "can explain to the Sandinistas how they could have their economic revolution without becoming a Cuban-style Marxist-Leninist state. He could be a *calming* influence in Central America." Then, re-

93

calling that he recently had been a member of the Kissinger Commission to Central America, Cisneros expressed regret that his dissenting opinion attached to the report had been mild. "I should have been stronger." Cisneros's weakest trait is that he tries too hard to please everyone.

"Would you like to meet González?"

"Absolutely."

"What do you think we should do about Cuba?"

"We should talk to Castro. We need normal relations. I'm an anti-communist and not tolerant of his exportation of revolutions, terrorism, and drug movements to our country. But until there is a basis for discussion, the mutual animosity will grow—there has got to be some better accommodation."

An unexpected scenario flashed through my mind of González and Cisneros solving Central America, Castro on the sidelines looking old—it played well. Yet, at home, Cisneros skirts the entry of religion into politics.

Before interviewing Cisneros, I visited COPS, a lay Mexican-American *barrio* association. During the past decade it has provided a power base for Mexican-Americans in San Antonio; through it they've obtained a better school system. A lay brother who had taken vows of celibacy, poverty, and obedience sullenly checked me out. Another member took notes of my conversation with the lay brother. The organization supports itself by tithing the local parishes on a geographic basis; they have done some good but I was concerned about church control of political candidates. I pressed Cisneros on COPS.

"I am appreciative of what they have done for our community and respectful of what they represent," Cisneros insisted. "They are almost a sacred force in my view."

"But I have been told that one of their major functions is the conducting of *accountability nights*. Politicians are asked to come to these meetings; then COPS grades them on their performance. Why can't politicians be accountable to the public through a varied press?"

Cisneros looked annoyed. "There are old people at these meetings: they are part of the empowerment process. Politicians should be accountable to the public."

"It's one thing to be accountable to the public, another thing to be graded by a political-religious organization."

"There's no punishment attached to it! I've been graded high and I've been graded low, and I'm still in public office."

"Do you think COPS allows for sufficient separation between church and state?"

Cisneros was silent, then spoke rapidly. "The most effective leadership organizations in our community are those who generate talent via church organizations. The church doesn't use COPS for religious purposes. But in the Mexican-American community the church is the most dependable organization. The answer to your question is yes—okay?"

Though a lot of the agitation and progressive strivings of the old, liberal enclave of Texas liberals made it possible for a Henry Cisneros to become mayor, Cisneros's career really was made by a combination of Hispanic power, the national politics of the Democratic party, and his acceptance by the conservative San Antonio business community. The San Antonio-Austin corridor is in the boom belt.

Raul Jiménez, Sr.—whose food factories are so sleek I like to think of him as the rotund king of the high-tech tamale—is one of the biggest supporters of Cisneros and of the national Democratic party. Jiménez is the true American success story: he borrowed two thousand dollars from his father, he and his wife started providing homemade sausages to the local grocery stores, and in record time he became a multi-millionaire supplier of Mexican foods. I met him and his son at their San Antonio plant on South Pan-Am Expressway. In the last eight years, Raul Sr. told me, they have been supplying huge amounts of hot sauce to the Saudis. "They like it hot, and they like it red. Some of them drink it." Then he prodded his son: "Now she needs you to say something." Despite the disingenuous grin under the big chef's hat that Jiménez likes to sport while posing for photos, he is very savvy in his dealings with the press. Although Jiménez owned his big estate in the fancy part of town a long time before he actually moved into it, preferring his old place in the Mexican-American *barrio*, he moved into it in enough time to throw a lavish bash for Fritz Mondale on his vice-presidential swing through San Antonio: a Mondale ice sculpture was the *pièce de résistance* along with huge bouquets of flowers floating in the swimming pool.

But old liberal Texas still means the Maverick family. They have added two words to the English language—in the nineteenth century Sam Maverick never branded his cattle, claiming all strays belonged to his herd; this is the origin of the word *maverick*. During the New Deal, as a Washington congressman, Maury Maverick, Sr. (most famous for having been the radical mayor of San Antonio) coined the expression "gobbledygook." "Well," Terelita Maverick, Maury's daughter said to me over the phone, "so you got yourself a fancy writing gig and came back to Texas—okay, I'll give a small party with tacos and deviled eggs." Terelita's mother, Terel Maverick, is a real *grande dame*, and after Maury died she married the historian Walter Prescott Webb. But Terelita is pure Maverick. She likes to drawl her address to new guests: "Honey, just get over to Hillcrest and ask for a streetcar named Satisfaction." In the 1930s Maury, Sr., bought the last trolley car in town for one hundred dollars and put it on his property on Hillcrest. According to Terelita, he also salvaged from a family graveyard the wonderful white wrought-iron New Orleans-type fence that now borders the trolley's porch. When I visited Terelita—small-waisted, round-bosomed, and peppery—she mused, "I think some of the other relatives were a trifle annoyed."

Seven or eight of Terelita's friends joined us at the Maverick Hillcrest trolley car, now Terelita's home, for the impromptu gathering on her front porch. "What do I think of the new Texas?" Terelita snorted, "Honey, it's all corporate America. You remember how it was—in the old days—why, it was a Texas custom to get laid once a day. Now, all that is on folks' minds is business, sports, and religion." She paused and glanced at two of her guests, one white and one black, Jim Cullum and Herb Hall, both jazz players at The Landing, which is one of the places on the riverwalk in downtown San Antonio. "White people," Terelita declared, "beat one three to jazz, and black people beat two and four."

At O'Neil Ford's funeral, Jim Cullum led the procession, playing "When the Saints Go Marching In." Ford is another name, like Maverick, that has special resonance here. The internationally known architect left his mark on San Antonio; the reason the town is such a visual gem is that Ford had an extraordinary imagination concerning the city. The funeral entourage stopped in front of every O'Neil Ford building in town before bringing his body to the Mission Park Cemetery, which is the way Ford had wanted it. Afterwards, Maury Maverick, Jr., wrote about it in his newspaper column.

Emma Tenayuca, another guest at Terelita's late afternoon, is a Texas legend. Trim, well-boned, she has the dark, intelligent looks of the sort one would see in women at a Hannah Arendt New School for Social Research lecture. She is in her sixties now, and has lived to see herself celebrated as a Texas heroine. But, at age twenty, in 1939, Emma Tenayuca, as the Joan-of-Arc leader of the pecan workers' labor movement here, narrowly escaped with her life; a mob of five thousand stoned the meeting she had led at the Municipal Auditorium. According to the *Texas Observer* account: "The mob demanded Mayor Maverick's recall, then marched to the Alamo and from there to City Hall, where Maverick was hanged in effigy. 'The civil liberties of everybody in San Antonio, even Emma Tenayuca, will be upheld,' Maverick later declared. 'The Constitution will be served.'" Emma, in those days, was involved with the Communist Party. Maury Maverick was never reelected.

Frequently sent to prison for organizing the Workers' Alliance and the pecan workers' strike, Emma was run out of town in the forties: no one would give her work. Several days after the party at Terelita's, I met Emma for lunch and she talked to me about those days. "After Texas, I drove up to California. At first—because there weren't enough jobs up there—the Californians tried to prevent the Okies and Texans from coming through. But the Supreme Court put a stop to that." Tenayuca worked at odd jobs, eventually became a teacher, and came home to Texas in the sixties. She spoke with little bitterness about the past. She has considerable reservations about the Communist Party, but retained a fondness for the Wobblies. Suddenly she smiled: "At heart, I had the soul of an Anarchist." The party clearly had been a side issue: the heavy baggage of those times. For her, the issue was that the average pecan worker in 1938 earned under three dollars for a 75-hour week. Although revered in Texas, Tenayuca's orientation is very different from the current firebrand Chicanas'. The word clearly makes Tenayuca wince. "I'm mestiza . . . Mexican-American." Not too patient about ethnic issues, she said firmly, "The English language has a height of purity and beauty that cannot be surpassed." At the end of the lunch Emma hesitated, then asked: "You know Mailer? I would love to talk to him. Tell him that *Of a Fire on the Moon* is an extraordinary book." She kept chain-smoking. Then she talked about how people had forgotten what a marvelous poet Robert Burns had been.

The grandchildren of hard-nosed Texas oil money have learned to do business with Hispanics and women and gays; the more sensitive also have begun to develop a social conscience. Marianne Bruni, the daughter of Corpus Christi business interests married to South Texas oil and ranching (the Brunis of Bruni), is accepted by the Chicano community because she has backed native Chicano talent. Marianne can corral Anglo heavies, like the Armstrong children from the King Ranch, into backing her programs for bilingual culture. I went to a theater group she had brought down from New York: the Repertorio Español. Afterwards, there was a fancy Texas hotel party. I watched the Anglo bankers, Chicanos, and blacks melded together on the dance floor. They tangoed to "Hernando's Hideaway," swayed to "Guantanamera," and did some swift salsa work, South Texas style, to the rhythms of Ramón Cerveras's band. "This couldn't have happened here five years ago," Marianne said.

"The men down here are better dancers than in the East," I mused. One of the society Anglo women guests joined us. "They tell me New York hasn't integrated its Hispanic population into the mainstream—why, that's sad."

Many of the *nuevo wavo* Chicano writers gather at Marianne's house. Some of them write in *calo*—Tex-Mex English. One of the poets read a section of his work; it was about his lost Jewish heritage. The poet's theory was that the Spanish settlers were Spanish Jews who had fled the Inquisition. He pointed out that Mexicans and Jews both eat unleavened bread. I turned to Marianne: "So the Indians were eating matzo in Aztlan?"

Peter Gonzales, a movie actor and director, had played young Fellini in *Roma.* "I learned a lot from Fellini. A lot from Europe. But I thought of my parents, my sister—I wanted to bring what I had learned back to Texas." Gonzales is helping to build the incipient Texas film and TV industry. He offered to take Marianne and me to hear music. Did I want Mexican conjunto? Jazz?

Country? We settled on country, and drove out on Bandera Highway toward Helotes. But Saturday night is tricky in Texas, and we detoured, dropping into the Lone Star. Its new owners are a divorcée and widow from the Northwest: Polly Hirschberger and Dodie Sullivan. One of the women came over and joined our group. She told us there hadn't been a fight in over two years. "Sort of brave for women to own the Lone Star?" I asked.

"Well, just say, we bought the Lone Star at a point in our lives when we needed it, and at a time when the Lone Star needed us."

We then drove on to the Floore Country Store. It's hard to see the big barn of a place because, over by Helotes, the highway has no lights. This is hill country. Hill people come in. Families. And Mexican and Anglo cowboys. They go in for progressive country here and lots of "Cotton Eyed Joe" and the frug. Some people think that Willie Nelson is from Austin, but it was the family who owned Floore Country Store that gave him his start. Right here.

A few days later Peter Gonzales and his sister gave me a lift up to Austin, where I asked State Treasurer Ann Richards (she is the highest elected woman official in the state, coming to power through the women's vote) what she thought about COPS. She blinked her blue eyes and remarked how fond she was of the organization. "I think people like to work in groups, don't you?" Never once did this purported feminist mention that COPS was militantly anti-abortion. When I tried to get out of her more concrete views about the direction the women's movement took in its early days, she drawled, Texas-folksy: "Ohh . . . whatever stuck its head up first—is the best way to shoot it down." But despite the blonde hair and her frilly "cute" style, Richards is an impressive state treasurer. When talking to bankers, she is a shrewd, nuts-and-bolts administrator. She tries to juggle support from minority groups in order to be in an A-one position with the new corporate bunch. Her ambition is to be the first woman vice-presidential candidate. What in Texas makes her seem more accessible—the Dolly Parton dress-up wigs, the bemused sayings (women should be obscene, not heard)—on a national level might prove off-putting.

The first time I came to Austin, because we were a family with all our things, we arrived by train. I remembered the long, flat ride through East Texas and how scared I was that we might have to live here forever. Texas then seemed so much farther away than it does now. After we left Ann Richards, Peter drove me through downtown Austin. I couldn't find the old tracks over by Third. Sixth Street—which now seems like Bourbon Street, with all the new cafés dedicated to "Austin sound"—amazed me. This part of town used to be so empty, you couldn't even locate a glass of water. I used to come here and take photos of the old grain buildings and the Goodwill shop. Sometimes in the evenings Hal and I drove to downtown movies, and because there was no place to go, we'd see mild, silly blue movies made in the twenties. There was a sign that read: EL PASO 585 miles. Now, in place of that old movie theater is a great rectangular glass skyscraper, the American National Bank. It's made of that type of glass that reflects the light; with the sun going down, it had turned rose gold.

I had promised I would attend a conference on Public Policy over at the LBJ Library. Kissinger was speaking; the place was heavily picketed. Central America is a big issue down here. After the conference ended, some of us were bused out to the LBJ ranch. Up East we would call the place an estate, because you can't seriously breed cattle in the hill country. At one point Lyndon Johnson's own voice was piped through the bus loudspeaker. The guide made us get out at his grave. There were lots of little buildings, as though someone had made a Lilliputian village in the hill country. Walter Goodman, of the *New York Times*, seemed confused by the guide's heavy accent. "Why does Mrs. Johnson want to protect wallflowers?"

"Wildflowers, Walter."

When our bus guide pointed out Lyndon's special white car, permanently enshrined in his garage, she failed to mention the crucial fact: Johnson had installed a special mating-call horn in his car; he loved driving visitors while honking at his horny herd stampeding behind him. The tour bus parked near the barbecue hangar. Lady Bird was perched on a white rustic fence. She wore a long red Laura Ashley-type calico dress. She asked us if we wanted her autograph, and said she would pose for photos. We thought we were her guests, but clearly Mrs. Johnson pegged us as her tourists.

Nobody ever dies in America; so we continuously rebury the dead. The barbecue became a eulogy for Lyndon Johnson. The country band played "Dixie." We guests had to stand straight while singing it. Kissinger seemed overcome with emotion at being at the Johnson make-believe ranch and singing the Civil War hymn of the secessionist Deep South. Did he think he was Clark Gable in *Gone With the Wind*? Though they don't agree on politics, Kissinger and Cisneros, both men still slightly ill at ease in America, are *moved* by it; but they have no sense of national laughter. All of us are immigrants; it is our glory and our shame, our vulnerability, our strength. It is what makes our politics wacky, volatile.

I was headed the next day for Houston. Diane Trevino, a Houston student at LBJ, offered me a lift. That day Texas had one of those paradise-wide, white skies that make people keep coming back to the place. We congratulated ourselves for managing to be on the Texas highway just as the bluebonnets were hitting their peak—also in bloom were the Indian paintbrush, wine cups, and primrose. We drove through pine and oak country, and there were patches where the trees were thickly covered with balls of moss. In Lagrange (the town of *The Best Little Whorehouse in Texas* fame) we stopped for a sandwich at the Bon Ton restaurant. It was late afternoon when we reached Simonton, an hour out of Houston. Marianne Bruni had flown down to visit Bob Frost, a friend of hers from South Texas, and suggested we drop by for the Saturday night rodeo. The roundup was a few miles from the Frost ranch, Pecan Acres. Marianne had hoped I would talk to Bob about his connection to the Alley Theater, which is one of the best things in Houston. Diane was wearing a sweatshirt with ten "I hate Reagan" buttons; Bob Frost was wearing a polo shirt. He said he liked to play polo down in Latin America. It crossed my mind that we weren't a well-blended group. We sat in Bob's living room, with his wife and children, watching the sun set down low among the pecan trees. Bob frowned and remarked that his father, Vernon Frost, had felt bad because he had liked Edna Ferber; after having had a nice time here she had turned around and made a bouillabaisse of Bob's father's friends and called it *Giant*. Marianne nervously fanned herself and said, "Why, Bob. You should meet Barbara's family. I mean, for Northerners they are positively Southern." "Oh, really?" Bob said. Then we straightened it all out, and had a good time at the rodeo.

I understood why Bob Frost thought his family background would be more important to me than his work in the Alley Theater: Houston is all about money. The atmosphere here has nothing to do with the Austin-San Antonio corridor. My first night there I nearly went out of my mind. The windows of my hotel room were sealed, there was a television set in my room, and another in the john, three telephones, and so many buttons on the air conditioner that I either baked or froze.

On a Sunday, downtown Houston is awful. There are no people in the streets; I felt defenseless in the face of all that Nazi glass architecture. So I was delighted that Lionel Castillo—the former Immigration head under Carter— offered to drive me through other parts of the city: he is in charge of the Hispanic International University and also of the Immigration Institute, both of which operate out of a small white building on Edmundson, in the Mexican-American *barrio*. Houston gets the raw immigrant population right from the border, which makes it more Hispanic than San Antonio, whose Mexican-Americans are assimilated. We drove through Houston's East End and Magnolia. According to Castillo whole villages of Salvadorans and Mexicans arrive here. But only two hundred Salvadorans have been granted legal asylum. Most aliens have little sense of their legal rights. "When we open a file with the government for them, we are buying them time. With the Salvadorans, this is crucial." Castillo parked his car in front of Fiesta Mart, part of a chain of enormous Latino supermarkets which functions as a mini-world for the Mexican-Americans. Everything except an American passport can be arranged through Fiesta Mart. Its bank, Monytron, is considered by Hispanics to be the most reliable way of sending money back to Mexico and El Salvador. I walked through the vast supermarket with Castillo. Many customers stopped to greet him; he is a hero of this new Latin subculture. "It's a cliché to think all illegal aliens are poor. Some do quite well." He pointed to the Luvs diapers and American beer stacked alongside of the *piñatas*, Florida water, mounds of fresh garlic, and saints' candles.

Later that night we stopped in a small Mexican restaurant, *Aguas Calientes*. At night this part of town is lit up with bright lights advertising Latino movies, Laundromats, and gasoline stations. Castillo lacks traditional liberal support (trade unions, ecologists, and political liberals) for his fight to gain amnesty for illegal aliens. But he also understands where the new Texas is heading. "In the end, the money to create institutions and foundations to help these people will come from Texas—from the children and grandchildren of the oil industry."

Kathy Whitmire, the mayor of Houston, Ann Richards, the state treasurer, and several of the Hispanic women politicians have come to power through a coalition of Hispanics, women, and gays. But most of these women are using a minority mandate to represent corporate interests. This is the first generation of Texans to have known affluence on a wide-scale level. Or to have experienced such huge shifts in population as have occurred with incoming Northerners and Hispanics. This means that political offices are up for grabs. Ironically, Sissy Farenthold, who perhaps is the Texas politician with the most stature and most authentic concern for the rights of Hispanics, is now out of office and, indeed, was defeated by her natural constituency, the Mexican-Americans. Despite having been the first woman to come in in second place for the Democratic vice-presidential candidacy (in '72), and her enormous national prestige, Farenthold ruefully admitted to me, on a hot Houston afternoon in her law office, that she is a politician without portfolio.

Farenthold had been president of Wells College; her style is reflective, her cheekbones high, her family elite, and her concerns not folksy. (At the present time, her priority is the one hundred thousand Salvadorans in a detention camp near the Houston airport.) She still speaks with considerable emotion of her '74 gubernatorial campaign, which she lost because she refused to back down on the abortion issue. It was hard for her because she is a believing Catholic and has five children. "But I don't believe I have the right to dictate to other women what they must do." What really got to her were the TV commercials in San Antonio of a baby's heartbeat; Sissy felt it was implied that she was a baby killer. "Also," she smiled slightly, leaning back from her desk, which was piled high with case work, "suddenly, the Mexican-Americans no longer needed an Anglo liberal—they had their own."

"Didn't that infuriate you?"

Sissy hesitated. "Well, my problem was that I understood them. I may not have liked it, but I understood where they were coming from."

When pressed further, finally she said, "Maybe Texas eats up its liberals." She complained about the real lack of investigative journalism in the state. Then we said goodbye.

I boarded my Delta flight back to New York. We taxied into position, then stood still for about ten minutes. I had only understood a small piece of what goes on in Texas. The Hispanic thing was complicated. Hispanic organizations like COPS in San Antonio do good because they get the streets paved in bad neighborhoods and fix up the schools. And they give the formerly dispossessed their say. On the other hand, these are church-controlled groups who insist that political candidates first be accountable to them: accountability nights, grades, and then informing the public who passes muster. In the next decade, Texans will be treading the fine line between minority rights and mob power. While I was thinking all this, and coming up with no easy answers, the jet's motor revved up and we took off. I looked back down. There, below, along the highway, was a Fiesta Mall. I wondered where the big detention camp was located. Near the supermarket was another one of those rose gold glass skyscrapers. Those who work inside the opaque office buildings find the temperatures agreeable. But those outside, walking below on the street, complain that they fry. There is controversy about it.

I.

Lewis Mumford

1984

I was just starting out, this was in the 1960s, and a magazine editor suggested that I try my hand at interviewing. He wanted a piece done on Lewis Mumford. But when I reached him, Mumford, somewhat frosty on the telephone, declined. "I never give interviews."

"Well, I've never written one—I'm not sure where one is meant to go for the facts, so maybe it's just as well."

"You don't sound like you come out of city planning." Suddenly he sounded friendlier.

"I don't."

"I've changed my mind—in that case, come up. Don't worry about the facts. *The New Yorker* taught me how to handle them." Before I had a chance to tell him I would be driving up by car to Amenia, Mumford briskly gave me train information and hung up.

When I called back Mrs. Mumford answered, and she gave me specific directions. "Lewis thinks everyone takes trains; the railroad is his favorite form of transportation."

Sharp New England late fall weather that day; the Mumfords' white house was set back off a dirt road, its shape molded and dominated by the rolling farmland hills and Amenia in upstate New York. Mrs. Mumford came to the door—*the beautiful Sophia Wittenberg*. Before coming up, I had immersed myself in the world of Mumford and had learned of the romantic story of their courtship. They had met in 1919 in the Village, both of them had worked for the old *Dial* magazine.

While the Mumfords gave me a tour of the grounds—I was shown the red oak planted by his daughter Alison for his birthday, the asparagus beds—I was aware that Lewis Mumford was not a person to allow himself to be passively interviewed without doing some sizing-up of his visitor. He said he had never granted a personal interview, and, obviously, he was undecided about this one. He threw out a test question, "Now, about Ernest Boyd—but, of course, you wouldn't know who he was?"

"No." Looking for a way in, trying to reassure him that I was on some speaking acquaintance with American cultural history, I mentioned that the grounds of my folks' summer home had been landscaped by Olmsted.

"From New England and you don't know your way to the Taconic Parkway?"

Clearly he had quizzed his wife about my second telephone call. While feigning casual aloofness, he scrutinized each detail of his interviewer's personality. This time, while presumably showing me a grove of trees, he mentioned his pamphlet, *Aesthetics*. Again he waited for my reaction.

I had done my homework. "Wasn't it published in the 1920s by Joel and Amy Spingarn? Troutbeck Press?"

Mumford pointed in the distance, "The Spingarns live over that hill."

"The twenties were the heyday of the little magazines. It must have been a wonderful time to have started out as a writer."

"Perhaps . . . or perhaps Troutbeck Press was just a rich man's whim." He seemed vexed, some bitterness in his voice, as though he had just remembered an ancient unpleasantness.

Of the two, it was his wife who struck me as more at ease in her relation to the trees and shrubbery. Mumford seemed almost jarringly separate from his chosen landscape; his relation to nature, to land, struck me as abstract, a man whose eyes were more visionary than visual, more morally committed to the *idea* of nature than connected to it physically. It had often been said that Mumford hated the city and loved the country. My impression was that he was passionately committed to the city, and therefore appalled by it, and therefore made do with the country.

We went inside and Mumford named the way I should perceive his home. "An austere place—" The large yellow kitchen, hand-adzed beams, abundance of books, and good view of the trees struck me as pleasant. Perhaps Mumford meant it was more of a writer's environment—Thoreau, Emerson could have lived there—not an artist's place. One sensed that its owners had an internal, moral, spatial vision—there was no room for lush, gratuitous objects of beauty.

The most spartan part was Mumford's study. He characterized it as disorderly; I thought it unusually neat. Angled on the desk was a photograph of his son Geddes, in soldier's uniform, killed in World War II.

After we returned to the living room Mrs. Mumford excused herself. We sat down, almost formally facing one another, Mumford waiting for our conversation to begin. What had fired my imagination had been his book on Herman Melville. He wrote it at twenty-nine. There was an inner music, a quality of passion and personalness that was absent in his earlier work. "You wrote a book on Melville—"

Mumford's formal, severe graciousness vanished; suddenly he looked like a delighted small boy and amazingly vulnerable. "I didn't realize anyone still remembered it."

I was silent. The pioneering book certainly existed for poets, writers—but perhaps not for urbanists and architects. In Mumford's salad days, good writers and vervy intellectuals aspired to become generalists; but now Mumford was in danger of being judged by the values of the breed he most despised, the specialists and technicians. He had already pointed out to me that he was neither an urbanist nor an architect. "I like to remind people that a person who investigates a crime is not a criminal. I couldn't have written my books on architecture had I been one."

"There is a quality of inner urgency both in your description of Melville, and of his novels *Pierre* and *Moby Dick*. Were there parallels, for you, concerning your own childhood?"

Mumford was unusually wary. "I didn't read Melville until I was twenty-one—yes, perhaps there were certain parallels."

In Mumford's earlier work—*The Story of Utopias, Golden Day*—in which a pre-Civil War, more generous America is celebrated, his writing struck me as static, simplistic. We had the good society, past and future. I suspected Mumford must have been the sort of lonely child who would have preferred identifying with an imagined paradise past, rather than cope with the sullen present. But, beginning with the Melville book, he found his voice. Utopia was replaced by a prophet's darker vision: man's struggle against evil.

"What happened to you after you worked on Melville? What changed your style, your thought?"

Mumford was pensive. I had been impressed by the special vividness with which he described Melville's rage at the loss of his father, of the humiliation of being cast out in the world, constant witness to his mother's economic deprivations and his anger at being denied his birthright, an education. There were the hopeless poor, the immigrants, and the genteel types, like Melville's family, who were down on their uppers, and once had known better; proud rather than optimistic, money for them was a hidden, embarrassing subject. With Melville in mind, I asked, "Did you have any brothers or sisters?"

"No," he hesitated, "there were some differences—I was an only child."

"Yes, that part puzzled me, because in your book you described Melville as though he had been one . . ." Something was askew. "You didn't have a father?" The phrase had awkwardly tumbled out of my mouth, or perhaps my unconscious had leaped ahead.

Mumford gazed at me, surprised. After a long pause he said, "Yes, I had a father." Again he hesitated, "He died before I was born." He thought over his answer, then gave me a slightly different explanation. "He was separated from my mother before I was born."

Then it flashed through my mind that the only possible explanation for all of this roundabout was that Mumford had been born out of wedlock. I was disconcerted; it certainly wasn't a point I would press with a man of Mumford's stature and aloof manner. I wasn't even sure whether he was aware what I was thinking and what had stopped me.

Mumford shifted slightly in his chair and went back to Melville, as though we needed his presence in order to continue our conversation. "But there was no blackness in my early life—I had to imagine that part, which made it harder for me to write on him."

"Oh?"

Mumford deftly sketched in some cheerful details—walks through the city with his grandfather, with a chipper Irish nurse—but if there had been no blackness, neither did Mumford convince me of plentiful happiness.

"Did you feel alienated as a child?"

"Alienated is a word of your generation," he fielded. I said nothing, but I remembered, in Melville, he had used that word to describe Shakespeare's and Melville's relation to their time.

"No," he continued, "we were never lonely, the city was a friendly place." In that abrupt shift of tone I had come to expect when Mumford had reached a personal decision to become more direct, he added, "The city seemed drab."

"And summers?"

"Vermont." Now his voice became more authentically warm. "Those were meaningful summers . . ." Again he hesitated, "About Melville—I did sympathize with his lying about his age during his time as cabin boy." He explained his own dislike of his job as copy boy for the *Telegram*—a job he had held when his interest had been in philosophy; and though he later had been offered other jobs on newspapers, he never again worked for the daily press.

We spoke of his own education—he had zigzagged back and forth between night and day school at CCNY. During that period he had bouts of TB and often had to work at odd jobs—an investigator in the dress and shirtwaist industry, a laboratory assistant with the United States Bureau of Standards. Although he took some courses at Columbia and The New School, he never got his degree. "The present emphasis on acquiring knowledge as an end in itself makes no sense. Knowledge is useless unless it is put to intelligent use. Now we have a new kind of knowledge, knowing how to get foundation grants. I see the present foundation system as essentially corrupting."

"You've done so many things, what was your real dream? Did you want to be a novelist?"

Mumford thought about that one, "A playwright."

"Did you write them?"

"Yes—long ago. I felt very akin to Hart Crane. I was also interested in the Brooklyn Bridge and I wanted to capture its symbolic quality in the theater."

Mumford had that complicated shyness that frequently emanates from quirky, overly intelligent people. I was quiet for a moment because I was aware that in a certain sense Mumford was reversing the truth. I had heard from poets who had seen Crane's correspondence that it was Crane who had been influenced by Mumford in his poem, and it was Mumford's book on Melville that had inspired Crane's interest in the novelist, causing him to write his memorable poem to Melville, *Elegy on a Tombstone.*

We both had avoided a necessary part of my visit: a long list of questions on city planning. Robert Moses hardly rated a shrug; Le Corbusier he saw as authoritarian, the imposition of personal will against human needs; Patrick Geddes became trapped inside his own philosophic system; and Jane Jacob's theories were wrong. Mumford paused over Gaudí: "Overpraised—but an interesting rebellion against the mechanism of modern society."

Later, when he walked me back to the car, he admitted, "Your questions on city planning bored me. But when you started out with Melville—I was touched. That meant something to me, we should have continued on him."

"On Melville? But you seemed to want to shift away from him."

"Did I do that?" He thought matters over, then replied, obliquely, as though we had been dealing with a puzzle. "Yes, but with Melville, you were on the right track." Then we said goodbye and I drove off.

Mumford's final caution impressed me. Certainly his spiritual connection was with the poets of America, Crane, Whitman, and Stieglitz. Unlike the expatriates—Hemingway, Stein, Fitzgerald—men like Mumford had chosen to rebel against the aridity of the American creative climate by rediscovering our native past, taking from Emerson, Thoreau, and Whitman the idea that the primary aim of society was the cultivation of the individual.

To separate the literary Mumford from the man who wrote on cities is false. In Melville, Mumford had started to develop the thesis for his subsequent major trilogy.

He wrote about *Moby Dick*: "In another sense the whale stands for practical life. Mankind needs food and light and shelter, and, with a little daring and a little patience, it gains these things from the environment: the whale that we cut up, dissect, analyze, melt down, pour into casks and distribute in cities and households is the whale of industry and science." He viewed the city as a living, traveling organism, as alive and as moving as the white whale itself.

But I was struck, at the heart of the interview, by Mumford's passionate identification of Melville as his alter ego, and the problem of Mumford's father. Attempting to clear up the haze, I contacted several people close to Mumford and, point blank, fired the question. By their Jamesian circumlocutions, I became convinced that my hunch was right. But the matter was not mine to pursue, and in censoring out the emotional center, my piece made no sense, and, eventually, I put it to one side. Then this spring I read Mumford's own autobiography, in which he states he was the illegitimate son of Lewis Mack, to whom, it turned out, his friend and neighbor, Amy Spingarn, was distantly related. I remembered our walk near the shrubbery bed of red myrtle. Mumford had explained how he had bought the adjoining fourteen acres from the Spingarns because he was afraid they would be selling it to the quarry people. And I recalled his frown when he referred to Troutbeck Press as "perhaps just a rich man's whim." Had Mumford already begun to suspect that he was connected, in some vague way, to the Spingarns? And, for a moment, I remembered him quoting a phrase from *Moby Dick*: "All are born with halters round their necks. . . ." He then was already at work on his autobiography. I realize, now, I must have walked in when the older man was struggling to set the young man free.

IV.
Fallen Angels

The Ordeal of Jean Harris

Adrift in Westchester

for Stanley Plastrik

1981

The Jean Harris trial has mesmerized Americans. It has received an unprecedented amount of publicity. Diana Trilling, Shana Alexander, and Lally Weymouth, daughter of Katherine Graham, owner of the *Washington Post*, have been commissioned to write books on the subject; in a Columbia University elevator was scrawled FREE JEAN HARRIS. Immediately after the trial Ellen Burstyn starred in a TV drama, "The People vs. Jean Harris." Jennifer Jones has contracted to do a movie on the subject. Why has this case aroused so much furor? An ordinary despondent, rejected, middle-aged woman goes to the home of her lover, who has replaced her with a younger woman—she makes a distraught attempt to kill herself—the only question to be solved is whether this was indeed a suicide attempt gone wrong, or whether it was a more conventional case of *crime passionnel*. How does this tragic mess end up becoming first-page news over a period of three months?

The Harris case shatters several American myths. Despite the cool instructions given to American women by modern analysts—by group therapy, sex therapy, and by that last great breed of valiant optimists, the American feminists—the human condition of the average American woman is closer to the universal condition of woman than most observers of the American scene would like to believe. As motherhood, wifehood, or grandmotherhood has no special status in this country, in many ways the typical woman, as she grows older, is deprived of a basic honoring of her life's "work." In a soap-opera movie such as *An Unmarried Woman*, Jill Clayburgh is rejected by her husband, looks younger than her daughter, and soon has a famous artist madly in love with her—urging upon Jill happiness and sexual fulfillment in his Soho pad. Meanwhile, after midnight, American cable television goes porno: "midnight blue" films, the ritual group-sex scenes, the hosts of the various sex clubs giving over the TV channels the telephone numbers of clubs and escort services for both men and women.

This barrage of zapped-up sex notwithstanding, many Americans are walking about still locked into the lonely sadness engendered by their old-fashioned nineteenth-century hearts. We are not a nation of Marilyn Monroes, Jane Fondas, with-it feminists, or Vanessa Redgraves; it is the very *ordinariness* of Jean Harris's ordeal to which Americans respond. She represents the misery of real life suffered, rather than the mythic American plan in which nobody gets hurt and everyone has the illusory option of a fresh start. It was as though Jean Harris's act of desperation had suddenly cut through our national puritanical censorship, which prohibits empathy for the aging woman, and every American woman "became" Jean Harris.

Another myth shattered in this trial is that America is a society of equals rather than a stratified society with class barriers. Jean Harris had upper-class mores; the jury, which found her guilty, was "just plain folk." Bolen, the prosecuting attorney, portrayed Harris to the press and the jury as an undemocratic and unrepentant member of the super-privileged class. Was reverse class prejudice a big factor in the jury's unanimous, harsh verdict of guilty?

We are used to writing impassioned protests concerning unfair treatment of blacks by white juries in the South; we know that Dreyfus was sent to Devil's Island because he was a Jew; but progressives have always been highly selective in their choices for compassion—the rights of the WASP upper class have never come high on the injustice priority list. But to understand who Jean Harris and Herman Tarnower really were, one must roll back to the America of their youth.

Both Tarnower and Harris may have been victimized by their *idealization* of upper-class values, but neither of them were from that background. Jean Harris came from a "nice" Cleveland, Ohio, family. She went to private school in a "nice suburb"—the Laurel School in Shaker Heights. Her father was a middle-rung army officer; she was one of those Midwestern young women coming of age in the late 1930s whose tremendous vulnerability was their awe of the magical East. The Atlantic Seaboard was mysterious territory to those conquered by Fitzgerald's Middle America Gatsbys—the East was the ultimate terrain of Ivy League colleges, New York "artistic culture"—a world peopled by exotic Jews and blacks. The model female writer would have been Dorothy Parker, the model movie actress Katharine Hepburn in *The Philadelphia Story*. Jean Harris believed in those myths. She graduated in 1945 from Smith, with top honors. She married, had two sons, divorced, and supported herself and her children by becoming headmistress in a variety of fashionable Eastern secondary schools for women. First she taught in Connecticut; at the time of Tarnower's death she was headmistress at Madeira, a huge sprawl of a school whose gracious buildings overlook the Potomac outside Washington, D.C. Traditionally, Madeira produces high-boned blondes—young Grace Kellys—who ride horseback well, have fine manners, and have been provided the polished rudiments afforded by an old-fashioned conservative school. The place has an indoor riding rink and eight tennis courts.

Last March, when Tarnower was shot, he was preparing to celebrate his seventieth birthday—Jean Harris, then, was fifty-six years old. For Harris, to be headmistress of Madeira, to be the mistress of a diamond-in-the-rough Jewish doctor, *was* the myth—and indeed one of the reasons the intelligent Jean Harris was so incapable of making concrete demands on those whose world she inhabited was that she lived inside her own myth. She never sought any of the protections of a more pragmatic woman. Like many Americans she was rootless—in Madeira she was living as handmaiden to the children of the rich, her genteel home of faded Southern grandeur was lent to her by the school's administration. On Tarnower's suburban Harrison, New York, estate she was also—over fourteen years—the shadowy female guest. Jean Harris ruefully commented to writer Shana Alexander, "My sons can say their mother died of dumbness."

Not dumbness—Jean Harris is an intelligent woman—but she was a Midwestern innocent severely hampered by being locked into the mores of another era. When Tarnower, in the early phase of their romance, gave her a ten-carat diamond ring to celebrate their engagement, and soon panicked at the idea of marriage, Jean Harris felt impelled to act the lady. She returned the diamond, and asked him to keep the ring for her in his bank. Eventually Tarnower sold the diamond and used the money for a down payment for a home for Lynne Tryforos, Jean Harris's young rival. A more realistic woman would have acknowledged to herself that she was Tarnower's mistress, that she was cash-short and he was rich, would have kept the ring, sold it, invested in her *own* real estate, and her own ego, and saved her own life. But American women of Jean Harris's background and time were raised to wear white gloves and become wives, not mistresses. By returning Tarnower's ring and telling herself that she continued to live with this man out of passion, out of weakness, Jean Harris managed to retain her image of herself as a lady, a part-time wife.

A New York City woman taxi driver commented to me on the case: "The guy's a mean bastard, uglier than Dracula. That's a sweet, refined lady who never did no one harm. I think she's innocent—but say, she got a little disturbed—what woman hasn't gotten disturbed at least once in her life? So, say, she was upset and the gun went off. Hasn't she suffered enough already? With all the nuts and murderers walking the streets of New York, going free for the most brutal crimes, they got to make an example of this one? Why? You call that jury normal?—all those women, and not one says, okay, I'll save her life. Okay, so Jean Harris didn't weep. Listen, woman to woman, all that business about weeping means nothing—the worst bitch can break down and cry. But that woman is not evil. So, what's with that jury? Listen, somebody ought to tell her lawyer, when she appeals the case, get it away from that rotten bunch in Scarsdale; in Manhattan where we got real killers to worry about, we would have given Jean Harris a break."

But the case was tried in White Plains, Westchester County, which was Tarnower's turf. Although Tarnower's lush estate was in Harrison, New York, his medical practice was in the nearby suburban town of Scarsdale. After World War II many members of the middle and upper classes moved to suburban communities within commuting distance of New York. The suburbs had neither the variety of the big cities nor the individuality of the small town. In the early 1950s Herman Tarnower moved his practice to Scarsdale and formed the Scarsdale Medical Group. He established himself as a society cardiologist, and apparently—although a cold man—was a good doctor to the rich. In the last few years he became a minor national celebrity as "Diet Doc," the author of the *Scarsdale Diet Book*, which grossed millions. Tarnower's well-heeled society patients seem to have adored him. This benign view of him was not shared by many others. One of his male colleagues described him as "one of the most killable of men."

Tarnower had his problems: he had been born ugly, dirt poor, the child of immigrant Jews, and was a man of overwhelming social ambition. Jean Harris was only, as she put it, "dumb" because she misread the cultural signals of the world she had joined in her great "East Coast adventure." Just as black men stood for sex and jazz, Jewish men, in the eyes of wistful, wondering, adventurous Midwestern women, were the symbol of the "good male." Jewish men were considered to be wonderful husbands, loyal mates, good providers, and intellectually superior. Women are shrewder about men from their own cultures; Jewish women rarely romanticized the macho Jewish male and, indeed, managed to survive by making heavy demands on their men, which their WASP sisters, fearful at being considered possibly anti-Semitic, would have thought "unfair." Women from minority cultures intuitively understood that the terrible feelings of social and professional rejection experienced by their men as they ran the rocky road of assimilation frequently produced revenge love affairs.

All cultures have a secret love story that embodies their covert national history. Mexicans perceive themselves the illegitimate sons of Indian mothers raped by Spanish conquerors and they frequently cast their women in the "Malinche" role. (Malinche was the Maya princess who deserted her people for Hernán Cortés.) Of the South, Faulkner dryly observed, "it's truly about miscegenation." The nineteenth-century European drama circled around class and ambition. But in the United States, more often than we admit, our hidden romance involves miscegenation, assimilation, and ambitions of class. An old American love sport has been the cross-cultural, cross-racial *affaire du coeur*.

But just as Jean Harris didn't notice that she infuriated the jury by behaving uppity, she failed to realize that much of what motivated Tarnower in his sadistic relation to a variety of women was sour vengeance. Instead, Harris tried to make her Jewish lover fit her notion of love writ on a perfect Greek vase— "Herman read Herodotus," she explained to the jury. But Tarnower had more driving him than a fine appreciation of the classics.

In Tarnower's pre-World War II America, the battles between the German Jewish bourgeoisie and the poor Jews of Eastern Europe, from which his family came, were ferocious. The German Jews who arrived in the United States in modest numbers early on had made a secure place for themselves within Protestant America. At the turn of the century, millions of Jews from Eastern Europe crowded into New York; as Irving Howe pointed out in *World of Our Fathers*, the Lower East Side suddenly had a density greater than Bombay; these Jews, with lice in their hair, their Yiddish, their Zionism, their overenthusiasms for God, religion, anarchism, socialism, threatened their discreet German co-religionists. Although the German Jews did good works among poor Jews, the social barriers were impenetrable. How was a poor young Jew to climb up the social ladder and become an "American" if even his own ethnic group denied him access? (Blacks, Chinese, Italians also maintain sharp class distinctions within their own groups.)

The cross-cultural love affair is a handy route. Woody Allen, Philip Roth are more than a generation younger than Tarnower; even so, their novels and movies reflect the dilemma of the young man on the way up. In *Goodbye, Columbus*, Roth's hero loses his true love object, the rich Jewish princess, Brenda Patemkin, who is standing firmly on prime Eastern territory, Radcliffe, to whose brother college the unpolished Rothian hero has no entry. In subsequent Roth novels, the Rothian antihero—confused and bitter over his loss of his original dream love, the Jewish princess—assumes an attitude of a plague on all your houses. The blonde WASP women are shown attempting suicide for him, the Jewish women are depicted as quarrelsome. Woody Allen, portraying Woody Allen in *Annie Hall* and *Manhattan*, also perceives his love affairs with naive Midwestern beauties as proof of authentic Americanization.

Jean Harris clearly had no more of a clue what Tarnower was about than the heroine of *Annie Hall*. Late in life Tarnower, through his medical practice and his elaborate entertaining, was able to establish friendships with people important to him, among them the longed-for German Jewish bourgeoisie of his childhood. Jean Harris berates Tarnower for his adulation of women like Iphigene Sulzberger, but WASP Jean Harris was never part of Tarnower's true goal—she was merely part of the decor he established in order to impress key people he fantasized about in his youth.

The *Scarsdale Diet Book* made Tarnower a celebrity and a multimillionaire; at seventy he could afford to dump his WASP upper-class Jean, and prove himself with her rival, his office assistant, thirty years his junior, good-looking but uneducated Lynne Tryforos. Tarnower—who during his fourteen-year liaison with Jean Harris had affairs with many other women—clearly was something of an exhibitionist. He enjoyed rotating the visits from his women and fomenting jealousies: his Belgian domestic staff was instructed to remove each woman's belongings from his bedroom before the visit of the next rival. Suzanne van der Vreken, his housekeeper, also was instructed to keep detailed guest lists, menu lists, and a record of the visits to the Tarnower estate of his two steady mistresses. Jean Harris was aware of his other women and finally began to suffer from severe depressions. Tarnower had her on increased dosages of amphetamines, which, if taken over a long time period, can produce dangerous behavior. Jean Harris had puritanical notions of integrity and good behavior, and for many years chose to ignore Tarnower's waning interest in her, as well as Lynne's overt attacks. (In a jealous rage Lynne slashed a wardrobe-full of Jean Harris's elegant clothing.)

Finally Jean Harris's own anger broke through: she wrote Tarnower an upset, furious letter referring to Lynne Tryforos as a "psychotic whore" and berating Tarnower for his behavior. That same day Jean Harris drove the five hours from Washington, D.C., with a loaded gun at her side. Her story is that she intended to see Tarnower, say a quiet, despairing farewell, go to the water lily pond on the estate grounds, and shoot herself. Instead, in a bloody, embattled bedroom, Tarnower was killed by four bullets, which left none for Jean to take her own life. Harris had a suicide note in her purse; she had left letters of resignation as headmistress at Madeira; several days prior to the event, she had made out her will in favor of her two grown sons.

Jean Harris undoubtedly fantasized that at the final moment Tarnower would save her life, and their love would be rekindled. Instead—perhaps it was the sight of Lynne's nightgowns and clothes in what she considered her bedroom—Jean Harris lost control, and one form or another of a suicide-cum-*crime passionnel* occurred.

At the trial Jean Harris's problem was that instead of fighting to save her life, she decided to save her love; she sought to explain to the jury and the press the *reason* for her existence. The just-plain-folk jury was shocked at her upper-class ways, which they held against her—the jurors, and indeed many observers, were appalled that she had referred to her young rival as a whore. We Americans are more phobic than Europeans in our use of strong language—Jean Harris damaged her image in the press by describing her rival as a whore. In hypocritically egalitarian America, one woman sleeping with a man is presumed the equal "sister" of another woman sleeping with the same man. Ironically, poor Jean Harris was more the victim of her puritanical, suppressed upbringing than of snobbery.

If one can imagine oneself into the troubled heart and mind of Jean Harris, undoubtedly she inflicted self-torture by placing herself on personal trial for her own failure to adhere to the value system of her own time and her own place. In referring to Lynne Tryforos as a whore, she wasn't making a social distinction but was being old-fashionedly female: Am *I* a whore? she was asking herself. No, I am Herman's wife—*she* (the other woman) is the whore. In the face of a tremendous media blitz, this totally private, unknown, fifty-seven-year-old matron struggled to desexualize her relation to Herman Tarnower. She had two grown sons testify to the healthy family ambience of her relationship; she came dressed to the trial some days as a proper headmistress of a fine girls' finishing school; other days she showed up in the tweed suits and mink scarfs expected of suburban housewives of her age and class. In her puritanical imagination she was attempting to resolve: Am I a whore? Am I a lady? Should I have let Herman pay for all those trips to Paris, Nepal, and the Caribbean? Should I have let him pay for my expensive wardrobe? But I did return the ring. . . . We shared Herodotus, it was an *amour spirituel*. American women are reasonably casual about going to bed with a man—it can be considered "love"—but they become uptight if men pick up too many of the bills. We do not have a mistress psychology. American women are very puritanical about money; both liberated and nonliberated women are ambivalent about what they would permit a man to pay for. Thus, all the energy Jean Harris should have used to keep herself out of prison was spent appeasing the Middle America of her childhood—Jean Harris tried to convince the jury she was not Tarnower's mistress, but rather his wife/soul mate.

In crisp headmistress style Harris reprimanded the prosecutor for his bad grammar; she freely admitted, under cross examination, that she was not the sort of person to make friends with the servants (many observers feel that this piece of snobbery cost her the trial). She acted as though the jury were Madeira students to whom she was explaining a Platonic ideal of life. She tried to be gallant à la Katharine Hepburn, witty and rueful like Dorothy Parker; under a barrage of questions she deemed undignified, she lost her temper but never wept or sought mercy from the jury. Jean Harris remained her idea of a lady. One of my women friends who comes from the South informed me that many Southerners felt that Harris had disgraced Madeira by having the fourteen-year affair. She should have either remarried or done without. In the South, my friend pointed out, Harris would have been ostracized for her *private* behavior—but of course no jury would have convicted her for killing Tarnower, since he hadn't behaved like a gentleman.

Unfortunately, Jean Harris gave a Southern defense in a Northern court. She infuriated the jury—instead of making clear to them that she was no whore, she convinced them she was a snob—and she lost her case. Whatever happened in Tarnower's bedroom, I believe Jean Harris is telling the truth when she claims she is innocent, meant to kill herself, and accidentally shot Tarnower. Her problem is that four bullets were fired. In those final distressed weeks no doubt Jean Harris struggled to bridge the split between the idealized lover she carried in her head and the actual Tarnower who was rejecting her for Lynne Tryforos. After the death of the cold imposter, the man who got in the way of this all-consuming passion, the split within her mind could heal, and in her memory Tarnower is permanently fixed as the idealized lover. When Jean Harris maintains that Tarnower died trying to save her life, I do believe she is telling the truth as she now perceives it to be.

When the jurors announced the harsh sentence—guilty of second-degree murder—Americans were stunned. Suddenly it occurred to us the drama had been for real. The backlash to the verdict was immediate: the jury claimed that after an eight-day deliberation they had wept copious tears before arriving at a unanimous decision of guilty. Still one detects a touch of bad faith. The press flip-flopped and more sympathetic interpretations of Jean Harris began to appear. Many Americans, especially city dwellers, felt outraged. The criminal courts in New York City are in total chaos, hardened murderers are going in and out of prison as though through a revolving door. The same week that Jean Harris was convicted, John Lennon's killer was sent to a psychiatric hospital. Because of his mental confusion he will not stand trial. Two lower-class women were acquitted of crimes similar to Jean Harris's.

Americans have no provision for *crime passionnel*—what we do have, and what many criminals use to their advantage, is "plea bargaining." The defense attorney and prosecutor "bargain" for a shorter sentence; the defendant pleads guilty, and is rewarded for not using the state's money in an elaborate trial. The questions being asked by thinking people are: In an attempt to prove the "fairness" of the system, are people such as Patty Hearst and Jean Harris penalized by receiving stiffer sentences than the average citizen? Does the indiscriminate use of plea bargaining prejudice the rights of those who consider themselves innocent? Are defendants penalized for *not* plea bargaining? Why wasn't psychiatric evidence given for Mrs. Harris? Why wasn't she indicted on a lesser charge of murder, such as manslaughter? Could a plea of temporary insanity have been used?

To have plea bargained or admitted to temporary insanity would have meant, for Jean Harris, the death of the heart, the relinquishing of her idea of Herman Tarnower, a public invasion into the privacy of her troubled mind.

Ironically, this woman so phobically afraid of being mistaken for a mistress or whore may spend the next fifteen years of her life in the company of hardened prostitutes. But despite her lost freedom she has remained oddly loyal to her love. Whether she has landed in jail for the next fifteen years because of her inner guilts, or because Tarnower was shot, or because of the unseemly intensity of her passion, or because of reverse discrimination against her upper-class manner remains unclear. Since her incarceration at Bedford State Prison for Women Jean Harris has been permitted to watch the TV special based on transcripts of the trial. "Now you can be the judge: guilty or innocent" ran the advertisements for the hastily put-together drama. More ominous is the news, since the Harris case, that under a new ruling future trials now may be televised. Are we back in the Middle Ages, *auto-da-fé* and public trials to be used for mass entertainment? A less spectacular piece of information, but news that may have more bearing on the events that led to Jean Harris's act of desperation, is the report in the *New York Times* from social welfare agencies that women over fifty-five are classed among the most economically underprivileged groups. Unfortunately, Jean Harris identified with a privileged group when, in reality, without a job, without a home, without a man, just before she shot Tarnower, she was at the bottom of the heap.

Fiction or Nonfiction?

1984

Frequently I have been asked whether the books I write are fiction or nonfiction. The last two—*Arriving Where We Started* and *Short Flights*—straddle categories. This is on people's minds because so many contemporary writers—Max Frisch, Mailer, Doctorow, Renata Adler, Vargas Llosa, Capote, Frank Conroy, Francine du Plessix Grey, Ishmael Reed, Exley, and Vonnegut—are writing books with a shape puzzling to some readers. In England, Thomas Keneally's *Schindler's List* was considered a novel; here, nonfiction. And we do like to pin things down. Are these novels? Memoirs? Nonfiction? Fiction-nonfiction? Or, that dreadful word, faction? (Nonfiction is also non-English. What would it mean to write "nonpoetry"?)

But even if we were to divide books into more sensible categories, the point is that many of the sorts of writers who, had they lived in the nineteenth century or the earlier part of the twentieth, would have been shaping their passions about the world and human nature into clearly defined novels, now go about matters in a different way. The news of the external world provided in the nineteenth century by novelists—the stuff and look of life—now is provided by mass media. We are living in a post-Freudian age, and internal news of the self, which seemed the great discovery of the first part of the twentieth century, is taken more for granted.

If we look at the changes in the novel since the 1950s—the same period in which the French were engaged in an abstract involvement with the *nouveau roman* (interesting at times, though something at the heart of really grand novels is resistant to this pursed, thin-lipped, Cartesian logic; the novel is more untameable, bad-mannered, and imperfect than the contained world of fable, po-

Delivered as a talk in spring 1984 at Books & Company in New York City.

etics, and linguistics permits) and the English stubbornly continued to write class novels (albeit now more frequently lower than upper)—Americans seemed to concentrate on a heightened use of personal voice and on autobiography. Indeed, we were showing as much discontent with conventional notions of narrative as were the French.

Along with the autobiographical went an increased use of real names. Some writers, like Bellow, do this only occasionally. Other writers use it more extensively. But the need of so many writers to do this doesn't mean that we have ceased being imaginative, or are only interested in our personal lives; it is that a deepened use of personal autobiography has become a literary technique. One of the ways a writer can get rid of all the cumbersome stops and pauses and "made-up" quality of conventional novels is to insert real names: it acts as a condensation—and is as much of a device as use of the first person (which also was once considered a questionable practice). This sort of use of real names has to do with a writer's inner sense of arrangement, and is akin to the artist who inserts newsprint, a written phrase, or perhaps a "real" object like a nail or piece of cloth into his canvas in order to create a new arrangement. What is fiction but an ordering of reality? And it is the successful way in which the writer frames his or her series of objects and thus creates a new order which is the test of the imagination—not whether or not some of the objects named seem to resemble real things. Although such techniques in art have been with us for most of the twentieth century and real names in fiction have been with us since Proust, publishers are prickly about such matters. When they see a bunch of real names they assume these to be books of literal information or straight, old-fashioned memoirs. But, by this logic, a film like *Star Wars*, which doesn't name our friends (not quite yet!), could be considered imaginative, while Fellini's *Amarcord*, because we can locate what we perceive as real events—Mussolini, the rise of Italian fascism, Fellini the child—could be considered autobiography . . . or my *bête noire*, nonfiction.

The way in which we arrange our writing puts us in touch with our deepest selves. My own journey has had to do with the losing and refinding of the firm, unembarrassed voice I had at ten. Then, at prepuberty, I knew who I was:

> *Chapter One. To begin with I am a girl. The girls in our class through the years have formed a certain group. The kaffeeklatch has formed various clubs, all lasting not more than three weeks. We have an overflowing amount of ideas, which never take place. . . . My best beloved friend, Mildred A., has a knack for getting the Boys. It has caused long never to be forgotten fights with boys who are conservative with the matter of love at our age . . .*

At the same time I was writing about life and love in the fifth grade of P.S. 6, I was making notes in a wonderful, odd book given to me by my favorite aunt: *Read But Not Forgotten.* Apparently unaware of the incongruity of grouping these two authors together, I wrote that "The Raven" was "the most inspiring thing I have ever read. In a class by itself," and that *Mary Poppins* "was my bible. I could open any page and soon be lost to the world. This is the best I can say for any book." My next entry was a curt dismissal of a book intended for female adolescents. "Idealistic for girls interested in careers. Not exceptional." The child wanted Edgar Allan Poe, not feminist position papers.

But nine years later, that sturdy child's voice was lost to me. At nineteen, how could I know, with the world's great literature, ideas, life, and learning pounding at me, who I was? The psychic energy I had used to make what in those days seemed an incredible leap from a New York childhood to Paris days at the Sorbonne had wearied me. Rather desperately in the margins of my notebook on Descartes (all I remember learning at the Sorbonne), I wrote about his famous formula: *Yes, but who is this* HE *doing all that thinking?* I meant: Who was me?

Europe, just staggering to her feet after the Second World War, was one big tragic bazaar. Everyone had his awful private history. With all this dropped at my doorstep, and Spain, too (I was living with a politicized Spanish student, thus underground politics took place in our hotel), I felt fraudulent. I never had suffered unduly. In the face of all this, did I have a right to my more ordinary feelings? Then, too, there were my secret lacks. I hoped that no one would ever notice that, except for a few poets, I had eliminated English writers from my consciousness. I never had seriously pursued Shakespeare, Hardy, George Eliot, Virginia Woolf, or Dickens. With such shortcomings, would I be "allowed" to become a writer? Even worse, Colette bored me.

What would I write about? Not a war book; I hadn't been a soldier. Nor a victim of the American Depression. The Jews that had been wiped out hadn't been upper-class, assimilated Manhattan types. I wasn't even a Southerner! Meanwhile, my English was losing its snap.

In a back-handed way, I did learn from Sartre and Beauvoir. Like all students in Paris in the late forties, I was fascinated by them. But it was already clear, despite their dazzling brilliance, that they both wrote dreadful novels. I grasped that their aim was to write "plain." Eliminate literary artifice. Wasn't that, after all, the eternal message of Stendhal, Flaubert? What I did (and continued this habit for some time; Beauvoir's *The Mandarins* came out in the early fifties) was to rework their novels in my head.

Had Beauvoir used real names, I felt, in *The Mandarins,* she could have produced a valuable book on how French intellectuals, and France, unraveled themselves from the German occupation. A *roman à clef* was thin going and the wrong choice for her material. Precisely because the genre depends on insinuation, it too often collapses into gossipy caricature. Though Sartre was later to write lovely things like *The Words,* and might have *thought* as Flaubert, *The*

Fiction or Nonfiction?

Age of Reason remained a novel of modern concerns with the old-fashioned construction of *Les Thibaults* without any of Robert Martin du Gard's narrative gift. But one magical day I discovered Céline. The opening paragraph of *Journey to the End of the Night* dazzled me. Céline had a *voice*. So, that's the *organizing* factor—that's how you hold together the disjointed fragments of a mad, modern world. Over and over I read his opening paragraph: "It all began just like that." And, boom! I was off. I was beginning to learn.

In my room in the Hôtel Observatoire, I stuck with Proust and Céline. Proust's world and novel ended with the First World War, which was just where Céline began. I was also part of a generation which had experienced a break in time; we had been children, not heroes, in the Second World War. That war had changed the world; I was beginning to locate myself. If I was to be a writer I had to find a way of communicating this new landscape; I had seen rubble in Germany, Dachau before it was fixed up, and, willy-nilly, had been thrown into the Spanish Resistance. I needed a new vocabulary for my Spanish experiences precisely because Americans had such solid images about Spain connected to García Lorca, Hemingway, and Orwell: my vision was more urban, less exotically "Spanish." Finally, like most Americans, I went home. And, after all that culture, all that Sartre, one day, while riding the Madison Avenue bus, I read *The Catcher in the Rye*. I recognized my own adolescence; Holden Caulfield was a soul mate. European techniques were fine, but I had missed our American direct artlessness. Through Salinger I had understood that even if I wasn't a war hero, a demi-mondaine, or even an exotic Southerner, it was allowed—I could become a writer.

In the mid-fifties I took some writing courses with Martha Foley at the School for General Studies, which, in those days, was a very unfashionable part of Columbia. During those silent McCarthy years our class formed a small enclave; we hung out at the West End Bar. Martha Foley and her then ex-husband, Whit Burnett, had created *Story* in the early thirties and forties. That magazine had been midwife to the short story in America. Cheever, Mailer, Lowry, Saroyan—everyone had published in it. One of the best things Martha did for her students was to make us send out at least a story a week, which meant we got a rejection a week. But wasn't it worth getting rejected just to hear Martha's stories of Vienna? Her wonderful nuggets of how Lowry recuperated in her apartment after his Bellevue breakdown cheered me on. Knowing how much I admired him, Martha suddenly found I had a gaze which reminded her of Lowry. None of the students had published; we described each other in heightened literary terms. When a slightly drunk visiting literary critic singled me out as the class Temple Drake, I was secretly ecstatic. In this half fantasy land of literary delights, overnight I had acquired the sensitivity of Malcolm Lowry and the abandon of a Faulknerian wild girl. Week after week I raced back to Columbia. Perhaps next I might be named Cleopatra on the Nile.

Right near me in class sat Tony Perkins, who hadn't yet become a film star. He wrote stories about white slavery. Martha, her hair dyed flaming red, waving a long jade cigarette holder, coolly inquired: Did these stories come out of Tony's knowing and feeling? "Yes, Ma'am." Perkins had met the Foley test: "Well, then, fine," she said, blowing smoke rings.

She tried to throw her female students a few practical lifelines. "Invent eccentricities—avoid the world's chores. Never marry male writers—or you will end up a typist." In her best Boston Latin School voice, she would mutter: "Anaïs Nin is *ridiculous*—read Jane Austen." Carson McCullers, who had been discovered by *Story*, dragged Tennessee Williams to our class; in order to get attention, she would mewl like a stuck cat, moaning: "Te-yun, yew read from mah woik, I jest ca-hunt." Martha hissed at her former protégée, "Pull yourself together, Carson."

At the end of the year a group of editors made the trip uptown to discuss with us the real world of publishing. The meeting was held in the large auditorium. They complained there was no real talent to be found. A middle-aged woman who taught another group abruptly stood up. She shook her black umbrella at the guests on the platform, "Scum, vermin, hypocrites—you have the nerve to come here just to tell us you are bored? Answer me one question— why haven't you published my work?" And, pointing her awful damp umbrella in our direction, "Or them?" She had given her soul to literature, like the fated heroine of a Russian novel, and literature—that evening on 116th Street—gave her nothing back. She had cried out what was in the heart of us all. But, ashamed of such open admission of need, we sunk back in our seats, pretending not to have heard.

One week my rejection package didn't arrive. Instead, a thin envelope. I brought it to Martha. She seemed to regard the acceptance as being as normal as the pile of rejections. "Well, we will have to find you an agent." I felt a pang, suddenly realizing that probably neither she nor anyone else would ever again tell me that I had Lowry's gaze or was Temple Drake. I was going downtown. To have lunch with real publishers. They wrote they wanted to meet me. I had crossed the divide.

It wasn't until many years later, during the writing of *Short Flights*, that I finally rediscovered the ten-year-old: the voice of the firm child who started me on my voyage. While I was growing up, my mother frequently left me to go to Europe. Around the time I was ten I thought I might lose her forever because war was breaking out and she had a hard time getting back to America. I attended acting classes for gifted children. (At the end of the Depression, if your father coughed up tuition, you were a gifted child.) I got a confused idea of a technique popular in the late thirties and forties—the living newspaper theater. And when it was my turn to improvise, I pasted newspaper headlines on my body about Europe at war, flapped my wings and called out that I was the voice of history. Perhaps I believed that if I performed furiously enough, if I became that Europe at war, my mother would come back to me. I'm not really sure. But while I was writing *Short Flights*, I suddenly became aware that my juxtapositions were not new, but a reordering of my childhood universe; the book takes place during the last days of Franco and the immediate transition. And it's all there—what was originally important to me: Europe, history, politics, the newspaper scraps, the child, all wars, a wandering adult, partings and returns.

My autobiography and Spain's intertwine. As I'm not fond of information-giving dialogue—"The revolution started at five, dear . . . could you make me a cup of tea?"—I reversed the use of diaries, which are frequently inserted to convey condensed intimate thoughts in a novel. I used a political diary for outer events, and let my dialogue remain aimless, which is very important to me.

About the business of what is and isn't fiction: publishers are constantly suspicious about what doesn't look exactly like what they had the year before. Instead of being puzzled that so many books have a different shape, publishers should ask themselves: Isn't it "funny" so many books are like what was written fifty years ago? We don't wear the same clothes—a bathrobe I bought in Bloomingdale's ten years ago now seems to me to be an overcoat—or lead the same lives, or inhabit the same spaces; every other art form has changed—why not writing?

Too frequently a rendering of reality is confused with literal reporting. I was asked by one Spaniard why I had made a "mistake" in describing a character wearing tweeds and drinking Scotch—when the character *he* knew drank wine and didn't wear tweeds. But to give an American audience an *authentic* impression of modern Spain, I needed the Scotch and tweeds, not the wine. Another reader insists her cousin owns the yellow dress I describe myself as wearing in the Chicago scenes. Still another, who tells me she would like to have a love affair just like the one "in Chicago," says she realizes, now, that she should own canary yellow diamond earrings. But those diamonds never existed. For purists who insist that a novel must be "made up," perhaps they are my proof: I pinned those splendid canary diamonds in the earlobes of my recreation of my younger self, because at that time I was rather broke. It pleased me that the character I was bringing to life had them, and that she was of an age when she believed left-wing politics and youth were her personal attributes: middle age was some other class, not the sort she was bound to meet.

Horse-Trading in
Female Ecstasy

1986

To appreciate what the gifted Mexican novelist Elena Poniatowska is up to in her extraordinary novella, *Dear Diego*, it helps to know an earlier classic, *Ifegenia: The Diary of a Young Girl Who Was Bored*, written in the early 1920s by the Venezuelan novelist Teresa de la Parra. In *Ifegenia*, which has never been translated into English, de la Parra examines the psychological and sensual state of a liberated Venezuelan woman just after her return from post–World War I Paris. Although Paris in the 1920s was full of North Americans, European culture didn't dominate them in quite the same way it did Latin American expatriates. In addition to the tango, wealthy Argentineans transported their cows to France so they could drink milk from the pampas while imbibing European culture. Their difficulties began when they had to return home to a far more stultifying society.

In her novel about one female exile's return, de la Parra leapt past the perennial feminist theme—a woman in search of herself—and established her character as already liberated and sophisticated. Ifegenia bobbed her hair, lived the bohemian life in Paris, and learned to regard both sexual pleasure and intelligent conversation as her right. Using the technique of letters and diaries, de la Parra conveys the intensity of Ifegenia's rebellious voice, the range of her intelligence and the degree of her sexual obsessiveness. But de la Parra also anticipates Simone de Beauvoir's warning that brains and sexual liberation don't matter at all without a firm economic base. Sacrificed by her adored love, who marries a woman with money, Ifegenia must also make a loveless bourgeois marriage in order to survive.

Elena Poniatowska's *Dear Diego*, set during the same period and reminiscent of de la Parra's *Ifegenia*, is about a heated *ménage à trois* between Diego Rivera, his Russian emigré common-law wife, Angelina Beloff, and the jealous third lover, art itself. Poniatowska's narrative—also a series of letters—blends real documents with her own imaginative reconstruction of Angelina Beloff's relation to Diego Rivera. Exactly how much of this is Poniatowska and how much is drawn from actual documents is not made clear, and since Rivera was a real person, the reader can't help filling the gaps in this impressionistic novella with what is already known about him. But whatever the proportion of fact to fiction, the novella is appealing because Poniatowska is so good at capturing the sadness of third-rate French hotels, the wet Paris fog, and the *cafard* so familiar to bohemians long on soul and short on cash.

Sent to Paris to study at age 20, Diego Rivera stayed fourteen years, living the last ten with Angelina. He was a part of the group that included Picasso, Gertrude Stein, Guillaume Apollinaire, Élie Faure, Diaghilev, and Ilya Ehrenburg. Angelina's letters start in 1921, just after Rivera abandoned both her and the Parisian art world. In *Dear Diego* he emerges as a real character, albeit a voiceless one. The reader senses Angelina's suspicion that Rivera's abandonment of Europe was caused by traumatic disappointment as well as practical advantage. Did she also suspect that he thought his Cubist work inferior to that of his friend Picasso? Certainly his decision that he needed neither the romantic Russian soul of Angelina Beloff nor the world of French Modernism was abrupt. In his next phase Rivera became his country's chief social realist, celebrating both Mexico's newfound national identity—*Mexicanidad*—and his own artistic one.

Angelina's complex reaction to his total rejection provides Poniatowska with the true subject of *Dear Diego*, the psychology of female ecstasy. Angelina's ecstatic obsession with Diego is capable of being interrupted only by her obsessions about other lost love objects. She constantly resurrects vivid memories of her adolescent trancelike adoration of the Russian Orthodox Church; even more significantly, she turns normal mourning for the tragic death of her and Diego's infant son into an almost romantic obsession with grieving itself. The only form of ecstasy that she uses to release herself from Diego is her desire to lose herself in her art. During the course of the novella Angelina shuttles back and forth between these competing passions. She reaches a high of sorts whenever they induce in her a fervid state of self-abnegation, often accompanied by extreme loneliness, hunger, and cold.

Like Teresa de la Parra's heroine, Ifegenia, Angelina Beloff was an uncommonly liberated and intelligent woman. But like many bohemian women of her time she tried to "upgrade" her sex life from the simply carnal to the classier state of "free love" by infusing herself with soul and her lover with talent. I think that, like many such women, she secretly hoped all that soul would bind her man to her in a union even more lasting than ordinary marriage. The romantic notion that a woman can liberate herself without economic underpinnings has proved every bit as dangerous as Isadora Duncan's romantic solution to the inhibitions of clothing (ironically, she died choked by her own diaphanous scarf). Women's magazines often have preferred to publicize women with a fondness for the sensational—women who have undermined the traditional domestic roles of their sex by pushing charismatic ecstasy in the form of artistic self-discovery, multiple orgasms, group euphoria, and the like. That these magazines were able to get away with the startling omission of economics meant that they became fabulous horse-traders in female ecstasy.

Angelina felt she had sacrificed herself in order to nurture a genius, and she was devastated when he broke their unwritten bargain and dumped her. In the first letter Angelina attempts to immolate herself: her talent, her sketches are nothing. Then she switches tactics and slyly insinuates that their Paris friends consider Diego a rat for leaving. Her trump card, her blackmail, is the argument that by deserting her, Rivera is also deserting what she sees as his "Art"— the formidable third member of their original trio.

Poniatowska's tone is perfect:

> *I love you, Diego, right now I have an almost unbearable pain in my chest. In the street, there are moments when I am suddenly struck by your memory and then I can't walk and I feel so afflicted that I have to lean against a wall. The other day a policeman came up to me: "Madame, vous êtes malade?" I shook my head and was about to answer that it was love, you see I am Russian, I am sentimental and I am a woman, but then I realized that my accent would give me away and French functionaries don't like foreigners.*

Angelina's attachment to Diego is so great that in her trancelike states she becomes him: "For the first time in four long years I feel that you are not far away, I am so full of you—that is, of painting. I plan to return to the Louvre in the next few days." Through her feverish painting Angelina believes herself possessed by Diego. She describes him as being inside her: she swells up, her breasts become engorged, she feels Diego on top of her. When not indulging in sexual imagery in her letters to him, she incessantly recalls the image of their dead son. At other moments, she conjures up her dreamscape (another version of him), Mexico.

Angelina uses every device to let Rivera know that she is, in the eyes of their friends, becoming pale with the sickness of love. She tells him that during a Russian Easter celebration in Paris, a fellow Russian takes pity on her poverty and her hunger and gives her a Russian hard-boiled egg. Finally, braced up by memories of religious celebrations during her Russian Orthodox childhood, she begins to retrieve her sense of identity. With filial pride she reminds Diego of her excellent bourgeois liberal-radical parents. She shakes herself loose from him and asks her first coherent question: "Does my love now have an object?"

As Angelina regains her strength, she recognizes that she has lost Diego. She then describes to him a scene in which her current teacher, the artist André Lhote, in front of many students, pronounced the magic words to her: "You have an extraordinary talent." She thus obtains permission from another powerful male to become an artist. She has also come to accept Rivera's power in the world outside Paris. In a new tone she writes to him: "Juan Gris is going to Mexico and he is counting on you for help." And she adds that Élie Faure has said that Europe has dried up: the bohemians miss Rivera's fables about plumed serpents flying through the skies. Rivera never answers her letters, but he does send money. In a real-life postscript to this book it is noted that Angelina Beloff's Mexican and European artist friends helped her to visit Mexico in 1935. Diego Rivera walked by her in a theater lobby without noticing her, and she chose not to intrude on him.

Pierre Jean Jouve's
Paulina 1880

<u>1973</u>

It's a general rule that novels having love between a man and a woman as a central theme succeed insofar as the writer has something else on his mind. The passion then works because what gives it its heat is the concern with, say, good and evil, a corrupt society, romanticism versus realism, and so forth. We Americans have never done well with the high-class love affair in fiction. The involved passions of men and women have been the stuff of lending libraries. The perfect example of what a love story ought not to be is Erich Segal's *Love Story*.

The two countries that reign supreme in the fiction of passion are, of course, Russia and France. Tolstoi, pursued by private demons, his obsession with land reform, which is what he thought he was writing about, produced the unforgettable Anna Karenina. How he hated her, and how marvelous she was when she hurled herself in front of the train! But it is the French who have made high art of the love of men and women. It is the very essence of their literary tradition, and Stendhal gave it its modern form—the psychological novel with passion and anti-romanticism at its core. We believe in Julien Sorel, as we believe in the feckless Madame Bovary, because in both Stendhal and Flaubert we are moved by the obsessive attempt to use all the forces of rationalism and realism to wipe out the specter of romanticism, which tempted and terrified both writers. Romanticism is damnation. The charming Julien Sorel must be destroyed; so must Madame Bovary. In the process they are brought to life for all time.

Paulina 1880

Paulina 1880 is a brilliant tour de force in this tradition. It was the first novel of a French man of letters, Pierre Jean Jouve, and when it was published in France in 1925 it was a huge success and quickly came to be considered something of a classic. But in spite of its enormous appeal in France, it made no dent on the English-speaking world. Now it has been made into a movie in France by Jean-Louis Bertucelli, and on the strength of this, the novel, admirably translated by Rosette Letellier and Robert Bullen, has been published in English for the first time.

Like Stendhal, Jouve chose Italy as a setting for his romantic and anti-romantic exploration of the madness and masochism of Paulina Pandolfini. (1880 is the year in which she shoots her lover.) Paulina is shown first as the capricious daughter of a wealthy Milanese man, who, with her four elder brothers, alternately watches over and indulges her. In this atmosphere of male attentiveness, constrained by deep taboos, Paulina willingly lets herself be "ravished" by a family friend, Count Michele Cantarini, almost under her father's eyes. Paulina acts as though in an adolescent trance, on the one hand moved by pure carnal pleasure, on the other by a morbid desire for total purity. *Paulina 1880* is a far more subtle novel than *Story of O*, which, when the stagey erotic trappings are removed, is a meat-and-potatoes book about a 100-percent masochist involved with 101-percent sadists.

Count Michele does nothing so murky as leaving Paulina. Indeed, the things that happen to her are not particularly tragic, except for her interpretation of them. Her father dies of natural causes, which arouses in her the same terror as the possibility of losing her religion. Michele's wife dies, leaving him conveniently free to marry Paulina, except that her voracious guilt demands that she do penance for the dead wife as well as her dead father. Jouve is skillful in suggesting all sorts of possibilities with the marvelously brief strokes that delineate the wife. Michele is not a bad sort—or is he? His wife went mad shortly after their marriage, through no fault of his. But then Paulina, whom he turns to for life, also goes mad, again through no fault of his. Is it Michele's bad luck, or is there something in him that is either drawn to demented women or produces them? Finally, at the age of 31, Paulina shoots Michele for, as she sees it, his daring to tempt her away from her religion. At last she pays the longed-for penalty—imprisonment—for the side of her nature that was carnal.

All this is done in brilliant modern style—abrupt switches of tenses, chapters a few sentences long, a lush description of the interior of an Italian villa, terminating in the dry words, "The inventory is over." The style makes the book. With its swift, jagged endings, its precise economies, it was made to order for the French New Wave directors. I imagine they would also appreciate the irony of a stylistically pure and perfect novel in the service of the message that purity is a savage killer of life.

Sylvia Plath Remembered

1982

1962 is a landmark date. Within a span of months, Doris Lessing's *The Golden Notebook* and Sylvia Plath's *The Bell Jar* (1963) were published in London. These two women, who have had an extraordinary influence on us, seem to have crossed each other in time. Though both were profoundly concerned with the place in the world of the woman writer, their literary sensibilities were of a very different order.

Lessing is eleven years older than Plath. When I first read *The Golden Notebook*, I was enormously energized by her use of explicit, almost tract-like political vocabulary in the arguments expressed by her men and women—this and the book's innovative structure. I was struck by this direct, nonpoetic approach. It interested me because, in my own writing, I had wanted to convey a world in which men and women thought and talked about politics and ideas; but coming from the "Silent Generation" of the 1950s, to whom such unwieldy language was considered bad literary form and a throwback to the leftist propaganda novels of the thirties and forties, it never occurred to me to grant myself literary permission to be that direct. But Lessing had grown up in Rhodesia during the late thirties and forties. She had been a member there of the Communist Party—her forthright concerns with world events and belief that she could effect a change came out of her early experiences.

In London, after she became disillusioned with the party, her subsequent, somewhat polemical, interest in women as being *the* central political problem of our time took the urgency of her former commitment to Communism; her style of looking at women was filtered through a Marxist-didactic way of

Based on a talk given at Barnard College on the fiftieth anniversary of Sylvia Plath's birth and in celebration of the publication of her journals.

viewing the world (just as *The Second Sex* has an existentialist aura to it). Though Lessing's placing of women firmly and angrily on the central battle ground was admirably suited to the foment of the sixties, what I liked least about her novel was the values expressed by the women characters. I had read that Doris Lessing in her own life had left behind in Rhodesia two very young children, taking with her to England only her third child. Also I found her portrait of the adolescent son in *The Golden Notebook* ungenerous. Lessing's "free women" reminded me of the Greenwich Village mothers of high school friends of mine. They were the sorts of women who assumed that by training their children to call them by their first names and by treating them like sexual peers, always chit-chatting about sex and Freud, they were transformed by the progressive stance into great mothers. They were disasters.

I have brought up Doris Lessing on this occasion meant to honor Sylvia Plath—somewhat changing my original talk—because other speakers have criticized Plath for her lack of political perceptions, and I don't think this is quite fair. The overt style which became popular after the success of *The Golden Notebook* didn't take hold until after Plath's death. Though my reputation now is of having always been political in my concerns, in the late fifties, before I read Lessing, I wouldn't have had a clue how to introduce "ideas" directly into my fictional work. My first novel, in 1960, *The Beat of Life*, frequently has been grouped (and taught by Tillie Olsen and others) with Plath, I suppose because we were contemporaries. Like most of the fiction written at that time the novel was very oblique. When I recently reread it, I was amazed at how private was the world depicted in it. Viewed in the literary context of that period, Plath doesn't seem excessively unengaged. Indeed, in the opening paragraph of *The Bell Jar*, Plath deliberately locates her narrative as happening the summer that the Rosenbergs "fried"—I don't recall any other novel of that period that actually mentions their electrocution. I don't believe it ever comes up in Bellow, Updike, Malamud, or Roth—Doctorow's *The Book of Daniel* came out in the seventies. In her poem "Daddy," Plath explores her obsession with her German-American father and her guilty fascination with the Nazis. The decisive events for our generation (which made Ginsberg's *Howl* such a success) were Hitler, the Holocaust, and the Rosenbergs.

Sylvia Plath worked within the literary metaphors of the English poets and those very literary American 1950s which replaced the political realism of the Depression and World War II: the exemplary models were Salinger, Carson McCullers, New Criticism, and Henry James. Though the muffled literary style during that period undoubtedly was exacerbated by political fears engendered by McCarthyism, the primary reason was taste: too much directness and realism were considered old-fashioned. Changing the world through literature wasn't to become a viable option until the activist sixties. Though I generally don't like to use catch words to describe a generation, most of the writers who started out in the fifties were alienated from the main drift of Eisenhower America. We were interested in finding our own kind: sympathetic readers and friends. By her personal choices—settling in the literary world of England and marrying Ted Hughes—Plath was taking for granted her negation of Mc-Carthy America and wouldn't have thought it necessary to over-explain any of this in her work. In the fifties categories were important, sharp distinctions were made. Southern was a category; other categories—war novels and the literary "anti-literary" Beats—were male turfs. The elite literary establishment which favored the oblique and symbolic had no relation to the mass-circulation women's magazines which stressed "women's problems." It is interesting to remember that Betty Friedan was a product of that women's-magazine world—since she was popularizer, wanting to reach vast numbers of women; for her, women's fiction was a tool to be incorporated into her movement. Friedan saw her first audience as suburban housewives, and in 1963 she published *The Feminine Mystique* for that audience. In order that they perceive themselves exclusively as victims, Friedan had to convince them that they had been incapable of making proper choices because they had been *innocent* of what life was all about. Perhaps. But sometimes the word "innocent" was used to erase the acquisitive materialism that these women, with their husbands, willingly had embraced. Sylvia Plath, at least, held herself responsible for her choices.

In her *Journals* she conveys what it was like to have been young and female and a writer during that time of stern literary do's and don'ts. Her sensible autobiographical prose reads like the novel she always had wanted to write. Straightforward and uncoy, she asks the fundamental question: What does a young woman of modest means need to do if she is to become a writer? Jane Austen would have approved.

Sylvia Plath unsentimentally outlines in her *Journals* a woman's basic predicament—her economics and her biology. It is, she points out, imperative for a woman writer to establish a safe niche that will allow her, without prematurely fatiguing herself, to give proper attention to her work, her man, and her children. In her own case, she must have been acutely aware that she also had mental problems. The hysterical idolatry of Plath after her death was obviously unhealthy, and, in angrily blaming Ted Hughes for her death, grossly simplified her characterological makeup—obviously she had had longstanding serious mental problems. Her narcissistic inability to achieve some normal autonomy from her children, whom she mistakenly regarded almost as an extension of her own body, was as extreme in its way as was Lessing's abandonment of her children. But Plath's awareness in her *Journals* of life's limitations also reveals her healthier side.

She must have considered her journals as being off-hand casual notes to herself—in them she is amazingly candid. After four months of marriage to Ted Hughes she concludes that her jealousy of his success will make it impossible for her to help further his career during his stint as visiting poet at Smith College. In the manner of a crafty old Frenchwoman, she makes a pragmatic assessment of her own more limited choices. She observes her own place in the world as well as noting her jealousy of male freedom and the male ability to be out in the world in order to make successful use of that experience in their work.

Plath expended enormous psychic energy to get herself, early on, the fellowships that gave her the chance to study in England. In an astonishingly short time she absorbed a new culture, found a mate as intelligent as herself, gave birth to two children, refined her own literary voice, and produced—still in her twenties—a dazzling output of poetry. While all that was going on, she also used up considerable strength in dealing with her ever-present mental problems. Her nemesis was the breakup of her marriage—she simply wasn't emotionally equipped to handle it. In a London flat with no heat, during the coldest winter England had had in this century, Plath, depressed, envisioned her future as being lonely and poor, and she killed herself. Probably she thought her coded message for help would save her, but the trouble with codes is that to the outside world they remain codes. Probably she suspected that her children's *au pair* would return in time to find her, or that a neighbor would smell the gas. She had not that luck.

The prospect of spending her life in grimy poverty didn't kill Plath, but I do think it haunted and depressed her. Sadly she mistook her yearning for economic and emotional stability to be a private, almost cranky concern, which she worked out in secret in her journals; she didn't seem too aware that she was entitled to worry about these basic fundamentals, entitled to ask real people in the real world to help her find real solutions. She killed herself just before university jobs for writers became available and before it became okay for women to acknowledge their fears about lack of money.

Plath has been criticized for her dual sensibility—on the one hand the gifted poet, on the other, her desire to write a potboiler or at least a commercially popular novel. Why not? How else would she have gotten through? She had small children, and since she didn't envision that her own poetry would earn fortunes, she needed to find a second career, or second husband, or both, in order to float her establishment. In that period, to be not only a woman but also a woman writer was a hardship. A woman lawyer, doctor, or teacher at least could look forward to not leading—at the end of the road—an economically marginal life. Plath never wanted to live a skimpy existence, she liked nice things, her lack of financial mobility gnawed at her. In the end she stopped looking for a solution and instead she used all her force for her last burst of poetry. The best of it, and the *Journals*, remain with us. My private criterion has been whether it matters to my soul that a certain writer existed and wrote. Plath does.

Ellen Hawkes's
Feminism on Trial

The Ginny Foat Case

1986

Back in the midseventies Clancy Sigal and I wrote a *série noire* detective spoof. While we were inventing our narrative, Clancy asked me: If a woman had committed a murder and wished to hide out, start a new life under a new name, how would she go about it? I suggested that she go to a booming new Southern city like Atlanta, join the local chapter of NOW, enlist the feminists' help, telling them she had to use an assumed name because her husband was a wife-beater and she was on the lam from him. Clancy thought a man might do well to join a chapter of AA in a medium-sized New York suburb like Mount Vernon. Although our *homage* to Dashiell Hammett never got published, it occurred to me after reading Ellen Hawkes's gritty account of Ginny Foat*—of mobile, violent America from the sixties through the eighties and the new breed of California fast-track feminists—that my Atlanta notion wasn't too far off the mark. Ginny Foat's own saga, as described by Hawkes, is true Ida Lupino with a *soupçon* of Mildred Pierce and Jessica Lange doing the paler remake. Hawkes recounts the story of a woman who essentially hid her past by using the feminist movement to invent a new self.

But Ginny Foat could no longer totally conceal that past after her second

*Ellen Hawkes, *Feminism on Trial: The Ginny Foat Case and Its Meaning for the Future of the Women's Movement*, William Morrow, New York, 1986.

husband, Jack Sidote, in 1977, confessed to Nevada police two 1965 robbery-murders. He alleged that his ex-wife (then known as Virginia Galluzo) lured an Argentinean businessman, Moises Chayo, from the bar in Bourbon Street where she worked as a go-go girl and Sidote worked as a barman, into their car, where they bludgeoned him. The couple fled to Nevada, and there (according to Sidote) Ginny Foat found another victim in a Reno casino. He also was killed. In 1977 in a Nevada court Sidote plea-bargained: his sentence was lightened in exchange for his testimony against his ex-wife. Later he reneged, and refused to testify against her. Foat, who had been under arrest in Nevada, then returned to Los Angeles and to her third husband—a caterer, Raymond Foat—and to her new career as president of California NOW. Though the Louisiana courts seemed remarkably indolent about the Chayo Bourbon Street murder, eventually they caught up with Ginny Foat in California. The Los Angeles police knew of her not because she was a prominent leader of NOW, but because in 1969 she had been with a small-time hood, Richard Busconi, when he got pumped full of bullets in front of a San Pedro bar. Foat had been called by the police as a witness in their investigation of the Busconi murder. Ginny Foat's past had been *varied*.

During Foat's unsuccessful attempt in 1983 to fight extradition to Louisiana for what later turned into her sensational trial for the Chayo Bourbon Street murder, her NOW spokeswoman, Jan Holden, primly told the press: "We want to stress who she is *today*, not who she was before."

But it is, precisely, the rise of Ginny Foat that is so fascinating. She met husband number three (after him there was a fourth, eight-months-long marriage to a California businessman, Jack Meyer), Raymond Foat, an Englishman, while working as a waitress in a floating San Pedro restaurant, Princess Louise. For a while they ran a catering place near Disneyland. Then, in 1974, Ginny Foat drifted away from Foat and joined with an old pal, Danny Macheano, to start a new catering business: Affairs Unlimited. Her first step into the middle class was in Anaheim, in Orange County. There, she joined a group of businesswomen: the Soroptimists. And from there, it was just a quick hop to California NOW. Her marriage with Raymond Foat had gotten her a big suburban house, with a Jacuzzi, a pool, and a sunken living room. NOW members recall liking the place for their spaghetti dinner meetings. With your own Jacuzzi, who cares about the past, about having to face a court trial for a remote, murky murder?

Ellen Hawkes belongs to a second generation of women feminist writers who now are questioning the values and goals of the feminists of the early 1970s. In *A Lesser Life: The Myth of Women's Liberation in America* (William Morrow and Co., 1986), Sylvia Ann Hewlett, the economist, points out that women's liberation is just another American myth; she concludes that women would have been much better off to have devoted their energies to basic social reforms that would have obtained for them the social protections that are taken for granted in England and most of Western Europe. Lenore Weitzman's *The Divorce Revolution: The Unexpected Social and Economic Consequences for Women and Children in America* (The Free Press, 1985) has been a milestone document in proving that the no-fault divorce has actually impoverished women and children. Also notable is *Women and Children Last: The Plight of Poor Women in Affluent America* by Ruth Sidel (Viking Press, 1987).

Hawkes's main question in *Feminism on Trial* is: What is the nature of NOW that a woman so extraordinarily lacking in ordinary credentials—either moral or educational—was able, with so little effort, to become president of the California chapter? She depicts Foat as having a chameleonic, almost psychopathic personality—she apparently was able to instantly mimic the look and attitudes of whatever social group she found herself in. Thus, when it occurred to her that the feminists were the next step up, and she noticed that these women weren't wearing her sort of polyester clothes, she bought a new wardrobe—and read three feminist classics. My one quibble with Hawkes is that she has shaped her book like a novel. Precisely because she gives such a devastating picture of the California NOW, I would like to know whom Hawkes is quoting in her portrait of behind-the-scenes savage politicking and "trashing" of women by rivals.

In order to save her skin in Louisiana, and to give her colleagues in NOW a chance to defend her (the women were split: one group wanted nothing to do with Foat, others defended her), Ginny Foat came up with a new version of herself: she became the symbol of the "battered wife" syndrome. In the version she presented of herself to the court, while married to Jack Sidote she had been a passive wife who felt obliged to follow the commands of her brutal, domineering second husband. Ginny Foat's tactic worked and she finally was acquitted.

But the real thrust of Hawkes's account—and in this, she more than amply proves her point—isn't whether or not Ginny Foat committed murder: Ellen Hawkes is a native Californian, and what she considers lethal is the *combination* of Los Angeles rootlessness, lack of history, and the quick, easy optimism of the feminist movement on the West Coast. One of the most amazing incidents in the book is that Ginny Foat, quite a while before being extradited to Louisiana, apparently mentioned to her NOW sisters during dinner at a Los Angeles restaurant that she had been accused by her ex-husband, Jack Sidote, in Nevada, of being his accomplice in several car murders. She told the women that her only involvement in the crime had been helping Sidote clean up pools of blood in their car. In her version she had spent an hour cleaning up the mysterious bloody mess because she had been a meek, subservient wife who had no mind or thoughts of her own—not even enough imagination to inquire of him: was this roast beef, a run-down dog, or a corpse? What is so extraordinary is that her NOW companions treated her story as an unreal, dream-like event, with no relevance to their own dreams and ambitions and to their agenda for NOW. Hawkes feels it is a cop-out for feminists to hide behind a rhetoric that relieves them from assuming responsibility for their past choices. If Foat had been an ex-waitress and go-go girl who then had made a serious commitment to another way of life—and had given real time to becoming educated—of course she could have gone on to NOW leadership. What made her such a bizarre choice for state president of NOW (and until the murder charges against her were revealed she had intended to run for national president) was that she never went through any educative process that might have given her even the slightest qualifications as an enlightened leader of women. All of Foat's metamorphoses happened overnight, and were accomplished through changing husbands. I am curious to know what the caliber was of the women she defeated for that position. And if it was high—why was Ginny Foat elected? *Feminism on Trial* is an extraordinarily original and valuable document of these, our times—and the questions Ellen Hawkes asks of the women's movement are piercing and long overdue.

2.

Norman Mailer

1981

Norman Mailer has done much of his writing in the various homes he has lived in on Provincetown's Commercial Street. In the early part of the twentieth century, American artists came to live in the New England Portuguese fishing village because the curved bay of Provincetown, jutting far out into the Atlantic, has extraordinary light. And "P-town" was cheap. Eugene O'Neill worked out of a small room in the east end of town (where his plays were first produced by the Provincetown Players); later writers like John Dos Passos came to live in the cape cottages along the beach. Provincetown has always had honky-tonk, tourists, and college kids roughing it; the town has never possessed elegance, just the great beauty of the sand dunes and the pink light. During the last twenty-five years, Provincetown has been Mailer's summer domain.

After graduating from Harvard, Mailer did a stint in the South Pacific during World War II. In 1948, with the publication of his war novel, *The Naked and the Dead*, at the age of twenty-five, Mailer was immediately considered to be among the finest of American postwar novelists. Twenty-two books later, he is still considered our most varied, intense, gifted American writer. He has won two Pulitzer Prizes (*Armies of the Night* and *The Executioner's Song*) as well as The National Book Award (*Armies of the Night*). He has acted in and made three movies. On July sixteenth I flew up to Provincetown to interview him. It is an advantage and disadvantage to interview a friend. The good part is that you have already developed a mutual rhythm of talking. The hard part is to get the sort of spontaneous electricity that is more likely to happen when two people don't know each other. I thought about this as the small P-town plane glided into the weedy dune-sided airstrip.

During dinner at his rented house on Commercial Street, Norman turned to me and asked if I could give him a sentence on the general thrust of the interview. He, too, sensed we would need an element of surprise. So I was oblique in my reply. He continued to help his wife, the actress Norris Church, serve beef stew to a crowd—Norman's mother and a good selection of his eight children, ranging in age from two to thirty, were present. After dinner we went into one of the children's bedrooms and set up the tape machines. Then we started.

Solomon: Frequently critics have divided your work into categories, journalist and novelist, and I wondered if we could consider your work as though all these books are novels. We don't say that Picasso isn't an artist when he collages newsprint, or that Shakespeare has turned to biography in *Antony and Cleopatra*. I would like to discuss your work in terms of them all being novels. In choosing these innovations of form—with the emphasis on *event*—you took a very different direction than what the Europeans have been doing during this same period. Have you ever thought about your writing in this context?

Mailer: No, I haven't, but it might be interesting. All right, let's look at it. Part of the difficulty is that I think of all journalism as being fiction, most of it dreadful fiction. There is the general assumption that journalism limits itself to what actually happened—faithful or at least accurate record of the event—and that novels are made up. Are about events that never took place. Granted there is a tremendous amount of overlapping. People are familiar with the ways in which novels often are close to reality. A novel often is straight journalism if you know the characters' real names. There are funny conventions about this; I've said several times, of *The Executioner's Song*, that if I changed the names, no one would argue that it was not a novel. They would have said it's not a terribly imaginative novel; it's awfully close to real events. But they wouldn't have said how dare Mailer call it a novel.

Solomon: Yet we accept musty literary conventions, such as the *roman à clef*, in which the writer has merely changed the names of the characters. What interests me, though, in what you've done is that you have been aware these past twenty years of the muchness of experience, during a period most other novelists have chosen to exclude experience. Were you conscious that the forms you were adopting were shaped to the experience of that moment?

Mailer: No. I was working the way you usually work—I was finding my way. The journalist writing that I did started with "Superman Goes to the Supermarket," a piece about Kennedy and the Democratic Convention in 1960. If there was a style that followed, it began there. I think what happened was I saw that I didn't know how to write about political conventions—at least not in conventional terms. I wasn't really interested in the politics; I thought they were boring. The politics were the same I had been suffering through in the fifties. But what seemed fascinating to me is that Kennedy was a protagonist rather than a candidate and that he offered something new to American lives—this daring and romantic and surrealistic and cockeyed idea that the president could be a young man and have an attractive wife. The only thing that I'll take credit for is that I had enough sense to see that this was more important than all the politics. There were going to be profound changes in the very inner style of American life. Because I knew that I, as an American, willy-nilly looked upon the president as one of the centers of my dream life. And it seemed to me that a lot of history is made in this country by the way people react to their dream life. In other words, the shifts in public opinion come out of many elements that are not available to the historians. One of them is whether the president of the United States gives people energy in their inner lives, their dream lives, their unspoken lives. Or whether he takes it from them. Carter was detested by everyone precisely because he took energy away from everyone. It was like having to listen to a dull minister or to a high school principal, always talking to you. Reagan is liked even by people who can't stand his politics because, in some odd fashion, he seems to give us energy. Just by his presence. Because he is interesting to think about. Problems that are interesting to think about give us energy. So we tend to hate those politicians who take our energy away. Like Carter. And tend to love those politicians like Kennedy who offer us energy because they are intriguing. Out of this vague perception, I blundered into a way of writing about that convention. Which was writing about them as though they were a great novelistic event. It was an incredible world with all of these incredible people in these unbelievable places.

Solomon: In *The Deer Park*, you are still paying your dues to past novelists. The War, Hollywood, they had been the traditional terrain for the American novel. *The Deer Park* is a fine novel—but after you hit Washington, you're not paying dues to Nathanael West, Fitzgerald, or Hemingway, and you do this new thing.

Mailer: Well, I didn't hit Washington until I did *Armies of the Night.* Until then I was writing about political conventions or about prize fights, but not about Washington.

Solomon: You did start to write in this new way in *Advertisements for Myself.* You wrote a novel that was much more open there. Had you remembered, at all, when you wrote *Armies of the Night*, the Living Newspaper theater experiment of the thirties and forties?

Mailer: I never saw any of their work. I was aware of them, but I don't think I was thinking of them.

Solomon: But Wolfe has a conventional narrator and you do break with that tradition.

Mailer: Until *Armies of the Night* I was very much in the background. You could feel that there was somebody looking in on all these events, and presumably it's the author, but I wasn't a formal narrator as such. However, one of the things I began to feel was wrong with journalism is that immense events were boiled down to 300 words. There's no way to write about an immense event in 300 words or 3,000 words unless you're a poet. So the trick was not to boil it down but to expand it, to blow it up and to use 30,000 words or 20,000 words to write about events usually described in 2,000 or 3,000 words. What I began to feel next is that the character of the narrator or the personality of the narrator was probably more important, or as important, as the event. Not because the narrator is important in his own person; it was not that I, Norman Mailer, was equal to the Democratic Convention, but that I had a set of prejudices. These prejudices were terribly important, and you as the reader couldn't begin to understand this event unless you understood me enough to reflect upon my perceptions. By being able to take account of me as a narrator, the reader could say, Oh well, Mailer is impossibly romantic, or Mailer is outrageously nihilistic, or Mailer is a fool—the reader could make his own interpretation of the events. It occurred to me that that's the way we always read. When I read my contemporaries, I'll say to myself, well, Vidal or Updike or whoever it is, is good on this and not very good on that. I thought it's the least we can do in journalism, so-called—let the reader be aware of the bent of the writer. That is objective reporting.

Solomon: After the publication of *Armies of the Night*, the reader is alive to your liberation. As though it had suddenly occurred to you that there are no narcissistic techniques. What caused your new writing freedom?

Mailer: I think the only thing that liberated me is that I had no respect for the people who were telling me what the world was like. It seemed to me that on the one hand the people I felt closest to when I was younger, the Marxists, were caught in the insoluble knot of trying to explain every deviation from Marxist prediction, and it had got to a point now where it was getting to be high comedy. Interpretations within interpretations. And the psychoanalysts I considered a bunch of plumbers. They were fairly good at dealing with psyches badly in need of a certain relief of pressure here, or the fixing up of a leak in this joint, but they were absolutely hopeless when it came to understanding the demands of a personality, the larger demands. They were inadequate when they came to a place where the psyche met the spirit in some of us. The average psychoanalyst secretly believes there is something obscene about religion. Anyone who is religious is a dubious case and probably psychotic. Now, they won't admit it, but those are their deepest sentiments in the case of nine out of ten of the psychoanalysts I've known over the years. The Marxists were useless, the psychoanalysts were useless, the imperialists in my own country were certainly useless. The political writers were mediocrities, had very little to say; and then on top of that, as I very quickly learned, one of the most dreadful things that goes on in conventional reportage is that the reporters all get together afterward, exchange stories with other writers. In other words, you give them the stories that you know your paper can't print and in return they give you the stories they know you can use, that their newspaper or magazine won't print or is not interested in. So what happens is everybody winds up using everybody else's stories—even worse—everybody arrives at the same interpretation. To wit, Jack Kennedy is a lightweight, Nelson Rockefeller is a wonderful guy—whatever the interpretation is for that week comes out as gospel. So you soon realize that their political wisdom is nil, a consensus of the marketplace, of the journalistic marketplace. Since you have the confidence of being a novelist—and a novelist is used to getting along with projections of what the universe might be like—it's very easy to take the large step. Just say yes, the way in which I saw this event is as likely to be right as the way anyone else sees it. You proceed on that basis. I think if there was one thing that separates me from the others it was this confidence.

Solomon: Of a Fire on the Moon is, I feel, your most undervalued novel. In that book you carried these ideas even further; you are battling not only the journalists but the new use of information-retrieval systems. It seemed that in this book you were in combat with whole systems of machines that were used to record that event. I felt that book must have taken enormous energy.

Mailer: Well, it did. Of all the books I've written that one probably took the most energy. Since I grappled with the largest opponent and the opponent was huge. I mean the opponent was nothing less than NASA and the particular information systems that NASA had to develop and the almost total impossibility of coming up with a real story. The real story involved the personal life of these few astronauts who had succeeded in going to the moon, and they were hermetically sealed away from the press. You couldn't get near them. You couldn't talk to them. So you had to write a work that was ninety-nine percent speculation—but it had to be well based because you were dealing with—I put it in quotes—"scientific matters." Technological matters. Certainly you had to become familiar to the best of your ability with all the technical knowledge that you could digest. And so the work on one hand was an immense work of speculation and on the other hand it was a prodigious job of digestion. Since the two were incompatible, speculation and digestion having little to do with one another, I had just a tremendous difficulty writing that book, and I did expend more energy in that year that I wrote it than I spend usually in five.

Solomon: You were like a runner running with the facts and the speculation. Do you feel that the energy that went into that book has been understood?

Mailer: No, but every writer has his terribly sad story; I'm not looking for tears. I think if I had to do it over again, I might not do that book, because I think I may have taken away some of those stores of energy that you reserve for other work. I think that book delayed me for several years from getting back to more serious work. If I hadn't done that book I might have been able to embark on my long novel a few years before I did.

Solomon: Don't you think that control of information systems is one of the problems novelists will be grappling with in the next twenty years?

Mailer: Oh, I think they will. But I'm just not sure they'll be successful.—*Of a Fire on the Moon* makes a great demand on the reader as well, and I'm not sure that it has enough to offer at the end in terms of answers. You can compose the most fascinating questions in the world, but finally you have to give a few answers.

Solomon: You have mentioned groups of people you haven't admired, that were of no use to you: the Marxists, the analysts. Clearly you do not feel that way about Henry Miller. I wonder if in the lives of Hemingway and Miller—and you contrast the two—there is a cautionary tale for yourself?

Mailer: There was nothing cautionary about Miller's life because Miller has a talent—or had a talent—and an energy that I just can't pretend to share. I never thought I was very much like Henry Miller. I find him a little hard to understand. I loved him but he seemed too good to be true. I did write a book about him, but I never thought I came near the man. I admired him and I love his talent. His talent is wonderfully enriching. You can read Miller and feel as if you had a good meal. But there is nothing he did in his life that would warn me.

Solomon: No, I meant it the other way. In *Genius and Lust* you wrote, "The difference between Hemingway and Miller is that Hemingway set out . . . to grow into Jake Barnes and locked himself for better or worse, for enormous fame and eventual destruction, into that character who embodied the spirit of an age. Whereas Miller . . . proceeded to move away from the first Henry Miller he had created. He was not a character but a soul—he would be various."

Mailer: Yes, Hemingway is cautionary to me. Several times in my life I think I stopped doing different things or veered away from doing certain things because of the example of Hemingway. Hemingway's suicide stood over us all like the suicide of our own father. He's the father of modern American literature, at least for men, and to commit suicide . . .—John Gardner has that marvelous remark that when a father commits suicide he condemns his son to suicide. Well, of course, you can suicide in more ways than killing yourself. You can destroy yourself with too much drink, too many cigarettes, too many failures, too many wild and unachieved alliances—and so Hemingway was a great cautioning influence on us.

Solomon: When Hemingway went to live and write in Europe, writers were not like governments, they were not nationalistic. One felt that during the twenties writers and artists of different countries had something to say to each other. They weren't waving flags. Americans and Europeans don't talk to each other very much at this point—do you feel our novelists have gone in very different directions?

Mailer: Yes, I think so.

Solomon: European writers have been more influenced by developments in linguistics. American innovators—and you have been a leading force—have gone in another direction. What do you think about this?

Mailer: I think of Borges, who is doing something else altogether, which I think of as very European. I don't know enough about South America to decide how much Borges speaks for Argentina and South America—but I think of Borges finally as European because to do what Borges does you need a culture that is profound. Almost none of us in America has that kind of culture. It's possible Saul Bellow is among the best-read of American novelists; John Barth, maybe. I can think of a few others, but none of them has been able to take that culture and use it effectively in their work. It hardly matters that Bellow is conversant with probably all the great and medium-great and small-great writers of the Western world since Plato and Aristotle . . . it doesn't get into his work. It doesn't enrich his work. The way Borges's culture enriches his work. Borges poses to us, I think, the nature of the difficulty of comprehending reality, because he shows us how every time we approach reality we are writing a scenario and these very scenarios are the equivalent of propositions and hypotheses in physics. That is, they are correct until the evidence subverts them. But in the course of the evidence subverting them we have learned a great deal because the next hypothesis, ideally, should be superior. So in Borges you have this wonderful business of immensely elaborate hypotheses destroyed by the one fact that turns the hypothesis inside-out, into its opposite. There is this marvelously sinewy dialectical vision of the interplay between culture and history, the two almost being . . . not artifacts, but separate organisms. Borges gives us an immensely vivid inner life which I think is all one finally cares about in writing. It is what I look for in other writers, what I expect I should be able to give others in my own writing. It is to make that inner life not only more vivid—but by making it more alive and stronger it becomes more able to stand as proof against the attacks of the world upon it. The attacks of the world now upon our psyche are not so much aggressive as subtle, insidious—we're leeched out. We're not destroyed from without, we are sucked out. Our spiritual souls, our social souls, are sucked out of us by the mass media, by information retrievable. I think Borges is the best when it comes to fighting that. Try putting Borges in a computer. Now, the ways in which the Europeans have been going at it have come out of a profound weariness with the novel, with plot, with all the impedimenta of writing a book. It's very boring to sit down and put people in a scene and have something come out of the scene and have them go on to the next step. Everything that is detestable in the best-selling novel comes to visit you every time you try to tell a story. It's getting harder and harder. A story lives just on one level. So you look for ways to get away from it. I suppose I've looked to other fields. To journalism. To historical events that I could write about as they were occurring. Because it's another way to attempt to apprehend reality. My fundamental stance in all this is that the attempt to apprehend reality is more interesting and more useful to other people than the success or failure of the attempt. Because we can learn from the attempt. We can't learn that much from the final product. All we can do is argue about how successful it is.

Solomon: Do you think that some of the weariness of the Europeans as writers is that they're basically more tied to upper-class and aristocratic values?

Mailer: Yes.

Solomon: You wrote, in *Armies of the Night*, that what saved America was our humor, the belly laugh. "The noble common man was obscene as an old goat and his obscenity was what saved him . . . The guy who says, 'Man, I just managed to take me a noble shit.' " That cadence is at the heart of the American vernacular; in thinking of Europe I remember Simone de Beauvoir's remark in *The Mandarins*, in describing the American writer (Nelson Algren is assumed to be the model) she meets in Chicago. She writes, "He was one of those interesting, self-made American leftists." Do you feel all this European weariness comes from an essentially nondemocratic society? Where writers feel their connection to the upper rather than lower reaches of society?

Mailer: I think it has a great deal to do with it. I think it's also impossible to live with a culture as rich as the culture of the Western world without being aghast at one's own temerity in trying to write something. Americans have a saving instinct—we're not that near to European high culture, we can avoid it most of our lives. Sooner or later we suffer from having ignored it, we feel the paucity of our own means, but at least we're not living in the shadow of the great beauty. Which is the shade, let us say, that sits over the light of European literary endeavor. Americans can live and work on a different street. We don't have to contemplate the beauty every day. In America one can still have the illusion that one is doing something brand new. One can feel like a pioneer. Which is the American sentiment that I think all Americans try to arrive at. It's getting harder here—because we didn't start with much culture and we never achieved a truly rich and various American marrow—we're now in terrible trouble because we're getting to the point where we are destroying the culture at a much greater rate than we are building it. And on top of that, we are exporting it to the rest of the world. The primitive and cultural heritage is in danger of arriving on the main historical stage all but cultureless; and Europe is beginning to be attracted by the novelty of America's cultureless culture—taking our architecture, our superhighways, our plastics, our McDonald's, our Coca-Cola, and all of it. They're destroying their culture. But in Europe, at least, they have something interesting to burn. So it's going to take them much longer. I make a prediction that European literature is going to get vastly interesting a little further down the road, about the time that more European culture is being destroyed. I think a talented European writer is going to be struck by the tension between the value of what is being destroyed and the ferment of the destruction itself. There are some very interesting works that are going to come out of it.

Solomon: So you think the balance of tension is going to shift because of their fascination with America?

Mailer: Not so much because of America. I think it's going to shift because they won't be living in the shade of their culture any longer. That culture is going to be destroyed to a degree where Europeans will be able to breathe again. At a terrible price to that culture. But they'll be able to breathe again and of course, breathing again, they're going to value that culture for the first time in decades, rather than feel awe, resentment, and reverence for it.

Solomon: You were influenced by a European, Jean Malaquais?

Mailer: Yes, very much.

Solomon: In *Armies of the Night*, which was published in '68, you wrote, "Communism would continue to produce heretics and great innovators just so long as it expanded. Between Poland and India, Prague and Bangkok, was a diversity of primitive lore which would jam every fine gear of the Marxist." You seem to be proved right.

Mailer: Yes, perhaps.

Solomon: That doesn't interest you?

Mailer: I think it would be more Malaquais's idea than mine. Jean Malaquais is the first person I knew who talked seriously and coherently about the inner contradictions of Soviet communism. That is, the very forces that would ultimately destroy communism. But the language in the *Armies of the Night* is not his but mine. I don't know that Malaquais pays as much attention as I do to primitive lore. I can't take credit for the idea but feel satisfaction as I read it. I think it's a fairly good description of what's going on now, but it isn't as if I invented all of it.

Solomon: Yes, but you can take credit for the ideas that you choose. We're always choosing somebody else's ideas.

Mailer: I think in choosing some of Malaquais's ideas, I chose well. Better than I usually do.

Solomon: In *Armies of the Night*, when you are in your Washington hotel room in Hay Adams, you reflect on Federalist architecture, and suddenly what swam in front of my mind was *The Federalist Papers*, *Democracy*, and *The Education of Henry Adams*. In that section you mention Adams's influence on you—did you mean his novel *Democracy* or *The Education of Henry Adams*?

Mailer: The influence of Adams on *Armies of the Night* was a most peculiar one. To the best of my recollection, I never read much Adams. I know for certain that I read one long chapter of *The Education of Henry Adams* in my freshman reader at Harvard. I remember thinking at the time what an odd thing to do, to write about yourself in the third person. Who is this fellow, Henry Adams, talking about himself as Adams—and being struck with it in that mildly irritable way freshman have of passing over extraordinary works of literature. It's possible that I then read more of *The Education of Henry Adams* sometime in my freshman or sophomore year, although I have no clear recollection and wouldn't claim that I have. I never wrote about Adams, never thought about him particularly, would never have mentioned his name as one of the writers that were important to me; and yet in *Armies of the Night*—one starts reading it, and immediately one says—even I said—"My God, this is pure Henry Adams." What the hell is going on here? It's an absolute takeoff, as if I were the great-grandson of Henry Adams. As if Adams was all of my literary life. You don't have to posit any other author but Adams for *Armies of the Night*. So look how peculiar is influence: Adams was stuck in my conscious as a possibility, the way painters do much more often than writers. A painter can look at a particular Picasso, or Cézanne, and say to himself, That's the way to do it. But the work might not pop out for twenty or thirty years. When it does, they say Oh yes, that was a Picasso I saw at MOMA twenty-five years ago, and I've always wanted to try a palette of such and such, and I decided to use it here. In effect that's what happened.

Solomon: Adams seems to have been one of the few good American writers who thought of putting Washington, D.C., and an American president at the center of his novel—*Democracy*. Which I also thought of in connection with you, as the protagonist discards Washington and ends contemplating Egypt. So I felt that Adams subliminally was reaching to you on all levels.

Mailer: Well, he is and he isn't. I feel absolutely at a loss before Henry Adams. I mean, on the basis of these facts, it's spooky. I didn't know about Egypt, for instance. Yet one of his books ends with a character going there.

Solomon: Madeleine Lee gets disgusted with Washington and then goes off to Egypt—it is the end of the book. You do seem more like Henry Adams's great-grandson at this moment than you do Hemingway's son.

Mailer: Yes, because here I am going off to Egypt . . . for the last ten years.

Solomon: Did any of the elasticity of the Jewish historical experience help you make that imaginative leap into Egypt?

Mailer: I don't know why I started writing about Egypt. I've been working on that book off and on for ten years. I feel only now as if I'm slowly beginning to understand Egypt, the Egypt of antiquity. You can very often write well about matters that you don't understand too well. Most of my life I've written about matters in advance of my understanding of them. Often, years later, I would come to understand the subject as well as I'd written about it years before and would be amazed that I could have done it at all when I did. Because I didn't have the knowledge then. Oddly enough, now that I have the knowledge, I probably couldn't write about it. There's some potentiality in all of us that we tap when we write. The best writing comes out of that. I don't know that the work I'm writing about Egypt now is better than the stuff eight to ten years ago when I knew very little about Egypt. But something in me was drawn toward Egypt. Nothing in my past was even remotely related to Egyptian problems. Their problems are not ours. I'm known as a tremendously contemporary writer and all my interests are contemporary. I'm certainly not a man of classical education—in relation to most writers not a man with historical concerns. Yet in this Egyptian book I wish nothing to be contemporary. I find that what appeals to me about Egypt is that there is nothing in it that is of the least use or relevance for ourselves. It is a totally different culture. You have to take in account that it's a culture that existed long before Jesus, so there's absolutely nothing of a Christian notion of compassion, which is the very center of all Western thought. There is also nothing of the Judaic tradition. At the time I am writing about, the Jews are a tribe of barbarians who occasionally give a little trouble on the borders. Moses comes in the book for a page. He's mentioned as this fellow who went wild out on the Eastern desert and helped some of the Hebrews to pull off a massacre and then took off further east. That's all we know about Moses in my book. I can't answer why I've been so fascinated with Egypt. I sometimes think that the only way you can be sure that you're attracted to a subject that's valuable to you for literary purposes is that you know so little about it. It's almost as if you have to have one deep instinct into the subject but really not be too familiar with it. Let me give you an example of what I'm talking about. It's more fun to pick up a mystery novel and read it if, early in that book, you decide you have a clue that the average reader is not going to have. If you and the author share something that no one else does, then you are going to get more out of this book than anyone else, you are going to come up with the answers even though you know nothing about the material or the crime. I think something of that sort works in historical research. You have to feel that you do know more than the average historian about one aspect of the subject. In Egypt I think that I felt I knew more about burial customs than the average Egyptologist. Not more about the details of them, which I hadn't learned then, but more about the reason for them.

Solomon: Did you need a subject of the dimension of Egypt to be able to pull yourself away from America? Up until now America has been a big character in your novels.

Mailer: Yes, America has been the character in my books. I have found that it's been not altogether a successful pull away. I've resented it and I've resisted it and sometimes I've gotten terribly tired of this Egyptian book because there's nothing to say in it about America today. *The Executioner's Song* was written as a reaction against that Egyptian book. At last I could immerse myself again in daily matters of American life. I went out to Utah, a place whose inhabitants have hardly heard of New York and where they certainly never have heard of me. I learned again how Americans who don't live in the media do in fact carry on interesting lives and I steeped myself in all the minutiae of American life. When I went back to the Egyptian book, it was in a certain sense a refreshment. Now, I don't have to think about America for a while. There's been this alternation over the last ten years, between writing about Egypt and writing about matters that are very American. Marilyn Monroe, Muhammad Ali, Henry Miller, Gary Gilmore.

Solomon: Gilmore was certainly a rebellion against the Egypt you had chosen to write about.

Mailer: Actually I was at a good spot in the Egyptian novel when Gary Gilmore came into my life, so I gave up the Egyptian book with a slight sense of woe and at the same time a vast sense of relief. Because now I could write about America again.

Solomon: Do you physically *see* Egypt?

Mailer: Yes, oh yes. I see it so clearly that I can't stand going there. I went there once for a visit and said, I have to get out of here. Because it's ruining my vision of Egypt. I was in Cairo in '75 and the city was six million people where ten years before it was two million people. You couldn't move out of Cairo on account of the military situation. It was just after the war of '74, and so it really was an Arab country. It had nothing to do with the Egypt of antiquity. I got out fast.

Solomon: Language has always been very important in your books. What do you hear in the Egypt book? What vernacular?

Mailer: I've been studying the Egyptian language a little bit, not in a very serious or concerted way, but I've been living with an Egyptian dictionary and I find it fascinating. Ancient Egyptian is a wonderful language and they have an extraordinary use of words. It is a very dialectic language. Often the nearest cousin to a word means the exact opposite. One example: The word for dung also means the bleaching of linen. And you find this all through the language. That's not just an isolated instance. The word for magnetism is also the word for you or thou. It's a tremendously sensuous language, rather existential. You feel that mankind at the very beginning of civilization had already articulated one highly complex and wonderful and rather magical civilization—but still so close to the primitive beginnings, in that every word in the language is a revelation. Every word is related to every other word in a fashion that we don't have today. Like this example of "you" and magnetism. The reason the two words were the same is because when people look at one another—and certainly in those days it was even more true—they would feel the play of forces between them. Today we have that crude expression, you have good vibes or bad, but that's a pale reflection of the idea that the same word would serve to indicate "you" and magnetism.

Solomon: In *The Executioner's Song* you mentioned that at one point you were concerned with getting the chronology right because you felt that you had to be very accurate in terms of the motivation of the people.

Mailer: The motivation was determined by the chronology. In other words, if Gary Gilmore saw Nicole smiling at someone—smiling at another man—and it got him so agitated that he picked a fight with somebody, that had one meaning; he was very jealous and he was reacting to Nicole's flirtation. If, on the other hand, Gary picked a fight with this fellow and Nicole smiled at another fellow afterward, you have a different story—which is that Nicole, disheartened by Gary's getting into fights for no apparent reason, starts flirting with people as an expression of her irritation with Gary. These little matters of which came first were crucial in reconstructing the emotional logic of the story.

Solomon: As you are a writer who does show a healthy respect for chronology, how do you feel about the fact that so many writers play hopscotch with time, and consider chronology meaningless?

Mailer: Writers are notoriously sloppy. The danger of being a writer is that every flaw of your character has a rich culture on which to feed. We're all like bacteria: at our worst give us a proper culture and our most awful diseases will blossom forth. It's even more true with journalism. Every disagreeable, second-rate, or meretricious element in the character of a journalist is encouraged to take its vengeance in writing. What is said about good writers is that they tend to have characters somewhat better than bad writers only because their work takes more mental organization. If they're evil, at least they are evil at a higher level. It's so easy for bad writers to express their bad character. So in that sense it doesn't surprise me that chronology is sloppy.

Solomon: Very few novelists, excepting Saul Bellow, seem to make any attempt to write expansive books. Most novelists do not so insistently include America in their novels.

Mailer: Well, it's hard. It's hard to write well on a large subject. Actually, most large subjects are handled by best-selling novelists. Best-selling novelists will have a cast of forty or fifty characters. They'll have stories that go over fifty to one hundred years. They'll have several world wars. They'll have startling changes in the lives of several families. The reason they do all that in a hurry is because they can keep their book moving. What characterizes a best-selling novel is that there's nothing in it that you haven't come across before. At least if you're a reader of some experience. Most writers tend to fix smaller and smaller canvases and expatiate upon them with more and more clarity because at least you have the confidence that what you are doing is accurate. And that's terribly important. At least you're contributing to knowledge rather than adding to the general sludge, cultural sludge that lies over everything. So it's very hard to take a large topic. At the moment the only great writer I can think of who can handle what I've described, forty to fifty characters and one hundred years, is García Márquez. *One Hundred Years of Solitude* is an amazing work. García Márquez succeeds in doing it, but how, I don't know. In my Egyptian novel—although it's very, very long—not that much happens in it. As I said before, it takes me ten pages to go around a bend in the Nile.

Solomon: But you have made the attempt to perceive of the modern world in a new way, to ask the essential questions. Now the average person lives in more homes, has more wives or husbands, more jobs. Though their lives may be more superficial, more *things* are contained within a person's lifespan.

Mailer: Yes, but in the same way that the expert knows more about a subject than the amateur and often has less feeling for it, everybody alive today who has a television set knows more about how people in the world look and how strange people look and how political leaders look, how experts in various fields look and how people talk. We know all that and we don't know anything. People who have led terribly impoverished lives half a century ago have had more intense inner life. It's not the size of our experience that's relevant, it's the intensity of it. My feeling is that the nature of the twentieth century world is to give us more and more superficial entry into more and more modes of experience and at the same time leech out the intensity with which we used to comprehend a few serious and central experiences.

Norman stopped talking and suddenly looked up. During an hour—nonstop—he had answered all my questions. We went downstairs to join Norris. It was a nice night. We spent the rest of the summer evening on the porch of the big white wood house, facing the Provincetown curved bay, waiting for the 10:30 eclipse of the moon. When the sky darkened we passed a pair of binoculars, wondering what certain shadows on the craters meant.

V.

Spain Lost,
Spain Found

1948

The Resistance
Goes Modern

1986

In August, at the side of the Gavina swimming pool in S'Agaro, in the Costa Brava, a Catalonian journalist asked me to explain the reason for my long involvement with Spain: it was nearly fifty years since the end of the Civil War and young Spaniards were becoming interested in its history and the subsequent Resistance. I glanced at a woman sunning by the pool, topless, her head covered by a straw hat. In my head was an askew vision of Catalonia—sleepy medieval towns, the Jewish quarter of Girona, La Platja D'Arco, Catalonia's cheapo Las Vegas strip along the coast. It blurred together: the nude bathers, the blazing sunshine, memories of defeat, exile, and fascism.

But the next day, while strolling through Saint Felieu de Guixols, I noticed a bright yellow casino next to an esplanade with palm trees. The sea, the bright colors suddenly seemed oddly familiar. As a child I had collected travel tourist folders. The best one had been about the Spanish Mediterranean. I had wanted to play on one of its bright blue-skied, palm-treed beaches, and begged my parents to drive me to it. "It's on the other side of the Atlantic Ocean," they said. "No one goes there because of the war." In my mind, war and beauty

In 1986 the Sunday literary review of *Diario 16* ran a series about the many phases of the Spanish Resistance between the end of the Civil War in 1939 and Franco's death in 1975. I was asked to write a piece explaining the nature of my personal involvement, and to describe the beginnings of student resistance in the post-World War II generation.

were mixed. One of my favorite story books was *Ferdinand the Bull*. During that same period my parents let me stay up late for one of their dinner parties. A New York couple just back from the war in Spain was the center of attention. One of the other guests joked *sotto voce* that the husband was a lazy type who he doubted had gotten any closer to Spain than Biarritz, adding that the wife, Ruth, was a magnificent woman who had been a nurse and had driven an ambulance at the front. I noticed how Ruth didn't have to *do* anything: everyone at the party seemed in awe of her. I thought she was marvelous.

I was furious that in World War II I had been too young to be part of the main action. I managed, though, to be in Times Square the night the war ended— my girlfriends and I kissed hordes of strange servicemen in the crowds. We felt as we gulped down champagne that the world was being reborn. As soon as I could, I applied for a passport without my parents' knowledge, and requested passage on the *Jon Erickson*, a converted troop ship. The State Department informed my family that their runaway daughter was headed for Europe. My parents finally were sympathetic to my pleas that being part of the immediate postwar would be more important for my future development than school, and in 1948 they agreed that my mother would take me to Europe and leave me in Paris.

Aboard ship my mother made friends with Norman Mailer's mother, who was traveling with *her* daughter Barbara. My mother read the galleys of *The Naked and the Dead*. When she told me that she felt it would become the great American war novel, and Norman was a genius, I thought she must be crazy. (I hadn't read it.) My mother tried to convince me that I would find the Europe I was searching for through Norman and his wife, Bea. I didn't pay much attention to her, but when the boat docked, and Norman came to meet his mother and sister, I saw how good-looking and full of gut-energy he was. I immediately decided to read *The Naked and the Dead*. After six weeks in Paris, my mother put Norman in charge of me and left for New York. She also gave me the addresses of Sartre and Beauvoir, which had been given to her by Gerassi, a Spanish exiled artist living in New York whom Sartre had used for his portrait of the Spanish general in *The Age of Reason*. I wanted to be independent of my parents—alas, I ignored her introduction.

Norman took charge; as soon as she left he asked Barbara and me if we would mind driving his Peugeot to Madrid, to help out some Spanish students he had met; they wanted to assist some of their friends in escaping from a slave labor camp near Madrid. Barbara and I commented how different Europe was from America: nobody in New York had ever asked us to assist them in a prison break.

Two distinctly different heritages had formed me. As an American I belonged to a nation that had just emerged victorious from the Second World War. We felt good about ourselves, we felt it had been a moral war; we had an optimism, a gaiety about the future. Just before Barbara and I left for Spain, I went to Louis Armstrong's first postwar concert in Paris. The French gave him a dazzling welcome. When he played "When the Saints Go Marching In," it was like the war ending all over again. The French students went crazy, they hung from the rafters of the concert hall, the audience was wild: a new era had begun.

But the part of me that was Jewish was not victorious. Like Spain we weren't celebrating at the end of World War II, but were a defeated and diminished people. Out of a family with vast numbers of relatives in Europe, only three members survived: a cousin in Brussels who had been hidden by his Belgian Catholic wife in the basement of a friend's factory; and, in Paris, my cousin Lea and her mother. Lea was heartbroken that her father had died of malnutrition right after the Americans liberated him from Auschwitz. She was two years older than I and was among the first to wear a bikini. She had an affair with a French Jewish Communist to make up for her losses. The rest of the relatives had become soap, so to speak. I had never been to Vienna, where my father's family came from, nor to Kolno, between Gdansk and Königsberg, the town where my mother's father was born. I was given, though, a little memorial book about Kolno, whose entire population, like Liddice, was massacred by the Germans. The book begins: "Kolno, my hometown, I see you in a dream . . ." My grandfather's family is listed in it.

My natural European past had vanished; German, my second childhood language, I forgot. What country, or countries, I would feel close to in Europe was for me to discover anew. Begin again. In Spain. As an American I felt *confident* we could rescue prisoners. As a Jew, I felt *impelled* to do so. Franco, Hitler, and Mussolini were associated in my mind as a triumvirate. Having frequently asked myself why Europe had done so little to save the Jews from genocide, I obviously had to do what I could to save Spanish students who were still trapped in a fascist prison.

Paco Benet, the novelist Juan Benet's older brother by ten months, organized the escape. He was twenty, and I two years younger. Norman introduced us in Paris. In his baccalaureate Paco came out first in Spain in philosophy, and got one of the first postwar scholarships to the Sorbonne. His mother had been delighted to get him out of Spain. She was certain if he remained he would land in prison. Paco didn't define himself as being part of a political group. His idea in using Barbara and me—though I wasn't flattered by his description of us—was that we were perfect because we looked like naive, well-protected American girls whom the police would never suspect. Nor would they have suspected him. He was tall, lanky, and had thick straight yellow hair which fell at a slant across his forehead. In his tweeds he looked British. Actually, all of us were on the blond side, including the student prisoners; we felt this upper-class armor was an advantage over the police.

Paco had many different things on his mind: the Faulkner novels he was bringing to his brother Juan, his desire to make his family understand that anthropology was a "real" profession, like being an architect or a doctor. His father, a Barcelona-born Madrid lawyer, had been shot in the beginning of the Civil War. His mother's divorce from his father and his father's murder were crucial events in his life. He talked about his childhood in Madrid during the war; he and Juan would take a bus at the university city to the front—they wanted to see the war.

We both had been very young during World War II: we perceived people in the Resistance as a much older generation. The day before the prison escape, we went to the caves in the Sierras. Paco urged Manuel Amit, an important CNT (Anarchist) leader hiding there, to escape Spain with us. Poor Amit looked at Barbara and me, in our pink and blue summer cotton dresses, as though we had dropped to his cave from Mars. Sadly, he couldn't conceive that we knew what we were doing; instead he joined the regular political underground, was caught, and died in prison. Paco said to me that afternoon, near the caves, that in his heart he realized the political leaders were deluded: they were still dreaming of a popular uprising. He said it was all over, it would be at least another twenty years before Spain would be rid of Franco. He took for granted that a brilliant intellectual career lay ahead of him; he knew his fate wasn't the same as an Anarchist worker huddled in a cave. On the ground in front of Amit's cave, he took a twig and drew in the sand a plan of a house he wanted to build in the future after Franco's death. His goals were to get as many people as possible out of prison, to do this in such a way as to alter the assumption that Franco was omnipotent and the Resistance always lost. He wanted to commit an act that was a *success*. He wanted future generations to have some concrete pieces of history that they could respect; they shouldn't feel his generation had done nothing. He later wrote in the magazine *Peninsula*:

> *Neither youth nor history can pardon failure. In order to prevent the next generation from losing their way in a Stalinist quagmire . . . we need to overcome the past, forget those Spanish liberals who were unable to convert their energies toward a productive future. We must create that future ourselves, with our bare hands—all, now, we possess.*

On Sunday morning we drove to the Escorial which was next to Culegamuros, the slave labor camp where Nicolás Sánchez Albornoz and Manolo Lamana, who both had participated in student resistance, were in a stalag which Franco used as a source of construction workers for his monument, The Valley of the Fallen. Manolo's girlfriend Aurora had given him Paco's instructions: to evade the guards during their Sunday morning march to Mass at the Escorial. They were to be the last on the line, and were to duck around the corner where Paco would be waiting for them. Our car would be ready to go, motor running. The hard part in escaping prison in the 1940s was to be able to rapidly navigate through Spain; there were roadblocks everywhere. I was behind the wheel. It happened very quickly. They jumped in the car and hid. I immediately drove right past the guards, but all they saw were three foreign tourists, two of them young women, sightseeing in a Peugeot with French license plates on a Sunday outing at the Escorial. As we sped past Madrid—not going into the city—I saw Nicolás wave. It was nearly thirty years before he saw Madrid again. After Franco's death he brought back his father, Claudio Sánchez Albornoz, the president of the Spanish Republic-in-Exile, and one of its last symbolic leaders. It was a very different sort of occasion at Barajas airport. Spanish officials and TV newsmen were everywhere. The newspaper headlines were: SPANISH REPUBLIC COMES HOME. I went with Paco's sister Marisol—Nicolás wanted her, because Paco had been killed in his thirties in a desert jeep accident, on an anthropological expedition.

But Paco also had desperately wanted the escape to be *fun*. The night before it, Paco insisted we go dancing at the Villa Rosa; it amused him to samba and rhumba at the favorite nightclub of rich young Falangists. He broke into laughter on the dance floor, because we were surrounded by right-wingers and black marketeers. He was gleeful at the thought of how mad Franco would be at news of the escape. Apparently Franco did go into a rage when he heard about it: he adamantly had refused international demands to release Claudio Sánchez Albornoz's son because of his macabre personal desire that his old enemy's son be used to build his tomb. Of course at the time we didn't know anything about Franco's temper tantrum.

Paco took some time off to show me the amusement park in Tibidabo when we got to Barcelona. He didn't want me to miss Gaudí, so we did that too. We distributed propaganda leaflets in both Madrid and Barcelona which we had stuffed into the springs of the car. In the end it wasn't easy getting Nicolás and Manolo across the border; they got lost in the Pyrenees for nearly a week. Paco was shot at when he left San Sebastián in a boat of Basque fishermen headed for France.

He was the last one of us to leave Spain. When his friends from the student resistance met his incoming train on the platform at the Gare de l'Est in Paris, they yelled into his compartment, "We won, we won!" The escape was a landmark event. It was the first action that had been planned jointly by Spanish students who had grown up in both the interior and exterior of Spain. Carlos Vélez and Enrique Cruz Salido were sons of exiled Spanish Socialists (Cruz Salido had been executed by the Germans); they had grown up in Mexico. Pepe Martínez, who was to join Paco in the publication of *Peninsula*, had just gotten out of prison in Valencia; he arrived in Paris in September. (Pepe later formed Ruedo Ibérico, the famous Paris-based Spanish exile publishing house, whose books and magazines have been said to have educated a whole generation.) Jo-

sep Pallach, the Catalan Socialist, who furnished the false papers used for Nicolás and Manolo, had been in the Spanish and French Resistance in Montpellier during the German occupation. The Culegamuros escape cemented relations between Spanish students who had grown up in the interior with those
who had grown up in exile—before '48 there had been no contact between the
two groups.

There were many meetings that fall of 1948 of the student resistance group,
the FUE. Everyone was in agreement that the time of the Maquis was over.
The entire central committee of the CNT had just fallen and been arrested inside Spain; the old anarchist movement in Spain finally was permanently
crushed. Paco and his friends recognized that the divisiveness and ghetto-like
atmosphere of the older political exile groups in France had been a disaster.
They felt that creating a magazine—*Peninsula*—which didn't follow any political line was the most constructive thing they could do. They would smuggle
it back into Spain; it would be a cultural bridge in a country which was on a starvation diet of Franco propaganda. I wrote about what I knew—America, the
Actors' Studio, Tennessee Williams, and Arthur Miller. Juan Benet published
his first poem—"El Bosque"—in it. The playwright José Ruibal told me years
later that he read it during his military service in the north of Spain—he said his
whole group waited for its arrival, there was only one copy for all of Galicia.
He said he read very seriously my pieces on the American theater, and assumed
I was an older person, an expert. It never occurred to him I was just an American kid scribbling away in Paris.

Paco, as a future cultural anthropologist, decided to do extensive interviews
with the different exiled political groups in Paris. He thought it was important
for the future. By then we were living together. He took me with him always—sometimes he met with his professor, Merleau-Ponty, and occasionally *L'Esprit* magazine invited all of *Peninsula* to their place outside Paris for
Sunday picnics. Paco always said that the real revolution in Spain would come
when women left the kitchen, and he told me to pay attention because I was living through history. But I don't believe that while he was taking down the histories of the Socialists, left-Republicans, Anarchists, etc., they realized they
were being preserved for oral history. Nor did any of us in the group around
Peninsula—Pepe Martínez, Paco, and Pallach—have any reason to believe that
after Franco's death they too would be dead, while I, the stray American,
would be the one left to explain those days.

My last day in Saint Felieu de Guixols, I walked by the acid-yellow casino
again, and I stared at the palm tree-lined Esplanade in front of it. I have long ago
lost my childhood collection of travel folders, but I kept Paco's globe of the
world he bought second-hand. It is beneath my study window. I see it when I
write, and perhaps that was it: I went to Spain because I wanted the world.

Spain After That War

1963

If the internal chaos of Inquisition Spain served as a climate to produce the complex character of the split hero Quixote, Spain's second inner psychic wound, the Civil War, did just the reverse. The missing factor in post-Civil War literature is the personality of the hero.

During the forties writers within Spain remained cut off from one another and the outside world. It was a period of fear, personal turmoil, and apathy. Direct reference to Church, politics, and sex was taboo. The regime, however, was too Spanish to promote an affirmative doctrinaire literature. Primness remained a native prerogative, and at least Spain was spared the false hero and false optimism of iron curtain fiction.

What happened was that the central character simply disappeared from sight. Unable to show their feelings directly—both because of outer censorship and an inner sense of failure—writers chose to concentrate on groups of people rather than individuals, to show situation in lieu of emotion. A literature emerged that was harsh on the surface, with an overall effect of cold remoteness. Ghost-like men with vague pasts, no future, and little present predominated.

The two outstanding novels of this period are *La Colmena* (*The Hive*) by Camilo José Cela and *Nada* by Carmen Laforet. By making Madrid itself the hero of *La Colmena*, Cela solved the problem of lack of personal focus. With brilliant photographic detail he etched a portrait of life barren beneath the artificial glitter of Madrid. *Nada*, which unfortunately has never been translated into English, is one of the few serious books of the early postwar to actually have a protagonist. A young woman on a visit to Barcelona discovers with horror the grotesqueness of the life around her. Perhaps it was easier for a young woman to express overt disgust in a voice clearly her own. Spanish males were paralyzed by what they considered to be their own destructive role in the war (this applied to both sides), and a woman might turn more readily into sensibility what a man might find necessary to cast in terms of politics.

In the fifties, with the exception of Ana María Matute, whose pictures of desolation are often presented in delicate, fairy tale-like stories, most of the younger generation continued to use Cela's format of super-realism. The most gifted, in my opinion, is Rafael Sánchez Ferlosio. Just as Madrid dominates *La Colmena*, the river El Jarama holds together his novel, which bears the same name (printed in America as *One Day of the Week*). Sánchez Ferlosio evokes the mood of a Sunday outing on the outskirts of Madrid for people whose lives are drab and restricted. They converge on the river, trying to find a bit of sun, a bit of a good time. Out of the simple material of a young girl's accidental drowning Sánchez Ferlosio conveys the tragedy of these young people's wasted lives; the quality of tenderness mixed with a sense of futility reminds one of some of the early postwar Italian films.

For my taste both Juan García Hortelano's and Juan Goytisolo's work suffers from a too didactic use of allegory. In Hortelano's *Tormento* (*Summer Storm*), which won the Formentor International Prize, the point about the apathetic attitude of the middle class is made by showing their evasive reaction when the naked body of a woman is washed up on the beach. Unfortunately, Hortelano's people remain shadows. Goytisolo's work is uneven. *La Resaca*, about the poor, is his best and least pretentious novel. *Juego de Manos* (*The Young Assassins*) is a terse account of youth at war with the previous generation. Their boredom and lack of purpose end in a gratuitous act of murder—the explosion of pent-up energy Spaniards call "*gamberrismo*." Goytisolo obviously dislikes *la dolce vita* so intensely that in *La Isla* (*Island of Women*) he doesn't even bother to write about its sybarites. Having the bored wife of a journalist tell this tale of the decadent rich doesn't help, either: she sounds too much like a female Humphrey Bogart with intellectual overtones. Both *La Isla* and *Juego de Manos* have received greater acclaim in France than in Spain, where his more abstract and less sensational work is preferred. The chief criticism leveled against him is that he has a tendency to over-glamorize Spanish Beat youth and Spanish indolent rich and to not truly reflect the current situation. In fairness to Goytisolo, he is obviously one of the writers most chafing under censorship. His talent is one born out of direct anger, but until he can find a way of communicating this more openly, his characters will appear oddly unreal.

Goytisolo's use of a female narrator in *La Isla* perhaps is not unrelated to Hortelano's and Sánchez Ferlosio's drowned women. Blocked in their attempt to describe the male situation, modern Spanish novelists often turn to female tragedy. Indeed, what more horrible indictment of war than this literature in which there are no heroes, no fathers, no men? There is something female about total defeat: women are traditional symbols of passive suffering and the inability to participate actively in the world. Even Cela shows his women with more detail than men. He has myriad portraits of girls forced into prostitution in order to help tubercular lovers, of neurasthenics, and of women destined to spinsterhood for lack of men. In the films, *Viridiana* is the symbol of the corrupted innocence of ignorance; and in *Calle Mayor* an old maid desperately seeking love is forced into complete withdrawal from life by the malicious pranks of a cruel, indifferent society. The angry young man comes only after there is the possibility of some improvement in a bad situation—e.g., England.

In two recent works, however, the authors emerge as the central characters and the writing has a more personal tone. Perhaps the distance from the war can be measured in this return to the Spanish comic sense. Neither of these two young protagonists has a father, neither has any relation with the previous generation. In the title story of *Nunca Llegarás a Nada*, by Juan Benet, the hero, the only child of a silent mother—of a family doomed to extinction—remarks that the strongest influence in his life has been his mustached aunt, the guardian of the family virtues. She suffered tragedy as a young girl when her fiancé, on the eve of marriage, drank too much at a bachelor party, had a seizure, and vomited his insides into the toilet. A military man, his final "noble heroic" gesture was to pull the chain, eliminating the evidence before expiring. The aunt, while waiting to join her lover in heaven, constantly admonishes Juan, as does the rest of the world: "Nunca llegarás a nada"—"*You will never get anywhere.*" In resisting this whirlpool of virtue, he develops his character. He is, indeed, a total calamity. He and a friend, Vicente, spontaneously set out for Paris, and from then on the story is a mixture of adventures that happen and nearly happen, mysterious appointments at cafés, strange females, and even stranger Englishmen.

Xavier Domingo, like Benet, has a bitter comic sense of life. *Villa Milo*, also written in the first person, was published last year in Paris and recently in New York. Because of its content there has been no Spanish edition. Paco, an orphan adopted by a Catalonian madam, has grown up in the sensual atmosphere of a Barcelona whorehouse, which at times resembles the establishment in *The Balcony*. (I have the impression that Genet had Barcelona in mind: many references and political allusions in his play seemed to be of a specifically Spanish nature, including what sounded like a description of the Valley of the Fallen.) Domingo's tone, however, is not Genet's. Sensuous, bawdy, blasphemous, and religious in the pagan style, he mixes the odors of love, cooking, and lust into a brew of ferocious sexual imagery. The outside world of clients—the law, priests, and police—is corrupt, the inner world of the bordello a paradise. Says the hero: "Sometimes I think I am only a witness, the envoy of some fu-

ture age, sent by it to mine to be that age's conscience during an absurd historical past, our present. When I return to my time, I'll be able to say no matter
how much I looked, I saw only two things around me, nonsense and death."
When the government edict announces the closing of the whorehouses, a sat-
urnalia takes place during which everyone's true personality is revealed. (One
whore blasphemes with a flow of language that should send Henry Miller back
to Brooklyn.) Before going out into the real world, Paco tells the daughter of
one of the whores: "Remember always who your parents are. It will help you
a lot. It's a way of getting ahead, knowing where you come from, something I
don't know myself." (He believes he may be the bastard son of the cleric and
the madam, a microcosm of the Spanish condition.) In the end he reflects: "You
live and you nibble . . . I had known in my bones that changing places and
names doesn't create a mutation of substance: a place isn't luck. They spat me
out of the Villa Milo, and since then I've gone from bad to worse. And now I'm
in this whore of a country, France, and I don't know if I should become a spit-
toon for a left-wing party or join the Foreign Legion to die with a warm meal
in my belly. Amen."

Also published outside of Spain are Manuel Lamana's more autobiographical novels, *Los Inocentes* and *Otros Hombres*. The first recounts his childhood
during the war, the second his prison experience during the forties. In order to
combat censorship difficulties, a group of young Spanish writers and intellectuals formed their own publishing house, Ruedo Ibérico, in Paris last year. Besides publishing fiction and nonfiction, they undertook to translate foreign accounts of the Spanish situation; their first was Hugh Thomas's *Spanish Civil
War*. Reading their collections of the poetry of Angel González and Gabriel
Celaya (arrested in Spain last spring), I was reminded more of the young Russian and Polish poets than of the French or American. The lament, in tones violent and sad, is for all dead—from the Spanish Civil War to the gas ovens of
Germany.

From the thirties to the present Spaniards have held various attitudes toward
their own condition. During the war their differences with one another seemed
irreconcilable. Immediately afterward the feeling was: no victors, all van-
quished. For foreigners Spain remained the great lost cause, and in their accounts the positive qualities were stressed—individual courage, the strong
stand against fascism—but Spaniards both in and out of Spain saw themselves
in a harsher light. A generation which had learned the bitter lesson that Spanish
courage often meant Spanish death did not wish to pass on the values of this
heroism. Paradoxically, because of this inverted idealism of never speaking
well of themselves, they passed on a totally negative view of their own history.

Now another generation has come along, and their preoccupation is with a
reexamination of the past. It is not an attempt to rehash old political debates,

but a deeper search. "Who is my father?" is the recurring theme. *Año Tras Año*, by Armando López Salinas, is the first novel published by Ruedo Ibérico. Significantly, it is dedicated to "mi padre, viejo luchador obrerista." Salinas throws light on the feelings and actions of that lost Spanish generation which came into maturity directly following the war. He shows how they viewed the progress of World War II from the isolated vantage point of a Madrid infested with Germans. He records the fear of the police, the confusion, the lack of work. More important, he explores the politics of this group, the organizations they belonged to, the risks they took to reorganize the workers and students, actions which were to end often in prison. Though the book has no special literary merit, it is a decent document of a period which up until now has remained a blank. It is a beginning of the clearing of the air, an opening of a dialogue between Spaniards without which no true literature can emerge.

As for the younger generation which grew up inside Spain—of whom it was said that they would never want to hear of the Civil War, never want to know of the exiles—it was members of this group—among them Hortelano, Lamana, and Goytisolo—who last February picked *Año Tras Año* for the first prize for fiction and González's poems for poetry. The place they chose to award it, settling their own account with memory quietly and without fanfare, was the small French border town of Collioure, where after making the long march across the Pyrenees in 1939, the poet Antonio Machado died.

Spain

Who Really Won?

1977

"Spain herself has won her new election"—so went the euphoric slogan on June 15. The Spaniards had not only brought off their first free vote in forty years but had satisfied their suppressed hankering for the new, the modern, the young. Juan Carlos, at thirty-nine, is a young king; President Adolfo Suárez—whose Center coalition (UCD) won with the slogan "vote Suárez, vote Center"—is forty-four. Felipe González, the Socialist leader of the opposition, is only thirty-five.

Suárez won—but then he did not win. His loose coalition of twelve small parties got 33.8 percent of the vote; but the three principal leftist parties together accounted for just over 42 percent. (González's Socialist Workers Party [PSOE] had 28.7 percent, the Communists 9.2 percent, the Independent Socialists 4.3 percent.) Suárez knows, moreover, that he faces a more severe test when the municipal elections take place at the end of the year. The delegates just elected to the new Parliament, or Cortes, will be much occupied with a new constitution. The municipal elections will give voters a chance to sweep away much of the old bureaucratic apparatus which still heavily controls Spain; and here the Socialists may do better than even they would like.

Still Suárez won a remarkable victory—not against the left but against the right. He put together his assortment of twelve parties, most of them new, in order to have a convincing base from which to defeat the *Alianza Popular* led by Manuel Fraga. This is the well-financed party in which prominent supporters of Franco were most visible—the party that the London *Economist* last

May estimated would get 20 percent of the vote. Suárez was brilliant in the way he demolished it. During the election the Popular Alliance was turned into the symbol of forty years of Franco. Fraga, Franco's former ambassador to London, found himself in the role of the *ancien régime* villain; he lost control of his party, became bitter and strident, and during the last ten days underwent a collapse that reminded some American reporters of Richard Nixon's.

Cast as Franco's unpopular heir, Fraga no doubt wondered: why me? After all, Adolfo Suárez, only a few short years ago, was himself secretary of the Falangist party. But when Fraga was Minister of the Interior in Juan Carlos's first cabinet, he was somewhat of a bully. And running with him this election were former Franquistas such as Arias Navarro, Franco's brutal military prosecutor after the Civil War who was fired as premier by the king to make way for Suárez. Some of them openly defended Franco's record. They could not shake off the smell of Fascism. The Spaniards took their revenge, giving Fraga's party fewer votes (8 percent) than the Communists.

Suárez is younger than Fraga, more quick witted and agile, less compromised, far more dashing and handsome. More important, he is the king's man, appointed president by him in 1976 and still one of the inner circle. Stendhal would have appreciated his rise to power. He comes from a modest family in the Castilian province of Avila, and worked his way up through the Falangist party organization. Much has been made of the way he attached himself to several reform-minded older officials, members of the lay Catholic network called Opus Dei, who helped bring him to the attention of Juan Carlos. Quite as useful, it seems, was his friendship with Carmen Diez de Rivera, the beautiful blond daughter of a Spanish duchess, a determinedly modern young woman who took a job at the State Telephone Company in the late 1960s and there met Suárez. "She took him up," a knowledgeable friend told me, "gave him advice on how to dress, introduced him around, gave him a new style, a shrewder sense of how the old cliques were changing, how one could have 'class' and be 'progressive' at the same time." When Suárez was promoted to director of national television, Carmen went with him; when Juan Carlos appointed him president, Carmen became "special president" of his first cabinet.

Some of the old guard officials grumbled at this. Apart from her connections, her casual chic, and a few courses at the Sorbonne, how was she qualified to run the administrative affairs of the cabinet? Yet, she soon became a popular figure, fitting in perfectly with the prevailing mood of *destape*—the spirit of social and sexual permissiveness that followed the dictator's death. Recently, however, she moved off on her own, campaigning for Tierno Galván's small Independent Socialist party, and Suárez was advised to ask her to resign. (Before he was appointed president, Suárez had been semi-officially separated from his wife. During the campaign all the candidates' wives were noticeably kept out of the public eye, as if Spain were still Moorish.)

During the week following the elections Suárez met privately with the politicians of the Center coalition and insisted they face some hard facts. The Center could crush Fraga and the right—but in the coming municipal elections the Socialists could well demolish the Center. If they were to survive, Suárez said, the members of the coalition would have to act pragmatically and form a real party. The Center has no clear-cut base and no specific shape. Suárez and the twelve parties appealed to the widely different groups of Spaniards who, while having little or no affection for Franco, had not done badly under him: state employees, professional and business people, would-be entrepreneurs, rural voters, particularly from the center of Spain, and much of the "new middle class." But during the campaign the Center coalition had to rely on paid help. The PSOE, roughly equal in membership to the Center coalition parties, was able to draw on a sizable pool of impressive young middle-class volunteers, and their party is evidently growing fast.

At the moment the Center coalition can be divided into two wings—one is led by the more civilized officials of the old regime who have now become respectable liberal conservatives; the more progressive wing includes social democrats like the economist Fernández Ordóñez and a scattering of bona fide Spanish Republican intellectuals. The well-known architect Fernando Chueca, for example, found that the small liberal party he belonged to was suddenly absorbed into the Center coalition. (Running for the Senate in the traditionally very conservative city of Toledo, he beat Blas Piñar, the fanatical leader of the small ultra-right-wing group called *Fuerza Nueva*.)

Suárez's coalition, as he pointed out, will have to unite, recruit, and organize if it is to stay afloat. But meanwhile he has not only the king, but also the army behind him; he no longer has reason to fear a military coup, as he apparently did during 1976 and early 1977. His technique for dealing with the army has been to shift around officers, making sure that the principal appointments in the lower echelons went to the men who would resist a coup. Whenever some of the hardline generals became obstreperous, Suárez confused them by taking even more aggressive steps toward liberalizing the system: his last such act was to legalize the Communist Party.

No one now expects a military takeover. The United States has promised Suárez substantial backing; the West Germans have already given much to the Socialists. Manuel Gutiérrez Mellado, now in charge of all the military services, is the most reasonable for the Spanish generals, close to both Suárez and Juan Carlos. Suárez is itching to appear as a man with a sophisticated foreign policy, one aimed at the Common Market countries, overturning what he has referred to as the "junk heap" of Francoist foreign relations. "Since Portugal worries about being poor cousin to Spain," he said, "let Portugal enter the Common Market first. If France is worried about Spanish agricultural competition in the Common Market, then we won't sell our melons in the Common Market. Why fight over melons?" The tone of cool reason.

The dilemma of the Socialists was made clear early on election night when the results from the major cities started to come in, showing them winning in Barcelona, Seville, Valencia; this produced a *frisson* of panic at headquarters, for the projected vote seemed dangerously high. A few of the Socialist strategists even tried to get some of the last-minute voters to switch to the Communists.

In no way did the Socialists want to win this election. They are confident that they will be the main party in Spain's future (as are the more perceptive writers in the Spanish press, e.g., in *El País* and the weekly *Cambio 16*). But their own strategists admit they have grown too fast. In May the polls predicted they would win 24 percent; just before the election the figures jumped to 28 percent. Early on the night of the election, it seemed they might win 30 percent—an upset and a potential disaster, for Suárez's step-by-step restoration of democracy would be threatened; some in the army and the police might have taken the vote as an excuse to cause turmoil. Felipe González wants only to be able to be the strong leader of the opposition, leaving Suárez to deal this autumn with Spain's urgent economic problems, including nearly 30 percent inflation, high unemployment, a large foreign debt, and the need to devalue the peseta. He does not want, moreover, to take on the entire task of undoing forty years of right-wing bureaucratic authoritarianism.

The strength of the Socialists, the embarrassing failure of Suárez to do better, probably accounted for the curious delay over the election results. After desultorily announcing some early returns, the Spanish national TV simply acted as if the election had never occurred. The Spanish weeklies and the international press were left to publish misleading figures giving the Center coalition 39.5 percent, the Socialists 26.9. During the week that followed, the industrial vote in Barcelona and the Basque country filtered in, showing clearcut and by then wholly expected Socialist victories.

Madrid was something else. For the capital, the home of the government, with its thousands of bureaucrats, not to give Suárez a decisive victory was distinctly awkward. After a week of suspense, and much dispute over "mislaid" ballot boxes, the Center squeaked into the lead with 32.3 percent of the vote against the Socialists' 31.6. So in Madrid, Suárez is even more sharply outnumbered by the combined vote of the left parties than he is in the country at large, making the coming municipal elections a grave threat to his claims to national support.

Why did PSOE and Felipe González do so well? Some Spanish experts maintained their vote was in large part "accidental"—the workers, knowing little or nothing about the new PSOE, simply chose the party that seemed to stand against the Franco past and for the poorer wage earners. But this seemed far too simple an explanation why the PSOE was chosen out of the half-dozen leftist parties on the ballot. The PSOE, after all, was the largest political party during the Spanish Republic, and many of its traditions remained alive. Suddenly, during the second week of the campaign, the "International" began to be played on the loudspeakers of the PSOE campaign cars as they drove through the Spanish towns. This was startling and much remarked on, as if people were hearing an echo from the old days.

The PSOE inherited much else. Since Spain is now a constitutional monarchy, it is illegal for "Republicans" to organize a separate party; they gave their votes to the PSOE, as did the remnants of the Anarchist movement. Many young and old Communists were furious at the Communist leader Santiago Carrillo for banning the Republican flag. This was no small matter, since the flag for which so many thousands died is still held as sacred. Yet Communists who carried it at some of their PCE rallies were beaten up by Communist special security police—causing resentment, mutiny, and the transfer of many Communist votes to the PSOE.

On the last day of the campaign I saw Felipe González drive through Vallecas, the working-class quarter of Madrid, to make his final speech. His motorcade played the "International" and carried the old Republican and Socialist Labor Union flags through the city that Suárez counted on winning. González's chances in Madrid were often discounted, even by those who acknowledged his strength elsewhere. That the Madrileños have by now "gotten in the habit of supporting the established order" was taken for granted by some of Suárez's supporters.

But Madrid was not always a proud Fascist city. As I remember it from the late 1940s, it was the most desolate, grim, and miserable place in Spain. The Basque and Catalan workers, because of the unifying regional passion for autonomy, could feel some kinship with the factory owners who employed them, some sense of security. The Madrid workers in Vallecas had nobody to protect them. When González's procession arrived there on 15 June most of the people simply stared, then some in the crowd gave the old clenched fist salute of the Republican days, then hundreds did. A policeman directing traffic made a V-for-victory sign, and pulled a Socialist insignia from his pocket and waved it. Soon it seemed as if the whole quarter was literally running toward the stadium where González was about to speak. Not a few men and women were crying. It seemed hasty to conclude the Socialist vote is explained by opportunistic, ahistorical choices of the moment. In fact the voting pattern in the cities is proportionally fairly close to the one that prevailed in pre-Civil War Spain, although then the Communist Party barely existed.

Still Felipe González, a former labor lawyer, is something new—as good-looking as Suárez and with more enthusiasm, a populist who can behave as if he is in a Hollywood movie, campaigning throughout Spain in a Lear jet, eating on the run. When I talked with him a year ago he told me that he had no interest in visiting officials or impressing leftist intellectuals in the United States—only the masses and the mass media interested him; and indeed within a year he became Spain's first mass-cult political hero.

His campaign was remarkably shrewd, and not only in reviving the old Republican Socialist emotions. Unlike the older and more rigid Socialist leaders he displaced, he and his young allies never attacked the Communists, although some of the Socialist leaders regard the PCE as conservative and unimaginative; nor, after much talk about it, did they ever form a coalition with the Communists. The only coalitions González organized were with potentially threatening parties claiming regional autonomy. Barcelona, for example, has both a strong movement for Catalan Socialism and large numbers of Andalusian workers who would automatically vote for González, who comes from Seville. The PSOE therefore joined forces with the Catalonian Socialists headed by Joan Reventos and won a heavy victory.

As the chief editor of the most respected publishing house in Barcelona, Reventos carried along with him most of Catalonia's impressive group of writers, intellectuals, and artists. In late June he met in Madrid with the king, Suárez, and González in order to negotiate for autonomy, starting with the return to Spain of Josep Tarradellas, the exiled president of what was, under the Republic, the autonomous state of Catalonia. Now that Tarradellas is back, the prospects for Catalan home rule seem likely and, if achieved, would set a precedent for a similar arrangement with the more intransigently separatist Basques. (In this election González made a coalition with the Basque Socialists similar to the one with Reventos.)

As for the Communists, they have done very poorly. Their "boom" was in the 1960s when they organized the underground unions called Workers Commissions and attracted many intellectuals. By 1964 two of the most gifted PCE leaders had been tossed out of the Party for revisionism—Fernando Claudín, the Party theoretician, and Jorge Semprun, the Spanish novelist and scriptwriter (*La Guerre Est Finie, Z,* etc.). Semprun, who comes from one of the most distinguished political families in Spain, did much to rebuild the PCE underground in Madrid during the fifties and early sixties. His account of those days—*The Autobiography of Federico Sánchez* (his political alias)—will be widely read when it is published in the fall and will not help the Communists.

Most of the intellectuals who were in the Party during the sixties are now out as well, while the bureaucrats remain. For example, Alfonso Sastre, who could have been one of the principal Communist planners in Madrid, and was one of Carrillo's closest friends, will never forgive the Party. When his wife Eva Sastre was arrested for subversion, the PCE lawyers were forbidden to defend her since she had been involved with Basques. (She was released during election week, having spent three years in prison without trial. She told me she was nearly tortured to death at first, and credits Amnesty International with saving her life.)

The PCE in fact has been in great difficulty since Carrillo secretly returned to Spain in early 1976. Most of the younger Communists would like to see him depart and the Party reformed from within. But the Party's centralized structure is as tight as ever, notwithstanding Carrillo's admirably independent stand against the USSR on the virtues of pluralism and Eurocommunism. He has chosen as his heir apparent the highly unpopular forty-four-year-old economist Ramón Tamames, who made a substantial fortune working for the government and was formerly a close friend of Fraga's. The Workers Commissions, now dominated entirely by the PCE, face growing competition from the revived Socialist union organization, the UGT.

Unlike those of other Latin countries, Spain's best-known writers avoid the Party. Arrabal loathes the Communists; the novelists Juan and Luis Goytisolo supported Joan Reventos. The Madrid novelist Juan Benet belongs to no group at all. For many young Communists, and indeed many old Communists, Carrillo's arbitrary decision banning the Republican flag was a final intolerable sacrilege. The PCE is thus undergoing a crisis far more serious than even its low vote shows. The vote is expected to improve in the municipal elections but the party remains crippled by rebelliousness within its own ranks; and taking note of its vulnerable state, the Russians have launched an open attack on Carrillo. To form an alternative party, should he fail, they hold in reserve a man called "Eduardo García," who now lives in Paris and is hardly known in Spain, except to a few top Communists or former Communists. But no one believes García has much future.

Still, the Communists are very much part of the self-congratulatory celebration that is now taking place in Spain. Only a year ago, they all risked jail or worse; so did many Socialists. Recently, even in a deeply conservative town like Toledo, where the Civil War fighting was most brutal, the leaders of both parties could meet with politicians of the Center coalition and drink two common toasts: first, to Toledo's Communist hero Luis Lucio Lobato, who spent twenty-eight years in prison; and second, "to Spain—which won the election." And it did. To keep up this happy mood, however, everyone must assume that the Socialists will only come to power in a few years—gradually, conveniently. But what will happen if the Socialists win the municipal elections toward the end of 1977 and the supporters of Suárez, and the Francoists to their right, find the edifice of privilege itself crumbling around them? The Madrid vote can only be mislaid once.

The Lively Literary Revival

1984

Despite severe unemployment, cultural life in Spain is booming. Spaniards now have a firm sense of national pride; a recent flurry of articles in the European and home press characterized Madrid as the new cultural mecca, and tastes now are more eclectic. Unexpectedly, Anagrama, a small, prize-winning independent literary house, found it had a year-long super best-seller with John Kennedy Toole's *Confederacy of Dunces*. Good writers are making their prose more accessible. Both Eduardo Mendoza and Manolo Vázquez Montalbán have experimented with the detective novel, now a very modish genre.

Fernando Savater, Spain's most popular young philosopher, also wants his ideas to be understood by the general public; in addition to his essays, he writes plays, novels, and detective stories. Bypassing linguistics with casual aplomb as though all that jazz had never happened, Savater has assumed real prominence by dusting off the old-fashioned study of ethics and presenting it to the Spaniards as being just what they need. Both physically and intellectually all over the place, Savater jets around Spain, talking to newly created lecture-circuit audiences. Instead of citing imperialism as the enemy, he points out to his countrymen (as did generations of thinkers prior to Spain's Civil War) that their primary enemy is Spanish fatalism. What most excites Savater is that his generation of writers has found a brand new and enthusiastic public at home; the lecture circuit is a new phenomenon for Spain.

At last, Madrid has regained the life style with which the city was comfortable before the Civil War—Socialists and aristocrats mingling, a very literary press, gossip, and good conversation. Although the success of the Socialists occasionally makes them seem exasperatingly smug, a special symbiosis exists between them and Madrid. Precisely because of this, the government has been perplexed that the established writers have chosen this time to seize their privacy and get on with their own work; prominent officials grumble that the intellectuals are selfish and lacking in civic responsibility.

I believe the reason none of the established writers, such as Carmen Martín Gaite, Juan García Hortelano, Miguel Delibes, and Camilo José Cela, has followed the Latin American example of becoming a part-time diplomat and political spokesman is complicated. Since, for so many years, Spanish intellectuals were the orphans at some sort of international tea party, it is extremely important for them to give all their energies to writing in order to reach the new, large readership at home. The enthusiasm for Latin American writers peaked here about a decade ago; there is less general interest in their work now, as well as a tendency to let the government represent Spanish writers in political and cultural matters regarding Latin America; individual participation in conferences is way down. Also, major Spanish publishing houses such as Bruguera and Seix Barral began to go bankrupt because of the inability of Mexican and Latin American publishers to pay them for foreign rights, which meant they could no longer manage the huge advances they had been giving Latin American writers.

Even several years ago it would have been almost impossible to publish in Spain a piece as explicit as the Barcelona-born Juan Goytisolo's account, published by the literary magazine *Quimera*, of the breakup in the early seventies of the Latin-American left's political-literary dominance over the issue of Castro's imprisonment of writers. In its heyday, the vogue for Latin American writers in Spain included formidable talents—Mario Vargas Llosa, Gabriel García Márquez, José Donoso, Carlos Fuentes, Octavio Paz, Severo Sarduy, and Julio Cortázar. In what was apparently a series of violent verbal battles, Juan Goytisolo and Mario Vargas Llosa led the anti-Castro faction. Criticizing Cortázar and García Márquez for succumbing to left-wing rhetoric and flashy political high life, Goytisolo described the former's metamorphosis from literary stylist to a writer of pro-Castro verse as "sounding like a tango with lyrics by Vishinsky." Ruefully, he writes of García Márquez, "Without our recognizing the changes taking place, the international García Márquez who was to become the intimate friend of political heads of state and espouser of presumed 'advanced causes' was about to be born." Ironically, in Spain, it took Franco's death to finally emancipate intellectuals from the emotional blackmail dealt out by the authoritarian left.

How much of the present cultural flowering is due to the Socialists now in power? Some of their improvements have been a benign form of window dressing. As they have been unable to afford what it would take to make profound social and economic changes, they have pushed culture, which gives them immediate results at bargain prices. Thus, there are free concerts and a new children's theater in Madrid's Retiro Park, and plans are under way to begin next fall the construction of a big new music center there. Some projects of real intellectual merit have also been initiated. Arab, Jewish (some from Israel), and Spanish scholars have been meeting at the universities of Granada and Madrid. For the first time in this century, there will be the much-needed pooling of their investigations concerning the Middle Ages, which, in Spain, was an amalgam of these three cultures.

To fully comprehend the significance of Madrid's emergence as one of the major centers of the Spanish-speaking world, one has to first go back a bit and put into perspective what the legacy of the left has been in Madrid and Barcelona, two cities with very different histories during the sixties and seventies. Although Marxism clearly is on the wane throughout Europe, the Spanish cultural-political process has been unique. Unlike Latin America and most countries of Europe, Spain never really had many well-known Marxist intellectuals. But over the past two decades the shadowy, Paris-based Spanish Communist Party developed what appeared to be a stronghold in intellectual and university circles. Some were attracted to the party for idealistic, anti-Franco reasons, others assumed that their choice in life was limited to the Roman Catholic Church, the Opus Dei, or the Party, and quite a number of intellectuals gravitated to the Communists—with their cultural links to Mexico City, Paris, and Havana—because they ran the best literary agency in town.

In this period, which was a mishmash of Franco propaganda and Communist pseudo-underground propaganda, Barcelona—not far from the French border, prosperous, and with a thriving publishing industry—seemed the natural headquarters of the left. The occasional visiting Latin American writers and intellectuals rarely went deeper into Spain. As the major publishing houses then had all sorts of economic ties with firms in Latin America, most of the intellectual excitement centered on the sort of international literary-political Third World cultural junkets popular during that period.

But as most of this generalized left-consciousness had little to do with the concrete specifics of Spain, two basic facts were ignored by the left. Before Franco, the Spanish working class had always been Socialist, and Barcelona, despite the enormous talent of its individual artists, had always had a conservative industrial tone. Indeed, a series of amazing myths took root during this unreal time. The notion of geographical goodness and evil had enormous currency. Thus, Barcelona, near France, was "good" and had lost the Civil War to Madrid, a city that was "Spanish and Fascist." In those days nobody seemed interested in statistics; during the Civil War there had been many Fascists in Barcelona, just as there had been many who had defended the Republic in the rest of Spain.

After Franco's death in 1975, when elections became legal and the Communist Party failed to attract the working class, these myths collapsed. Then, suddenly, being near France counted for nothing. New York became the foreign cultural mecca, the second language for everyone under 40 was now English, and the latent anti-French feeling that has always existed in Spain exploded into real rage because of France's blocking of Spain's entry into the Common Market and its failure to help control terrorist attacks against Spain by Basque separatists. Manuel Gutiérrez Aragón (Carlos Saura, Victor Erice, and he are now the three most interesting movie directors) shares the prevalent dislike for things French. "Their movies are too dead, too literary. My generation learned from John Ford and Francis Ford Coppola." Laughing, he said, "Sometimes I think that Spain makes the best bad movies in all of Europe." Then he added, "But Hollywood made the best bad movies of the 1940s and think how wonderful they were."

During the sixties and seventies intellectual buzzwords for "bad" included anything too Spanish—gypsies, flamenco music, and bullfighting were dismissed as "folklore." In the more eclectic 1980s, intellectuals wanting to indulge their secret passion for bullfights have come boldly out of the closet; last November, the organizers of the Seville Film Festival—after dutifully opening with Jean-Luc Godard's *Prenom: Carmen*—felt relaxed enough about themselves to run as homage to the actress Juanita Reina a series of her somewhat cornball flamenco movies of the 1940s. There is enormous diversity and opportunity for artists here. Carlos Saura pointed out to me that if he left Spain for Hollywood, he would lose his ability to be completely in charge of his films. Opera, which never had much of a following, is all the rage among the young.

Most of this general burst of creative energy has centered around Madrid precisely because many people who normally would have been drawn to Barcelona have been discouraged by Catalan becoming the official language there. Ironically, those who feel the most victimized by the switch away from Spanish are the Barcelonans themselves. Groaned one writer, "It was one thing to shout 'Down with Franco' in Catalan, quite another to have to listen to 'Dallas' in it." The serious problems caused by imposing Catalan as the region's official language haven't yet been sorted out.

But what has been the political history of Madrid? In the sixties and seventies the place certainly was a cultural backwater, and, perhaps because of that, the Communists never gained the toehold they had in Barcelona. In those sleepy, slow-moving times, one person might tell of having had tea with García Lorca's sister, another had a story about Luis Buñuel's brilliant brother Alfonso, and a third, sighing wistfully, mentioned that in the old days Madrid had had a great newspaper called *El Sol*. During long, dusty afternoons the novelist Juan Benet (who hadn't yet become "the Proust of Spain") would caution me: In writing about the Spanish opposition, indicate to your readers that though the Communists organize well underground, the Socialists would probably be very strong overground. "So, where are these Socialists?" I asked skeptically. Benet's own father had been killed during the Civil War and Juan was steeped in its history. (The publication of his long novel about the war—*Herrumbrosas Lanzas*—was one of the major Spanish literary events last fall.) Puffing on his Dunhill pipe, staring out the window, as though imaginary legions were about to descend on us from Calle Serrano, Juan would wave his hands and say, "Just leave a tiny space in your piece for them. . . . They'll come, they'll come!"

They came. And now Spain suddenly seems bathed in a sort of optimistic cultural glow. The British are enthusiastic about a new group of Madrid architects; there has been much talk in the art world about the verve of the peppy Madrid Figuratives; and the brand new feisty newspaper, *La Luna de Madrid*, recently ran a questionnaire: Is this the city of the future? Despite the down-to-earth replies, including "nope," there is no doubt that Madrileños are delighting in their city's cultural renaissance.

Museums, previously empty, are packed. One of the most successful shows· is that of Guillermo Pérez Villalta at the Picasso room of Madrid's Bellas Artes. Luis Gordilla, Gerardo Delgado, Chema Cobo, and he are the main figures in the current explosion in art. Pérez Villalta, like several of the others, was trained as an architect. Born in Tarifa, a hair's breadth away from North Africa, he paints in a style that blends long, almost North African vistas, Murillo, a dash of Max Ernst—and recalls Andalusian architecture, in which Arabic, Gothic, Roman, and Spanish styles were jumbled together to produce marvels. His retort to an American artist who had suggested that he expand a single element—"As we are a poor country with limited space, we accumulate many ideas in a single picture"—is less to the point than Spain's abiding affinity for the Baroque, in which paintings within paintings are commonplace. During the twentieth century we have come to think of Spain as synonymous with a simple style in art—stark browns and blacks—but that really has to do more with Cubism and the 1920s than with anything intrinsically Spanish.

Certainly, Spanish architecture has been a continuous celebration of the idiosyncratic. El Gran Teatro Del Liceo, Barcelona's magnificent opera house, built by nineteenth-century industrialists and aristocrats as a place to see and be seen, is a wonderful example. Inevitably, the history of the place has included mob violence, political intrigue, and a turn-of-the-century Anarchist bombing. Death and *Amor* have also been given their due. Death was accommodated in the secluded mourning boxes from which the wealthy could enjoy their opera-going while being hidden from the general view. The main tier of boxes, with their adjoining private salons—some have private bars, others have Japanese divans, nearby bathrooms complete with bidets—were perfect for the second. The most coveted of them, right next to the proscenium, to this day maintains its strict bylaws which prohibit the presence of wives. One of its present six owners, Antonio Pares, the president of the Barcelona Ritz, showed me its adjoining "second box," which has a secret door leading directly backstage, all the easier, in former lush times, for the ballerinas' visits. "Do you think, under the Socialists, these bylaws might be changed?" I asked. Mr. Pares shook his head, "No—not even in Socialist Spain. After all, some things remain sacred."

And, I thought, despite Barcelona's temporary transition difficulties, this is a city that has produced one of the world's greatest architects, Antonio Gaudí, contains the wonderful treasure trove of old books at the flea market of San Antonio, and has urban planners who make sure that dream spaces continue to be built. Thus, the designer of the new plaza in front of the Sants railroad station has created slopes in order to provide children with rain puddles, while an iron cat stalks above the station roof. And still another square has been built solely as homage to a splendid lone grandfather of a palm tree. Sometimes, it is best just to wait and let history unfold.

A Diary of the New Spain

The Spanish Elections

1983

We are still traumatized by the Spanish Civil War. It was the first military proving ground of Fascism and Stalinism, with democracy squeezed and smashed
in between, and for most of us Spain continues to mean *For Whom the Bell Tolls*,
Ernest Hemingway, George Orwell, André Malraux. I've been back from
Spain for more than two months now, and my friends' questions about the Socialist landslide in the 28 October general elections have shown me how abiding are the gut fears we Americans have about that country's destiny.

What kind of political animal is this grave, boyish Felipe González Márquez, who has become the first Socialist Prime Minister of Spain since the
Spanish Republic of the 1930s? What kind of socialism will his party seek to establish now that it has an absolute majority in Parliament? Will the defeat of the
right-of-center government that had been in power since the 1977 election
tempt its military supporters into a coup, like the one led by Gen. Francisco
Franco in 1936? Is there danger of another civil conflict, such as the one that
took a million lives from 1936 to 1939? Are there really two Spains, one leftist,
one rightist, at endless war with each other?

I have found it difficult to reassure my questioners that the stark conditions
of the 1930s no longer exist. I could not find words evocative enough to describe the remarkable change the country has undergone in the seven years
since the end of the Franco dictatorship. Perhaps the best answer I can give is the
diary I kept during the three weeks I spent in Spain last October, revisiting the
people and places I had known in the past and following candidates of different

parties in their election campaigns. In those crowded weeks, a jumble of impressions of a kind that often evades the headlines added up to a conviction on my part that Spain is finally at peace with itself—sure at last that the democratic process can hold.

Despite vague new threats of a coup, most Spaniards came to believe as election day approached that it was possible to vote for political change without inviting violent overthrow. The fear that had existed in the 1977 elections—especially in small towns, where everyone remembered who did what to whom, and that there could be reprisals—was over. Nearly 80 percent of the population voted. To the average citizen, what seemed even more important than who won was the novel right to vote for a group of his or her choice—and, if he or she didn't like the new government's performance, to vote "for another crew" at the next election.

A Spanish woman I knew in Madrid once told me that during the two years and nine months she spent in prison for political activities under the Franco regime, she was never permitted to see her face in a mirror. That, she said, was the severest deprivation: "After a while you feel deformed, a monster." In a sense, all of Spain, during that era, was not permitted to see its true reflection, as the dictatorship polluted the institutions of press, literature, and public life that can explain a people to itself. The 1977 elections were only a first glimpse. This time—during the campaign and the voting of last October—Spain saw its face clearly in the mirror. My Spanish diary is an attempt to convey the disparate elements of that political image.

Madrid, 13 October 1982
A Spanish couple took me to Sacha's, one of those restaurants where they are fussy about white lace tablecloths, china, smoked salmon, and caviar. My hosts recognized a friend, an engineer, who joined us. We also recognized several members of the Spanish Socialist Workers Party at the next table. "Hunting for cadres," the engineer said.

The Party, he explained, "will get millions of votes. But they know they are going to need good men in their ministries. So some of them arranged this dinner with a group of engineers, to see whom they could pick up."

My mind went back to a scene I had witnessed on the night of the 1977 elections: In a crowded café, students shouting, "Long live the Socialist Party!"—and policemen staring at the students, both groups staring at each other, apprehensive, unsure. And suddenly it occurred to all of us, for the first time: Why, the Socialists are *really* legitimate now! Up from the underground, free of their miserable hiding places, more than just tolerated—so legitimate that it is all right to acclaim them in the very presence of the police.

And now, five years later, there they sit, neatly dressed, in a fashionable restaurant, recruiting managerial help from the country's technocratic elite.

Actually, they are only resuming an old role. The Socialists have the longest tradition of any of the country's present political groupings. The 1936 elections, the last held by the Spanish Republic, gave them the largest bloc in Parliament. In 1977, they lost to the Union of the Democratic Center coalition by a small margin. Since then, many municipal posts have gone to the Socialists; Madrid has long had a Socialist mayor, the region of Andalusia a Socialist local government. If the Spanish public is reacting with a certain placidity to the likelihood of a Socialist regime, it is because, to them, González & Company is not an unknown quantity.

14 October

This afternoon, I visited the offices of *Cambio 16*, the weekly news magazine that played such an extraordinary role, along with several other publications, during the first year after Franco's death in 1975. No one group had real power in its hands in that murky time—not the new king, Juan Carlos, and his palace entourage, not the fledgling political parties. *Cambio 16*, the sociocultural magazine *Cuadernos*, and the new post-Franco daily *El País* provided the only forum in which Spaniards could follow and comprehend the shape of the new era.

A new move toward a military coup has just been reported in the press; three alleged ringleaders have been put under house arrest. I asked Juan Tomás de Salas, the publisher of *Cambio 16*, if a coup were still possible.

"Well," he said, "I don't think we are out of the woods yet, but . . . no, I don't think a coup is likely." He said the extremist faction within the military is even angrier with the king and the conservative members of the present government than with the Socialists. The *ultras*, he explained, feel the conservatives have betrayed them by colluding with the opposition to obliterate the vestiges of Francoism, which for them remains the symbol of the "true Spain." The Minister of the Interior, Juan José Rosón, is on their lists of those to be "neutralized"—killed—for having arranged an amnesty for one faction of the Basque independence movement ETA. The threatened conservatives, with their allies in the armed forces, have been keeping close watch on the restless minority among the military officers.

Tomás seemed more concerned by the question of relations with the United States after the voting. It would be nice, he said, if the American embassy had a staff capable of developing closer ties to the incoming government, which he assumed would be Socialist, as well as closer cultural ties to Spain in general.

"What you want," I joked, "is Jackie Kennedy."

Juan Tomás seized on the idea. "A Socialist government and Jackie Kennedy—yes! Madrid would be full of parties; everyone would get to know each other. *Dios*, it would be stupendous!"

Fernando Claudín is the director of the Pablo Iglesias Foundation, a sociopolitical research group. He has also been, for many years, the leading theoretician of the Spanish Communist Party. Receiving me in his office, he said he had finished writing a critical biography of Santiago Carrillo, the party's leader for a quarter of a century and, before that, chief adviser to Dolores Ibarruri, the legendary *La Pasionaria* of Spanish Communism. He smiled apologetically when he told me the work was being published by Planeta, a group that had had the reputation of being very pro-Franco during the Franco years.

Another example of the topsy-turviness of present-day Spain: Planeta, in search of prestige and a clean bill of health, has been publishing many books by the leftist opposition. And the left, short of cash, wants the fattest publishing contracts it can get.

Claudín's book will, I am sure, be another shot in the long political war between him and Carrillo, an extension of the ferocious hostilities that took place inside the Spanish Communist Party in the 1960s. Many Spanish Communists engaged in clandestine activities inside Spain had begun to rebel by then against the authoritarian control of the party exercised by Carrillo from exile in Paris. Their point of view was represented most strongly by Jorge Semprun, the Spanish novelist who wrote the screenplays *La Guerre Est Finie*, *Z*, and *The Confession*, and who was sent back to Spain to help rebuild the party in intellectual and university circles, and by Claudín, the party's "thinker," who spent the Franco years in exile in Russia, Mexico, and France. What they wanted was more autonomy, and a change of political orientation to what we later came to know as Eurocommunism.

Claudín, particularly, sought to persuade Carrillo that the old dogma, under which the working class would rise up and rebel, no longer made any sense. He insisted that the party take account of the economic miracle of the Franco years, the emergence of the Spanish middle class and the relative success of capitalism in the United States and Western Europe. Claudín and Semprun were expelled from the party, along with their intellectual followers within Spain. Eventually, during the Prague Spring, Carrillo switched over to the Eurocommunist position, but by then the party had been riven by bitterness and Claudín was the leading voice of an amorphous rebel faction.

Talking to me today, Claudín put down his coffee cup and said harshly, "I will never forgive Santiago Carrillo for his destruction of the Spanish Communist Party."

The party is certainly in a period of collapse. Yet is this entirely Carrillo's fault? For many years under Franco, the Communists maintained the fiction that theirs was the only resistance, and they became victims of their own propaganda. Actually, Spain, unlike France and Italy, has never had a sizable Communist Party. Before the Civil War, there were 1.7 million members of the Socialist trade union, *Unión General de Trabajadores de España* (UGT), 1.5 million in the Anarchist labor union, *Confederación Nacional de Trabajo*, and only 40,000 Communists, who did not have their own labor union. The Anarchists are no longer a force, but their heritage tends to favor the Socialists more than the Communists. The Communists had exaggerated hopes for the post-Franco era; reality has caught up.

15 October
Lunch with an old friend, Fernando Chueca, an architect by profession and a member of the Liberal Party, a part of the governing Democratic Center co-alition. Chueca was elected to office in 1977 but is sitting it out this time. "It's no use," he said. "The Democratic Center has fallen apart. Suárez has had it."

Adolfo Suárez is the politician who led Spain through the transition. He had been the No. 2 man of the Francoist *Movimiento Nacional*. The new king appointed him prime minister, and he put the Democratic Center together with scissors and paste. Growing increasingly liberal, he was increasingly at odds with the coalition's right wing, and finally resigned as prime minister in January 1981, just before an abortive military coup. Last summer he quit the coalition and formed his own party, the Social Democratic Center Party, which seems to be getting nowhere in this campaign, despite Suárez's personal populist appeal.

"The petty ambitions and internal fights in the Democratic Center made them lose credibility with the public," Chueca said. "There were too many vestiges of Francoism in it. That they should have permitted themselves to disintegrate this way is a disgrace."

Madrid has been plastered with political posters. Wherever I walk, the faces of the principal candidates seem to be grinning at me: Felipe González, more ubiquitous than any; Landelino Lavilla, the Democratic Center's candidate for prime minister; Adolfo Suárez; Manuel Fraga, leader of the right-wing Popular Alliance. The television spots of the various parties are very similar: young romantic Spanish couples embracing the future, images reminding me of American shampoo ads. Trucks and cars, festooned with party flags and slogans, toot through Madrid, blaring their campaign songs. Neither the Communists nor the Socialists make much use of the "International." All the parties favor songs that sound like singing commercials.

The morning papers report a new flourish by the military extremists, who placed a bomb in the Democratic Center headquarters in Toledo. They begin to sound more like juvenile terrorists than serious plotters.

Barcelona, 16 October
A change has crept over Barcelona, not all of it to my liking. With their distinct history, their own language, and this beautiful city as an expression of their separate identity, the people of the region of Catalonia perceived themselves as an oppressed minority under Franco, keepers of a tradition of liberty closer to European culture than to centralized Spain. Franco even suppressed the use of

Catalan. Now that their home rule has been restored, the Catalans have been imposing their language with equal vehemence on a no-longer heterogeneous population: About half the people of present-day Catalonia are workers from other parts of Spain. These workers understandably resent having to send their children to schools where only Catalan is spoken. It would have been much more sensible to make Catalonia bilingual.

Perhaps it is only a temporary overreaction, but if this Catalan exclusivity lasts much longer, Barcelona will risk destroying itself as one of Spain's principal cultural centers. Already—what with the current punitive attitude toward writers born in Catalonia who choose to write in Spanish—much of Barcelona's literary activity is shifting to Madrid.

17 October

This afternoon, I drove to Cornelia, one of the factory towns in Barcelona's outer belt, to hear Santiago Carrillo on the stump. In a town of one hundred thousand people, about three thousand were gathered in a movie theater to hear the Communist chief. They were members and followers of the *Partit Socialista Unificat de Catalunya*, the historical vessel of Catalan Communism, a sister party to the national Communist organization. As usual, Carrillo was dressed in the neat dark suit of a moderately successful small-town Spanish businessman. His speech was heavy on bourgeois values and his party's loyalty to Spain.

There was a press bus to take us back to Madrid. Carrillo himself joined us, sitting directly in front of me. His followers in the street cheered him, threw bouquets of flowers through the bus windows and sought to shake his hand as we pulled away.

Carrillo stared silently out the window. He was having his troubles in Catalonia, I knew. The independent Catalan Communist Party had split into two groups, the breakaway faction consisting of old-fashioned Communists. Confused by Euro-this and Euro-that, ill at ease with the anti-Soviet line of both the national and the Catalan Communist parties, these were people who wanted clarity: Cognac should be Cognac, a woman should be a woman, and Communists should be Communists, loyal to Moscow.

Carrillo turned around to talk to me. After several generalizations about the need to improve the position of Spanish women, he said that although he wasn't always in agreement with my country, he thought we had fine writers.

"Who?"

"Steinbeck. Hemingway. Dos Passos."

"Our classics."

He looked surprised. "That group—you already call them classics?"

"Of the living Spanish writers," I asked, "whom do you admire?"

"Francisco Umbral."

It was my turn to be surprised; Umbral was more of a newspaper column-ist. It must have showed, because he added: "And Cela."

Like his reference to America's greats of the 1930s, his afterthought showed him to be locked into another time. Camilo José Cela is one of the more gifted realistic writers of Carrillo's generation, out of fashion today in a country hell-bent on being modern.

18 October

Miguel Roca is running for re-election to Parliament as a deputy of Conver-gence and Union, the local Catalan new centrist party. Today, I watched him meeting morning shoppers at a food market in a residential area, moving suavely through the crowds.

I asked an older man whom he was going to vote for.

"Roca," he said. "Don't worry—everyone in this market will vote Catalan center. No extremes."

He grinned. "I bet you would never guess it, but in 1936 I was an Anarchist. Can you imagine? With a gun, and everything. But you give a man two duros, and '*Adiós Anarquismo, adiós Comunismo*.' Here, in this market, everybody has his two duros now."

Seville, 21 October

Seville is euphoric. This capital of Andalusia, its population still at a civilized 630,000, remains one of the most perfect cities in the world. It also could be called the home base of Felipe González; many of the current Socialist leaders are from Andalusia. The first telephone call I got was from a Spanish friend: Did I know that Felipe had made the cover of *Time*'s international edition? Even people who don't intend to vote for the Socialists share this local pride in "our boys." In fact, there is a strong conservative vote in Andalusia that is ex-pected to go to the Popular Alliance.

The rumors today were that an unidentified military column had been seen marching on the Zarzuela, the royal palace in Madrid, and that Morocco might try to take advantage of the election period to reclaim Ceuta and Melilla, the Spanish enclaves in North Africa. Both rumors turned out to be false, but the question on everyone's mind is: Can the Socialists assume power without in-terference from the military?

22 October

Much of the campaigning is done after 10 at night: the candidates need to reach the workers after their working day is over, and in Spain everything gets off to a late start. Last night, I drove out to Torre de la Reina, a town of about eight hundred people, with Manolo Manches, a man in his early forties who had

done scientific research at the University of California at Davis and was working in the Socialist campaign. The olive trees smelled good in the night.
Manches told me all the houses in Torre de la Reina look alike because they were
built by concentration-camp labor during the Franco dictatorship.

Several hundred people of all ages were waiting for us inside a small movie
theater. Most of the talking was done by Felipe García Chaparro, who had
started in the early 1970s as an underground organizer of agricultural workers
and who now was running for deputy in the Andalusian local government.

"We are going to do things very slowly," he told his attentive audience. "We
can work no miracles. Remember Portugal: Things started there with a big
flurry, then boom, disaster, and a right-wing government. We don't want to
do things that way. We want to be realistic." He got tremendous applause.

Later, he joined us in a small café. It was warm; our group, including some
families with young children, sat around a few outdoor tables and he remi-
nisced about his clandestine career. He would go to a workers' bar, he said, carrying a copy of the old, long-suppressed Socialist newspaper, *El Socialista*, under his arm. He'd stand at the bar with a glass of wine. A worker would
approach him, then another, asking about the newspaper, and a conversation
would begin.

"I wouldn't want to repeat that experience, and I am glad we are being
elected," he said, "but those nights rushing around, dodging the police—they
were beautiful."

23 October

Five days left before the election. The Socialist campaign workers have been
distributing truckloads of fresh red carnations—along with leaflets—to
crowds in the streets. It must have cost the party a fortune. But, then, in Spain,
election campaigns are largely financed by bank loans, which run in proportion to the party's strength in the previous election.

Last night, one of the Socialist candidates drove me to El Rubio, a depressed
town of four thousand population an hour-and-a-half away. Alfonso Guerra
was to speak. Guerra is the party's top intellectual, its second most powerful
man. Working together, he and González rebelled in the 1980s against the ideologically rigid course set by the party's leadership, in exile in France. Seville
provided them with their power base; a left-wing Madrid faction lost out in the
party congresses after Franco's death. By 1977, the national organization was
under the firm control of the Andalusian team, with the enthusiastic support
of Western European Socialist figures like Olof Palme of Sweden and Willy
Brandt of West Germany.

The Andalusian sunset, orange and pink above the olive trees, made me forget I was following a political campaign. Again, a movie house. Out in the
street, a loudspeaker blared flamenco. Inside, the speechmaking began. One of

Guerra's aides told me to wait for him in his car. His chauffeur and, I assumed, a bodyguard sat in the front seat. A police car provided security.

Alfonso Guerra came out of the theater and worked his way through the welcoming crowd. He got into the car and we drove away, back to Seville.

Casually dressed in a maroon sweater and gray flannel slacks, he had the intense affability of a man about to embark on some historic destiny. We had met once before, in Madrid, at a book party for Gabriel Jackson, the American historian of the Spanish Civil War, and Guerra reminded me of that meeting. Everything seemed heightened to him; he roared with laughter quoting one of the speakers, who had said that everyone in Spain now had to work twenty-four hours a day, "Eight hours, ten hours, twelve—but twenty-four? I couldn't believe what I was hearing!"

He seemed surprised when I said I was related to Gabe—he had been Hal's cousin (Harold died in 1967).

"So two members of your family have to do with Spain?"

"That's right."

Abruptly, he asked me if Americans understood the Socialists' position on NATO. Once in power, he said, the party might not push for Spanish membership in NATO, but that did not mean it was against the Western alliance. The Socialists, according to him, were not for upsetting the natural equilibrium of things. For instance, he said, it was too bad that both the Democratic Center and the Communists seemed to have suffered such a loss of following. "There is a natural, small percentage of workers in this country who vote Communist, and a natural center vote; both need rebuilding," he said.

I asked Guerra: "There is so much good feeling about the Socialists now, but what will happen if in six months or a year you can't deliver the goods, if you can't stop unemployment and inflation?" He paused, and said: "There is so much to be done. What we don't need is ideology. We need a raising of social consciousness. Spanish intellectuals—and I mean the left—are appallingly narcissistic. Selfish. We've had four centuries of a total separation of classes. That feudalism has got to be changed."

Did he mean, I asked, that the first period after Franco's death saw the liberalization of the Spanish upper class, and that now the country as a whole needed democratizing?

"Yes," he said, "that's it, precisely."

We drove into Seville, past the Giralda, the astonishing cathedral that incorporates the Gothic with the earlier Moorish mosque and tower. *Totus tuus*—"All is yours"—said a billboard on the cathedral wall, the Government's welcome to Pope John Paul II, who is to arrive in Spain three days after the elections for a ten-day tour. This will be the first papal visit to Spain. Guerra's enthusiasm spilled over. "To have the beauty of the Giralda and a Socialist Spain—it's extraordinary, isn't it?"

Before leaving Seville, I called on Ricardo Bernal, a leader of the Andalusian branch of the Popular Alliance and a candidate for the Andalusian Senate. Aware that the party frequently has had a bad press as perhaps the most right-wing major political grouping in Europe, the candidate wanted to make clear to me that it was, nonetheless, a democratic party.

Most of my Spanish friends regard the Popular Alliance as a party of the "civilized right." It has been surprising to hear so many average people say they would vote either for the Socialists or the Alliance, they weren't sure which. The reasoning is simple: For personal needs, the Socialists; for tougher policies against crime and juvenile delinquency, the Alliance. People instinctively want some form of insurance. If things get out of hand under the Socialists, they want to retain their option for a more conservative solution.

Yet there are real worries about the Popular Alliance. The party does contain some extreme-rightist elements, and many Spaniards wonder how these former Francoists would behave in a critical situation.

Madrid, 25 October

The Popular Alliance arranged a breakfast meeting at which businessmen and housewives could chat with Alfonso Osorio, one of the party's candidates for Parliament. The women had very concrete questions about the party's position on women's rights in regard to work and divorce. Osorio, a lawyer, responded in legalistic generalities, seeking to assure them that the Popular Alliance was sympathetic to women's needs. It is interesting to see how even the conservative parties in this campaign try to present a "modern" image.

The businessmen did not sound like the ideological right. From their questions, they seemed to be concerned with economic security and preservation of the status quo. What they were afraid of was the threat of terrorism, street crime, an uncontrolled military, and free-floating morals.

One woman asked, "If the Socialists win, is there a danger they would stay in office permanently?"

Osorio resisted the opportunity to hit below the belt. No, he explained, there would be another election in four years' time, and the Socialists could be voted out of office.

Felipe González spoke this evening at the nearby town of Cuenca. He went part of the way in the press bus, and was interviewed by the French state radio. On the question of his relations with President François Mitterrand—rumor has it that they don't get along too well—he said frostily, in good French: "The French have their culture and their Socialism, and we have our culture and our Socialism." He added that the Spanish Socialists did not work in coalition with the Communists—an apparent dig at Mitterrand and his election alliance with the French Communists in 1981. And he chose that moment to ask: "Why shouldn't Spain have close ties to the United States?"

González spoke in a gymnasium filled with about two thousand people. He is at his best with large crowds—his style, calm, reasoned, and intimate. But what impressed me most of all was the candor of the local speakers. The mayor of Cuenca gave an extraordinary speech. He said the Spanish had to give up their "irrationality," their "intolerance." "Do not forget," he said, alluding to an outburst by a Franco army general during the Civil War that has echoed down the years, "it was in this country that we said, to our disgrace, 'Death to the intelligentsia!'" The mayor got tremendous applause.

I asked Miguel Boyer, one of the top Socialists, what the new Government's three main problems would be. His reply: "The economy, the economy, and the economy."

28 October
Election day. I was finally able to get to Fraga. He is a man of contradictions. A former ambassador to London, he affects an admiration of Anglo-Saxon government that hardly jibes with the bellicose manner he has carried over from his Francoist past.

Fraga clearly objects to the Francoist label pinned on him today. He reminded me of the many reformist positions he took under the dictator. "What about everybody else who was *Franquista?*" he asked—a fair question, considering that half of Franco's followers turned up as flaming leftists the morning after his death. What Fraga resents is being singled out as a scapegoat for the country's bad conscience.

Election night. The Socialists held their rally at the resplendent Palace Hotel. When I got there, around midnight, Alfonso Guerra was announcing victory. There were mobs outside the hotel. Inside, I found one of my oldest friends, Carlos Vélez, whose father had been Secretary General of the Socialist trade union UGT. Carlos said his mother, who now lived in Mexico, dreaded the prospect of a Socialist government. "To her generation, the Socialists are a reminder of the Civil War. They can't see that it is all very different now." We went to watch the festivities in the Plaza Mayor.

29 October
The outcome is a political landmark. The Socialists won 202 seats in the 350-seat Parliament, almost doubling their representation. But the biggest gain was scored by the Popular Alliance: up from 9 seats in 1979 to 106, making it the strongest opposition party. Its advance came mainly at the expense of the Democratic Center, which suffered a disaster: from 168 seats down to 12. This leaves Spain without a strong right-of-center force of a clearly liberal stamp. Another fiasco awaited the Communists, who fell from 23 to 4. Adolfo Suá-

rez's Social Democratic Center got only two seats. Convergence and Union, the Catalan new centrist party, went up from 8 to 12, making its leading figure, Miguel Roca, a man to watch. The few remaining seats were divided among various regional parties.

I had lunch with three women friends, all of the Spanish upper class, all well off. One of them had voted for the Socialists, another for the Popular Alliance, and the third for the Democratic Center. They discussed the question of whether they should keep their investments in Spain. The first two said yes; the third said she would wait a few months before deciding whether to move her money to a safer place abroad.

1 November

The taxi driver who drove me to the airport, for my flight back to New York, took a roundabout route to avoid the heavy traffic within Madrid caused by the Pope's presence. "In this country," he said, "we do everything at once."

3.

Gregor Von Rezzori

(Interviewed 1985)

1988

Gregor Von Rezzori, the author of *The Death of My Brother Abel*, called by some the great epochal novel of Hitler Germany, is a complicated man with witty eyes. He was born in 1914 in Bukovina, that part of the Carpathians that became Rumania; he looks like what Saul Bellow would term "a dapper gent." Tall, courtly, casual, and rueful, his accent is nifty Londonesque, befitting a wandering, stateless aristo who grew up in five languages. His family originally were Italian nobles who became Austrian during the spread of the Hapsburg Empire in that part of the world. His themes are the loss of that world, a permanent sense of dislocation, the nature of art, and European history. He refers to *The Death of My Brother Abel* as being the story of Germany's "Ice Age." He was in his early twenties, dabbling in Vienna's café life, hanging out among Jews whom he alternately treated with adoring awe and Middle European aristocratic anti-Semitism, when Hitler invaded Vienna: ". . . that day in 1938 that cut off the first half of my life . . . the total demolition, the annihilation of everything, of all cities, all so-called values . . . the state, the social fictions, and image of mankind."

Von Rezzori is at his most appealing when he speaks of what he lost. "In everything I write, I write of having lost a world. I am a ghost of myself. I come from an empire that vanished nearly a century ago. When I was a child we had to go away from Bukovina, because the Russians came. I miss that past, that place. I've never spent one day of my life without a pang of nostalgia for that part of the world. It sounds ridiculous, but I lost practically everything. I was thrown into a totally new world after this last war. I was in Vienna when I got the news that Bukovina was given to the Russians in 1940. My ambassador said, If you want to die for Mr. Hitler, go back to Rumania, where you will be drafted. So I stayed through the war in Germany—unfortunately the idea I had right after the war to write a book on that experience I have never done. I wanted to give it the highly sarcastic title of *A Sense of Humor*. Of somebody spending those atrocious years in Germany, where the utmost horror was linked to the utmost ridiculous. . . . What do you do when you have nothing left, no hope for the future?" Seated to one side of my desk, he stared mistrustfully at my collection of gadgets—as though my word processor, printer, and cassette machine were alien objects. Then he smiled sardonically: "Of course. You marry and produce children." His first wife was German, his second Jewish, and he presently is married to the Italian art dealer Beatrice Monti. They live most of the time in Tuscany. "I stayed in Germany until the early 1950s, then I went to France, and from there to Italy."

A conservative in dress—which he would consider part of his "style"—he likes to be outrageous in his remarks. In *Memoirs of an Anti-Semite*, he writes in a disarmingly candid way about his youthful anti-Semitism toward the "yiddles." His tone is both disarming and disturbing. Obviously he is telling the truth of the Jews' pre-war position in Central Europe. In his journey of discovery and metamorphosis are many flashes of cruelty—the complexity of this aristo who eventually falls in love with the Yiddish language and Jewish women while, on the same pages, confessing to having thought his Jewish friends' flight from Vienna just before Hitler invaded to be "Jewish fear." His class had meant to confine their anti-Semitism to social prejudice, but because of that they failed to bolt the barn door against *Mein Kampf*: Hitler went beyond the boundaries of their imagined universe. In *Memoirs* his metamorphosis is complete. Minka, who seemed to have been a sort of adopted older Jewish sister during pre-war Vienna days—and the one woman he truly seems to have adored—traces him to Hamburg in 1947. She sends him a ticket to visit her in London. For him she gets suitcases of old clothes, which he will then barter in Hamburg for money. She has cancer. "I went back to my hotel carrying two large suitcases full of old clothes that I hoped to sell in Hamburg like a *handalē*, to make enough money to follow Minka to America. She died there a few months later." And the aristo finally becomes the stateless Jew, wisecracking in Yiddish, *handling* for survival.

Von Rezzori is a chameleon writer who *becomes* his subject. So, as soon as we started to talk about his Germany novel, *Abel*, he sounded less ruefully middle-European and more Teutonic: more metaphysical. He said about Germany right after the war: "There was a perpetual struggle for survival, which meant one lived very near to reality. And there was the possibility, then, of forming a completely new society . . . which was lost." He paused, as though wondering how to describe this Germany to me.

I explained to him that, though American, I had lived large parts of my life in Europe: "Look, I also lived in Germany in 1948. What you were going to eat that day, or how you were not to be cold, or how you were to get from one place to another, that was what life was about."

"Of course," he broke in. "The war was also the 'Ice Age' in Germany, but these were the most bitter years. There was also the weight, that Germany must be punished, whether justly or unjustly. Even as a non-German living there one had the feeling of being punished for collective guilt. The sheer reality of having to live underground, in shacks, in huts, to find your food and a piece of wood or coal made it very similar to pioneer days here in America."

"I have to interrupt you. I think it was a very different situation."

The most troubling part of *Abel* is Von Rezzori's description of the Nuremberg trials as a failure and "claptrap," from which he draws his rather grandiose conclusion that good and evil no longer exist. "You can't criticize the ethics of Nuremberg. But the procedure was wrong. The Hague Convention didn't allow for war crimes. Unfortunately you couldn't judge the Germans according to Anglo-Saxon code; they had their own law. But, by describing it the way I do—I have made it clear that there is no more possibility to judge good and evil because it becomes a matter of quantums. If you kill one person it is murder and horrible, ten is even worse, if you kill fifty thousand, it becomes a statistic."

I wanted Von Rezzori to slow down. I heard myself sounding down-to-earth, very American, uncomplicated, and not clever. "I don't know that I follow you on that. Your description of those trials in *Abel* puzzled me."

Von Rezzori's head went back, he laughed like a gleeful small boy. "Everybody got hooked on that."

"Well, it seems to me that you are mixing many things in there. Now, let's take the idea that the Nuremberg trials possibly may have been inadequate. All right. But that doesn't have to have anything to do with the existence of good and evil." I continued rather flatly, "It just means that the Nuremberg trials were inadequate."

"But this is not *my* opinion. It is the opinion of the narrator of Book One. In Book Two you will find out that it is more Schwab's [a character in *Abel*] papers than the narrator's. In the end you'll find out that the narrator doesn't exist. He is Schwab's invention; through him he writes his autobiography."

I felt I was listening to a stylistic, metaphysical, human roller coaster. "As an author, as yourself, though, do you feel that there is good and evil, and that one has the right to judge?"

"Absolutely. Mind you, there is also the possibility that a character, when he thinks, and even when he speaks, expresses himself in a totally different way than how he really lives and acts."

"But the reason that people are, as you say, 'hooked on this point' is that you are dealing with a major event of the twentieth century."

"What? The Nuremberg trials?"

"No. The whole thing with Germany. What went on *before* the trial."

"The war."

"Yes, the war."

Von Rezzori said, "I think, for America, for changing attitudes in America, the Vietnam war was much more important, but never mind."

"Vietnam was a more traditional war, it was a *war*."

"But then there is the question of good and evil. What is traditional?"

"Well," I said, "do you make a distinction between genocide and war? Perhaps you don't."

"Yes and no."

"What do you think of Claude Lanzmann's distinction?" I asked. "Have you seen *Shoah*?"

"No, I haven't. There might be one reason for killing another person, and only one—self-defense. I'm afraid that self-defense couldn't be applied to Vietnam."

"But you are the one who told me that for *you* the central fact was Germany—so there is no reason for us, today, to be discussing Vietnam."

"*You* said that fighting Nazis was one of the main events in American history."

"No," I answered. "I said that that period in Germany and that genocide was a major fact of the twentieth century."

Then Von Rezzori pulled back, as he did so often during the interview—torn between delight at uttering the outrageous and self-censorship when he went beyond the limits. More thoughtfully he added, "There might also be made a distinction between something that happens in Asia and something that happened in the core of European culture. I wish that I would never be misunderstood: genocide, and the murder of the Jews, was a crime beyond words. The Germans have suppressed that time—between the end of the war and the currency reform—just as much as they have suppressed the memory of what happened before. And Nazi crimes. But it is a simple fact that you can't conceive that crimes of that dimension could be committed. Let me say something absolutely horrible. That for most people it has become what the French call a *façon de parler*. Not really felt. I make the narrator experience the killing of one man in a displaced persons' train. Because to imagine six million Jews being killed is too abstract."

"Okay . . . but then we get to the real history of your book—and after all, you are a witness to that history, and an intelligent witness. You also have an advantage in that you are not Jewish and you are not German. You are at one remove. Though we have referred to the genocide of the Jews, others also were killed in the gas chambers. So let us say we are discussing the invention of a methodical means of extermination that included the Jews, but wasn't necessarily meant to end there. The Nazis created a machine that would have just gone on finding new groups of people to exterminate. Again, we are not referring exclusively to what happened between Germans and Jews. No, we are referring to extermination camps. You have made that a point in your book. And yet, in the end, you seem to give a sort of cosmological shrug. I don't know whether that was your intention."

"Yes, it was my intention, mind you. And particularly because in trying to sketch the portrait of a narrator, I was also trying to give a picture of his despair. If you look backwards from 1968 to 1919, those fifty years of European history, which is the end of Europe from a certain point of view, of a form of Europe, you come to the conclusion that if form doesn't count, well then, evil doesn't exist any longer."

"Why?"

"Because form is a result of the choice between good and evil. When, as a European, you look back over those fifty years, with all you know about good and evil, you must realize that it didn't exist. It exists as a perpetual dream, not as a reality."

Von Rezzori's flow of words, his nonchalant British pronunciation, was so graceful, it would take me a moment to figure out that I didn't agree with what he was espousing. "I don't see that. You have said that without form there is no good and evil. Yet you would probably say that the extermination camps were evil."

"But of course."

"What had they to do with form, or lack of form?"

"I mean, form is also a way of living, isn't it?"

By this time I felt we were in a game of intellectual chess; I felt he was just curious to see how I would pick up on his phrases. In self-defense I went off on my own tack. "Sometimes America has done things that are evil, wouldn't you agree?"

"Absolutely," Von Rezzori smiled. "Think of the Indians."

"All right. But we did it without form—does that mean we were innocent?"

"No-o-o, yes. . . . But it was not without form." Von Rezzori is a man who thinks quickly. I watched the light in his eyes as he concocted an explanation. "Yes, it was the form of the white man's way of thinking based on Christian ideas . . . no, not of Christian ideas, but ideas of the Church. A genocide for religious reasons, for instance."

"In *Abel* you repeatedly accuse the French of having too much form. Do you believe they have good and evil as a result of too much form?"

"They *had* it."

"Do you think that the French, who have been more allied to form, have more good and evil, more morality than a country with less form? I don't see it."

"Well, this is now stretching a metaphor a bit far. What I said about French form is that it is fossilized. And it's not only French, it's a fossilized European way of thinking, based not only on Christian ideas but on the Enlightenment and the French Revolution. I will say not for myself, but for my narrator—who has read his Nietzsche—that, in the end, moral and ethical qualities are, at their utmost, highly aesthetic."

I rummaged around in my head. Nietzsche can be served up to account for almost any point of view. So I steamed forth with what came to mind: "Yes, but Nietzsche cautioned that his ideas should only be read by the French, who, unlike the Germans, would not misapply them. Your narrator is not French, therefore he would not properly qualify as a person who could apply Nietzsche according to Nietzsche."

"For goodness' sake!" He positively jumped at hearing his Nietzsche dragged in as if from some other planet. "If people quote from one philosopher, it doesn't prevent them from picking up ideas from another philosopher and making them rather personal. You pick up things that apply to yourself. You can't just follow one line . . . and say, I am completely Hegelian, or completely Nietzschean."

"Yes, but you want it both ways. You want to be cosmological when you want to be—but when I jump over into the metaphysical, you say now, here here, you are going too far. You're very brilliant at—"

"Changing positions?" Von Rezzori seemed to be suddenly enjoying his cold cup of coffee; he was laughing and no longer eyeing the cassette machine as though it were his mortal enemy.

"I admire in your writing the way, with a quick sleight of hand, you switch mirrors. I was merely trying to ground you a little."

"You want me to confess?"

"I am bothered at how your literary shrug towards good and evil can be interpreted."

"May I say something in parentheses? One of the reasons modern theater is so utterly boring . . . is that it never discusses established moral values. Let me give an exaggerated example: Let us take a play which discussed the point of view of a Nazi, who considers genocide justified, and who doesn't on the stage say that yes yes, we know it's evil. . . . No, let me jump back just for a split second to my second volume, which will follow *The Death of My Brother Abel.* Olendorf was a Nazi who discussed Nazism inside the Nazi party, and for matters of obedience still killed ninety thousand people. And there was an extraordinary dialogue between him and the American judge, who became interested in him almost like a scientist. He asked Olendorf: If the Führer asked you to kill your mother, would you have done it? And Olendorf said, yes. This is a phenomenon which is unheard of in our time. You can't just skip over it by saying, well, he is the personification of evil. You have to discuss it within yourself. Perhaps that means inviting the devil for a tango. Just dare it."

"You are a very different writer from Grass," I said, "but still there is that thing in your writing and his where one suddenly comes up against 'Mother Nature.' The force of Mother Nature. I don't understand that formulation as an explanation for what went wrong in Germany."

"My dear, you are an American and you are embedded in a world of established values. But when you come out of a world in which every bloody value was mired, and put into the mud and destroyed and broken, you have to find your way out of the rubble. You were completely formed in America. No— you said you lived in Germany in '48, then you must have noticed what was going on around you."

"Of course, and I have written about what I experienced then. Also I think what formed me was very complicated. But I don't think that is part of this dialogue. I think it's too simple for you to say I am an American. I mean, I wouldn't dream of saying you are just a Bessarabian."

"No, no, my dear, now please don't misunderstand me. You are lucky enough to have been a human being brought up in a world of established values. Sometimes, I must say, values are so well established that one doesn't realize they are resting on rather unsafe ground."

"Your book—*Abel*—is brilliant. It does not elude me, but somewhere in it, I feel an abyss."

"In its conclusions? You see, there is another theme in this book, which puts an emphasis on things happening collectively. Influences on us which we can't control, which we aren't even aware of. The narrator reflects on the secret of style, which comes close to the secret of form. Handwriting in the nineteenth century has the same characteristics all over the world. What makes ideas spring up at the same time? Mother Nature not only devours, she creates funny things. The simple fact that a people can get into a collective nightmare by killing millions of others, and then wake up a day after as if out of a dream, goes beyond all philosophical discussion about what is good and what is evil. I didn't pick the Nuremberg trials at random. It is a neuralgic point. I am grateful for any kind of contradiction. I want this book to be discussed."

The light outside my study window was changing—as though everything had been said on that subject. We turned to the style of *Abel*: huge, sprawling, dominated by the narrator's rasping invective. For a moment the narrator's voice melded with Von Rezzori as he berated the French and their modern novels. Then, in the jesting style of a Viennese café writer, mocking yet serious, he leaned forward and asked me: "Tell me. Do you think it megalomaniacal of me to believe that in some way this book is a form in itself? That I have invented a new form?"

I thought about it. "In *Abel* you answered that question yourself. You said whenever a man thinks he has come upon a brilliant idea, he can be sure ten others are thinking the exact same thought."

"Exactly. Well there you are."

"With your own reply."

He abruptly got up to leave, with the sudden abruptness of a person who feels he is disappearing—exuding the melancholy of a man who has been telling his readers for over six hundred pages that the world as he knew it was over before they were born.

VI.

France,
Its Occupation,
and the Barbie Trial

Paul Nizan

1973

There are those rare novels—Henry Roth's *Call It Sleep* is one—for which the label of masterpiece always seems slightly beside the point. Both *Antoine Bloyé* and *Call It Sleep* suffered the similar fate of being lost literary classics that had to wait a generation or so after their publication before being restored to their rightful literary place. *Antoine Bloyé*, although of an entirely different literary tradition than *Call It Sleep*, has the same obsessive, wounding power.

Paul Nizan was Jean-Paul Sartre's closest friend when they were students together, first at their lycée and later the École Normale in Paris. During Nizan's short life he wrote eight books—some novels, some polemics—which made of him a dazzling young literary star of the French Communist party before he broke with it in 1939 over the Hitler–Stalin Pact. As foreign correspondent for *Ce Soir*, Nizan was in touch with the top echelons in the Union of Soviet Socialist Republics and the French Communist party. He recognized that the French Communist party's optimism concerning the Pact was a piece of tunnel-visioned lunacy—France, the party, and French workers were going to be crushed by the Germans. Nizan tried to persuade the party to alter its position and failed. In the heated days of 1939 the party condemned Nizan as a traitor, and after the war they did much to annihilate his literary reputation. In 1940, at the age of 35, Nizan was killed at Dunkirk while acting as an interpreter for the British. According to Sartre, a British soldier buried Nizan's body at Dunkirk along with his own written answer to the Communist party, his personal diaries, and his last novel, *La Soirée à Somosierra*. Although the British made some attempt to inform Nizan's widow of the whereabouts of Nizan's grave after the war, it could not be located.

Written when Paul Nizan was 29, *Antoine Bloyé* is his one truly great novel, and was considered as such when it appeared in France in 1933. Much has been made of *Antoine Bloyé*, being the only Marxist novel to rise to the level of literature. Nizan was, of course, a Marxist and he did use his Marxist intelligence—although, thank God, never the jargon—to show the economic and emotional cost of the life of Antoine Bloyé, a working-class railwayman who made the painful rise to become a railway functionary and a member of the petite-bourgeoisie. But the power of Nizan's novel is pre-Marxist, for he had two torturing obsessions in his life: One was his father; the other was France. *Antoine Bloyé* is Nizan's lyrical eulogy to both.

Nizan's true subject in this novel is his own rage and fear, as a young man, at bearing witness to his adored father's premature emotional disintegration; *Antoine Bloyé* is the story of Nizan's own father. A lesser novelist might have written the novel from the more direct and obvious point of view of a young man's anguish at his father's life and death. But Nizan wrote this novel at that marvelous moment in a novelist's life when he has all the feelings and rage of childhood and all the techniques of a mature novelist to control them; and it is that tension between child and novelist which gives the novel its power—not Nizan's Marxist framework. By making Antoine Bloyé the central character, rather than Bloyé's son, all Nizan's fury at the society that contributed to the attrition of the character's flesh, soul, and senses is sublimated into creating the world of Antoine Bloyé. His rage is held in perfect control because he knew his literary aesthetics. The tone is cold, precise Flaubert. But the child in Nizan helps the novelist Nizan win the battle. Beneath the lyrical but subdued prose we are aware of a child's conviction that the only universe which exists is the universe of Bloyé—Nizan's father—and that Bloyé's death is a total death. The fate of the young intellectual son is irrelevant. Nizan knew we are doomed by our father's generation; our contemporaries are of less consequence.

In that respect he was very different from his friend Sartre, who suffered no such obsessions. Sartre was queasy at being a bourgeois, while Nizan suffered from being a hybrid: working-class father, Catholic petit-bourgeois mother, and himself a talented bourgeois intellectual. Certainly during their lycée and École Normale days Sartre and Nizan were very close. They studied philosophy together, outranked the other students, and playfully thought of themselves as young intellectual supermen who would divide the world between them. They often thought of themselves as one person and at the start of their literary careers were often taken for one another—though at the time it was Nizan who was well in the lead, and it seems to have been Nizan who brought news of the world to Sartre, rather than the other way around.

Modernism, theories of negativism as a literary technique, André Breton, Marxism, experiments in film—all were grist for the mill. Nizan shocked Sartre by wanting to abandon the world for film making. Although Nizan's name is permanently linked with Sartre's—Sartre, in his famous introductory essay to the 1960 French edition of Nizan's 1931 work, *Aden, Arabie*, has willed it so (always claiming Nizan as the better writer of the two)—in sensibility Nizan is not at all like Sartre. He comes much closer to Jean Vigo (whose own father was an Anarchist who was killed in prison), who was filming *Zéro de Conduite* and *L'Atalante* around the time *Antoine Bloyé* was published. Both Vigo and Nizan were more precise, more personally involved in their criticism of prewar France than was the more metaphysical Sartre.

In the first marvelous scene of this novel, Nizan renders the exact cost, smell, and formality of disposing of the body of the 63-year-old corpse of Antoine Bloyé. The nuns to the widow: " 'Madame, all I ask of you is to put his pants on. . . .' 'What an outstanding show of modesty.' Ann commented later: 'How prudish these nuns are. After all, a dead man is no longer a man. . . .' "

After this funeral prologue Nizan gives us an exact accounting of Bloyé's life. The film director John Grierson once said of Vigo's *L'Atalante* that he could find his way around that barge blind-drunk on a wet night. After reading *Antoine Bloyé*, you could, in the same state, find your way around the French railway system of two decades before and after the turn of the century. We learn exactly how a French workman rises to the ranks of minor managerialdom. We discover how a railway man amuses himself, how he educates himself to his craft, and we see Bloyé's slow apprenticeship into the niceties of lower-middle-class existence through his sexually stifling marriage to the daughter of a railway official. Bloyé becomes an old man young. His sexuality is crushed, he is alienated from his own class, his companions, and his family. When the industry changes, Bloyé is kicked down; emotionally he disintegrates, he makes a few feeble attempts to revive his emotions by seeing old companions and wistfully entering a bordello; finally he dies of a coronary. The novel ends abruptly. "Ann called him, she placed a mirror to his lips. She pierced the lobe of his ear with her scissors: no blood flowed."

Sartre's essay discusses Nizan's relation to his father brilliantly. As he points out, Nizan *becomes* his father in this novel (Bloyé's own son is a bleak shadow)—when Bloyé dies, the son as a character in the novel virtually disappears. Indeed, there is not the slightest suggestion in the novel that Bloyé's life might be redeemed in any way by *having* a son. Thus the strangely abrupt ending and—after Bloyé's death—oblivion. Nizan was clearly haunted by his identification with his father. During Nizan's adolescence Nizan's father made several semi-suicidal attempts, as described in the novel. Paul Nizan himself then made a more drastic attempt at suicide by driving his car into a ditch after his return to France in 1930 from his youthful flight to Arabia.

When, in the same essay, Sartre writes meta-history about French youth, Nizan, himself, and the French Communist party, he is maddening. The French Communist party did indeed wage a hate campaign against Nizan after the war. Sartre, in 1960, claims Communist perfidy as the reason Nizan did not reach the attention of the young after World War II. Yet France was not then culturally monolithic. Most of the influential reviews and presses were in the hands of the nonconformist left. Sartre simply had more clout among the "young" than the babblings of the French Communist party. If he had wanted to publish or write about Nizan, he could have done so. The real reason Nizan was eclipsed was that the French were then on a binge of literary abstraction, and the king of it all was Sartre himself. Nobody needed a pessimistic writer who said France was putrid and rotten to the core, and who then went ahead and died for the bankrupt country he inveighed against.

Klaus Barbie and the Conscience of the Literati

1986

World War II continues to haunt the French. Unprepared, the French military capitulated almost immediately to Germany, and France was the only major European power to be occupied. The coming trial in Lyons of Klaus Barbie, the head of the Gestapo in that city, will resurrect France's deepest trauma: its noble and ignoble history during the German occupation.

The Barbie affair, in particular the accusation that in 1943 he tortured and murdered Jean Moulin, the head of the French Resistance, has threatened to destroy the myth of the Resistance because of the claim that Moulin was betrayed by his fellows.

The public prosecutor of a French court ruled that three war crimes against Resistance fighters allegedly committed by Barbie fell into the category of crimes against humanity, which carry no statute of limitations. As a result, Barbie will be charged with those crimes, in addition to crimes against Jews: the deportation to death camps of almost eight hundred people, most of them Jews. The court-broadened definition of crimes against humanity to include crimes committed against members of the Resistance opens the possibility, alarming to some French, that former collaborators, who had considered themselves safe, could now be tried.

All this has raised painful questions for French writers concerning their roles during the occupation. Since I was planning to cover the trial, I wanted to talk to French writers and intellectuals about it.

Jerome Lindon, Samuel Beckett's publisher at Les Editions de Minuit, is among those who oppose trying Barbie, whose lawyer, Jacques Vergès, Lindon told me recently, "will mix in all sorts of things that have nothing to do with Barbie. He will bring up Algeria, and say that as the French did thus and so there, they've no right to try Barbie. I'd be content to see him die in prison."

Claude Lanzmann agrees. Though known here for the film *Shoah*, a nine-and-a-half-hour oral history of the Holocaust, he has been for many years an editor and a member of the inner circle of *Les Temps Modernes*, the literary-cultural monthly magazine founded by Jean-Paul Sartre after the liberation of France in 1944. He told me that, in trying Barbie, "the special significance of the deportation of the Jews will get drowned out by Vergès's tactics of putting France on trial. The notion that 'all of France was in the Resistance' originally came about when the Resistance had no presence in France, and needed to legitimize itself"—during the liberation, when it was important for the French to delegitimize the Vichy Government. "Of course," he added, "that was not true—but those who maintain 'there was no Resistance' are completely crazy. After 1942 it was considerable. What you had between the Pétainists [those who supported Marshal Pétain and Vichy collaboration during the war] and non-Pétainists was an undeclared civil war. Remember, two-thirds of French Jews survived. My brother, sister, and I were saved by a French family in the country." Lanzmann considers the *nouveau roman* the moral opposite of the aesthetics of *Shoah*. "I don't like a plethora of babbling images. It is inauthentic."

There is a profound split in consciousness between Sartre's generation—*Les Temps Modernes*, *L'Esprit*, Camus, Raymond Aron—who were publishing by the end of the occupation, and the practitioners of the *nouveau roman*, who came forth a decade later, in 1954, just after France's defeat in Dien Bien Phu. A new myth which needs a little sorting out is that France felt so humiliated about her role during World War II that she immediately sank into total silence and evasion about those years. True and not true. The French cinema, unlike the Italian, never dealt with the occupation until the late sixties, when Ophuls made *The Sorrow and the Pity*. But the film industry shouldn't be confused with what was going on among French writers. Until the mid-fifties they were obsessed by the war. Much of the best material on it was published immediately after, before the amnesty laws of the mid-fifties made it impossible to write about collaborationists who had been tried and later amnestied.

Specifically, the French didn't want to be reminded of the savage reprisals which took place directly after the liberation, and the immediate catch-as-catch-can trials which resulted in some overly rapid executions (such as of Robert Brasillach). But until the early 1950s they saw themselves as victims of the Germans; the important Oradour trial of the French Gestapo didn't take place until 1953. It was *after* the humiliation of the French military debacle in Indochina that the country embarked on a course of de Gaullist grandeur, anti-Americanism, and historic amnesia. Sartre, in his 1960s essay about his boyhood friend Paul Nizan, fretfully noted the evasiveness of a presumed leftwing literary generation which avoided all societal and historic reference: "After five years their future was beginning to thaw. They had the ingenuous hope of renewing literature with despair, of experiencing the distaste of long trips around the world, of the unbearable boredom of earning money. . . . Nizan had nothing to say to them. He spoke little about man's condition, a great deal about social matters. . . . He was an intimate of terror and anger as opposed to the languors of despair. The Cold War went straight to the heart of this generation of dancers and vassals. The rest of us, the old ones, merely lost a few feathers and all our virtues."

The *nouveau roman* group solidified its gains during the mid-fifties; its antihistoric stance and rarefied prose style perfectly suited France's new mood of grandiosity and amnesia. Alain Robbe-Grillet, one of its most celebrated practitioners, has recently written an oddly jolly memoir, *Le Miroir Qui Revient* (*The Recurring Mirror*), about his pro-Pétainist, Anglophobic, anti-Semitic family. Sandwiched between lyrical references to his childhood love of kings and Kipling and his admiration for Roland Barthes is a thoughtful definition of his parents. They believed that Jews threatened to destroy the old Europe and create social and political disorder. The Nazis, for them, represented order, decency, and a chance for a united Europe. Though Robbe-Grillet insists his parents never would have condoned the death camps, he also says that until their death, in the 1970s, they believed the Holocaust was merely propaganda invented by the Allies to justify their victory.

Since Robbe-Grillet waited forty years to tell this story, he may be nervous about his revelations. During the two occasions we talked, once in his Manhattan apartment and once in mine, he asked me not to record our conversations. No matter—it is all in his book.

Robbe-Grillet's classmates nicknamed him "K" for *Kollaborateur*—for his willingness to join *Service du Travail Obligatoire* (STO), the French labor force that the Vichy Government sent to work in German war factories. He recalls that before he was shipped off to Germany, the STO gave him a pair of new boots, a can of sardines, and a ticket to hear Edith Piaf sing. Though he saw an ominous sign in the factory where he worked ("You are a number and that number is zero") and a companion told him of the existence of the death camps, his general impression was that he was in a country of orderly adults and pretty blond children—until 1945, after the liberation and after news of the gas chambers became widespread, when his faith in the idea of political order collapsed.

Robbe-Grillet's recollection of the occupation is that almost everyone was pro-Pétainist. According to this logic, no one is at fault; and it is precisely this air of normality he bestows on people who were pro-Nazi that is disturbing. Robbe-Grillet tones down the horror of Hitler. He discusses his postwar disillusionment with the abstract idea of political order, which was what Hitler represented to him, but he makes no mention of confronting his parents about their unrepentant admiration of Hitler. Nor does he tell us what happened to him and his family after the liberation. Instead, he converted his last year at Maschinenfabrik-Augsburg-Nuremberg into *L'Année dernière à Marienbad*. He likes to play with word games in which people are manipulated like objects.

Robbe-Grillet also likes to manipulate puns in a blindman's buff with his public. In a recent edition of *Le Monde* the critic Bertrand Poirot-Delpech pointed out that Robbe-Grillet was the mysterious "Jean Berg," author of *L'Image*, which was published by Les Editions de Minuit two years after *L'Histoire d'O* as a similar erotic-porno tale and dedicated to its presumed author, "Pauline Reage." Poirot-Delpech said, "It doesn't take much to conclude that 'Jeanne' (Berg) is Catherine, wife of the author of *L'Image* . . . when one knows Robbe-Grillet's predilection for literary hide-and-seek."

Poirot-Delpech was referring to *Cérémonies de femmes* by "Jeanne Berg," which had just been published by Grasset. The difference between *L'Histoire d'O* and *Cérémonies de femmes* is that the former was presented to the public as a novel, and the latter as an actual account of a sado-masochistic whipping club in Paris of which Jeanne Berg was the dominatrice/owner. *Liberation* ran lurid photo stories portraying a pinioned black "slave," purportedly willing to accept death if it pleased his white mistress, with a coyly semi-masked author/dominatrice holding the appropriate torture items, entitled: "Black slave with masked lady of *L'Apostrophe*." 1940s Nazi racist sadism had been rehabilitated and honed into 1980s chic racist decadence. What was awful about the *Apostrophe* program was that the "masked Jeanne Berg" was only masked to the noncognoscenti, the general French public; it is the worst kind of French intellectual rottenness. Françoise Sagan, who was on the same program, refused to join in. She frostily pointed out that she wrote about erotic love, another subject entirely.

Ironically, at the same time Robbe-Grillet was looking forward to his sojourn in Germany, Claude Simon was escaping a prisoner-of-war camp in Saxony. Simon, an independent leftist sympathetic to the Spanish Republic, spent time in Barcelona at the beginning of the Spanish Civil War. He remained opposed to Gen. Francisco Franco until the dictator's death, in 1975, and has always been much admired by both the French and the Spanish for his above-reproach moral and political positions; this may have been a factor in his winning last year's Nobel Prize in Literature. Perhaps because Simon has nothing in his past to conceal, his novels have been more overtly autobiographical than those of other *nouveau roman* writers.

At the PEN Congress in New York last winter, Simon talked to me about *The Flanders Road*, considered by critics to be his masterpiece: "It is what happened to me in the war—the literary inventions of the nineteenth century bore me. Reality, autobiography, is what it is about. In 1940 [he was 26], I was mobilized in Collioure. I took a train and two days later I was in the cavalry, in the rain. On May 10, we crossed the Meuse River on horseback and entered Belgium. On the 14th, Hitler attacked. We were in a pine forest along the frontier. We were surrounded by German tanks and planes. It was a massacre. All that remained of our regiment was a colonel, a lieutenant, two troopers, and myself. Then the colonel and the lieutenant were killed by a sniper—in the end there was just one other man and myself." Simon described the surreal images of frightened horses surrounded by the machines of modern warfare. "Can you imagine?" he said. "The French still believed they could win a war with the cavalry." He added that when he was in Stockholm to receive the Nobel Prize, he "didn't like the Swedish press referring to *The Flanders Road* as a war novel. It is about many things. Erotic experiences, women, people, flowers. My novels are not political."

The bits and pieces of the world I remember having seen in 1948 are evoked in *The War: A Memoir* by Marguerite Duras. The book is about the period just before and after the liberation. Duras, a Communist when she was a member of the Resistance, saved the life of President François Mitterrand, then a Resistance leader, tortured members of the Gestapo herself, and was responsible for the death of a Gestapo agent who befriended her during the occupation. Though she wrote the memoir in the 1940s, she also waited forty years to publish it. Her description of trying not to overfeed her emaciated husband, returned from a concentration camp, is shattering.

It is now easier for French writers to write more overtly about the occupation because their country is now stressing reconciliation, forgiveness for whatever wrongs were done then, and these confessional books foster a national catharsis.

A striking example of the change in the French view of what is acceptable is the sudden boom in the popularity of Louis-Ferdinand Céline. Though he was always acknowledged as a literary genius, until recently his raving anti-Semitism was an embarrassment to the French. Now, for the first time since

World War II, the prestige of Céline is equal to that of the contemporary he most hated—Sartre.

In this rehabilitation, a distinction is made between Céline the fascist and Céline the liberator of the French language. *L'Evénement du jeudi* points out that a recent biography by François Gibault whitewashes Céline, that it extols him for his prescient remarks concerning the dangers of world communism while neglecting to say that he also ranted against the "dangers" of Jews and Freemasons. Philippe Sollers, a novelist and the editor of the dominant intellectual magazine of the sixties generation, *Tel Quel*, now reborn as *L'Infini*, considers the present approach to Céline inadequate. In Paris recently, he said that "though Céline is a great genius, his widow's refusal to let anyone see his inflammatory 1930s anti-Semitic pamphlets is censorship." Sollers, who was young during the war, believes that the trial of Klaus Barbie will have tragic results, because it will reawaken old conflicts between rival groups in the Resistance, chiefly the Gaullists and the Communists.

Herbert R. Lottman—who lives in Paris and who examined the role of writers during the occupation in *The Left Bank*, and whose new book, *The Purge*, is about the punishment of collaborators in France after the war—said to me that another problem is that there are still former collaborationists holding high government positions. "A real roadblock for historians writing about that period is that the French government has an odd amnesty law. This means that if a person was sanitized—pardoned—you can no longer mention in print that he was sentenced for collaborating. Many French don't know that people got sanitized."

A younger generation, those who were children or adolescents during the war, is searching out the past in highly accessible novels or memoirs; the abstruseness and emphasis on linguistic games associated with the *nouveau roman* are out of date. In his novels—*Les Boulevards de Ceinture* (*The Avenues of the Outer Belt*) and *De Si Braves Garçons* (*What Great Guys*)—Patrick Modiano pursues the fate of his Jewish family; and in his novel, *Cat's Grin*, the French publisher François Maspero, whose brother was in the Resistance and whose family was then sent by the Germans to concentration camps, describes his anguish at being too young to join the underground.

How strange, as this century draws to a close, with the Dreyfus affair still being re-examined (as witnessed by the recent popularity of *The Affair: The Case of Alfred Dreyfus* by Jean-Denis Bredin), that France has defined as its two great novelists such polar opposites: Marcel Proust, the passionate defender of Dreyfus whose *Remembrance of Things Past* ends with World War I, and Céline, the obsessed anti-Semite whose *Journey to the End of Night* starts at the point Proust stops. If excessive delaying tactics prevent Barbie from being tried, that fact, like the Dreyfus case, will become an important piece of French history.

Klaus Barbie and the Conscience of the Literati

Though it was not so long ago that many literati felt that Jewish writers harmed the purity of French culture, ironically, in the second half of this century, the fate of the Jews has become intermingled with the fate of France as it is portrayed in French literature in a way I would not have dreamed possible when I first arrived there, after those dark times that seemed like the end of the world.

Lyons

1987

On a gray wet day, the nineteenth of May, the week after Barbie refused to appear in court, the case, for me, suddenly took shape. The media rush was over. Barbie's brief appearance was unsatisfactory. In his glass box all that could be truly noted was that indeed he does have the remote intent stare, so remarked upon later by the witnesses, that one might associate with a somewhat disintegrated personality. To many in a younger generation, whose image is of young and dashingly uniformed Nazis, he seemed, confusingly, to resemble "a grandpa." The Palais de Justice had begun to empty. Pierre Truche had called in two German experts in Nazi crimes—Alfred Streim, Director of the Nazi Documentation Center in Ludwigsburg, and Rodolph Holfort—to establish that Barbie willfully had acted on his own initiative in rounding up the 43 Jewish children from their refuge in Izieu, and to confirm that the telex describing their roundup for Drancy had been sent by him. In the Lyons trial the Final Solution—the genocide of the Jews and other "sub-human" groups—has been defined as starting the moment that Jews (the 43 children of Izieu and 86 Jews from the Jewish headquarters at rue Sainte-Catherine) were rounded up. Barbie also has been charged with the deportation to Auschwitz and other camps of over three hundred Jewish prisoners from the "Jewish barracks" at Montluc prison. During pre-trial, the court ruled to widen the definition of crimes against humanity to include another three hundred prisoners—Resistance members who survived the torture process at Montluc prison and who were deported with the Jews on the last prison train from Lyons to Auschwitz on August 11, 1944.

Streim and Holfort are in their early fifties; their stance is direct, they are not afraid to pause over questions. Fassbinder would have cast either of them as the uncompromising professor, or the head of an enlightened political magazine in postwar Germany. Streim contended that when Barbie placed the children on the train to Drancy, their murder had begun. Drancy survivors testified that the debased conditions at the detention center were part of the planned beginning of a system of physical deprivation and intentional personal humiliation necessary to the Final Solution. The train ride to Auschwitz, Streim emphasized, *continued* the murder. Food, water, heat, and air were deliberately withheld: when Czechs tried to throw provisions into the trains, the guards threw the food back. The deportees traveled with the corpses of those who died en route. Barbie had to know that the children, due to their ages, had to have either died or been in a weakened condition by the time of their arrival at Auschwitz.

Holfort informed the court that Heydrich, on January 20, 1942, at the Wannsee Conference, made the plans for the Final Solution explicit, though they had been decided well before that. Since the language for the Final Solution was coded, he argued—there is no record of a document signed by Hitler ordering the extermination of the Jews—the SS argument that "they were only following orders" is spurious: the only men who understood these orders were to be carried out were those who had been clued-in as to what the coded initials of the various telegrams meant. Therefore, they knew of the Final Solution. They had either been at Wannsee or the information had been relayed verbally to them. Streim and Holfort described the meaning of "*Nacht und Nebel*"— Night and Fog. Those judged able to work were Fog; those judged not able— and this included the children from Izieu—immediately were sent to be gassed. That was Night.

"Was it certain that Barbie knew this coded language?" Truche asked.

Holfort said yes. In Germany they now had in their files Danneker's personal diary which indicated an extensive knowledge of the Final Solution. "Danneker headed the anti-Jewish section of the Paris Gestapo—Barbie's position in Lyons was on the same level."

Streim said: "The thesis maintained by those accused in Nuremberg that they were following the Führer's orders, and which had some credibility until 1960, has been discarded by those who have continued to investigate Nazi records. We have compiled many instances of SS who refused to carry out this kind of order. Their only punishment was that they were sent to the Eastern Front. Not a single SS was killed for disobedience." Streim described the principles of National-Socialist doctrine. "It was the destruction of all life that they considered without worth. Not only the mentally ill or fragile, but the destruction of all races they deemed inferior. The theory of the supremacy of the Aryan race meant that all non-Aryans had to be either exterminated or slaves. Barbie remained a fervent supporter of this doctrine. In 1969 we heard about a German in La Paz who boasted of being a Nazi, and, when drunk, said he had been sentenced to death in absentia by the French. At first we thought it was Danneker; then we found out it was Klaus Barbie."

Streim and Holfort outlined the structure of the SS, which by 1936, under

Himmler, had maneuvered itself into a position outside of German law. The destruction of the Jews was by then an integral part of its philosophy. Streim showed how the SS manipulated propaganda to spread the idea that Germany had to defend itself in a war being waged against it by Jews, portrayed as a world power. In a trial tense for the multitude of subagendas never explicitly stated but always there, and that included the defense attorney Jacques Vergès's extremist anti-Israel position, Pierre Truche's question to the Germans had a special resonance: "And did those ideas have any basis in fact?"

"No," one of the two replied: "There was no basis in fact that the Jews were a world power, or a power, or had declared war on Germany."

Emphasizing always the role of choice, Streim dissected Barbie's career in the SS. One could choose to join or not join it. Once in it, men also made choices. One could belong to the Waffen-SS—army—or join the extermination-camp forces. There was always some leeway. Obviously no one in Germany had ever heard of a specific Jewish children's shelter in Izieu, nor was the remote mountain village known to the Paris Gestapo who, by then, had other problems—Germany was losing the war. Streim and Holfort also gave a detailed explanation, based on records of the Nazi system of hierarchy and of coding telegrams, confirming that the telex to Paris reporting the roundup of the children of Izieu for deportation and signed by Barbie had to have been personally transmitted by him. According to them, the contention of Barbie's lawyer, Vergès, that the telex could have been sent by an underling, was not possible. They cited examples proving this wouldn't have conformed with Gestapo regulations concerning important communications involving the Final Solution.

Vergès, despite his pre-trial reputation for brilliance, couldn't flap Holfort and Streim: his style depended on rapid, rapier flashes, a knowledge of his opposition's weak points, and rolling French rhetoric. His "disruptive tactics" needed as a foil the quick rhythms of Paris entwined with eternal left-wing guilt; right before Lyons he had unnerved the capital with his theatrical, albeit unsuccessful, defense of the Arab terrorist Abdallah. His sarcastic *bon mots* took too long to translate into German. Vergès taunted Holfort: "Did the great German anti-Nazi experts know that the truck which picked up the children from Izieu had been 'Flak'—the German anti-aircraft battalion?"

"No, I didn't know," said Holfort.

"Now that you do know, why don't you demand a trial for crimes against humanity for the Wehrmacht?"

Holfort slowly replied, "We will study the affair, and we will see what conclusions should be drawn from it." Streim and Holfort consulted with President Cerdini; they decided to stay several extra days in order to answer Vergès's accusations. I obviously preferred them to Vergès, so I was disappointed with the casualness of their eventual reply. They simply said that the trucks must have been requisitioned by Barbie, because the Wehrmacht, on its own, had no power to raid the Izieu children's home. Vergès had touched on a thorny issue for the Germans—had the Wehrmacht "helped out"?

The child in me had firmly led my adult rational self through the long trip to the trial of Klaus Barbie in Lyons—a child whose needs I hadn't always fully recognized. I liked sitting in the Palais de Justice and hearing the Germans and French talk about the genocide of the Jews. I greedily lapped up their self-condemning phrases; I couldn't get enough of it. The books on the Holocaust, the Eichmann trial, *Shoah*, were Jewish statements. This was different. This was the French and Germans. Day after day, I came back, put myself in the pressurized tunnel and just listened.

The proceedings in Lyons reverberated with the obsessions of children firmed into the passions and actions of adults: Serge Klarsfeld's father had been deported; his wife, Beate, was of the next German-born generation after the Holocaust. The Minister of Justice, Robert Badinter, had placed Klaus Barbie in the same cell in Montluc prison where Barbie had put Badinter's father before deporting him to Auschwitz. Among the American observers: Ted Morgan's father had been killed fighting for the Free French, Marcel Ophuls was the son of Max Ophuls, Elie Wiesel was the only member of his family to survive Auschwitz. Everyone had *some* connection that went deeper than the press assignment that got you your place in court. This was the first trial of Nazi war criminals in which my generation played a leading role. Our age group has no memory of "before Hitler"—the children of Izieu could be our children, but also they are ourselves, the shadowy missing part of our world that had no chance to exist. Lyons, we knew, was the crucial final moment when there was maximum information available and survivors of the Holocaust still were alive. It had to be got right, it had to be marked. The century was ending.

I had a privileged American childhood. My parents were cosmopolitan, highly assimilated Jews. They were formed by the twenties. They had money, optimism, style, a faith in modernity, and rational ideas. I knew about Europe because my father had been a World War I hero, a reconnoiterer. Most in his unit were killed. He was gassed in the trenches at Château-Thierry and after the war spent three years in a French hospital before coming home to New York. I also knew about Europe because my mother, during the thirties, liked to live there from time to time. In the late thirties when I was eight and my brother eleven, she wanted to take us to Italy to see sculpture. I remember sitting in the living room, my arm swollen from typhoid shots, listening to the grownups: the exiled Berlin photographer Lotte Jacobi, Einstein's friend, was there with her husband, Eric Reis, who had been in one of the early concentration camps for political prisoners. They and my father persuaded my mother it would be a bad idea to take us to Europe. I understood from what they said that Germans wanted to kill Jews. Roosevelt was calling Americans home.

My mother had some problems when my older brother, Mark, was born that made it hard for her to take care of children. In my parents' eyes the most reliable substitute-mother for my brother and then me would be German. They imported a young girl, a Lutheran from Prussia, who spoke no English, and she raised us. In the thirties she went back briefly to Magdeburg and got herself engaged to an SS. Though she decided to return home to us (and remained forever), I always wondered: what would she have done if she had been taking care of us in Germany? What choice would she have made? During the war she hid the photo of her fiancé in his SS uniform, but we all knew she had it, that she would take it out and cry. She said she was glad her father, a Marxist, was dead and didn't live to see Hitler. It was confusing. After the war we found out that her family and the SS fiancé were dead. My family consoled her. I was in high school, at the same time the news came in about the extermination camps. I had wanted to talk about the six million dead. My father's answer was you couldn't condemn a whole people for the mad ideas of its leaders; in the First World War he felt he had contributed to the death of men that were no different from himself (his family originally came from Austria), and the war had been fought for nothing. I loved my independent-minded family and I understood where they were coming from, but their muffling of the six million left no room for the expression of my equally valid feelings. After I graduated high school I took one of the first boats to post-war Europe. I wasn't particularly ideological; I wanted to find out what had happened, to get it straight.

"Come to the Roosevelt," Alfred Streim's friend, Hans Schäxtler, a lawyer from Bonn, urged me. "We like the Roosevelt—the German crowd has picked it for the trial." The names in Lyons had a surreal logic: I was staying at the Place de la République; Tamar Golan, the Israeli correspondent, at the Hôtel des Etrangérs; we met at the Café des Négociants or the Bar Américain. Barbie had tortured Jews and Resistance members at the Hôtel Terminus. I was disoriented during the beginning of the trial—I went to find the Hôtel Terminus, which I located on a small street, rue de la Lainerie, in the old quarter. It was small, the windows were wide open, it still suggested violence and decay. But I had gone to the wrong Terminus. The right torture hotel had been splendidly refurbished, its mood *Belle Epoque* and traveling salesman *moderne*. It is next to the Gare Lyon-Perrache, where you get the TJV *rapide* for Paris. When I went back to the first Hôtel Terminus, I realized what I thought I had seen had been a delusion: there was nothing violent about it. The graffiti near it read: LE ROCK EST CRETIN and N'OUBLIEZ PAS L'ARMENIE.

Schäxtler, who spoke English, was late. Streim came down. He spoke neither English nor French. "Sprechen Sie Deutsch?" I blinked. Streim wanted me to speak German? "Ich kann nicht Deutsch sprechen," I replied. "Sie können sprechen," he insisted, like a professor giving me a language lesson. "Ich verstehe Sie." "Speak," he insisted, "I can understand you." I stared at him blankly. How was I going to talk to him about the trial? Then I started to think. It would make no sense to Streim that someone with a name as *echt* German as Probst, enough of a linguistic duck to easily follow a French trial and write about it for the Spanish press—*Cambio 16*, a sort of *Time* magazine of Spain— couldn't speak a word of German. I had even lived in Germany in '48. I remembered hearing it, but not speaking. I hesitated, but Streim persisted. Then suddenly I mustered up some collection of words out of the kitchen and nursery; it felt like going over the edge of a cliff and yet gliding at the same time. Streim kept saying, "Ich verstehe Sie," as I answered him in German.

And in doing so, I had a sudden insight into Hannah Arendt's definition of the Eichmann trial as the banality of evil. Lyons reinforced my conviction, which I wrote about in the early sixties, that she had been deeply wrong: during six weeks of excruciating description of torture and humiliation we heard nothing to indicate evil was either banal or ordinary. In Jerusalem—so orphaned from her mother German, forced into an alien English, hearing an equally unfamiliar Hebrew—when Eichmann spoke, didn't some part of her feel reassured? He must have sounded so *familiar*—did she repress this feeling and substitute "banal" and "ordinary"?

When Schäxtler came to the Roosevelt he looked green. Stroudze, one of the witnesses, had testified in the Palais de Justice that after the Allies bombed his last camp, an underground munitions plant, the inmates had been forced to reassemble from bits and pieces of nothing—a hand, blood, skin—the dead bodies, so the guards could count to make sure there had been no escapees. Do you know what it is like, Stroudze asked the court, to put together a body from dead pieces? We were beginning to hear from the women who had survived their children's extermination; witnesses described Barbie's technique of using drowning baths and dogs trained to eat live human flesh. At twenty Schäxtler had been in the Wehrmacht, a flier; at twenty-four he had been a young lawyer recruited to assist the defense at Nuremberg. Amazing how all of us in Lyons—give or take five, eight years—were of the same generation. "We knew everything at Nuremberg, but the trials were more formal. We didn't have the witnesses—it's Lyons that makes the incredible credible."

Schäxtler explained Streim's work to me: during the past ten years at the *Zentrale Stelle der Landesjustiz* they had set up a system which centralized all the documents pertaining to the Nazi period. "This solves the problem of venue. If three Nazi war criminals involved in the same crime need to be tried now in three different parts of Germany, we can send the local courts the centralized documents."

"*Centralized?*" I blinked. They were using their own new system of centralization to indict the Nazi centralized system of extermination! Lyons resonated repetitions: the day before in court a crippled man recalled it was forbidden to be sick in the camps. He kept refusing the chair President Cerdini offered him, appearing not to notice the connection. Another witness, who had been deprived of water during the train trip to Auschwitz, carried his flask with him into court; he couldn't be without. Past and present fused. Nothing ended in '45.

Schäxtler suddenly turned to Streim. "Our system is good, but there are gaps—we've had such good documents we haven't needed the victims. We never knew what the victims experienced when they stood on the *Nacht und Nebel* selection platform. Lyons is more human, more authentic. Now that I am here, I think: Who are we to decide when and for how long and under what circumstances the victims should speak?"

Though Schäxtler was commiserating over the fate of the Jews, the same uncomfortable feeling came over me that I once felt as the victim in a legal complaint, when my lawyer said to me, "There, there . . . at least you shall have your day in court." A day in court wasn't enough! My "German paranoia" surfaced—who, really, was Schäxtler? Why was he there? "You were a flier during the war?"

"We flew over France. It was horrible, when we found out later . . ."

"But when the Jews put on the yellow stars? Didn't you notice something was strange?"

Schäxtler was silent. Then he said, ". . . That was a bad moment."

I looked past the Germans, through the glass windows of the Roosevelt, and remembered being in Germany in '48. It was cold, there were no cities left, people going nowhere gathered in train stations. The American Army posted odd signs: DRIVE CAREFULLY. DEATH IS SO PERMANENT. JAVA JUNCTION FIVE MILES AHEAD. I got scared on the highway near Munich—a bus rolled by: DACHAU EXPRESS. I found the camp. It wasn't fixed up yet. The spaces there were small. I saw and I didn't see. There were pockets of horror. But I was just a kid not long out of high school, far from home, adrift in nothing that looked like a normal landscape. The "Nuremberg crowd" was still there—but they were grownups with a permanent place in the American Zone. I had no identity. In Dachau I had no defenses to see more than I did, there was nothing between me and it. Now it was different. I have raised two daughters, I even have grandchildren. I had come to Lyons with assignments, I had a computer, a printer, and a typewriter in the Carlton. I wore a Press badge and some people knew my name. The next morning I called Vergès.

Jacques Vergès

1987

Why did so many Parisian intellectuals persist in spreading rumors that the trial would never take place; or, if that didn't convince, that it *should* never take place? The reason frequently given was that Barbie's lawyer, Jacques Vergès, would use the trial to besmirch the Resistance. But this never happened. France, besides, was never *that* worried about the Resistance: countries simply don't melt at the threat of the revelation of national wrongdoings that occurred over forty years ago. It comes as no news that France was chock-a-block with collaborationists. What never was explained, particularly in the American press, was that Vergès's real quarrel was not with the by now remote Resistance (very few French intellectuals ever were connected to it), but with his former friends, those Parisian ex-leftists with whom he ideologically had stormed the barricades in the 1968 student revolution, and to whom he has become a pariah (he hangs out with Pol Pot) and an embarrassment. During the Algerian war Vergès became a hero to the French left, including Sartre and Beauvoir (the literary establishment in the sixties was monolithically left wing), because he defended the Algerian FLN terrorists, including his future wife, Djamila Bouhired.

Vergès was accustomed to moving in the best French circles. Beckett's highly respected publisher, Jerome Lindon, was his friend and publisher— Vergès has written a book of political essays and a novel, *Agenda*. But by 1979 leftists of his generation had dropped Marxism for an establishment place in the sun: Regis Debray, Che's old buddy, became one of Mitterrand's chief advisors, and helped Serge Klarsfeld negotiate the removal of Klaus Barbie from Bolivia to Lyons. Jerome Lindon, like most French intellectuals, finally was horrified by Vergès. But he insisted that the reason he didn't want a trial was that Vergès would get Barbie to ruin the image of the Resistance. (Never did Lindon mention to me the fact that he had been Vergès's publisher.)

The real fears remained unexpressed—in '68 Vergès had been one of the inner sanctum. With what language would French intellectuals now attack him? Not only Marxism but also flirtation with terrorism has long been scuttled; the French, these days, are mildly pro-American: former communists like Yves Montand adore Reagan. But these new positions are somewhat *faute de mieux*—French intellectuals have no firm ideology that would make them feel secure in attacking Vergès. Many of their old demi-gods like Sartre and Beauvoir not only are dead but their myths have tarnished: it turns out Sartre was rarely with Beauvoir, but had a great harem of adoring women. Weren't some of the Paris rumors—that there would be no trial, or that there *must* not be a trial because of Vergès's omnipotent demonic powers—an understandable desire to make the "Vergès problem" disappear? Vergès remained almost childishly pleased that, of his former mentors, one had remained "faithful" to him: poor Jean Genet, aged, confused, and near death, wrote him a note—"I hear you are defending Barbie. More than ever I remain your friend." During the trial he called Marguerite Duras (who found a legal reason for her refusal to appear) to be one of his nine defense witnesses. This interested me and I telephoned him for an interview.

Vergès suggested we meet at the Sofitel, his hotel, at noon, before the trial's afternoon session. He is a short, compact man and wears sporty luxe and Peter Lorre steel-rimmed eyeglasses. He is well aware that in Paris these days his former friends call his ideas *rétro bolchevik*, and he often looks rueful, as though he is the misunderstood victim. Despite his radical baggage, in court he preens, strutting the traditional black robes of the law. Child of miscegenation and French colonial privilege, he was sent by his well-placed French father to the best schools. He speaks the over-perfect French of an outsider; like Duras he is an *outre-mer*. He gave one of his interviews on the Barbie case while being photographed taking a bath. But in provincial Lyons his statements sound askew, as though Jean Genet had attempted to bust up a good-cause Quaker meeting in Kansas City.

I figured my advantage was that he hadn't a clue where I was coming from. Vergès prides himself on the correct gesture, and offered me lunch. When I travel I frequently rely on magical thinking—I immediately evoked the presence of my father. A lawyer, he would have wanted me to hold my own, and so I would. I put the cassette machine on the table, near Vergès. We talked in French. I told him I came from a legal family and there was a matter I wished to clarify: "My father taught me, when I was a child, that the first thing you must learn is that a good lawyer must always be prepared to take the defense of a person with whose ideas he doesn't agree—"

"That's right. Yes."

"He gave me *Crime and Punishment* to read, and my education began. What I want to hear from you is whether you have taken on the defense of Monsieur Barbie in the spirit of that great legal tradition, or for other reasons?"

"First, because lawyers must defend clients. The graver the crime, the more interesting to me. One shouldn't confuse a lawyer with his client. Before Barbie, I defended Georges Abdallah. Obviously one can't say that in one case I am a terrorist, and three months later I am a Nazi." (According to *Le Monde* and Erna Paris's *Unhealed Wounds*, Vergès's close friend, Swiss banker François Genoud, controls secret Nazi funds in the unmarked Swiss bank accounts of *Die Spinne*, a group of former SS. Maître Berman—one of the forty defense lawyers in the Barbie trial—tried to call Genoud as witness. Berman claimed Genoud's funds come from the stolen property of Jewish extermination-camp victims. The Paris book indicates he used this money to bankroll Nazis and Arab extremist terrorist activities. Vergès never has hidden his closeness with Genoud. During the pre-trial period he persuaded Barbie's daughter, also visited by Genoud, not to use the French lawyers already provided her father. Vergès says he is contributing his services free.)

"So you feel you are here because of the legal tradition, but not because you identify with the ideas of your client?"

"At eighteen I joined de Gaulle's Free French Army in order to combat Nazi ideology—because, as you can tell from my appearance, I am Asian. Obviously I don't defend racist ideas." (Vergès is enormously proud of having served under de Gaulle: during the trial his pronouncements wildly fluctuated between bitter condemnation of all white colonials, in which he includes Israel, and sporadic patriotic utterances about defending "French honor.") "But my client wasn't legally extradited from Bolivia, and in France there is a legal time limit. You can't judge a man here for crimes that took place forty years ago. During the Algerian war I defended Djamila Bouhired. France has committed atrocious crimes similar to the Nazis'. I want to denounce those massacres."

"I am a writer. I must admit, when you talk about writers, this has a special interest to me. You wanted to call Marguerite Duras as one of your nine witnesses for the defense. Why?"

"Marguerite Duras, in *La Douleur*, wrote that she tortured a collaborator. When one reads her account of that torture, I believe this permits one to 'relativize,' to humanize the judgment one makes about the Germans. Barbie, not the Germans, is on trial. This is Marguerite Duras—a woman of the left."

"You like her work?"

"I am interested in the construction of the *nouveau roman*. I like Claude Simon—the others have only technical skill."

"I want to speak a little more about Marguerite Duras. You have read *L'Amant*?"

"Yes."

"And you have seen *Hiroshima Mon Amour?*"

"Oh, yes."

"And what do you think about all of that?"

"I liked both. Yes, yes."

"I find this most interesting—this indicates a certain ambiguity on your part. Because what impressed me about *L'Amant*, and, despite my great respect for Marguerite Duras, troubled me—" I paused and started intently at Vergès—"is that *L'Amant* takes place in the early thirties—a time in her Indochina of the great starvation and political upheavals—yet there is not *one* reference to any of that in her book—"

Vergès suddenly realized where I was heading: I was accusing him of admiring a book drenched in French colonial racist xenophobic attitudes, a book which totally obliterated the real human and political problems in Indochina. He glanced at the cassette and quickly interrupted me before I could go further. "Yes, yes, that is evident. It is my reproach against Europeans. Their vision of Indochina is Eurocentric. They lived in Indochina as though the indigenous population didn't exist. You are right when you said that the 1930s were the years of the great famine, when many people died—"

Now both of us spoke more rapidly. "None of which was in Marguerite Duras's novel, and—"

"Yes," he broke in. "It was a time of political revolt—"

"—But you said that she, as witness, would humanize things, and even humanize the Germans."

"She participated in a torture that was odious. I want you to understand what I mean. Because when we see what she, a woman of the left—and cultivated—was capable of doing, this permits us to have a more nuanced vision about what the Germans did."

"About what she *said* she did."

"About what she *did*."

"About what she *said* she did."

"All right. What she said she did. I hope for her sake that she lied. That is also possible."

"Well then—would she have been such a stable witness for you?"

Again Vergès quickened: "I didn't mean to call her as a favorable witness, but as someone I would have fought. I would have asked her, as she has done what she has done, how could she condemn the Germans for doing the same thing?"

"Do you believe she did those things, or, as a writer, she has chosen to write that she did those things?"

"She may have indirectly been involved with some of those things, but I think it is a fantasy that she is writing." Suddenly Vergès broke into uncontrollable, hysterical laughter—he seemed unaware he was defeating his own argument. "A sexual fantasy. Her description of the naked man sounds like a sexual fantasy."

What crossed my mind was the photograph of Vergès taking a bath while discussing the Barbie case, and his own love affair with the tortured Djamila, and his recognition of the Chinese lover in *L'Amant* as fantasy. But I didn't wish to digress into an analysis of Vergès's psycho-erotic makeup. "So what use to you would she have been as a witness?"

Vergès looked at me—his expression suddenly went blank.

The sexual fantasies in the novels of Marguerite Duras obviously are irrelevant to the Barbie trial. Vergès undoubtedly wanted to call her as part of his campaign to smear the Resistance; her appearance would have glamorized his provocative bluff. But he had read her with care. One of a pair of twins, he enjoys mirror images and doubles. Duras's *Hiroshima Mon Amour*, about the German occupation, is told from the point of view of a young girl, a collaborationist, who falls in love with a Nazi. The Nazi later is killed, the girl socially punished. The wrongdoers become the Americans and the Resistance; film images of Hiroshima and the Third World are superimposed on France after its liberation, the Third World is perceived as the Second World War's real victim. Duras's innovative technique of using geographic montage to falsify history—a crime committed in country A fades into horrifying movie shots of victims in country B, in another part of the globe—worked because France in the early 1960s was very anti-American, and liked switching the emphasis away from France to our bombing of Hiroshima. Vergès, who was formed by the ideas of the early 1960s, tried to use Duras's technique in designing his defense: he removed Barbie from the trial and—half-Asian, half-French—superimposed himself in his place: he also imported, as surrogate Third World victims, several lawyers—Nabil Bouaîta from Algeria, and Jean-Martin M'Bemba from Brazzaville. What he didn't take into account was that the Barbie trial was neither movie nor novel: unlike *Hiroshima Mon Amour* Barbie's real victims—Jews, the children of Izieu, and *résistants*—could not be magically removed by a literary device.

We had heard, day after day, in Lyons, the testimony of people who suffered atrocities that did not come from literary imagination—testimony so harrowing journalists were finding it difficult to convey its essence without overwhelming readers. Francine Gudefin, now in her eighties, has had to live her life with her face disfigured because Barbie and his assistants thought this would be clever to do to a pretty girl from the Resistance. Starved camp inmates resorted to cannibalism. A Frenchwoman imprisoned in Montluc recalled giving a ten-year-old a hard-boiled egg to eat. Her guard observed: "You like Jewish children?"—and in front of her cell beat the child to death. Vergès has no "secrets" to reveal about these victims. Their cacophonic voices repre-

sent no one political point of view, no one group, nor have they used their suf-
ferings for careerism. The witnesses shared a very human trait—they were less
obsessed with the absent Barbie than with mentioning aloud the names of
those who had been with them in Montluc and the camps and didn't come
back.

"Has it never occurred to you that the Nazis, by killing just those sorts of
humanists who would have defended the rights of the Algerian people, created
a void which left the road open to extreme right-wing French militarists?"

"No. The massacres in Algeria preceded Hitler."

"So you feel the humanists are the same as the military?"

"Yes—I am a pessimist." Vergès understood I was alluding to his dramatic
verbal clash in court with the Catholic historian, André Frossard. In *L'Aurore*,
the same paper in which Zola published his defense of Dreyfus, "J'accuse,"
Frossard had published, during the Algerian war, a famous piece that had saved
the life of Vergès's wife, Djamila Bouhired, who had been tortured and condemned to death. Frossard, whose grandmother was Jewish, had been imprisoned in Montluc. He described witnessing there the torture, humiliation, and
killing of his professor, Marcel Gompel, the French Jewish humanist who Einstein had claimed was one of the three men who understood him. Frossard
said: "What the SS did went far beyond racial inequality. It was killing someone just because of their birth, and that death needed to be preceded by terrible
humiliations. The Jews, in Montluc, before being killed, were forced to repeat:
'I am a parasite.' It was the abolition of all that was human." Vergès retorted
that what the Europeans didn't pardon Hitler for was the humiliation of the
white man. Indirectly, Frossard also was reminding Vergès that if the Barbies
are permitted to kill innocent men, women, and children because of their be-
liefs—so rooted in humanistic thought—who will write the letters for the future Djamila Bouhireds? Despite Vergès's retort, Frossard's presence in the
court was one of the few times Vergès seemed to lose his composure. At one
point he said in a low voice that he "owed a personal debt to Frossard." Because
of Frossard's testimony, the French press, in recalling the somewhat forgotten
Marcel Gompel, was instructing its readers to consider Gompel's life as the authentic symbol of French culture and heroism.

"You defended your wife, Djamila Bouhired," I said to Vergès. "Doesn't
this indicate that you aren't *always* a pessimist?"

His former friend Jacques Givet in "Le Cas Vergès" wrote that Vergès said
to him, apropos of his defending terrorists, "I would have also defended Anne
Frank." Givet replied that Anne Frank did not need a lawyer but an army to liberate her from the extermination camp.

"Oh, sometimes in real life I am an optimist. One can be an optimist and
have a pessimistic philosophy."

"You don't feel that the French, realizing what happened to the Jews because of racial prejudice, can benefit from the educative aspect of the trial to become more aware of their anti-racial bias against the Magrebs—the new marginals in France?"

"No. The trial is dangerous. France is filled with anti–Semitism. It is just there, all around, under the surface. People laugh at the trial."

"Really . . ." I stared at him somewhat cooly. Vergès frequently resorted to press statements warning that the trial was dangerous for France, dangerous for the left. As I was obviously Jewish, he assumed fear about anti–Semitism would be my Achilles' heel.

"The crimes against the colonials were more serious than those of the Nazis in the West," he insisted.

"You've given me no reason why you can't treat the Algerian cause as a separate matter. My friend Robert Lifton wrote serious studies on the effects of the atom bomb on Hiroshima. But it would be idiotic to reproach Lifton for writing on Hiroshima because the Russians had perpetrated genocide, too, on the kulaks."

"I don't talk of the treatment of the blacks, or the kulaks or Hiroshima, because the crimes against Algeria haven't yet been judged."

"I do not understand why, as a lawyer, you don't defend your cause in Algeria as a separate matter."

"Because I also want to make this a trial of what went on in Algeria."

"Every case, always, has to be tried by itself."

"A trial on Algeria isn't possible, it has been amnestied."

"All laws can be amended. No law is eternal and omnipotent." Obviously, Vergès knew the Barbie trial could be used as precedent for crimes against humanity.

"In France there is a tendency to close one's eyes to what one doesn't like."

"I repeat—all laws can be contested."

"In the United States you have had My Lai . . ."

"Do you think I am defending the United States? I simply said laws can be amended. Do you like our writers?"

"Very much. Faulkner. Hemingway. Dos Passos. Fitzgerald. I like Fitzgerald very much."

"You like our *traditional* writers . . ."

Vergès again brought up France's Nobel Prize winner Claude Simon. "Claude Simon did things, he was in Spain."

"Precisely. And he would have made a perfect victim for a Barbie. During the occupation, he was close friends with the parents of a Catalan friend of mine, Amadeo Cuito. They ran an underground railway to smuggle Jews from France into Spain. They worked with the Catalan Socialist hero, Josep Pallach. Simon dedicated one of his first books to the Cuitos."

"If Claude Simon had been a victim of Barbie, he would not have taken

vengeance against Barbie. As an artist he would have better things to do."
(Vergès in court just had had an inflammatory confrontation with Nobel Peace
Prize winner Elie Wiesel. Vergès had tried to turn Wiesel's evocation of being
a child in Auschwitz into proof that Wiesel and Israel were indifferent to French
torture of Algerians. Though his technique of mixing apples and oranges has
lost him credibility in France, it increased his prestige among his Third World
clientele.)

"I hardly think that 'vengeance' is the correct description for what is happening in Lyons," I answered him, "but neither you nor I can speak for what
Claude Simon would do or say about it today, we neither of us know."

"Yes. But you brought up Simon."

"I did not say what he would say. I said he could have been, in that period, a
victim of a Barbie." I abruptly stood up. I felt it was time for me to leave the
Sofitel.

Izieu and the Jews
in the
Resistance

1988

The gravest charge against Barbie was that with full knowledge of their fate he had ordered the deportation of 43 Jewish children from their refuge in Izieu, a small mountain town in the Ain *département* an hour southeast of Lyons; they were immediately exterminated upon their arrival at Auschwitz. The problem with the Izieu case was of misplaced focus—to understand how the deportation of the Jews was effected, and the enormity of the act, one needs to know how the Nazi net worked, which was from the top down. Nothing was left to chance; the deportation of Jewish children was inherent to the system; they represented the ongoing future of the Jews and it was imperative that they be wiped out. Children of *résistants* automatically were deported. Children also were used as part of the hostage system the Germans employed in France, their seizure a warning to both Jews and the general population. In emphasizing so heavily Barbie's act as exclusively his own—as though he had behaved *atypically*, ignoring his obvious connective links with his superiors (he was a small-fry within the SS hierarchy in France)—the historic point was lost. There was, tragically, nothing unique about the fate of these 43 children; at the same time they were being deported, Jewish children throughout France were also being deported, including others from Lyons.

Izieu was presented in court with the fixed rigidity of myth: 43 martyred children and one sadist. So much of importance had been omitted—just the tip of the iceberg of the history of the occupation (and no significant collaborationists) surfaced. I sent back reports each week to *Cambio 16* in Madrid, but I wasn't satisfied: if I was to make real sense of what had happened, I would need to do it on my own, after Barbie was sentenced. Though it hadn't been my original plan, I ended up spending the next eight months in archives in New York and Paris, reading, thinking, and talking to people. Slowly I got hooked. I would think: I'll just look up this piece, and check out X. But X led to Y, and Y to Z.

Finally I found myself mainly concentrating on the crucial elements that had been rinsed out of the trial: the Jews in the Resistance, both their own and the French, and the workings of the Nazi net, particularly the role of Otto Abetz—who as Hitler's ambassador controlled much of what happened in France from his Foreign Office on rue de Lille.

Whatever one could say about French behavior during the occupation, one could also point to the opposite. There are no obvious conclusions to be drawn. Nor is there any such animal as "Jewish behavior." Jews were in the top echelons of the French Resistance, which was centered in Lyons; some had key positions in the Communist Party, others such as Aubrac (Raymond Samuel) and Ravanal (Serge Asher) worked closely with de Gaulle and Jean Moulin. There was a secret Jewish Army, a Jewish Maquis, the *main forte* (the Irgun), Zionist resistance, Socialists, Bundists, the OSE, and so forth. There were also Jewish bankers and bourgeois. And sometimes the father was a banker and the son in the Resistance; other times the banker was the *résistant*. There is no correlation between those who were deported and those deemed "passive": many of the most well-informed, highly-politicized Jews were deported, and many dolts who hadn't a clue how to save themselves managed to survive. Approximately twenty-five per cent of France's Jews were deported, of which roughly forty per cent were *apatrides*—foreign born—and ten per cent French. (Part of the responsibility for the fate of the foreign Jews abandoned in France, which had no quota system, should be shared by the United States and Britain and their refusal to allow them to emigrate from there in any meaningful number to the United States, Britain, and Palestine.) According to SS Sturmführer Röthke's figures in the July 1942 Vel d'Hiv raid in Paris, his Gestapo rounded up three thousand Jewish men, nearly six thousand women, and four thousand children. Ten thousand women and children compared to three thousand men is a striking figure, particularly since many of the men were old.[1] Clearly the least mobile parts of the Jewish population were the most trapped; those in the Resistance generally were young. In *The War Against the Jews, 1933–1945* Lucy Dawidowicz makes the main point: the number of Jews saved in each country was proportionate to the degree of outside help they received.

The 43 very young children from Izieu were part of the nonmobile population: Switzerland wouldn't accept children under sixteen, nor could this youngest group easily be transported across the Pyrenees. French shelter had to be found for them, which was what Madame Sabina Zlatin was attempting to do when the Izieu raid took place.

My sense that there were significant splits in the trial—opposing perceptions of history within the Jewish community—sharpened toward the end of the Izieu testimony: after the shattering accounts by the few survivors who had witnessed the German seizure of the children, the trial seemed to slip into an odd hiatus—nothing much seemed to be going on. Serge Klarsfeld, the lawyer for the children of Izieu, had called witnesses concerning the two memorials made after the liberation, commemorating the children. Klarsfeld wanted to add the phrase "they died because they were Jewish." The first plaque, placed immediately after the war by the local mayor, listed the 43 names (obviously Jewish) and said the children had been deported to the gas chambers at Auschwitz. Underneath that was the troublesome phrase: *Que la Défense et l'Amour de Ma Patrie Soient Ma Défense Devant Toi Seigneur.*

I didn't see anything wrong with the second memorial, sponsored in 1946 by Sabina Zlatin and a special committee which included some of her friends from the area. Madame Zlatin had run the children's refuge with her husband, the agronomist Miron Zlatin. (He was deported with the children, the Zlatins having been part of the clandestine network of OSE, the Jewish Relief Organization, which saved thousands of children by smuggling them to Switzerland and Spain, or hiding them with the French.) The obelisk she commissioned had as its stone relief the Star of David outlining the carved heads of a boy and girl. Beneath it are engraved two verses: the first is a reminder of the martyrdom of innocent children, the second contains John Donne's *Every man is a piece of the continent, A part of the main; Any man's death diminishes me, Because I am involved in mankind* (which the judge mistakenly credited to Hemingway who'd used it for *For Whom the Bell Tolls*).

Neither I nor most of the other journalists quite grasped the relevance of the ensuing plaque-debate to Barbie's guilt. One witness, irritated at being questioned about the plaques, pointed out that after the war "everyone knew that Jewish children deported to Auschwitz were deported *because* they were Jewish." The court room became restive. A Frenchman seated in the row behind me—he knew I was Jewish—anxiously tapped me on the shoulder: "With the memorials—did we do something wrong?" Another American, not Jewish, chimed in that he felt the Star of David was not adequate: "Those plaques rob the children of their Jewish identities." Sullenly I mumbled back that Hitler didn't rob the Jews of their identity—in fact he had insisted on it. He robbed the children of their *lives.* "Identities is post-1960s stuff," I said. "After the war the State of Israel was being legitimized, and *that* was to be the identity, the memorial. People's minds in 1946 were on basics: food, shelter—getting the DPs to Israel." There had been no Holocaust language before the end of the 1950s, and, anyway, I felt inscriptions were tricky—if after the war the French had overly emphasized the separateness of the Jews, in a country where the Jews were so fond of their assimilation, it could have been construed as one more xenophobic insult, as if Jews still were being considered, as under Vichy, a "foreign unassimilable element." *Mort pour la France*, never meant to be taken literally, was France's highest honor—meaning France embraces all her children.

Lyons was disintegrating into an international meltdown, a cacophony of different voices, generations, agendas; a bunch of disconnected foreign passion plays were being enacted in a city rented out as a stage: Vergès was working the Algeria question, the German-born Beate Klarsfeld was involved in German guilt, we Americans tended to see issues with an overlay of the civil rights movement, while the British disliked the French legal system—the trial being run as a sort of Town Meeting, with individuals speaking at amazing length. Those of us covering the trial were glued together in the Palais de Justice as recorders of immutable historic suffering, but in terms of points of view and historic perception we were an oddly askew bunch with little common ground.

Bernard-Henri Lévy sat in the row in front of me. His family had left Algeria after its independence; he was part of the 1970s generation of French Jewish intellectuals who as a reaction to the extreme anti-Israel positions of the orthodox left had asserted their Jewish roots, something that had never happened before in France. He now also seemed confused; he asked me about the older generation of French Jews. Why had so many of them been so phobically opposed to the trial? And now that it had started, why, suddenly, was everything "all right"? Tamar Golan, the Israeli journalist, was surprised that so few of the top French Jewish establishment attended it, and at the lack of Israeli coverage. Most of the people I met in Lyons had come to the trial out of particular interest; if there was a cohesive insiders' point of view, none of us were in on it.

Confused, and still disoriented, I took refuge in my memories: I had arrived in France after I graduated Dalton—I didn't go to college. Abruptly I found myself in a new world that had nothing to do with watching Clark Gable and Carole Lombard movies in the Loew's Seventy-Second, a veritable Alhambra with revolving ceilings. A French friend of my mother had been on the ship with us, returning home to France (this was several years after the war) with her daughter Annie to reclaim the empty apartments of her dead relatives. Annie was about fifteen, and she and I went with her mother to those windy places on avenue Foch and rue Saint-Florentin. Her home in Saint Cloud still had huge swastikas scrawled on the walls; everything in it had been smashed by the Nazis before they retreated from Paris. I still hear the silence of those vast rooms, and remember Annie's mother's bewilderment that her sisters and mother had been considered Jewish. She made Annie and me go with her to the

Bois de Boulogne; the housekeeper at her sister's apartment said her nephew was buried there. Annie and I stood on either side of her as she said nothing; but the phrase *mort pour la France* was baked into my brain forever, no rational argument could dislodge it. Annie's mother was surprised her nephew had died a communist. Then my cousin Lea took me to the Jewish Quarter, to rue Rosiers; in the shops they were still talking about the Gestapo raid there, telling what had happened.

Halfway through the trial I realized I didn't want my memories of that time fixed up, modernized, detached from me. I glanced again at my copy of Serge Klarsfeld's book on the children of Izieu, at the photograph of the "for whom the bell tolls" obelisk. There was so much talk of Sabina Zlatin having been in Montpellier the day of the Izieu raid. I thought of my Spanish friends, Teresa and Josep Pallach, and Juan Bellsoleil (they had been in the Catalan youth movement of the POUM during the Civil War), who had been in the underground in Montpellier and Toulouse. And gazing at the obelisk pictured on the page, I suddenly recognized its meaning: the Izieu story *smelled* of the French Resistance—I never believed the nonsense that the children, since they were in the beautiful, peaceful countryside, would have been safe (but for one local collaborator). Since when has a good-looking tree stopped genocide or a war? The children's innocence was not determined by scenery, nor did guilt accrue to them because they were smack in the middle of Maquis country. They were being hidden—whether by Maquis, church, or individuals—because the Nazis wanted to exterminate them.

I never considered myself *of* the Spanish Resistance because I never felt I was at risk. But those twenty-seven years—1948 until Franco's death in 1975—of going back and forth between France and Spain, running errands for my friends in the Spanish Resistance and later writing about the underground, had marked me. The generation I had known—ten, fifteen years older than myself—had been as that of my professors. I was, in a way, a *child* of the Resistance; it was what I had instead of an alma mater, four years of college, and a university degree. It would have been hard for me not to have spotted its presence in France and Spain.

Only an anti-fascist would have used the "for whom the bell tolls" quote on a memorial for dead Jewish children in 1946. The very expression "anti-fascist" sounded outmoded, having lain neglected in history's attic, so dusty its original meaning conveyed nothing: Hemingway finally had become a victim of metamorphosis, the very thing that had obsessed him. The allusion to *For Whom the Bell Tolls* (though never a favorite book of mine) would have been perfect in 1946: the Star of David, the Nazi persecution of the Jews, combined with the Spanish Civil War (Jews and exiled Spaniards were the two largest *apatride* groups in France). Hemingway also exemplified the American role in the liberation of France—it all must have seemed so dignified to the people who planned it. But with the passage of years, and changes in moral fashion and language, the memorial, in this more blunt time, now was being questioned by Klarsfeld as a partial denial of the dead children.

Seven months after the trial I visited Sabina Zlatin in her apartment in Paris near the Luxembourg Gardens. I asked her if she had had Spanish contacts. She stared at me quizzically for a moment, then nodded. "What made you think so?"

I smiled. "Montpellier combined with the Hemingway." We traded names, but we hadn't known the same Spaniards.

She said she had sent some children prior to the raid through the underground railway which went across the Pyrenees. "One now lives in Canada."

Madame Zlatin confirmed my intuition that the children had been protected by the Maquis. She said that in the final three months before the raid, which was an extremely dangerous period because the unoccupied zone had been taken over by the Germans, her contact with OSE had been broken off; she had no money, she had already sold her jewelry and personal valuables. "During those three months the Maquis took care of us, they saw to it that the children had food. Our lives depended on them." When she talked about the past she brushed aside the easy, the sentimental; a strikingly handsome woman in her mid-eighties, her sunlit, spacious apartment reflects her cultural interests—she deals in rare theater and art books. The Zlatins were born in Poland, but well before the war owned their own property and established real roots in France. After the liberation Madame Zlatin was honored in Paris for her work in the Resistance.

I had felt bad at the trial that the plaques had taken such a beating—after all, Sabina Zlatin and her friends, with no fanfare, had tended that memorial for over forty years, quietly going up to Izieu every April. Those deaths for nearly half a century had been a private experience—now to have it emblazoned across the world, commented upon by strangers, to have Izieu converted into a national museum with all sorts of people clamoring to become donors, even if in the good cause of history, had to be hard, dislocating.

In Lyons I had been almost phobic about not asking survivors to tell me their "story." I had gone to Lyons expecting to keep my Spanish experiences very separate from the Barbie trial—but it was not possible: it informed the way I looked at things. After Franco's death and their return to Spain the Resistance had been lionized by the press; people who had coped extraordinarily well until Franco's death suddenly died from what some Spanish psychiatrists termed "transition deaths"—*catharsis* hadn't panned out. I had been nervous during the trial that the survivors of the camps, most of them now old, who recalled in court grueling torture and humiliations, would lose their defenses against those memories. If near the end of your life your total victimization is made public, and you become known *for that reason*, what have you left three months after the trial? After the press goes home? Is Barbie in a well-maintained French jail? It was the survivors, not Barbie, who seemed at the point of collapse. De Gaulle's niece, Genevieve de Gaulle, suffered a heart attack in court after her testimony about Ravensbrück.

So I merely said to Madame Zlatin that I had liked her plaque—its simplicity had reminded me of the *mort pour la France* plaques I had seen after the war; I mentioned the one for Annie's cousin in the Bois de Boulogne. "The Bois de Boulogne killings—" she immediately responded. "We knew about that." Talking to her in her light-filled apartment, bits and pieces of the past were validated, I felt *centered*.

For Sabina Zlatin the fate of the Jews and anti-fascism are linked. But this doesn't mesh with the Klarsfelds, who are involved in a different coupling: they have said they feel their children symbolize a unification of the German non-Jew and the French Jew, and that this yearned-for unification will be completed when the Germans and the French admit their role in the genocide of the Jews. This family romance, which nails a dollop of German romanticism onto the already complex issues of the French occupation, deals in mythic symbols that make no sense to the French, and it suggests that the Germans and French were equal partners in what happened.

When I cautiously mentioned to Madame Zlatin that I felt the presentation of Izieu had been too *la belle et la bête*, too Germanic, I struck a chord; like many French Jews she is at ease in France and feels grateful to those French who helped save Jewish lives. She, like Claude Lanzmann, feels the genocide of the Jews to be a profoundly German problem and she has been explicit about this on German television. She didn't like the humble note Klarsfeld had stressed in his choice of photographs for the Izieu book; she had been offended that he had used a picture of her husband, a distinguished agronomist, in his work clothes. She showed me her own photograph of Miron Zlatin—he was a good-looking, well-dressed, cultured intellectual. For isn't this inherent bias for the pathetic, or the pure innocence of children, an inchoate submission to anti-Semitism? It's particularly to be resisted precisely because Hitler succeeded so well in eradicating two-thirds of European Jewry at a high point or flowering of their European culture—leaving us pictures of piled cadavers and the walking dead, empty spaces for us to fill in the vital adult lives that preceded. Inevitably those increasingly shadowy lives exist in our imagination in a downgraded form.

Colonel Romans-Petit, who organized the entire Maquis for the Ain, and who had helped the Zlatins provide for the children, is on the planning board for the Izieu museum. "I definitely wanted him on the board," Madame Zlatin emphasized to me. "He tried to save our lives. I took in Jewish children—also gypsy children. I want the museum to reflect the history of what happened."

Romans-Petit's organization of a mass liberation demonstration in November 1943 in Oyonnax, a town of 12,000 in the Ain near the Jura mountains, is a famous piece of French history. By the end of '43 de Gaulle was setting the Resistance in place for the liberation of France; he needed to convince the general French population that the Resistance, and specifically the Maquis, were not "foreign terrorists," but patriotic peaceful Frenchmen. The first *parachutage* lifts, connecting the Maquis to de Gaulle's Free French forces in London, were started in the Ain; Romans-Petit's string of *parachutage* operations included the Col de la Lèbe, near Valromey and Artemare, to the north of Izieu. Jean Moulin, sent by de Gaulle to Lyons, had there put together his favorite plan (he was a former prefect): the NAP (*Noyautage de l'Administration Publique*), a super-secret inner claque of Resistance people inside the Civil Service. Moulin financed this and the other Resistance operations through funds made available by de Gaulle in London for this purpose. This meant that, in Oyonnax, Romans-Petit had the cooperation of the local administration—his men were able to lay the Cross of Lorraine at the World War I Memorial and shout: *Vive la République! Vive le Maquis! Vive de Gaulle!* without gunfire.[2] De Gaulle hoped the bloodless demonstration would help unite recalcitrant Pétainist French to the Resistance in the final push against the Germans; he was only partially successful.

The Ain *département* was truly Jean Moulin country—his job there was to unite all the southern Resistance groups. During the trial I had looked up members of the Franc-Tireur, one of the groups he worked with closely (mostly university intellectuals, many originally from Paris, of the independent left, and not to be confused with the *Francs-Tireurs et Partisans Français*, the guerrilla organization of the Communist Front National), because I had wanted to read what their clandestine press—started in 1941—had published in Lyons during the occupation. I found their August 1942 leaflet,[3] published after the July Vel d'Hiv Paris roundup of 13,000 Jews for deportation, a useful indication of what was known at the time. Its numbers were accurate: 13,000 Jews were rounded up—making the point too that the majority were women, children, and the aged. The leaflet clearly describes the conditions in Vel d'Hiv: babies, separated from their parents, were dying from lack of water and food. It warns that Hitler's demand for the slave deportation of 30,000 foreign Jews from the Occupied Zone, and 10,000 from the Unoccupied, is only the beginning. The tract, which employs a highly patriotic tone, calls for the French to prevent the deportation of foreign Jews by hiding them in their homes; by this act they will be behaving like "true Frenchmen." Though the Final Solution wasn't yet known, or known only to very few, it was already clear that by one method or another Jews and their children were being hunted down and killed.

Many assimilated French Jews were in the Franc-Tireur. Jean-Pierre Lévy, one of its founders, told me in Paris after the trial how strange he felt as a young man giving orders to the famous historian Marc Bloch. (Bloch founded L'École d'Annales and his work later was continued by Braudel; just before the liberation he was executed, and there is now an avenue in Lyons named for him.) Lévy worked specifically with Bloch and Moulin on the coordination of propaganda, so crucial to de Gaulle's plans. He told me he and Moulin had planned one trip together to London—they were to take off from the *parachutages* near the *barrage de Génissiat* run by the *Maquis du Gros-Turc* in the Ain; but the London plane couldn't land because the position of the moon wasn't right. Lyons, because of its closeness to Switzerland and the Jura mountains, was the natural heart of the Resistance movement, which de Gaulle hoped would function as the French army. Moulin's special Maquis, the Vercors, was in the nearby Juras. Most of its men ended up trapped, like the Glières Maquis in the Haute-Savoie, by lack of arms.

Serge Klarsfeld's efforts to draw attention in France to the genocide of the Jews has been commendable, one part of the positive result of his dedicated work being that the history of the occupation and its role in the deportation of the Jews now is a necessary part of French high school curriculum. But his presentation of Izieu, which was similar in plan to his *Izieu: A Human Tragedy*, suffered from a somewhat misplaced emphasis. In the back of his book he lists fifty additional children deported from Lyons during the same period as the raid on Izieu; according to his account, UGIF (*Union générale des Israélites de France*) placed most of them in the Hôpital d'Antiquaille, on the instructions of the Gestapo, pending their transfer to Drancy; presumably Barbie was also in charge of their deportation. Yet these fifty children, many of them infants, never were mentioned in court.

The UGIF issue has torn apart and anguished French Jews since the liberation. The Germans—and through them, Vichy—controlled the Jewish population in both zones by means of their combined *Commissariat Général aux Questions Juives* and its creation, the UGIF, which operated somewhat but not entirely like the *Judenrat* in other German-occupied countries. The Germans set up this apparatus in 1941 as part of the anti-Jewish laws which made existing Jewish organizations illegal. The Consistoire, which represented Jewish religious interests in France, as well as most of the Jewish relief and resistance organizations, vigorously opposed its creation precisely because they feared it would turn into a *Judenrat*; the Jews would be trapped into a ghetto situation. But the Germans, as elsewhere, forced its creation: their method has been amply demonstrated by Marrus and Paxton in *Vichy France and the Jews* and by Jacques Adler in *The Jews of Paris and the Final Solution*. Jews no longer had any financial or legal rights. Poor Jews no longer were considered part of the regular work force. This population had to be fed and cared for. The Germans threatened the Jews that if they did not accept the control of UGIF, non-Jewish officials, who would deal with them more severely, would be appointed. The Jews had no real choice but to run it.[4] Many UGIF leaders eventually were deported, among them supporters for the Resistance, including the *"Sixième,"* a group of young UGIF Resistance workers who acted as double agents against the Germans.[5]

In Lyons, during the trial, the Jews were split about UGIF. The most passionately opposed was the journalist Maurice Rajsfus. In 1942, when he was fourteen, he and his parents, Polish Jews, were rounded up at Vel d'Hiv. His mother and father were immediately sent to Auschwitz. Rajsfus and other children were instructed to report to a UGIF children's home, which he was warned by other Jews was a holding depot for the Gestapo. He ran away and found a place to hide. Three days later the other children were deported. He was fourteen years old at the time. During the trial he attacked Klarsfeld for attempting to convert the UGIF into *the* Jewish Resistance and to mask the true purpose of the UGIF homes. Rajsfus—who considers himself a Trotskyist—wanted Barbie punished; he dismissed Vergès's rhetoric: "Vergès says France hasn't judged Massu [the extremist right-wing general who tortured Algerians in their war for independence]. I say the opposite is true: when you condemn Barbie, you condemn Massu."

In his thoughtful preface to Rajsfus's *Des Juifs dans la collaboration: L'UGIF, 1941–1944,* the French historian Pierre Vidal-Naquet ruefully characterized Rajsfus's book as both inopportune and necessary. In assessing UGIF he quotes Georges Wellers, Vice President of the Memorial and the Centre de Documentation Juive Contemporaine and editor of *Le Monde Juif,* in his book *L'Etoile jaune à l'heure de Vichy, de Drancy à Auschwitz*: "At the time, I didn't hesitate to take a categorically hostile position to it, but during my years in prison I met UGIF people who had selflessly and courageously worked to help those who were trapped, who without money and resources would otherwise have been lost. . . . Today I am no longer so sure its role was really favorable to the Germans." (Translation mine.) But Vidal-Naquet, whose own family were *haute-bourgeoisie* assimilated Jews, nevertheless validates Rajsfus's point of view: that the notables who ran UGIF essentially controlled the destiny of the foreign-born Jews, who had no representation and who were the group most deported.[6]

Another ticking bomb in the trial was Kurt Ipser's testimony. Ipser escaped from Montluc prison and went to Grenoble, then occupied by the Italians. He sought refuge with UGIF, who informed the French police who in turn notified Barbie. Ipser was picked up, returned to Montluc, and deported. The UGIF story, then, is tragic and complex, but to obliterate the history of Jewish resistance in order to fix up UGIF is unthinkable—leaving us with only what was most tenuous and denying Jews a precious and necessary record of our past.

The press dossier put out by the Grand Rabbinate and the Jewish community of Lyons gave a more evenhanded account than the Klarsfeld book of the Jewish situation in Lyons during the occupation. Listed were all the resistance groups, both Jewish and French, to which Jews belonged; indeed, in Lyons, the Jews had a very heavy input in the French Resistance. According to it, most Jewish groups in Lyons had been opposed to UGIF. The dossier also mentions the famous attack led by Gilbert Weissberg and Abraham Rayski against the *Milice* (a French Nazi paramilitary group who worked with the SS) and Gestapo guards of the Antiquaille prison hospital; their militant unit of *Groupes Francs* rescued a group of Jewish infants and children about to be deported from there.[7] The Lyons group also bombed the UGIF offices and destroyed all its records during a lunch-hour, when its premises were empty.

In Paris the Resistance rescued a group of children from the rue Rosiers School for Young Workers (on the UGIF list) just before the Gestapo raided it; Resistance leaflets and radio broadcasts from London warned Jews not to register themselves at UGIF or other dangerous central points. As early as 1941, Georges Garel, in charge of OSE in the southern zone, gave orders that the children had to be hidden and dispersed.[8] Before the terrible July and August Vel d'Hiv raids, the French Communist Party warned the Jewish Communist underground of the impending raid, as did certain sectors of the French police. According to Jacques Adler's book, the various Jewish groups in Paris were in a frenzy of activity in the days before the raid, but only a certain number of the foreign Jewish population could hide themselves; there was no prior precedent for deporting women and children—another reason why so many women, children, and old people were taken. Because of these warnings, the Germans rounded up 12,000 Jews in July and August instead of their estimated 23,000. Adler scores UGIF for not warning of Vel d'Hiv despite knowledge of it, though he also points out they were hampered by their fear of worse reprisals from the Germans. But it is precisely the story of the children's homes that has been the source of the Resistance's biggest quarrel with UGIF. Adler points out: "The Comité d'Union et de Défense was convinced that the SD [*Sicherheitsdienst*, the notorious German security agency] was preparing new and massive arrests of Jews in Paris and felt it was imperative to warn the Jewish population. The fact that there were 350 children still in the UGIF homes became the first concern of the underground committee. It approached the UGIF leadership in Paris and offered to organize a mass escape of the children but [Georges] Edinger refused to accept the scheme. . . . The Germans deported more than 200 to Auschwitz on July 31, 1944. . . . The arrests over the four days in July [just three weeks before the Allies liberated Paris] were the

UGIF's worst indictment." After the August '44 liberation of Paris the Jewish militia, symbolically, placed Edinger for a time in Drancy, which was temporarily being used as a prison for collaborationists.[9] In Lyons in September 1944 the Jewish Resistance accused several members of UGIF of blocking their rescue of children who were being held by their staff prior to being sent to Antiquaille and Auschwitz.[10]

Perhaps there is a correlation between the *forgetting* by American Jews that Jews once were Communists, Socialists, Bundists, and members of the Irgun, an amnesia that started during the Cold War—and our increased unease with "Jewish passivity." In the fifties, just as we were uncoupling the words Jew and Communist, the Communist Party in France was expropriating the whole of the Resistance. The European left was slow, too, in their acceptance of the genocide of the Jews as a separate unique event—and both revisionisms have contributed to a lack of balanced perspective.

But what makes it hardest for us to understand what happened is something generational; the split starts with my contemporaries, who were children or adolescents during the war. When I ask friends my age when they knew Jews were being exterminated, they answer: "Always . . . from the start of the war." Obviously it would have been impossible for us to have known more than our parents, but children go to the heart of the matter; we knew that in Europe Jews ceased to be. The Holocaust is our central experience—we can no longer imagine the felt experience of Jews in a pre-Hitler time, we have no *before*. During the trial the French philosopher André Glucksmann said to me that we can only speak of the Holocaust in the negative: "Nobody has the right to speak for or in the name of its victims, but all of us have the right to speak out against an injustice done to us." The distinction is important.

Notes

1. Anny Lévy Latour, *La Résistance Juive en France, 1940–1944* (Paris: Stock, 1970), 50.

2. Henri Amouroux, *L'Impitoyable Guerre Civile, Décembre 1942–Décembre 1943* (Paris: Robert Laffont, 1983).

3. Dominique Veillon, *Le Franc-Tireur, Un Journal clandestin, un mouvement de Résistance, 1940–1944* (Paris: Flammarion, 1978).

4. Jacques Adler, *The Jews of Paris and the Final Solution: Communal Response and Internal Conflicts, 1940–1944* (New York: Oxford University Press, 1987).

5. Latour, *La Résistance Juive en France.*

6. Maurice Rajsfus, *Des Juifs dans la collaboration: L'UGIF, 1941–1944* (Paris: Études et Documentation Internationales, 1980).

7. Latour, *La Résistance Juive en France.*

8. Latour, *La Résistance Juive en France.*

9. Adler, *The Jews of Paris and the Final Solution.*

10. Erna Paris, *Unhealed Wounds, France and the Klaus Barbie Affair* (New York: Grove Press, 1986).

Otto Abetz

King of Hitler's Paris

1988

In 1930 the groundwork for Germany's future occupation of France was firmly begun: an obscure art teacher from Karlsruhe, Otto Abetz, went to Paris to meet Jean Luchaire, the vaguely leftist author of *Une Génération Réaliste*; both men were under thirty. Abetz immediately enlisted Luchaire's support for his plan for a united France and Germany.[1] By the mid thirties the eclectic Abetz also joined forces with Fernand de Brinon, a French rightist Nazi who had founded the *Comité France-Allemagne*. Abetz, concocting a complicated chess game *sui generis*, now had his two main knights in place. Brinon was the banker, Luchaire the journalist. Through Brinon, who had worked for Lazard Frères and had married the widow of a Jewish banker, Abetz now had sophisticated access to the financial holdings of wealthy French Jews. Luchaire, the son of distinguished university scholars, introduced Abetz to writers and journalists (Céline, Guy Crouzet, Jules Romains, Jean Giraudoux, Abel Bonnard, Pierre Drieu La Rochelle, and Henri de Montherlant) who were willing to back his Nazi ideology. With Luchaire's help Abetz was able to start the collaborationist press.

In July 1939 the French government accused Abetz of creating a fifth column of Nazi sympathizers inside France; he was deported as a spy. That same month the writer Paul Nizan, friend of Jean-Paul Sartre and Simone de Beauvoir and prescient about world events as they were not, warned in *Ce Soir*[2] that Luchaire was heading Abetz's collaborationist press; Nizan demanded an inquiry into the financial source backing *Les Nouveaux Temps*. But France had blinked at the press takeover too late, and Nizan (who had broken with the Communists over the Hitler–Stalin Pact) was killed shortly afterward, in the battle of Dunkirk. After the French defeat Abetz made a triumphant return to Paris: as Hitler's ambassador to the occupation, he was now one of the most powerful men in France.

In his book on Izieu, Serge Klarsfeld explained that he had found the original of the telex from Barbie concerning the children of Izieu in Otto Abetz's folder in the *Centre de Documentation Juive Contemporaine* (CDJC). Klarsfeld assumed the telex to have been placed in Abetz's folder by mistake: "It is likely that a CDJC staff member, having an appointment with the examining magistrate in the Abetz case [Paris 1949], had brought with him the original of the Barbie telex . . . to show what had befallen the Jews during Abetz's terms as ambassador. The magistrate would not have kept the document in his possession, there being no direct connection between the activities of Abetz in 1944 and this initiative of the Lyons Gestapo, so the CDJC staff member must then have brought the folder back to the center, omitting to return the telex to the place where it had been filed alongside the photocopy." Thus Abetz was identified during the Barbie trial by the French and American press as the German ambassador who had nothing to do with the deportation of the children. Abetz is dead—in 1949 he was sentenced to twenty years of hard labor and served five. Four years after his pardon he and his wife were burned to death when their car mysteriously exploded. Barbie is alive, but if we are to understand what happened to the Jews in France during the occupation, it is crucial that we understand Abetz's true motives and role in their deportation.

I think it unlikely the Jews would have so casually misfiled one of their few remaining precious documents about the deportations, and which told the specific tale of a massacre of more than forty Jewish children. Jews are not careless about the Holocaust. Not in 1949, so soon after the war, with the sad knowledge that none of the French trials had alluded to the deportation and genocide of the Jews. On the contrary, what evidence was there that Abetz was *not* related to this event?

In the early thirties Abetz quickly made himself Hitler and Heydrich's right-hand man in France; he fomented the early Nazi-French Fascist alliance and anti-Semitic propaganda. He was an early enthusiast for the Final Solution—the Anti-Jewish Bureau in Paris started as a branch of his Foreign Office, which he staffed with experts on the subject. When the SS ran out of transportation for the deportation of Jews in the unoccupied zone, Abetz, who wanted the deportations to go more rapidly, found the necessary trains for them. He was the chief architect for the anti-Jewish laws passed by Vichy.[3] He immediately established the *Commissariat Général aux Questions Juives*, which controlled its creation, the UGIF, in both zones; its "aryanization" of Jewish assets was an excellent mechanism of laundering those assets into the Reich while leaving some of it in the hands of Abetz and his group. In effect Abetz made Luchaire a gift of his newspaper, *Les Nouveaux Temps*. Part of the billion-franc fine he extracted from the Jews through the *Commissariat* and UGIF helped to cover the cost of his *Propagandaabteilung* in Belgium and France (aimed against them), which included Luchaire's newspaper.[4]

Abetz had many rivals inside the Reich and at one point he was recalled to Berlin from Paris. He understood that, as neither a soldier, an SS, nor a professional diplomat, he needed to make himself useful to Hitler, to Ribbentrop, and to the French. Goebbels considered Abetz's *Propagandaabteilung* a rival to his own propaganda machine; the military felt he interfered with their intelligence; the other anti-Jewish departments felt he was horning in; he constantly quarreled with Alfred Rosenberg and Metternich over his penchant for helping himself to French art. Like the Scarlet Pimpernel turned diabolic, he was here, there, and everywhere: he managed to be at Ribbentrop's side in the Poland invasion—he personally supervised the immediate seizure of France's Bor mines in Poland, a rich plum for the Reich, and a detail the French did not overlook in their charges against him in his military trial in Paris in 1949.[5] Though Abetz is now remembered mainly for his more visible persona—his seduction of the French literary world—he superbly understood modern methods of moving around money; he transferred French and Jewish assets through to the Reich with ease, grace, and swiftness at a time when the Reich needed quick injections of cash. His relations with the French were astute; while stealing, he seduced, corrupted, and earned the admiration of a not inconsiderable number of them.

Even dead, Abetz is worth considering precisely because he wasn't the blood-and-guts Nazi, but an elegant one—he filled his embassy with the literati, artists, and cinema stars; he enjoyed having the French literary world and press under his thumb, and instantly put them in his debt by doing favors for them. He was a special mixture of his idea of *mondaine*, plus the ability to give the most brutal orders when it suited the strategy he had mapped out. Hardline and soft-line are not applicable terms for him. The question frequently has been raised: Why did the Germans continue the deportation of Jews even when this meant lessening their chances of winning the war? We know some Nazis were fanatics, but there were other reasons to continue the monstrous policy. Nazis of the Barbie type wanted to impress their superiors; they were thinking in terms of a raise in rank for a job well done. Others, like Abetz, had so involved themselves in the takeover of Jewish property that the fewer victims who returned, the fewer problems they would run into after Germany lost the war (which they accepted as a given). Abetz opposed the wearing of the yellow star not out of mellowness to the Jews but because he considered it a useless detail that would only serve to alert the French to Germany's plan to exterminate the Jews. He was a big advocate of "correctness in the West." Shrewder in assessing the French than Sauckel (who, as *Gauleiter*—a Nazi provincial governor—was in charge of foreign labor for the Reich), he opposed the mandatory conscription of French youth into the STO—the French forced labor in Germany. He accurately predicted the policy would be making a gift of French youth to the Maquis. General von Choltitz testified in his behalf that Abetz helped him circumvent Hitler's order to destroy Paris. True enough. Abetz didn't join the Nazi party until 1937; he was a Francophile and probably hoped to end his days there. On his terms.

So could the opposite have been true?—had a CDJC official put the telex in the Abetz file so that his name would be forever linked to the massacre of the children of Izieu? I looked through the Abetz trial folder at CDJC; the materials in it pertained to Abetz. If the telex purposely had been conserved there, what in the original had been so precious? I made a blow-up of it. My conclusion was that the right question about it had not been asked at the trial. The real question wasn't from whom, but *to whom*, and to how many departments in the Nazi hierarchy in Paris had it been sent? Depending on the translation, the address could mean: "To the B.DS—Department [Abteilung]—IVB—Paris" *or* "To the B.DS—entire division—IVB—Paris." The Nazis were exceedingly precise in the coded language of their telexes. No other telex I saw carried the abbreviation for Abteilung (ABTL) before the IVB.

During the trial both the prosecution and the defense were astonishingly lethargic about another unanswered point: the telex was stamped with three different stamps of receipt. One was marked April 6 in French. The other two were dated April 7, one in French, the other German. I was amazed that so substantive an issue had been left hanging in mid-air, with a lot of mumble that the telex might have gone to a mail sorting room. The *Judenreferat* was on 31 bis avenue Foch, Knochen's office on 72 avenue Foch, and the German embassy on rue de Lille; the three offices worked jointly on Jewish affairs.[6] Obviously the telex had been sent to three different departments.

On April 6 the telex appears to have been initialed A.A.—Auswärtiges Amt, the German Foreign Office. The next day it was signed for by IVB. At some point in the life of this telex someone had added an O over the A.A. (Otto?). I asked myself why the lawyers were so indifferent as to who received the telex. The prosecution had spent so many years developing their case against Barbie, they might not have wanted it diluted by emphasizing additional Nazi involvement. But, historically, it is important for us to consider what relation the Foreign Office had to the Barbie telex; particularly as Abetz managed to destroy most of the Foreign Office documents pertaining to the last two years of the occupation. As this telex was presumably sent on to the IVB, it wouldn't have been in Foreign Office files. Now, what about Vergès? Why hadn't he made more of an issue of the three different stamps? While I was in Paris I went to see him again, in his office on rue Vingtmille, between L'Opéra and Clichy. Vergès dismissed the question of the stamps as irrelevant: his position (which didn't seem to have a firm basis) was that the telex was fake, therefore its details didn't matter. He also shrugged off my questions about Abetz; who the telex had been sent to didn't appear to interest him. I wondered: did Vergès's friend, the Swiss pro-Nazi banker François Genoud, hire him to defend Barbie—or to keep Barbie quiet? Vergès had insisted on being Barbie's only lawyer; through his diversionary tactics about Algeria, etc., he managed to keep Barbie mute: we learned nothing of Barbie's Nazi connections.

According to reports in *Le Monde* and Erna Paris's *Unhealed Wounds*, after the end of World War II Genoud managed the Nazi treasury in numbered Swiss bank accounts run by a clandestine former SS group, *Die Spinne*; Genoud also acted as a financial intermediary and courier for Nazis imprisoned in France for war crimes after the war.[7] Logically the imprisoned Abetz would have been one of the main Nazis Genoud would have contacted in France. Like Abetz (who wrote his memoirs in prison), Genoud recognized the value of the written word: during the Nuremberg trials the youthful Genoud immediately (and amazingly) acquired the rights posthumously to the writings of Hitler, Goebbels, and Martin Bormann. Maître Berman, one of the prosecuting lawyers in the Barbie case, in a sharp courtroom exchange with Vergès, demanded (unsuccessfully) that the court call Genoud as a witness. His point was that Vergès had been hired by a man who handles the financial interests of Nazis whose funds come from property and money taken from Jewish victims during the occupation; after the war the French prosecuted the collaborationist press, but did not go after collaborationist businessmen, which was much more important, as so many Jews had been deported because of financial machinations.

One of Abetz's staff in the German Foreign Office testified in the Abetz pretrial disposition that Abetz wasn't an anti-Semite but was essentially indifferent to the Jewish problem.[8] A bitter irony is that there may be a small element of truth in it; I doubt he believed in Nazi theories of racial superiority. He married a Frenchwoman, the secretary of his friend Jean Luchaire. According to Claude Lévy's *Les Nouveaux Temps et l'Idéologie de la Collaboration*, Luchaire wasn't particularly anti-Semitic; his wife's family was part Jewish. He hid and gave employment at *Les Nouveaux Temps* to two young Jewish women, one of them an aspiring actress named Simone Signoret.[9] But he was cash-short and his big dream was having his own newspaper; Abetz gave him both.

Yet Abetz's 1942 message to his rival in the Foreign Office, Under Secretary of State Martin Luther, is clear: "It isn't a question of reserving a privileged position for French Jews, since they will, in any case, disappear in the plan to eliminate Jewry from Europe. . . ."[10] What was new about Abetz (and what made his actions hard to grasp) was his use of ideology as a tool in the acquisition of financial assets—he was a strategist, not an ideologue. So the French Jews, familiar with French social anti-Semitism and shaping their arguments to it, didn't understand how completely they were victims of a modern money scam. The Final Solution was set in place *after* the laws stripped Jews of their property, and in France it was a consequence that flowed from it. Maurice Rajsfus in *Des Juifs Dans La Collaboration* pointed out that different types of anti-Semites were used to run the *Commissariat Général aux Questions Juives* depending on the objectives; Xavier Vallat, who was a snobbish sort who liked having connections among the wealthy, including French Jews, was good for the early negotiating stages when UGIF was being set up; later, when the French Jews were being deported, he was replaced with Louis Darquier de Pellepoix, a thug with an abiding hatred of the bourgeoisie. Marrus and Paxton pointed out in *Vichy France and the Jews* that the Germans were keenly aware that Jewish charities were a tremendous source of money; by putting these institutions under the control of the CGQJ, this enormous amount of money was easily siphoned off to the Reich. By labeling the assets of French Jews, and of their charities and hospitals, "Jewish," rather than French, the Germans found a handy device for seizing French assets without raising alarm. The Jewish children in UGIF homes were doubly at risk because of the high deportation quota set by Abetz and Berlin and because the Germans used UGIF to aryanize Jewish charitable funds.

Not all the money went to Germany. In his 1941 embassy memo Abetz's specialist on Jewish affairs, Carl-Theodor Zeitschel, laconically pointed out: ". . . I suggest we get rid of as rapidly as possible the Braques and other similar ones (24 paintings) which we still have at the Embassy before Rosenberg inundates the art market with paintings, hundreds of expressionist paintings which he still has in his possession. In any case, if we do this now, we would be in a position to obtain better pieces in exchange than later on"[11] (translations mine). The Foreign Office sold considerable quantities of "degenerate art" (Braque, Max Ernst, etc.) through Switzerland.

During his trial Abetz, never repentant, maintained that the two world wars had been the fault of the Jews; he argued that their property had been rightfully shipped to the Reich because the Jews were obliged to indemnify its victims.[12] Abetz convinced Berlin (at times the Reich also had trouble understanding his plans) to let him create French trusteeships to run Jewish businesses. His excuse was that he wanted the bulk of Jewish property used to indemnify the French.[13] Gérard Chauvy in *Lyon 40–44* describes the way aryanization of Jewish firms was accomplished in Lyons during the occupation. He cites confidential documents from the archives of the Rhône Police Prefect. Well-placed Lyons industrialists (former members of Brinon's pre-war creation, the *Comité France-Allemagne*) met with Abetz's economic advisors in the Foreign Office at rue de Lille to discuss their willingness to run industrial firms in Lyons (the jewel of French industry) for the mutual benefit of France and Germany. Technically Abetz's office represented German interests, which now included occupied France; while Brinon (whom Abetz had made Pétain's ambassador) was the channel for French interests in the unoccupied zone. Obviously Abetz and Brinon were laundering heavy assets by using a complicated system of business agreements between the two zones.

Both Luchaire and Brinon were immediately executed after the war; Abetz managed to stall his trial until the milder climate of 1949. The French military judges conveniently forgot to append Abetz's gold embassy book, which contained the personal list of collaborationist industrialists and politicians he worked with while ambassador, to his dossier.[14] Abetz's connections were excellent, and he never gave information in his deposition or trial about the well-placed collaborationists who helped him in return for business payoffs. He was convicted of having been one of the individuals most responsible for the deportation of 80,000 French Jews and seizure of their assets; of the orders for the murder of former Minister Georges Mandel and the attempted murder of Minister Paul Reynaud and the former President Léon Blum; it was his order that caused one hundred hostages to be shot per each German killed; he had demanded the deportation of French prefects, members of the Resistance, Gaullists, and *franc-maçons*. He had seized French publishing houses, in particular Hachette. After the liberation nearly three thousand valuable art objects were found in his embassy. When Abetz took flight with his inner circle and members of the Vichy Government to Sigmaringen Castle in the Black Forest, he traveled as a Napoleon with the riches of France; he brought one hundred and fifty of the most valuable paintings for his own use; he attempted to take the Gobelins tapestries from the Louvre, but Metternich stopped him.

In Abetz's pretrial deposition, though he mentioned knowing even minor French writers, I noticed he left out Louis-Ferdinand Céline, the writer whose name had been on the Embassy's special list of top consultants for their Anti-Jewish Institute. With good reason: Céline had shown up uninvited at the bizarre Götterdämmerung at Sigmaringen; he was a shrewd, albeit paranoid, observer of events there. And his trial came up after that of Abetz, whom he had no reason to help.

Céline's biography, written by his lawyer, François Gibault, sheds light on Abetz's fluid relation to the SS. During the Barbie trial the Paris hierarchy of the SS was depicted as functioning in such rigid terms that it was assumed that only Knochen could have received the Barbie Izieu telex; the three different department stamps on it were shrugged off as oddities, as was the fact that Knochen was never charged with Izieu, though the existence of the telex was known at the time of his trial.

According to Gibault's account, which reproduces direct testimony from Céline's trial, the reason Céline was questioned about his participation in the notorious Anti-Jewish "scientific" Congress organized by Abetz in May 1941, which prepared the way for the Wannsee doctrine of the Final Solution in 1942, was that Abetz's correspondence about it to Knochen was discovered among Knochen's personal papers. In 1946, when interrogated about it, Knochen admitted that Abetz was in charge of the French Bureau for Anti-Jewish Affairs, and had employed Céline and other writers to work for it.

Céline's notes and letters written during his Sigmaringen and Danish sojourn record his anxiety: ". . . Jules Romains, Maurras, La Varende, Pierre Benoit, Chardonne, Farrère drenched up to their ass in Vichy where they don't get out except through the BUREAU—Develop the habit of never saying what BUREAU . . ." (Otto Abetz's Bureau for Anti-Jewish Affairs). Later, from his prison in Copenhagen he wrote an ironic note to his friend Maurice Escande, who had just received the Légion d'Honneur for actors who had been veterans of the first war: ". . . I enter . . . the German Embassy's in the orchestra pit in full force . . . That ode . . . La chanson de Roland! . . . Dear Escande! Always in the breach, in the parapet of the sublime! . . . It's the least one could expect! . . . For Abetz! . . . consider the bad end of always playing the wrong tune at the wrong moment in the wrong play! . . ." During Céline's 1951 trial he constantly resorted to ironic double entendres; Abetz remained very much on his mind. "*Mais oui!* I was Hitler's mistress! . . . I delivered Pas-de-Calais to Keitel! I organized Oradour [the French village massacred by the Germans in '44] with Abetz . . ." (translations mine).[15]

Céline's association of Abetz to the Oradour massacre is significant; in "De Rethondes à l'île d'Yeu," Maurice Vanino cites the propaganda speech defending the massacre made by Xavier Vallat, the anti-Semite whom Abetz had used as his first Vichy High Commissioner for Anti-Jewish Affairs. Vallat ostensibly had used his radio broadcast to answer the anguished letter of a thirteen-year-old French schoolboy who had demanded to know why his grandmother and five hundred other innocent women had been locked in a church and burned to death, but his real motive was to warn the French not to join the Resistance, and to define the Resistance as bandits.

Vallat replied: "Emile Juge, 13 years of age, drunk with ideas of justice and liberty—ho-hum!—has written me from Montpellier asking why Madame Canitrot, whom he loved so much, was burned to death. . . . My reply is . . . it is the French who are morally responsible for this woman's death. . . . If the French had not disobeyed the orders of the Marshal [Pétain] . . . the Germans wouldn't have been driven to make an innocent population endure the cruel consequences of acts [against the Germans] by individual bandits. . . . Therefore, reflect, young Emile Juge . . . on the Marshal's advice to French students on the necessity of discipline and obedience."[16]

Vallat was a complete puppet. The German Foreign Office kept him on a short leash—they denied him a pass permitting him to cross from unoccupied to occupied France. His murderous radio reply to his own countrymen (clearly written by German propagandists) indicates that, though the genocide of the Jews must be understood as a unique historical event, the use of anti-Semitism by Abetz and his circle was an integral part of their basic criminality. They used the same justification for Oradour as for their extermination of the Jews—the Nazis held all their victims legally responsible for their own demise.

In recent years the descriptions of Abetz have become fuzzy. He frequently is described merely as "the German Ambassador in France," a man with a great interest in French culture, ergo the "civilized Nazi"; we are reluctant to accept such absolute evil in a man so quick to help artists and writers. His own propaganda aide, Gerhard Heller, wept at the deportation of Jewish children, yet he idolized Abetz, who was responsible for it, for his sensitivity and polish. But in the end, Heller, though milder than most Nazis, accompanied Abetz to Sigmaringen.

While at Sigmaringen Céline became friendly with Laval and his wife Josée. In his notes he observed that Pétain and Laval were kept apart from the others; they weren't invited to Abetz's big banquets—Laval maintained that Abetz had taken him to Germany by force. In the film actress Corinne Luchaire's memoir (she was Luchaire's daughter) she describes Laval at Baden-Baden, just before the group went on to Sigmaringen: "I found Laval curiously changed . . . he was in Germany against his will and had resigned when Abetz had compelled him to leave Paris." Then in Sigmaringen: "Numerous French workers [sent as forced labor to Germany] had come by in large numbers. . . . Suddenly we saw Pierre Laval . . . going up to the group of angry French workers. He explained why he had [sent 500,000 workers to Germany] . . . he had to limit the danger. . . . These men, who foresaw the danger that was threatening him, told Laval to stay with them, and they would protect and defend him. Laval thanked them, but got in his car; as he drove off, these men waved goodbye."[17]

Céline seemed to grasp that he and Laval were in danger of being murdered at Sigmaringen; they represented evidence of how the Nazi net had worked in France. They both were outsiders, neither of them in the inner clique. Céline couldn't head back to France, he knew the enormity of what he had done, and he used every ounce of strength, every shred of influence to flee from his former patrons to Denmark.[18]

Had Laval, now considered by most historians to have been the least bad of a bad lot (he was summarily executed in 1945 with less than a full day's proceeding), been tried after Abetz and been able to testify, Abetz and many others would have been executed. In the CDJC Abetz folder where the Barbie telex was found are handwritten notes of one of its founders during Abetz's trial. One senses from these anguished fragments that the Jewish leaders felt they had little support in making France understand the enormity of what the Nazis had done to the Jews. One sad comment about the delay in trying Abetz tells it all: *Four years too late!*

Barbie boasted that he knew Nazis in high places; his main function was hunting down the Resistance in the key Lyons region. His work was as important to the Foreign Office as to the Gestapo. In 1940 Abetz outlined his political strategy for occupied France and Belgium (he was in charge of propaganda for both countries), which was a continuation of techniques he had developed during the thirties: "The goal of our propaganda must be the prevention of a united Front."[19] His plan fomented the growth and manipulation of regionalist movements (such as the Flemish), youth groups, World War I veterans, and social associations; his stated aim was to confuse the population by pitting one group against another—even, if necessary, to invent new groups and new polemics. "It is important to give the press, radio, and propaganda positions as varied as possible and to let them engage in polemics with one another. . . . The goal of our propaganda always must be to prevent the formation of a united front. A politically united France would be a permanent focus for international intrigue against the Reich, even if these intrigues aren't backed by military power" (translations mine).[20] He particularly advised to keep close watch on the Communists and Gaullists. The groups he felt should be held responsible for the war and exterminated without consideration were the French bourgeoisie, whom he profoundly hated: ". . . all government officials, all *franc-maçons*, all Jews, all clericals, and journalists." Had the war continued, the finances of the Church in France would have begun to be siphoned off by the Germans.[21]

In a certain sense, then, Abetz was the *anti-Jean Moulin*. At the same time that Abetz was attempting to promote disunity among the French, Moulin, for de Gaulle, was dealing with the same problem in reverse; the unification of France behind one solid front in the final phase of the war was crucial to de Gaulle. Moulin, who brought financial support from London, aided the growth of the clandestine propaganda press, radio broadcasts, and the pro-Maquis demonstration led by Romans-Petit in Oyonnax in the Ain (it took place several months after Moulin was caught), in order to convince the French that the Maquis was made up of patriotic Frenchmen: His base was Lyons. When Barbie caught Moulin in Lyons at the end of June 1943, Moulin was conferring with the leaders of all the Resistance groups to bring them under one organization.

Abetz in the meantime fought the Moulin–de Gaulle calls for patriotic unity and armed resistance through *Les Nouveaux Temps*, the official organ of his *Propagandaabteilung*. On April 6, 1944, the same day of the raid on the children's home in Izieu, Luchaire's newspaper reported seizing two terrorists in Tarbes; in March the paper published scare accounts of bands of armed foreign terrorists in the Haute-Savoie, defining the Glières Maquis (which had received a substantial quantity of light arms from London) as a secret army composed of

Polish Jews and Spanish Anarchists.²² The paper needed to deflect the news that in March eight thousand Germans with heavy artillery had attacked the five hundred *Maquisards*. Most of the Glières unit were savagely massacred and tortured by the Germans; a few escaped with the aid of local inhabitants. The British historian Alexander Werth pointed out: "Significantly, Abetz, in his account of the same operation, claimed that the local inhabitants thanked the Germans for having liberated them of the 'terrorists,' and insulted the few surviving French prisoners."²³ Abetz used the time-honored technique of cloaking his operations with respectability while delegitimizing his enemies. The name, *Les Nouveaux Temps*, suggested an older French paper, *Notre Temps*; anti-Semitism was judiciously used in *Les Nouveaux Temps* and then in careful language. As Claude Lévy points out in his remarkable analysis of it, the paper's aim never was the sensationalist anti-Semitism of *La Gerbe*—indeed, Céline, for whom anti-Semitism and its language was *the* purpose, made a nuisance of himself by writing letters to the paper protesting its lack of anti-Semitic juice. But Abetz's trademark combined concealment, thoughtfulness, and the ability to create confusion. The paper concentrated on heavy anti-American and anti-British attacks; French postwar anti-Americanism had some of its roots in its propaganda that America entered the war in order to destroy and take over France and Europe.

Abetz's role in the unoccupied zone has been underestimated because of confusion as to how the two zones connected. Abetz was less an ambassador than Hitler's all-purpose emissary in France—his Foreign Office was used in multiple ways. It involved itself more with the deportation of the Jews than in other countries; at various stages, particularly after the North African landings, it functioned in the unoccupied zone as intelligence and propaganda, and to supervise the military and the police. The SS also infiltrated into it. The German Foreign Office negotiated in the unoccupied zone through its appointed representatives—Brinon for Pétain and Laval (whom Abetz and Brinon considered too profoundly French to be of much use). This meant Abetz was in close touch with Lyons.

One of the main charges against Abetz was his deportation (which he concealed from Laval) of 14 prefects who belonged to the NAP²⁴—the super-resistance group of police, organized by Jean Moulin and Claude Bourdet in Lyons, to colonize the Civil Service in a Trojan Horse operation for insurrection against the Germans after the Allies and Free French landed. Abetz's activity against the Resistance in the unoccupied zone and the area in and around Lyons diminished in the final stages of the war, when the military took over, but it is hardly likely he had not been in connection with Barbie and vitally interested in the death of Moulin. Again, I am speculating on the Abetz-Barbie relation—but Barbie *was* hunting down the Resistance in Lyons at a time when Abetz was concerned with it. Would Abetz have deported the NAP and not been interested in the details of the murder of one of its creators, which had taken place just months before? Wouldn't Abetz, logically, have been the person to have given the order to have Moulin removed from Lyons in the unoccupied zone to Paris in the occupied zone? Technically, Laval should have been consulted in a move that involved both zones. But we know, because of information given at Abetz's trial, that Laval was never consulted by Abetz in his subsequent order to deport Moulin's creation, the NAP. Abetz's deportation of the fourteen Resistance leaders of the NAP is, in itself, very interesting. He was solely in charge of that operation and it was kept highly secret. After the war the French were unable to find out the fate of most of the group—they seemed to have simply disappeared. René Hardy, the Resistance member in the Lyons group who was twice tried by the French for having betrayed Jean Moulin, also was a member of the NAP.

In *Is Paris Burning?* by Larry Collins and Dominique La Pierre, the authors hold Abetz responsible for turning down Emil Bender's humane plea (he was an Abwehr—German foreign intelligence—double agent) to prevent the last train of Resistance prisoners from being shipped to the gas chambers; it seems highly unlikely Abetz wouldn't have been among those signing orders for the transfer of Jean Moulin. Indeed, Moulin's murder seems to be the only significant political murder Abetz wasn't tried with. Clearly his trial had all sorts of omissions. We know Céline's name was never mentioned, yet in the writer's own trial, a few months after Abetz's, Abetz figured prominently. If the French truly mean to examine the occupation period, they must begin with the case of Otto Abetz—not Barbie—and ask the real historic question: who let Otto Abetz off and why?

We are told that Barbie in 1947 eluded an American military manhunt, in Kassel, for a ring of SS who had escaped while being held for trial. He was the only one of the net not recaptured—he jumped out of a window just ahead of the Americans and bolted to the railway station. Kurt Merk, an Abwehr intelligence man formerly stationed in France (we are meant to believe), conveniently happened to be lurking in the station at the right moment for Barbie. Merk, already working for American intelligence, convinced American military intelligence to hire him. I happen to have wandered a bit through Germany in 1948. In 1947 one wouldn't have bolted to the railway station if one were in a hurry to get out of town, as transportation almost was at a standstill. But with the population using the stations as shelter, in bombed-out cities they made a fine prearranged meeting place. According to George Vassiltchikov's appendix to *Berlin Diaries, 1940–1945*, the diary of his sister Marie Vassiltchikov, Barbie surfaced in the services of the Americans together with the notorious Dr. Franz Six (later a publicist for Porsche) who was part of the German Foreign Office. He was one of their pseudo-scientists involved in anti-Jewish theories for the Final Solution. (The Foreign Office participated in the Wannsee Conference.)

A small-fry minor functionary like Barbie, whose chief characteristic was his appetite for sadism, wouldn't have been able to convince the American Intelligence to hire him as an expert—they had their pick of highly trained Nazis after the war—unless they had been sold a sophisticated bill of goods. My speculation is that Merk had been sent by top Nazis—such as Abetz, who were still awaiting their own trials, and therefore vulnerable—to dump Barbie into the lap of American Intelligence and thus prevent him from being tried at a time when he could have implicated them. Certainly Barbie's metamorphosis from small-time sadist to sophisticated international expert on communism, with contacts everywhere, enough to dazzle the Americans, indicates he had the guidance of top Abwehr people. I can't imagine that a fluid thinker such as Abetz, so agile as a long-range planner, would not have been busy making plans for his survival. Genoud, then trekking back and forth between French prisons and Nuremberg (where he was acquiring book rights, preventing the royalties from Nazi writings going to their victims), also might have helped out as go-between—Genoud has boasted that he helped smuggle the Belgian Nazi Léon Degrelle into Spain in 1956.[25]

Though this explanation for Barbie's intelligence career is only a speculation, it is interesting that, in the trial, survivors reported that Barbie boasted—while loading them on the last trains to the camps—that as soon as the Americans won the war, he would work for their Intelligence Agency. The court dismissed this as bizarre coincidence and just another indication that when drunk, Barbie bragged of his highly connected friends. To me it indicated that he might have been present at a few long-range planning sessions—according to *Berlin Diaries* Six and some others in the Foreign Office had been brokering their Communist savvy long before the end of the war in contacts with the Americans and British in Switzerland and Sweden; both Roosevelt and Churchill refused to deal with them. When I requested the materials on the Abetz trial at the *Centre de Documentation Juive Contemporaine*, I was told that historians working on Abetz had complained that the French government temporarily had blocked their archives on Abetz because of the Barbie trial. This was seven months after it ended. If Abetz really had nothing to do with events during the occupation in Lyons, why were his files blocked?

Abetz's modus operandi was to gain control by going after high finance, publishing, communists—but leave culture in place.[26] His acts were evil, yes; banal, never. And French "culture" has rewarded him by letting his memory, along with the rest of the occupation, sink almost unquestioned into history. The German embassy had gaiety under Abetz. But it is Nazis like him who permitted intellectuals like Heidegger their excuse: that there were two forms of Nazism—their own and that of the brutes, the hoi polloi. When Heidegger was asked after the war why he had joined in a banquet for Julius Streicher, the publisher of the virulent anti-Jewish paper, *Der Stürmer*, he named its baseness as proof of his distance from it: "*Der Stürmer? Pornography!*" Actually it tells us the opposite: Heidegger was acutely aware that the sensationalist racism excited its readers precisely because of its underlying pornographic appeal. When Arendt termed Eichmann "banal," not only did she panic—and confabulate her sense of the familiar, the German—but, in demoting Eichmann to a lower category, that of a *stupid* man, she found a way to wishfully endow her former lover and mentor, the brilliant Heidegger, with a clean slate. Their sense of superiority enabled rather than prevented intelligent men like Abetz to evolve the Final Solution and sign the deportation orders.

The philosopher Philippe Lacoue-Labarthe has noted that it's not Heidegger's early joining of the Nazi party that we judge, but his later failure to contemplate the meaning of Auschwitz. Intuitively we know this great German philosopher never did address it; had he, the words of his gifted Jewish pupil would not have come out misplaced. Arendt maintained she was a child of philosophy and of the German language; in order not to become a child of no one, she misnamed her own history. From her former professor she must have heard only the silence.

Notes

1. Claude Lévy, *Les Nouveaux Temps et l'idéologie de la collaboration* (Paris: Librairie Armand Colin et Fondation Nationale des Sciences Politiques, 1974).
2. Lévy, *Les Nouveaux Temps et l'idéologie de la collaboration.*
3. Michael R. Marrus and Robert O. Paxton, *Vichy France and the Jews* (New York: Shocken Books, 1983).
4. Lévy, *Les Nouveaux Temps et l'idéologie de la collaboration.*
5. *Centre de Documentation Juive Contemporaine*, File CXII-2 (Paris).
6. Marrus and Paxton, *Vichy France and the Jews.*
7. Erna Paris, *Unhealed Wounds, France and the Klaus Barbie Affair* (New York: Grove Press, 1986).
8. *Centre de Documentation Juive Contemporaine*, File CXII-2.
9. Lévy, *Les Nouveaux Temps et l'idéologie de la collaboration.*
10. *Centre de Documentation Juive Contemporaine*, File CXII-2.
11. *Centre de Documentation Juive Contemporaine*, File CXII-2.
12. *Centre de Documentation Juive Contemporaine*, File CXII-2.
13. *Centre de Documentation Juive Contemporaine*, File CXII-2 and Abetz folder.
14. *Centre de Documentation Juive Contemporaine*, Abetz trial: *Le Figaro.*
15. François Gibault, *Céline 1944–1961, cavalier de l'apocalypse* (Paris: Mercure de France, 1985).
16. *Centre de Documentation Juive Contemporaine*, Bibliothèque No. 8382.
17. Alexander Werth, *France 1944–1955* (New York: Henry Holt and Company, 1956).
18. Gibault, *Céline 1944–1961.*

19. *Centre de Documentation Juive Contemporaine*, File CXII-2.
20. *Centre de Documentation Juive Contemporaine*, File CXII-2.
21. Lévy, *Les Nouveaux Temps et l'idéologie de la collaboration*.
22. Werth, *France 1944–1955*.
23. Werth, *France 1944–1955*.
24. *Centre de Documentation Juive Contemporaine*, File CXII-2.
25. Paris, *Unhealed Wounds*.
26. Herbert Lottman, *The Left Bank* (Boston: Houghton Mifflin, 1982).

Design by David Bullen
Typeset in Mergenthaler Bembo
with Trump Mediaeval display
by Wilsted & Taylor
Printed by Braun–Brumfield
on acid-free paper